WITHOUT BORDERS

BORDERS

Syria   SUSANNE BURGE

Matador
9 Priory Business Park,
Wistow Road, Kibworth Beauchamp,
Leicestershire. LE8 0RX
Tel: (+44) 116 279 2299
Fax: (+44) 116 279 2277
Email: books@troubador.co.uk
Web: www.troubador.co.uk/matador

ISBN 978 1785898 471

British Library Cataloguing in Publication Data.
A catalogue record for this book is available from the British Library.

Printed and bound by CPI Group (UK) Ltd, Croydon, CR0 4YY
Typeset in 11pt Adobe Garamond Pro by Troubador Publishing Ltd, Leicester, UK

Matador is an imprint of Troubador Publishing Ltd

MIX
Paper from
responsible sources
FSC® C013604

Each time a man stands up for an ideal, or acts to improve the lot of others, or strikes out against injustice, he sends forth a tiny ripple of hope ... and crossing each other from a million different centres of energy and daring, those ripples build a current that can sweep down the mightiest walls of oppression and resistance.

Robert Kennedy

It was never my intention to write a story set in Syria. The subject matter is catastrophic and would have to do justice somehow to those it seeks to represent. But early in 2013, two news items hit the headlines that I could not ignore. The fate of Dr Abbas Khan was particularly shocking and struck a personal chord. He was a British hand surgeon, married with young children, whose punishment for going back to help his people in Syria was imprisonment and death by torture and starvation. Not long after this, we were presented with evidence that Assad's machine had systematically murdered thousands of his citizens in the same way and I have to remind myself with shame that, like me, President Assad is a qualified doctor.

Karen Blixon once said that "All sorrows can be borne if you put them into a story or tell a story about them."

"Without Borders" is about ordinary people and especially children, who happen to be in the wrong place at the wrong time. Though all characters in this story are fictional, they are inspired by real heroes who rise above depravity, demonstrating the power of the human spirit to overcome adversity and the redeeming power of love.

All proceeds from the sale of this story
will go to those who inspired it – the children of Syria.

susanneburge.com

CONTENTS

ZA'ATARI REFUGEE CAMP, JORDAN

She sits bolt upright and strains in the darkness for anything that will give them away. Silence. Not even a rustle. Only the sound of her pounding heart and the smell of mildew. She must have been dreaming. Who is Caleb, anyway?

He was so brave that little boy whose injuries she was treating. His face lit up when he spoke of this man, fast becoming a legend amongst the refugees. Of how he rescued them. In her dreams she became one of them, scared witless, traumatised and Caleb saved her too, from certain death.

The camp is quiet tonight. That lead weight sinks to the pit of her stomach, heightening her senses as she waits, hardly daring to breath. Too long in this desolate place. A lifetime. But, unlike them, I chose to be here, she reminds herself. No regrets. Nothing to lose.

She lies herself cautiously back down, shaking the terrors out of her head. It is cold, the blistering heat, an illusion chased away by the howling winds. She curls herself into a ball and pulls the damp blanket over her head, savouring what warmth she can draw from herself. Disregarding the nagging dread of childhood comfort.

It's over. They will never touch me again.

Ironic really. She once thought there could be nothing worse. If only. These children have suffered so much more. Just treat the injury, that's what they say. As if it were that simple.

Footsteps. Her heart skips a beat. Dead still. She waits for the intruder to pass. Silence. Someone fumbles with the fabric of

1

her tent and begins to unzip the entrance. She jumps to her feet, reaching for the knife and crouches in the corner, hardly daring to breath. Torchlight pierces inky black and her muscles scream for release but she resists the urge to run. The beam searches, dropping the instant it finds her and is replaced immediately by a voice – young, uncertain.

"Doctor, we need you."

Her heart settles back into her chest. Ashamed, she places the knife carefully back on the box beside her mattress. Incongruous – next to the photograph of her dogs and the friend looking after them, the bottle of stale water, the half empty packet of blue orbit, her alarm clock and her current evocative read, Maps for all Lovers.

He made her take it, Kai, and tonight, for the first time…

She holds her hands before her face but it is too dark to see how they have changed beyond recognition. Only their trembling connects them to her now, the vibration of them shaking her out of her trance. No. She couldn't have. She's tired. It's been another long day.

"I'm coming. Wait outside."

She reaches for a fleece and trousers, pulling them over her boxers and warm pyjama top. Then her wellies. Ties back her wayward hair. Grabs her medical bag and a torch.

Sleep beckons. It would be so easy to lie down again, close her eyes and escape from it all. What difference does she make anyway? It is all too big. Overwhelming.

"Pebbles." Her favourite quote has become a mantra to her now. Sometimes it's what gets her out of bed in the morning. Even a small pebble sends ripples of hope… With a start, she realises not knowing what happens next, doesn't bother her anymore and for once, her self-destructive alter-ego is not to blame.

It is a little way to the refugees. The aid organisations have provided the outsiders with an encampment of their own. Countless white tents float like lanterns in a sea of black. Twinkling stars bloom into

2

blazing campfires, with the ghosts huddled around them of those who could not sleep or had cause to stay awake. Sounds rise with smells drifting on the bitter wind. Smoke, sewage, coffee, babies crying, dogs barking, women wailing, snatches of conversation.

He wears a featureless tracksuit, this young man, once white trainers and a dark beanie that blends imperceptibly with his black hair and tender stubble. Stopping from time to time, he looks behind him, as if to check she is still there, then hurries off into the night again. They seem to be skirting the edge of the refugee camp and Ana wonders what he may be leading her to. Perhaps it is more than medical help he wants. She has heard stories and been warned. But it makes no difference now.

He slows down. It is a tent he leads her to, after all. One like all the others but noisier than most. Someone moans, children cry and, as she enters the crowded space, Ana sees a young boy talking quietly, reassuringly, stroking a woman's fevered brow.

"They have just arrived," her guide informs her, still in English. He points from the entrance of the tent into the blackness behind him towards the border with Syria and Ana knows already what she will find.

Despite the long black robes which exaggerate the woman's weight-loss, it is clear what the immediate problem is. She is in the second stage of labour, her body urging to push the baby out. "Can you ask her how many weeks she is into this pregnancy?" Ana asks the young man and the boy answers.

"Thirty four. Are you the doctor?"

He looks on her accusingly, desolate black eyes glimmering from bags that hang almost as far as the grim lines of his mouth. The soft squat nose of youth betrays the face of an old man, thick brown hair falling over a head far too big for its gaunt frame and thin muscular limbs protrude awkwardly from an outsized tee-shirt.

"Yes. My name is Ana, and yours?"

"Rahim and this is my mother, Lileth."

3

He says something to the woman and Ana listens carefully. She has become quite proficient in Arabic, almost fluent, her new friends flatter. Rahim is reassuring his mother, all will be well now that the doctor is here. Ana hopes it will. She turns to the stranger, relieved to see him still standing at the entrance.

"Do we have hot water, towels, blankets?" she asks and he shakes his head. "Could you get some please?"

He shoots her a look of resentment, turning to disappear into the night and Ana regrets not treating him with due deference. She is merely a woman.

Two scantily dressed little girls with bare arms thin as sticks, cower in the shadows. They will have to wait. Ana goes to Lileth, smiling reassurance as she introduces herself, and does a quick assessment of mother and baby.

Clearly Lileth understands no English. Ana resorts to Arabic, Rahim repeating and embellishing her simple phrases with such seriousness, that she has to smile. Lileth acknowledges neither of them.

"We walked five days to get here," Rahim tells Ana as she monitors his mother's contractions. "Without food or water after the second day, except what I could find." He considers Lileth with a frown, blinking back his tears then, looking around for his little sisters, clears his throat and takes a deep breath. "Luckily no-one was hurt ..."

Ana waits. Guilt lurks behind the pain in his eyes but she will have to gain Rahim's trust before he reveals himself to her. She nods, her eyes falling to his swollen feet as she pretends not to be affected by his appearance.

Lileth cries out, grabs Ana's hand and squeezes hard. The head is crowning. Soon it will be over. Extricating herself, Ana makes one final check. The cord is wrapped tightly around the baby's neck. It will suffocate if not released. Flinching as Lileth protests, Ana pushes the baby back, unwraps the cord and, when she lets go, with one push, the head is born.

The stranger has reappeared. Handing Ana a towel, he deposits a bucket of cold water at her feet. He has brought company but Ana is too preoccupied even to look up. Hopefully they will make themselves useful.

Lileth delivers a tiny baby girl and a cry of joy goes up in the tent, but the baby is not breathing and looks very grey. Ana wraps her in towel and rubs. "Come on little one, wakey, wakey."

Hush descends. Even the girls stop their whimpering. Time stands still and Ana prays once more. Please, let her live.

The baby gasps, coughs and starts to cry. Along with everyone else in the tent it seems, Ana releases a lung-full of air and braces herself against the joyful whooping rising around her. She removes the wet towel, wraps the baby in a dry one, gives it a cuddle and smiles into its open eyes as it settles to the sound of her voice. She takes it to its mother but Lileth ignores it so she places it on her tummy instead, watching, hoping. Slowly but surely, the tiny creature makes its way up to a breast and, as mother acknowledges baby at last, Ana finds it incredible once more, that the agony of labour is forgotten in an instant. She smiles at Lileth and returns to deliver the placenta.

Despite its prematurity, mother and baby are doing well. She is almost an hour old and has a name. Aamina, safety. Ana wonders what will become of her along with all the other children here who worked so hard for a future they will never see. The generation that was going to civilise Syria.

"Would you like a drink?"

She jumps, weary eyes open in an instant, but it is only little Rahim, concern on his face and a cup of something steaming in his hands. She takes it off him, flicking the hair out of her face so they can see each other properly, and smiles.

"Thank you." He looks relieved and so tired. "How old are you Rahim?"

"Eleven. Why?"

"I was just wondering. Are your sisters alright?" She has already checked them over and found nothing wrong that a good night's sleep, some fluid and food won't sort, for the time being anyway, but Rahim still won't let her touch him.

"Yes, it won't be long until they're asleep. They're tired."

"And you Rahim?" He looks at her in surprise. "Can you sleep now? Your new neighbours will take care of your mother and little Aamina. You need to get some rest too." She sees how reluctant he is to let his guard down. "So you can be there for them again in the morning," she adds, hastily. "You're all safe now, there's no need to watch over them tonight."

It takes seconds to sink in but then Rahim is transformed. The worry etched into his pale dirty face, melts away, along with the stiffness in his body and a little boy looks back at her. "Go get some sleep, Rahim. I'll stay until you're all settled and come back in the morning."

"Thank you." But he doesn't move. Something terrible haunts his black eyes. Ana cannot help herself. She puts her arms out to him and he falls into them. For an age they hold each other then, wordlessly, he withdraws, an adult once more. He nods at her, wipes the tears from his cheeks with dirty fingers and backs away.

She must have slept through her alarm-clock. Warm sunlight streams through the open flap of her tent and for a moment, Ana chastises herself for forgetting to close it. She hears whistling then footsteps approach. A giant shadow casts itself with confidence onto the wall of her tent, intensifying as it shrinks back, exposed. Finished off by a flash of sunlight and burst of warm Australian from that rugged, wind-burnt face.

"Morning Ana. Heard you had a busy shift." He smiles, crow's feet deepening the furrows in his brow, sky-blue eyes bright, white hair threatening to make off with the wind.

Ana hauls herself into a sitting position. How can it possibly be time to get up already? "Kai. How are you?"

"Ah – ya know …" With one step, he reaches her makeshift bed, steaming mug in hand. "Cup o' char m'lady?"

Rahim's face flashes before her eyes and Ana frowns.

"Not that bad, surely? Even used ya English teabags on this one."

She takes the mug with a grateful smile and he makes himself comfortable on the edge of her bed. Some might think this a bit forward. After all, though he has become like a father to her, they have only known each other a few weeks and this is an Arab country. They must be careful not to offend. Ana wraps her hands around the mug and sips gently. Too hot. She places it on the ground beside the mattress and finds a band to control her hair.

"What is that?"

She holds it up, surprised that he should notice its adornments. "Primrose and rose-hip."

Now is snowdrop time. The mists that lie low in the valleys will be lingering in the pale winter sun, coating everything with a thin layer of crystal ice. She misses those early morning walks with Ebb and Flow. The way the silly cocker stands beneath the springer when he feels threatened. The unconditional love her spaniels never cease to lavish on her. The way they seem to share even her most profound thoughts in those quiet moments when all to be heard otherwise, are the sounds of nature.

She misses her friends too, images fresh in her mind of how they saw her off, cramming her bag full of goodies when it was too late to stop them. Presenting her with this. A precious reminder of them and of home. Something small and practical that wouldn't compromise her bulging backpack.

"S'no place for a tender English rose." Kai shakes his head mournfully and Ana follows suit with a reluctant sigh. She's too tired for another sparring match.

"That's okay then. I'm not English, or even British."

"Mongrel, like all Poms."

"Thanks for the tea, Kai."

7

He picks up the knife and frowns. "Don't seem right – you having this."

"You gave it to me!"

She follows his puzzled gaze to the evil blade, gleaming in the morning light and a cold shiver runs along her spine. She wonders if she could ever use it. Last night she believed she would. Her brothers wouldn't hesitate. Flesh and blood, yet they've killed, and some. She shakes them out of her head. "Take it back Kai. It was good of you but I don't want it. More likely to be used against me." She smiles sweetly at him but he shakes his head. She shrugs. "If we're needed we go, right? That's the way it is. Why would anyone want to hurt me anyway?" He gives her a sideways glance. "Besides, when my time's up, it's up and there's nothing I, nor anyone else, can do about it."

"Bit defeatist. Bet ya brothers don't think that way nor ya dad, for all 'is faults."

Irrational anger wells up inside her and Ana struggles to be objective. I was only a child, she tells herself. I wasn't to blame. And look what he drove them to, their father. It was inevitable really that they would leave home as soon as they could. The only childhood friends he couldn't deprive her of, following his footsteps into the army, just like he trained them to. Through the ranks into the SAS. A general himself now, he must be so proud of them. Those sweet boys turned into merciless killers.

"We've got work to do."

Kai looks at her suspiciously. "Bet ya mum was a beaut! Shouldna left ya."

"He would have been the death of her. Look Kai, I don't want to talk about it, okay?"

Kai takes a good long look at her. "Anything I need to know 'bout last night?"

Ana heaves a sigh of relief. "Not really. A new family came over in the night. Weren't processed properly – just put into a tent. The mother was in labour. She came with three young children. No-one else."

"Heard 'bout them. They'll be okay. Good neighbours they got there. Want me to check on 'em?"

"No. I said I'd pop in, but thanks." He makes no move to go and Ana waits.

"Camp's growing so fast," Kai says with a frown, shaking his head and Ana nods.

It's a disaster. Hundreds come over and thirteen babies are born here, every day. The population of Za'atari looks likely to reach seventy six thousand by the end of January, seventeen thousand over maximum capacity with no end to the conflict in sight. And over half of the refugees are under the age of eighteen. It's a children's camp. There are children everywhere. Playing in the mud when it's wet, struggling to shelter from the unbearable heat and dust-storms that howl across the barren plain when it's dry.

They call this an internment camp. A self-sufficient people from a middle-class economy have escaped indescribable horror and death only to find humiliation and deprivation. To get in you need a permit. Each family is given a tent; mattress, pillow and two blankets per person and a licence for provisions. These can be got every fourteen days by going through three tents. The first to verify identity, the second to collect a temporary card and the third, to exchange this for food rations. Rice, sugar, lentils, oil, bulgar, dates and biscuits. Two thousand one hundred calories per person per day. Meat and vegetables have to be bought at a premium that many can't afford, from those who have managed somehow, to procure them.

Life here is bleak. The refugees live in constant fear of regime informers they say have infiltrated the camps and Jordanian police do little to maintain order, their main concern being to stop anyone getting out. Not surprisingly, smuggling is rife. Of people, goods, even aid supplies. It is said that Za'atari caravans and tents can be found for sale at favourable prices in local markets and it has become normal practice to tell newcomers, not only to look after their ID cards as they do their children, but to take care their tents don't get stolen.

Children dodge tear gas at almost daily demonstrations. They shake down water tanks to get their buckets filled first and throw stones at aid workers. Gangs have formed, looting doors and windows from trailers. Nine-year olds are coming to the playgrounds armed…

"Hey Ana, why's the Don after ya blood?" Kai brings her back with a jolt, stirring that uncomfortable feeling in the pit of her stomach.

"Is he?"

"Yep. What you done to annoy him this time?"

"He wanted antibiotics for a cold."

"Ahh. Guess the usual spiel 'bout antibiotics not killing viruses didn't go down too well, then."

She shrugs.

"Did he get 'em?"

She shakes her head.

"The Don always gets what he wants in the end, Ana," Kai warns. "You know that."

"That doesn't make it right." Anger sets her cheeks ablaze. "And I'm not going to condone the idea going around that he's the real mayor of this town. I wouldn't have given them to him either if it hadn't been appropriate, or the King of Jordan for that matter!"

Kai looks on her with concern.

"He's a crook, Kai. He openly admits to stealing electricity from the Italian hospital and then has the audacity to call us corrupt! Look at the way he lives. Even his children have a separate air-conditioned trailer to watch cartoons in and he has another just to store blankets and food. With three refrigerators! How is that possible when so many here have so little?"

"I'm not saying it's right. Just think you should be careful with him, that's all."

10

Reluctantly, Ana heaves a sigh and nods. The Don has a reputation for getting things done, God only knows how. People go to him, ask him to do something for them and it happens. Someone stuck at the border with Jordan or somewhere in Syria, even? No problem. He just makes the call on one of his mobiles and it's sorted. She doesn't doubt the rumours that abound about what else he is capable of. Ana feels a heaviness in her heart. Kai is genuinely concerned and she is too careless for her own safety.

"Did he call you everything under the sun?"

She rocks her head from side to side thoughtfully then looks at Kai and laughs. "Only mean and heartless."

"You got away lightly then. Perhaps he's getting to like you. I mean…who wouldn't?Go careful with him Ana or he'll be the undoing of you."

Ana frowns but says nothing. Everyone knows how it started of course. That the Don was one of the first to arrive when this camp opened in August last year, famously replying, when he was refused extra blankets without the required coupon, "give me the stuff now or I will separate your head from your body." Ana has good reason for her particular aversion to bullies and will not be made a victim again by anyone, let alone this self-styled mafiosa don.

Kai hasn't finished. "He claims to solve problems in the camp and that he can stop the riots. Looks like the management and he will have to reach some mutually acceptable arrangement."

"You mean work with him? Jan?" She couldn't bear to think of the tough German aid worker brought in to manage Za'atari because of his skill in resolving impossible situations, being compromised by anyone, least of all, the Don.

"Yes, Ana. Look…" Kai hesitates and apparently decides not to give her the lecture about a woman's vulnerability in the Arab world. "I worry 'bout you, that's all."

"Will do my best to avoid him Kai, promise."

"Good. That's settled then." Kai makes a meal of rising from her bed, crooked teeth revealed by a broad grin, reminding her of the injury some-one once dared inflict on him. "Meet for lunch?"

Ana laughs. They've only achieved this once so far.

"By the old tree?"

Another joke. There are no trees in this God-forsaken part of the desert. Apart from that in the Don's shaded courtyard, watered by the decorated fountain built by his workmen, of course. It is a particular cafe they refer to by the name of the old tree. One of so many shops and businesses that are springing up along the main avenue through Za'atari, that they are beginning to call this the Champs Elysees on account of the French hospital it leads to.

Kai nods.

"Two, at the old tree then. Have a great day."

"You too Ana, see ya later."

With the cheerful sound of him disappearing, Ana jumps out of bed, grabs her wash bag and towel and heads for the shower-block. Though not quite completed, it is comfortable enough. Like many in not so salubrious camp-sites back in England and far better than any facilities available in the third-world countries where she has worked. But like most of them, it smells. Of urine, mould and bleach.

Draping her towel over a bare breeze-block wall, dropping her wash-bag on the floor and throwing the soap into the shower, she turns the dial and waits for the water to heat up. It does today and, stripping, she steps happily under the warm stream, releasing her hair so that she can wash it properly. She regrets not having brought enough of the products that stop it frizzing up, her only consolation being, no mirrors with which to deceive herself. We are only ever as beautiful as we feel, she tells herself. By the time she finishes, others have joined her but she doesn't see anyone to speak with and hurries back to her tent.

Comfortable trousers, plain tee-shirt, polar-bear fleece, no wellies today. It's dry and sunny – hooray. She redresses, tying back

12

her hair, puts on her comfortable brashers, grabs her bag and heads out to meet the day. A few visits then to the canteen for breakfast.

The water trucks are unloading. Unreliable and expensive as they are, despite the newly dug bore-holes, they are still vital, for they deliver more than a million litres of clean water daily. They're working here on improving the water supply to surrounding towns as well as Za'atari, promoting all this new development in the hope of reconciling the locals to the inevitable without too much fuss.

"Morning Ana, how are you today?" Ghizlan's father catches up with her.

"Good morning Shahid. *As salam alaykum!*"

"*Wa laikum As Salaam!* And unto you be peace."

Ana smiles, her faith in humanity restored that little bit more for his courtesy. "How goes it with you and yours, Shahid?"

"Good, thank you, *Alhamdulillah!* Just two things I would be grateful for. To be able to return to my homeland." He points, as they pass it, to where the foundations are being laid for infrastructure to extend the camp and shakes his head. "No good," he proclaims mournfully.

"Why no good? They're making the camp better, more comfortable."

He shakes his head. "Bigger, more permanent. Soon we'll be known as the people of the water-resistant tents." Ana laughs at this description of the area he lives in. Recently flooded, with everything ruined as rain seeped in, their inadequate shelters have been replaced with structures which are supposed to be water-tight. "I want to go back to my home before that happens, Ana."

She nods. "And the second thing?"

"Syrian wheat and the facilities to make *Ghee*. Our *hrisi* doesn't taste the same without it."

"But it's delicious, as your customers clearly appreciate!"

"We own sweet shops in Daraa," Shahid tells her again. "When we return, you will come visit us and you will try hrisi made the right way."

13

She has been to his tent, a veritable factory with trays of pastries and cans of syrup neatly lined up, all remaining members of the family, including grandmother, fulfilling a role in the production line. While Ana admired their efficiency and hard work, Shahid told her how he couldn't sit around doing nothing. Now they have a thriving business and money to help pay for the plastic surgery their beautiful daughter will need on her face.

"How is Ghizlan today?" Only five years old, it took several operations to remove the shrapnel from her forehead and save her eye.

"Ghizlan is good thank you. Come by later. She can't wait for you to try her latest."

"Another new recipe?"

"Yes, but this one is all hers."

"I'll do my best Shahid."

"All good, no worries. We look forward to seeing you any time, you know that."

They separate as Ana heads for Rahim's tent. She has deliberately come this way, skirting the camp as they did the night before, to avoid too many distractions on the way, but someone is here already. Covered, except for her face, in subtle colours rather than depressing black, one of the camp's water and hygiene promoters has almost finished her talk on how to use water sparingly and keep clean. Little Aamina feeds hungrily from her mother's breast whilst the girls listen attentively but Rahim stands apart, his eyes flitting uneasily between them and the entrance.

A couple of plates, mugs and a half-eaten loaf of bread have been tidied into one corner of the tent. Ana catches Rahim's eye and smiles but he doesn't respond. She asks how they all are and if they would help her check the baby over, noticing as she opens her bag, the tension in him rising. Carefully, she takes out a stethoscope, gives it to the girls and shows them how to listen to each other's chests. Next a measuring mat, tape measure and finally, an opthalmoscope. Rahim startles, his dark eyes wide with terror.

"It's okay. Just a torch. Look." She switches it on and shines the light on her hand, changing the patterns by turning one of its dials. "If I look through this hole into someone's eye, I can see all the way to the beautiful blood vessels at the back." Rahim begins to tremble. Ana places the ophthalmoscope carefully behind her. "What is it?" she asks gently but he doesn't hear. She glances around. His mother seems oblivious to his plight so Ana makes a move towards him herself, just close enough to touch, and kneels. He doesn't see her. "Rahim," she whispers and he looks at her, but remains somewhere else. She reaches out, touching him gently on the shoulder and he jumps. He sees her now but says nothing. She waits. "Is there anything I can do?" she asks at last and he shakes his head. "Would you help me check Aamina over?"

He blinks back tears. "You do it."

Ana nods.

"She is beautiful and you're both doing really well," Ana tells Lileth as she hands Aamina back. "How about the rest of you?" The girls come forward eagerly but Rahim remains routed to the spot, watching like a hawk from one corner of the tent.

"And you Rahim?"

"I'm fine, thank you, and you?"

"Also fine, thank you. You look worried."

He shrugs, releasing the tension that held him as stiff as a board so that he seems to crumple before her eyes, but when the tears well up, he turns away. Ana looks to his mother but she is preoccupied with her new baby and the girls have retreated to play with toys someone left them. Once more, Ana is alone with Rahim in his distress. "Rahim," she entreats. "I can see you're really sad about something."

No response.

"Would it help to talk, do you think?"

He shakes his head but turns to search her eyes. He comes closer, hesitating then, throwing his arms around her, pulls her close. Ana rests a hand on his back and his thin body begins to convulse, tears falling unchecked onto her chest until there is nothing left. His breathing slows, becomes more regular and he stands back. He lifts the hem of his tee-shirt to blow his nose, wipes his eyes with the backs of his hands and looks intently into hers but neither of them say a word. Then he turns and walks away.

Should be rationing yourself, giving less to more. Fairer that way. More sustainable. It is Kai's voice that resonates around Ana's head though it wasn't him who said it in the first place. "I'm boss, not you." Saying it out loud lends it weight, makes it true. Even though it wants what's best for her – this part of her that tries to cut through her determination, she mustn't let it get the upper hand. Still, it makes her smile even when she shouldn't. It relieves that immense burden of sadness and breaks overwhelm down to manageable chunks.

She wonders if she will ever get used to the horror of it all and what she would become if she did. Despite her conviction that the most effective medicine is the person administering it, there is no denying that here, quantity of care has to take precedence over quality.

Even the smallest pebbles... In her mind's eye, a stone skims the surface of a mirror-calm pond. Ripples radiating from a dozen places of contact come together in little waves, churning, drawing and pulling on the water beneath until they form a powerful current. "Together, strong enough to sweep away the mightiest walls of oppression."

"We left everything behind," this pharmacist tells her. "Family, good jobs, property. An entire life. The soldiers found us." Luckily for them. Without the military, they would probably have perished, for many of the forty-five points where the refugees cross the border into Jordan are completely barren. There is no water, vegetation or birds, not even Bedouin and much of this land is traversable only by specialised vehicles, requiring extra manpower, increasing wear on equipment. Another huge expense for this poor country.

"We had to join a long queue to be registered. There were so many. We were all exhausted. The children were crying, my wife faint with hunger …" Ana nods, looking at him with concern, though she has heard this story many times before. The soldiers would have treated any injuries, given them water and blankets and put them on the bus that brought them here. A cold shiver runs down her spine as she wonders why Rahim sneaked his family in by foot.

"We heard Za'atari camp was big. There are more people here than in Daraa!" Ana nods, handing the baby back with a reassuring smile and looks out to the children playing in the dirt.

Beyond them, endless rows of dirty white tents and trailers set on chalk-white gravel, gleam in the blinding sunshine. Over five square miles of them now, all bearing the blue markings of the UNHCR and many, lines of washing hung out to dry. She can see a group of youths huddled around a fire, others wondering aimlessly. Structures that serve as mosques and schools. Stalls that are extensions of people's homes, selling goods of all kinds. Giant yellow bins. Water towers. Poles carrying wires and street-lights that seem to be multiplying and spreading, invading the streets around them.

Built on a disused military airfield a few miles from the Syrian border, by the United Nations High Commissioner for Refugees, following Jordan's claim to be able to house no more elsewhere. In July 2012 – only six months ago. And in just two weeks. This vast tented city stretching as far as the eye can see, that is swamped by muddy puddles in the freezing winter, overwhelmed by thick dust clouds in the unbearably hot dry summers and always windy.

A gang of youths waits for Ana as she continues on her way.

She recognises one or two of them. Mohamed lost an arm and still has a leg in plaster, his limbs shattered when a shell hit his home. "I will remember the pain until my dying day," he told her, "and I will never forgive."

Others must have come from another part of the camp. They are like young people anywhere in the world except for the loss and trauma they have experienced. No-one should have to suffer what they have, least of all, children. It makes her so angry, just like them. Here they have nothing to do, no future. A whole generation of traumatised children, vulnerable to fundamental Islamic views, is growing up without an education, bitter at the rest of the world for ignoring its plight and with the understanding that violence is the way to get things done.

One of the young men throws a stone which lands a few feet in front of her and Ana startles, her heart racing as she looks to see what their intentions are. Only a few weeks ago, aid workers distributing bread for breakfast were attacked with sticks and stones, the latest in a series of protests against harsh living conditions here.

Another stone. Determining to revive her martial arts skills, Ana puts her head down and continues purposefully on her way.

Some children play with home-made kites, wonder and delight on their faces, nothing but wet mud on their icy feet. Ana stops for a moment to take it all in. Scraps of material, plastic bags, wood and string, carefully put together and lovingly decorated, fly high above them in a deep blue sky. Ana wonders if these children imagine like she did, what it would be like to float away from it all.

She hears the distant drone of an aeroplane and the children freeze, the joy on their faces replaced by terror. One of the younger ones begins to cry, running to bury her face in Ana's legs and the delusion of normality is shattered once more. "It's okay." Promising that this plane will leave them alone, Ana helps them recover their fallen kites. She admires their handiwork encouraging them to talk about themselves, waiting until they settle before continuing on her way.

She passes a vandalised toilet block and wonders if it will share the same fate as so many communal structures around the camp. Even by the very next day, a new washroom can have been completely dismantled, carried off to the market and rebuilt into a new shop. Hundreds of new refugees arriving exhausted and confused to find no washing facilities, blame the management who can't understand what the complaints are about. So much confusion and acrimony results from simple misunderstandings like these. Yet many of these refugees come from working-class backgrounds. There is a plumber, bricklayer and construction worker in most streets. Ana wonders how long it will be until each community is given money to build its own facilities and responsibility for managing them.

Rida approaches, several of her ten children in tow. At only twenty nine years old, she is eight months pregnant again. As Ana considers how the size of this family reflects a society that values children as the greatest of blessings, the voice of grandmother Shweti rings in her ears. "They kill our children to break our hearts."

Grandmother Shweti. She must wake every morning worrying about those still left behind. Especially the twin she sacrificed to save the rest. She hadn't the money for a bribe so the officer demanded the child instead. One of her murdered daughter's twins.

Ana shudders despite the warmth of the morning but smiles at an old friend emerging from his tent. A tough Bedouin goat herder, he and his young family fled their village when it was viciously attacked. "Something inside you dies when you see innocents killed so brutally," he told her as he branded those images into her brain. A young man accused of desertion, tied to his motorbike and set on fire. Youngsters – anyone deemed old enough to fight for the rebels, dragged into the street and shot. Women and children, their throats slit and the dreaded *Shabiha*, Assad's muscle-bound, sadistic thugs who carried out this dirty work for him.

Ana doesn't make it to the canteen. Her last visit before that morning's clinic, is to the oldest resident in the camp. At one hundred and five years old, she has seen empires come and go. "I came out of the fire." Her wavering voice is so quiet that it is hard, at first, to make out what she is saying. "I saw so many young people lying dead on the ground. Somebody put me onto a motorbike, then into a car and took me out of my village. Now I don't know where I am."

The clinic is literally bursting at the seams, the marquee like structure that serves as its waiting room, overflowing into the mud outside. The volume of people is outdone only by the noise they make. Talking, shouting, coughing and crying. Right at the front of the queue, is the Don.

"I did what I could…"

Ana smiles graciously at her assistant. "It's okay," she lies. "I'm sorry I was late."

"Busy night?"

Of course. Ana nods.

"Why doesn't he go to the men's clinic?"

Ana shrugs grimly. Though they see whoever presents, this is supposed to be a children's clinic. The only one in the camp and by far the busiest of them all.

"Must have come especially to see you."

With a look of dismay, Ana prepares herself for the relentless need she is about to confront. "Guess he pushed his way to the front?"

"'Fraid so."

"Okay. Let's get him sorted and out."

But the Don isn't waiting to be brought in. Smartly dressed in a crisp white shirt, dark blue trousers held up by a belt that is undoubtedly leather with matching shoes that are remarkably clean and polished, he strides purposefully in. Slim but not much taller than her, his neatly trimmed beard perfectly complimenting steely grey hair that stands, apparently blow-dried, high on his head, he looks through cold blue eyes and Ana's heart sinks.

"What time do you call this?" he demands angrily, banging a clenched fist on her desk.

Ana resists the temptation to advise him it's time he learnt some manners. "What can I do for you?" she asks with forced politeness instead.

"Give me the antibiotics I need."

"Oh? So, how are you now, then?"

The consultation continues in this hostile confrontational way and the Don gets his antibiotics because, regrettably, he does now have what looks like a bacterial superinfection. Ana tells him he must stop smoking and he replies angrily with something in Arabic which doesn't sound particularly flattering.

Frowning at his back in exasperation, Ana shakes him out of her head. There is far greater need to contend with. Focus on the problem at hand. Don't get involved. But that is easier said than done and her patients' stories never fail to test her determination, challenge her resilience.

The sadness of a nine year girl who misses her father, a teacher, now in one of Assad's notorious prisons. Eight month old Bilal who, along with so many others born into this war, was never registered so doesn't exist. Twelve year old Ahmad who, like hundreds of children, took the perilous journey to Za'atari alone. "I would die to go back to school," he tells her. "I want to be a teacher or an engineer or a doctor like you. We studied so hard!" Ana nods. Before the conflict, over ninety per cent of Syrian children went to school, more than any other country in the Middle East.

Then there is the trauma, often deliberately inflicted. Children orphaned, maimed, even tortured. Struggling to recompose herself, Ana imagines wiping the board clean of her previous patient's story in preparation for the next. She reminds herself that children are resilient. That given the right support they can recover from the most traumatic of experiences. That here there is the practical help they need, safe places to learn and play, and structure to help recover a sense of normality. Above all, there are people who listen. She takes a deep breath and smiles as her next patient is brought in.

Lanky at sixteen, with inflamed acne, dirty baggy jeans and a tight blue tee-shirt, Wael looks like any teenage boy – except for his hopeless demeanour, his tormented eyes. He sits motionless, expressionless, as his uncle complains about how useless he is, that he hardly eats, doesn't sleep, is easily provoked to angry outbursts or tears and spends most of his time lying on the floor of their tent. Ana waits for him to defend himself. "What can I do for you, Wael?" she asks at last, but he ignores her. When she offers to examine him, he shakes his head but then his eyes glaze over, his lips quiver and his hands begin to shake.

"I knew a boy called Amal," he says. "He was only six years old. He didn't understand what was happening. I'd say that six year old boy was tortured more than anyone else in the room. He wasn't given food or water for three days. He was so weak, he used to faint all the time. He was beaten regularly. I watched him die. He was terrified all the time. He only survived three days then he simply died. They treated his body as though he was a dog."

The shock of it hits Ana like a punch in the stomach and she gasps as if the blow had been physical. An unbearable pressure threatens to burst out of her chest, tears forming in her burning eyes with the heat rising in her cheeks. She looks to the floor, struggling to regain control of her emotions and forces herself to focus on her patient rather than the terrible images now seared into her brain.

"I'm so sorry Wael." She reaches out to him, touching hands that lie limply in his lap and he opens them up to her. For a while they sit wordlessly but, just as the noise of those waiting outside begins to intrude, he continues.

"He was one of a group of small children whose parents were wanted. There were perhaps thirteen of them. They weren't allowed any food or water. When it was time for us to eat, armed men surrounded them to stop anyone giving them something. Those children were too weak even to cry. They just lay on the floor. The guards beat them repeatedly with sticks. More than us." Unable to prevent it, Ana lets her tears fall freely into her lap but she sits as still as a statue.

"In the beginning we could just about survive. We would go to the shelter and hide but now they are using different weapons. Before, the shelters were safe, but now the weapons destroy even those in the basements of houses. I couldn't stand it – the shelling, the destruction, the torture.

"We dug a hole in the garden of my home in Syria, just big enough for three people to crouch in. Whenever we knew violence was coming, our mother would take us to it, me and my brothers. She would cover it with corrugated iron and throw sand over the top and we would wait, sometimes for hours. The last time was from seven in the morning until five in the evening. It was terrifying. I was so worried that they would find us and kill us.

"We'd hide in the hole while armed men walked the streets and in the basement when they shelled us. That was almost every day. Thursdays are worst. A big day for massacres and crackdowns because prayers on Fridays can be a trigger for protest.

"Then I was arrested with hundreds of other people. They separated out the children. I was one of the oldest. There were many of us. They forced us into a small cell together. There was nowhere to go. No toilet, just a hole in the floor and there were bodies. They'd been there a long time rotting, full of maggots. It was so hot and the smell was terrible.

"Nights were worst. You couldn't lie down to sleep." Wael heaves a great sigh and gives her that look she has become too accustomed to. "You can't imagine what I've seen. What Syria has seen…Please help us. Tell the world, doctor. Please, please help us!"

THE JOURNEY
WAS DEATH

Kai finds her at four and dumps a sandwich on her desk. "How come you always find time for lunch?" she asks.

"Don't give 'em as much time as you do." She is too distracted to read the concern in his face. "You can't carry on like this Ana. You'll burn out."

"So, what should I do differently?"

"Treat the disease."

"I am treating the dis-ease. It's not just physical, they need to talk."

"That's not your job Ana. There are trained counsellors and psychologists for that."

"But I can't just tell them to stop talking, time's up, especially when they're upset. Besides, you know it takes ages to see a counsellor."

"Can't save 'em all, Ana."

She scowls at him and puts pen back to paper. "Know the starfish story?"

"Nope."

"Made a difference to that one and that one and that one…"

Kai heaves a great sigh. "Okay Ana, let me take over from here. You go get some rest."

She looks at him incredulously. "I don't need you to do my work for me." But he means well and she would probably be doing her patients a favour as well. "You've got enough of your own to do."

"S'finished!" he tells her smugly and she is grateful he didn't take her rudeness to heart. "To be fair, my waiting room wasn't bursting at the seams like yours is." He sits on the desk and pushes the sandwich under her nose. "Eat, girl. Now." He watches, waiting and she cannot refuse him. "Good. When you're done you can do some visits. Go see Rahim and his family." Ana frowns. "What?" he asks reluctantly.

"Something about that family."

"Yep."

She ignores him. "Doesn't feel right."

He raises his eyebrows. "Does it ever?"

"No, but there's something else," she persists.

Kai rolls his eyes to the sky and stands. "Perhaps best if you don't go see Rahim," he concludes. "Don't want you getting involved now, do we!"

Ana's assistant clears her throat loudly and looks pointedly towards the noisy waiting area.

"I'm worried about them."

"Okay, Ana," Kai concedes. "Go see to it. Make a nice change anyhow, to see some kids and women."

Ana frowns. "Not sure the women will be too happy to see a man. Best I see them before I go."

He shakes his head and Ana's assistant hurriedly agrees that would be best. "I'll find some space in the waiting room for you to see the children," she says.

"You sure?" Ana asks and Kai nods. "Thank you."

"No probs."

"How would I describe the journey? The journey was death," a mother of three tells Ana. She is trembling, her eyes wide, her voice broken. "We gave them sleeping pills, our children. We drove with the lights out and then we carried on by foot. Every time we heard a car or saw lights, we dropped to the ground and held our breath. When we came to the border there were soldiers. The baby started to cry. They told me to put a hand over its mouth. If the soldiers had heard that would have been the end. It was all of us or my baby... ." She bursts into tears and Ana puts an arm around her.

"Once we were in a shelter for twelve hours because the shelling would not stop. Then the shelter was targeted and the generator died. We sat in darkness, waiting, crying. Sometimes the shelling goes on for a few hours, then once an hour. To keep us on our toes, terrified.

"They started regularly targeting schools, mosques, clinics, hospitals. I saw the bodies. Schools! They target schools!

"There are no shops now. All destroyed. You cannot work. You cannot buy food. We tie belts tight around our waists to stave off the hunger. All you can do is run or die. I ran because I had to. Whole villages are surrounded even now. It is too late for those people to run, so they will die. Some have been shelled for months. There will be nothing left."

Thirteen year old Yana suffers from headaches that stop her from sleeping and make her cry. Mindful of Kai's warning, Ana takes a proper medical history, avoiding the question about any worries Yana might have, and does a thorough neurological examination. She gives some advice about fluids, exercise and sleep, then puts an arm around her and waits.

Yana describes armed men forcing her brother to the ground and stamping on his back until he could no longer walk, tying her father to a chair and making him watch. She falls silent. "Do you think I could be pregnant?" she asks at last. In a culture that places such high value on chastity, many don't report rape. Yana must know she and her baby are likely to be ostracised, left to fend for themselves.

It is normal for girls in Syria to be married between the ages of fifteen and sixteen, younger here in the camp to protect them. "Our daughters for our sons," one mother explained and that there are Syrian women providing girls to Arabs visiting from the Persian Gulf.

"We'll find out and make sure you get the help you need," Ana reassures.

"What have we done to deserve this?"

Ana searches bewildered eyes, anger vying with despair. "Nothing Yana. No-one ever deserves to be treated like this. Those who hurt you are guilty of the most terrible crimes and I hope they get the punishment they deserve." Even as the words leave her mouth, Ana realises she has gone too far. Not so much in what she has said, however unprofessional, but in the passion rising within her that wants far worse for those who inflict such harm than they are ever likely to suffer and the realisation of what she herself, might be capable of.

"Still here?" She looks at Kai blankly and he glances at their assistant with a frown. "Time's up. I'll see the rest. Any that don't want to see me can come back again tomorrow. I'm taking you out of here tonight, Ana. So go get some rest. I'll pick you up at seven."

She doesn't take it in, what he's just told her, though she's aware of him – the contented, secure feeling his presence invokes in her, and smiles. He sighs and comes to kneel before her. "Want me to come with you?" She frowns, blinking the tears away before he can notice them but it is too late. He lifts his hands to wipe them from her cheeks with his thumbs and, unable to help herself, she puts her arms around his neck, burying her head in his shoulder. Effortlessly, he lifts her to her feet and she snuggles into his warm chest, sobbing. He rubs her back, comforting her wordlessly and, gradually, the pain dissipates.

It feels so safe here but, as Ana wonders where Kai gets his strength from, she remembers what upset her and pulls away. "I'm sorry."

He shakes his head. "You okay?" She nods. "Was rather enjoying myself actually."

She turns to apologise to her assistant. "Kai can finish up here."

"Sure?" They both nod.

"Yes Ana, go." That authoritative tone again. "Seven, remember?"

"Seven?"

"Yes. Be ready to go for seven."

"Where to?"

"Out for the evening. Surprise." Ana feels uneasy. She is so fond of Kai, the last thing she wants is to hurt him and, though she believes he looks on her like the little sister he left behind, sometimes she worries it is more than her friendship he wants.

"S'okay, Ana. Friends have invited us for a meal tonight. They host a Syrian family so we won't be completely getting away from it, but it'll do you good to leave this prison for a few hours. What d'ya say?"

"Thank you Kai, that sounds great. Seven?"

"Seven."

Ana makes her way towards the main avenue in search of a small gift for their hosts this evening. A couple of doves fly overhead landing with a flurry and much cooing on the ground before her, and she smiles, wondering if their minder is far behind.

"Afternoon Ana!" She turns to greet the thirteen year old but he overtakes her and bows, his birds making way for him to do so.

"Hello Bashir, how are you today?"

Gentle Bashir flashes his toothy grin at her. "Good, thank you Ana." He turns to introduce the birds. "*Munya* and *Shahid*, Wish and Witness." Like many of the children here, his English is good.

"Oh?" She guesses what will come next.

"Yes. The birds remind me of Syria, as if I've taken a piece of it with me."

His older cousin taught Bashir how to look after birds on their rooftop back in Syria and now he has claimed a patch of desert behind their caravan for his aviary. A large wooden cage to which he likes to retreat with his sparrows, canaries, doves and pigeons.

He cares for the birds, feeding them, tending to the chicks and protecting them from unwanted attention.

"Aren't you afraid they'll fly away?"

"They won't go anywhere. They know where they belong. Even if they did, they'd probably go to Syria, to tell her to wait for me." Bashir smiles, his dark eyes sparkling mischievously. "You going to my dad's restaurant?" A little falafel place on the Champs Elysees.

"Another day. I've been invited somewhere else tonight. I'm looking for a present for our host. Any suggestions?"

Bashir's face clouds over and he shakes his head. "Sorry, but you can't have one of my birds."

"Oh no, I wouldn't take any of your birds from you!"

"I miss Syria so much," he tells her and she nods. She hears this sentiment expressed so often: I want to go home, Syria is my soul. Crouching down, he puts his hands on the muddy ground and the birds hop onto his thin wrists, settling there as he rises to his full height. He beams at Ana, wishes her a good day and continues on his way.

The hustle and bustle is audible from some way off but even so, the sudden noise as she rounds a corner into the crowded market street, halts her in her tracks. Taking a good look around her, Ana marvels once more at this semblance of normality.

Someone touches her elbow and before she can turn to see who it is, Laila stands before her, a big smile on her face. Ana's heart lifts. She looks so well now, this beautiful girl of seventeen who would wake in the night screaming, "leave me alone!" But now it is her fourteen year old sister who concerns her. Kareema stopped eating when they came to Za'atari. Like so many young girls who cope with the pressures of life by taking control of what little they can, she is starving herself because she thinks she is too fat.

"Would you come and see her Ana? She's not well."

Ana nods. "Of course. Lead the way. I'll never find your place otherwise."

Taking Ana by the hand, Laila steers her down the busy street. They pass bakeries, stalls piled high with shiny tomatoes and giant cabbages, a barber, a clothes shop, a cafe and a child selling sweets. Immersing themselves in the sounds of normality they breathe in deeply of delicious smells carried by the fresh breeze. Coffee, baking bread, barbecuing meat. On towards the other side of the camp where those who have been here the longest, including the Don, have settled into a relatively comfortable way of life.

"So, what's wrong with Kareema?" Ana asks, quelling her uneasiness before it has the chance to take hold.

"She's had diarrhoea for three days. We thought it would settle but she won't eat or drink."

It has been so hard to maintain Kareema's weight. As tall as Ana, she is only a pitiful forty three kilo-grammes and painfully thin. Every week she is brought to the clinic to be weighed and promises to try harder at least to maintain this, but Ana knows she is fighting a losing battle. The specialist counselling needed here is overwhelmed.

By the time Ana realises where they are it is too late and she can't help but look up to the trailer as they pass this abnormally fertile garden. The Don is deep in earnest conversation, a fierce look on his face. The odd Arabic word drifts close enough to hear, but the only ones that have any meaning for her are those they use to describe ISIS, the Islamic State of Iraq and al-Sham or Syria. This, she knows, is a terrorist group considered so violent as to have been disavowed by Al Qaeda from which it spawned, that is intent on creating a fundamental Islamic state in the Middle East and imposes an earlier form of Islam with strict Sharia law, on the people it controls.

The Don doesn't see her but the man facing the window does, catching her eye with a look that chills her to the bone. Probably in his early thirties, his black hair, moustache and beard tidily cropped, he bears elaborately patterned black tattoos that

30

cover his neck and hairless chest, aviator style sunglasses that perch above his forehead and has pierced ears, though he wears no jewellery that she can see. Muscular arms, almost bursting from the sleeves of his pale blue shirt, rest casually before him, his fingers, no doubt, drumming impatiently on the table. Jet-black eyes bore directly into hers. Evil. Interrogating. Invading her very soul so that it takes effort to break away. Putting her head down Ana hurries by, her heart beating an uncomfortable pattern in her chest. I will not be intimidated by another bully, she admonishes herself.

Kareema lies lifeless on a mattress in the corner of the trailer. From the doorway, Ana sees that she needs admitting for rehydration at the very least but she goes to examine her properly before delivering her verdict. There is little response when she speaks to her. Kareema can just open her eyes but is too weak even to batt her eyelids against the flies that crawl along them. "She needs to go to hospital," Ana tells her family reluctantly, then taking pad and pen out of her bag, scribbles a note which she hands to Kareema's twelve year old brother. "Run to the clinic and give this to the nurse. She'll organise an ambulance." Though nothing more than a modified estate car, that will serve its purpose here.

The boy comes to a stop at the doorway, dodges something and continues on his way undaunted. "She'll get over this," Ana reassures the family. "She just needs some fluids into her veins and feeding up a bit, then we can look after her at home." They thank her profusely and follow her to the door.

A dark shadow looms and even before she sees, Ana realises, with dread, what she is about to face. Blocking her way, the Don peers angrily up at her and behind him, his brutal companion, standing at well over six foot tall, his black trousers bulging in sympathy with the shirt as if they too, expect to be ripped apart by the muscles rippling beneath them.

"What you doing here?" the Don demands and Ana brushes

31

past him but she isn't going to get away so easily. With one hand, his minder halts her in her tracks, squeezing her shoulder until she pulls herself away crying out in pain.

"Don't you dare touch me," she hisses with a scowl then she turns on the Don. "It's none of your business what I do, or anyone else in this camp. There is a very sick girl in this trailer who needs to go to hospital and I have other people to see, so let me by."

The Don ignores her. "What did you see?" he demands.

She is so angry. How dare he. Who does he think he is?

"What did you hear?" he persists, the volume of his voice increasing with his anger.

"Nothing, now let me pass before I call the police."

The Don sniggers. "Think the police can help you, do you? Send you back where you belong, no doubt. Tell me, Ana, what right do you think you have interfering with our lives? We come, how do you say it, out of the frying pan into the fire, and the West sends us doctors, nurses, paramedics. If it wasn't for your world Ana, we wouldn't be in this mess in the first place! What do you think Qassem here, thinks of little western girls who come to our country and interfere with his work?" Qassem licks his lips, leering at her and Ana shudders to think what his work might be.

"Look." Laila's father intervenes at last. "We don't want any trouble. Our girl is sick and needed a doctor, that's all. Please leave us in peace. We have no intention of interfering with anything you're doing."

The Don looks from him to Ana. "If anything gets out, I'll know and there will be consequences," he warns, his voice full of menace.

"Are you threatening me?" she demands angrily and his tattooed thug looms over her, eyes wide and hungry. There is a strong smell about him. Animal. Like a zoo but more subtle. Dog, horse perhaps?...And liquorice. Ana pretends she hasn't noticed, dodging him easily now he is so close. She looks back at Laila's family, praying she causes them no harm, ticking herself off for allowing her fear to turn to confrontational anger. "Let me know when Kareema comes home again." Deliberately she retraces her steps past the Don's house into the Champs Elysees.

Shaken but determined not to let it show, Ana stops at a sweetshop to buy some *awwama,* honey balls, for Rahim and his family, then heads for Ghizlan's tent.

RAHIM

Even before she enters, Ana can tell something is wrong. Aamina cries inconsolably and one of the children pleads with their mother.

"Knock, knock!" Moving aside a plastic bag that reeks of ammonia, Ana taps an imaginary door. She lifts the tent flap and peers into the gloom, waiting for her eyes to adjust. Rahim, on his knees beside his mother, watches her rock backwards and forwards humming something tuneless to herself, whilst the girls do their best to comfort the baby. Behind them, everything has been tidied into one corner. Clean nappies, eating utensils, food, toiletries and two mattresses sandwiching blankets. The smell of freshly baked bread and something fried, rises above that of disinfectant.

"May I come in?" Rahim acknowledges her with a nod but does not take his eyes off his mother. Greeting them all with contrived brightness, Ana reassures herself that Aamina cries for nothing but food and goes to kneel beside him. "Hello Lileth," she says in Arabic. "How are you?" Lileth gives her a disgusted look and Ana tries a different tack, encouraging Rahim to help establish what is wrong.

It doesn't take long. Obvious really, in retrospect. Lileth is suffering from profound depression which, surprisingly, is neither reactive nor postnatal but a bipolar disorder, so called for the profound lows and manic highs it inflicts. Moreover, she has probably had it most of her life. Wondering afresh at what Rahim has achieved in motivating his mother to leave their home when all she wanted was to sit down and die, Ana does her best to reassure him.

She rises to a more comfortable position, stretching to release cramped muscles and the tent reminds her that there is not room even to stand up straight. A number of drawings have been piled neatly behind the mugs. Aamina appearing to settle in the arms of one of her sisters, Ana goes to look at them instead.

Similar to so many she sees produced by the children here, neither do these fail to upset. "Who drew these?" Rahim points to the girls. "How old are they Rahim?"

"Six and seven. And this one is mine," he says, a grave look on his face.

Painted in black and red, a tank advances on the bloody body of a baby, a warplane dropping bombs overhead while flames pour from buildings all around. "This is what happened when the army came to slaughter us," he says in that disturbing matter-of-fact way the children here have of describing the terrible things they have suffered. Ana is stunned.

The smell of richly spiced sweet coffee wafts through the entrance, a man's voice raising that of a woman's next door.

"What would you draw if you lived in a world without war?"

Rahim looks confused. His eyes flit about as he considers the impossible and then they settle. "There was a station where we lived," he says, losing himself to another place. "I used to watch the trains, wondering where they had been. What they would see next." He becomes more animated and when he smiles at her, a glorious light radiates from his eyes. "I loved to play football in the park with my friends." He hesitates and the spell is broken. "But now the park and my friends are gone."

"What was Syria like before the war?" Ana persists.

"Syria?" She nods. "A beautiful country with fresh air, vast plains where anything can grow, the highest mountains, deserts full of treasure, great rivers and a timeless sea. We saw whales and dolphins. And seals." He looks at her. "Dad used to take me on kayaking expeditions. Walking and climbing, too. I loved that. Not having to share him." A fat tear rolls down his cheek and he wipes it away without noticing. "The best bit was the evenings when we'd set up camp and made a fire. It was like all his worries disappeared while he was cooking. He'd laugh and joke, tell stories and listen to me. No-one else saw him like that. Only me. Special. Boys-time, he called it.

"One night, up so high you could almost touch the moon, there was a noise outside. Ssshh, he said, putting a finger on his lips. Wrap up warm and wait. It was ages 'til he came for me. We followed foot-prints in the snow without saying a word and, suddenly, there it was. A giant cat. The sun had set the mountains on fire and it was just sitting there watching, as if nothing could be more beautiful. There are big cats in Syria, you know, leopards, cheetahs, panthers …

"Some nights we'd lie awake listening to the wolves howling and once, we watched bears, fishing.

"Lots of interesting people lived in Syria. They'd come from all over the world to live there. Father used to say it was the cradle of civilisation." Falling silent, Rahim surveys the ground between them.

"What an amazing place Rahim! Will you show me one day?"

He looks at her as if she has gone mad but there is hope in his eyes and then the baby starts to cry.

"Foued?" Lileth reaches out in distress and Rahim hurries to her side.

"It's alright mother. It is Aamina cries for you, not Foued."

His sister brings the baby, holding it out to their mother and to everyone's relief, she puts it to the breast. Without hesitation, Aamina opens her mouth, shaking her head frantically from side to side until she is positioned well enough to draw the nipple in, then, settling with her eyes wide open, she gulps greedily, watching as Lileth recommences her rocking.

"Is Foued your father?"

"No. Father's dead. I must go back for him," Rahim tells himself, absentmindedly.

"Go back where?"

"Mmm?" He looks at her in surprise. "To Homs."

"Why?"

Rahim gives her a sideways glance. "For Foued." He turns to his mother. "I couldn't find him quickly enough." Though the torrent that follows is too fast for Ana to follow, he is clearly saying how sorry he is to have left his little brother behind. Lileth ignores him and he turns back to Ana instead.

"It wasn't your fault Rahim," is all she can think to say and he comes closer, hesitating. Her eyebrows try to meet despite her best efforts to control them and, before he can see the mist welling up in her eyes, she falls to her knees and gathers him into her arms. Long and tight he holds her, and though she doesn't notice him shake or hear him cry, she feels the wetness of his tears against her skin.

"Did you know that when you hug someone for twenty seconds or more," he says, withdrawing at last, "that causes a hormone to be released that makes us feel loved and secure?"

Ana smiles despite herself. "I'm not surprised. You're welcome to a twenty plus second hug anytime, Rahim. Where did you learn that?"

"I don't know. Somewhere." He looks at her thoughtfully. "Once I wanted to be a doctor. Like you, and father."

"That is something to aspire to, Rahim." He sighs. "What sort of doctor was your father?"

"A good one. He helped all those who needed him, including those who were against the regime. That was why they came for us." He falls silent again.

"Do you want to talk about it Rahim?" He shakes his head but she sees that he is desperate to offload and waits.

"We were trapped," he tells her at last. "Thirteen of us in one room. My little cousins. Aunties too. For ten days while they shelled and fired all around us. In the end father had to go out for food and water. A sniper shot him in the street. Just like that. One minute he was standing, the next, lying on the ground. I went to help. I went round the back so the same wouldn't happen to me. There was a policeman." He pauses and looks to Ana in bewilderment. "Where do you go when you can't trust a policeman?" She shakes her head with a shrug. "I thought he would help. He held his hands up and the shooting stopped but then he started to kick my father. I tried to pull him away but he was too strong and he knocked me to the ground with his gun. Then other men came.

"They set the building on fire but wouldn't let anyone out. I heard them screaming. I saw .... The heat burned my skin. Aunty broke a window and jumped with her baby. Then they took us away.

"So, you see, it was my fault."

Ana shakes her head, desperately trying to subdue her own pain. "No Rahim, it wasn't your fault."

"There was something else they didn't like about father," he continues. "He posted pictures and film of what they did to us, on the internet, so all the world could see. He was very clever. It took them a long time to discover it was him."

Ana doesn't want to know what happened next. Not yet. Not ever, though she will listen if Rahim wants to tell, but now she has taken all she can. He must have realised for he holds out his hand to help her up. "Thank you for listening," he says. "Can you make my mother better?" She nods. "Thank you, doctor."

"Rahim." He looks at her attentively. "Please don't go back to Syria. Your mother and little sisters need you."

"When mother's better, then I'll go," he replies as if it has already been decided.

"But how?" She has to know he couldn't.

"The way we came out but I'll be much quicker by myself."

"Would you remember the way?" Still she reaches for reassurance that is quickly ebbing. He proceeds to explain his route in minute detail. "But it's so dangerous!"

"More dangerous for Foued if they catch him."

"But what if they catch you, Rahim? What would your mother do without you?"

"They won't."

"How do you know Foued is still alive?"

"I just do. We used to look out for each other. He may be young but he's clever like me."

"Couldn't someone else get him for you? Friends, relatives?"

"All gone."

Clearly this conversation is going nowhere. Ana remembers the sweets she bought in the market and pastries from Ghizlan's family. "Brought you something." The girls come over, wide-eyed and she brings out the paper bags. "From someone who can't wait to meet you." She hands them over to their brother. "Rahim will make sure you don't eat them all at once whilst I go get medicine for your mother. Won't be long." She looks at Rahim, thoughtfully. "Don't go anywhere, alright?"

"Alright."

Kai is still busy though the waiting room is almost empty by the time Ana gets back to the clinic. Trying her best not to disturb him, she skirts the side of the tent to the drug cupboard but he sees her and shoos her away. "Seven," he mouths and she nods with a smile.

Something spicy and full of tomatoes bursts through with a damp warmth as she lifts the tent flap. Rahim is busy dishing up from a bowl of stew. "I give them our rations and they cook them for us," he explains. "Maybe we don't get quite so much back but at least it's edible. Want some doctor?"

"No, thank's Rahim, I'm being taken out to eat tonight. Call me Ana, won't you?"

He grins at her. "That's what my dad always said – to call him by his first name. He didn't like his patients to think he was above them. Each of us is as important as the other, he'd say and how would anyone survive a world of surgeons?"

"Your father was very wise."

Ana goes to Lileth still rocking on her mattress, the baby fast asleep in her arms. "Lileth?" She doesn't hear at first but the second time Ana calls, she startles and stares at her in terror. "I've got some medicine to make you feel better." Ana touches her gently on the shoulder. "It's called Sertraline. It won't harm Aamina when you feed." Rahim comes over to ensure his mother has understood, laughing at the funny way Ana says things in his language. "Take one tablet each morning, starting tomorrow." She offers to take the baby so Lileth can get some food but she declines. Ana tells her how important it is that she eats, pleading with her to no avail and Rahim tells Ana not to worry, he will keep trying. "Make sure you eat something yourself Rahim." He tells her he will. There is plenty to go around.

Ana goes to sit with Lileth while the children eat. Perhaps she will get used to her and open up. But Lileth ignores her. Ana picks up the children's pictures, noticing another pile almost buried beneath the mattresses and asks if she may see those also. Preoccupied, Rahim nods.

In another class altogether, both in their exquisite execution – with plain pencil, and their content, the effect they have is immediate and as she goes through them, Ana's stomach begins to churn. She looks up to check no-one is sharing this horror but the children are happily engaged and Lileth has settled back into her trance.

It is mainly faces Rahim has drawn, but there is enough detail to see how emaciated the bodies are. Skeletal, deformed. Contorted in agony. Adults, children and most disturbing, a recurring theme that runs through them all. The same face appears on every page, gaping black holes where the eyes should be. Seeing the likeness, Ana realises this must be Rahim's father. She looks up, grounding herself in the vision of a little boy busy with an everyday task, buries the pictures back under the mattresses and heads out for some fresh air.

When no-one can see, she starts to run, as fast as she can away from the tents, past the new building work and out to the perimeter fence. She puts her fingers through the wire mesh and looks up to the darkening sky, the razor sharp edge that prevents people climbing over, the saucer moon that seems to glow ever brighter, and then she begins to cry. Quietly at first for she doesn't want anyone to hear, but the wind, blowing away from camp, drowns her out. When there is nothing left, she falls to her knees, burying her face in her hands and takes some deep breaths. She feels better now but still there is madness in her and, taking to her feet once more, she sprints as fast as she can along the perimeter fence. It is about seven kilometres all the way and, though she makes it back in record time, she is hardly short of breath.

It is about an hour's drive to the village where they will be entertained tonight. Kai has borrowed one of the administrator's cars and drives them along the muddy road at a leisurely pace, chatting away as if his day has been nothing out of the ordinary. Entertaining Ana with funny stories and jokes, he watches her out of the corner of his eye, listening carefully whenever she has something to say, his face, the picture of unaffected happiness whenever he makes her laugh.

Malka is a quaint farming village tucked into the very north west corner of Jordan where its border winds with that of Syria and Israel along the Yarmouk river valley. A dramatic gorge that many refugees follow to safety. Rolling hills covered in orchards, are just beginning to spring to life and beyond them, to the north, the plains of Hawran, a rich agricultural tract, reach across the Daraa province all the way to Damascus. The honey here carries the taste of Citrus groves in Israel and fields of wild thyme in Syria, Kai informs her. Also that, with wonderful views over the Golan heights and Lake Tiberius, it is particularly lovely here in Springtime. His enthusiasm and the pictures he paints, lift Ana's mood, banishing Za'atari to another world far away. She wonders if she should succumb to his attentions after all.

Though already dark by the time they arrive, the bright moonlight clearly reveals the olive trees that surround this smart

41

villa and its carport enclosed by a grape trellis. A distinguished looking, bearded and moustached, middle aged man in traditional white flowing robes, opens the door. He introduces himself as Halim, greeting Kai like the long-lost friend he is, for they were students together at University in Melbourne. He takes Ana's hand but hugs her warmly instead of shaking it and kisses her on both cheeks before introducing those present of his family which, Kai has already informed her, goes back many generations and is well respected in the village.

"So good to see you again," he says in English with a faint Australian accent. "You haven't changed at all. And this is Ana. We've heard so much about you." She smiles and, taking their shoes off at the door, they follow him into a comfortable living area.

A heavily pregnant woman and her husband rise, bowing with welcoming smiles through their introduction as guests from Syria. Their two boys are already in bed along with his own children, their host explains, inviting Ana and Kai back during the day sometime to meet them also. Gratefully accepting a glass of chilled water, Ana tells them how much she would love to do this and settles herself next to the lady of the house.

Back home, the Syrian explains, they owned several corner-stores and a small farm. He had never imagined he would leave Daraa, let alone Syria but after the first year of the war, regular army units of local conscripts were replaced by unfamiliar faces from various branches of government security forces. The frequency of door to door raids, ostensibly to root out terrorists, and the violence with which these were undertaken, increased along with the looting.

He thumbs wooden prayer beads, his voice soft and slow, his eyes sombre, his smiles, flashing several gold-capped teeth, infrequent and tense. "It was like a medieval marauding army," he recalls. "They would move through a village with a truck beside their tank taking anything they wanted. Refrigerators, microwaves, furniture, jewellery – anything." They would barge into homes and take military aged men, no questions asked. Local watch groups, which began as bands of residents armed with farming equipment and kitchen knives, hardened into squadrons of rebels. As fighting intensified, regular citizens became trapped. They were used as human shields to protect the tanks, anyone who refused being shot on the spot. A strict curfew was imposed with snipers settling in the rooftops and daily life ground to a halt.

His businesses foundered as it became unsafe for customers to shop and employees to travel to work. Across Daraa, residents were confined to their homes, their resources dwindling as they were shelled. Two homes belonging to his extended family, were destroyed. "You did not know when you might die." Then his sister went into premature labour as a result of the stress. After a terrifying dash under sniper fire through the streets with their mother, for the army had warned no men to accompany them, she arrived at the hospital to find no experienced medical staff. The baby, born by emergency caesarean section, died soon after it was born and they buried it at home because open places, like cemeteries, are off-limits.

The family left in a hurry, packing one small bag for the four of them. He contacted the Free Syrian Army to arrange passage and at a pre-arranged time, a nondescript sedan fetched them from their home and drove them to a drop off point. Here, along with five other families, they piled into the back of a flatbed agricultural truck. "Under normal circumstances such a trip would have cost under a hundred dollars, but drivers are now charging up to one thousand five hundred," he tells them in disgust. The truck followed a route considered safe by the rebels, to a remote point on the border where they disembarked. From here they walked the rest of the way in the wilderness until they encountered a desert patrol.

They were taken to a military staging post where they were registered, then loaded onto a bus to Za'atari. After a few days, he decided a tent in the desert with unpredictable medical care was no place for a pregnant woman and contacted a middleman who arranged for the family to be bailed out by a Jordanian citizen. They made their way here on the recommendation of his uncle, a close childhood friend of Halim's father. "The Jordanian would take only twenty dollars but the middleman demanded six hundred for his part!"

He asks what entices foreign doctors to help the refugees and, as Kai relays their story, tantalising smells of frying food waft in from the kitchen. Ana's tummy begins to grumble loudly. "I'm so sorry to keep you waiting," Halim exclaims. "No doubt it is far too long since last you ate. Excuse me while I check on proceedings." To Ana's embarrassment, he rises but before she can protest, let alone rise to help him, his wife rests a reassuring hand on her arm. "Don't worry Ana, the kitchen is Halim's empire. He loves to entertain and today he has help. You are our guests here tonight. Relax and enjoy."

A young woman enters carrying a covered bowl, a thick towel protecting her hands from the heat. She doesn't appear to notice them at first but when she does, the effect is immediate. Paralysed, she stares at the ground, holding her precious load with trembling hands before her. She is beautiful, her olive skin set off by an intricately embroidered red dress, a matching scarf loosely thrown over long, silky black hair and deep brown eyes full of sorrow. She is introduced as Halim's niece and, reassured that no-one here will harm her, she passes with a shy smile. Ana wonders at the history this ancient family house must have witnessed.

They feast that night on a dish of meatballs in spicy tomato sauce, flatbreads and a cheese they call *ka'ak,* followed by yoghurt with honey and *baklava.* Inevitably, conversation turns once more to war in Syria and the strain its refugees are placing on Jordan. "The poor look at the camps and say, three meals a day and free shelter – that's more than I have," Halim tells them and of how people here are beginning to feel outnumbered.

"There is a standing joke," he says. "Oh look, a Jordanian. You don't see one of those every day!" Ana looks with surprise at his guests but they are not offended. "Yet you Syrians are the most enterprising, industrious people in the Arab world. Rather than taking them away, you do the jobs we consider beneath us at rates we would never accept and you bring business into our country."

Ana breathes in deeply of her fragrant coffee and takes a sip. It is strong, black and very sweet. She wonders if she will be able to sleep tonight and, remembering Za'atari with a jolt, finds herself asking if they think ISIS is recruiting there. "Undoubtedly. It is a children's camp after all and you know how hatred for Assad's regime rages in them. ISIS prefers children for they are easier to train and brainwash into followers for life, leaders of the future. The young are bored and angry. There is nothing for them to do. They look for anything that will break the monotony of day to day existence. Why do you ask?"

Ana frowns. "I heard something." The Don's warning rings in her ears, Qassem's sinister eyes boring into her soul and the smell of him is suddenly so powerful that she urges. Kai frowns.

"Oh?"

"Nothing much." She recomposes herself, anxious to change the subject. "Just the name being mentioned in conversation somewhere. What was Syria like before the war?"

"A wonderful place. With such horrific human loss, it is all too easy to overlook the history that is also being destroyed," the Syrian tells her sadly. "Sites that have stood since the dawn of civilisation and survived millennia of insurrection, steadily being reduced to rubble. Exquisite mosques where, throughout the ages, people have prayed and lived. Ancient marketplaces including some of the oldest souks with miles of covered shopping alleys and thousands of historic livelihoods, in ruins. There is no sentiment towards our heritage. It has become as disposable as our lives." He turns to their host. "Neither is Jordan a stable country, is it?"

Halim shakes his head. "We too, have all the tensions of the Arab Spring and a stagnant economy. With the cost of living rising much faster than wages, this war threatens our very existence. Since its creation, resource poor Transjordan has depended on international assistance yet, increasingly, this comes with strings attached which pull our king in directions opposed to those that best serve his country. Qatar and its allies want to topple Assad to diminish Shi'a influence in the region. They expect us to support the rebels, yet hesitate to help with the refugees. If the Qataris want to play kingmaker in Syria, they should at least pay the bill and tip the waiter, don't you think?"

"I hear women at Za'atari are beginning to stand up for themselves," Halim's wife informs Ana and she tells them about a qualified nurse who has turned one corner of her trailer into a beauty salon. A woman who makes wedding dresses. A place that rents evening wear and a hair stylist. All making good money to supplement their meagre rations. There are workshops too, that teach women and girls gender equality and life-skills as well as how to produce goods that will sell in the bazaars.

"Did you have a good evening?" Kai asks as he drives them back to Za'atari and Ana nods dreamily.

"Lovely. Thank you Kai. I feel so much better now. Shouldn't be needing your help again tomorrow."

"No probs., Ana. Any time. It's a pleasure. Ya far too hard on yaself, ya know? No-one else works as hard as you do at Za'atari. If ya wanted my advice, I'd say don't get so involved and give yaself a break now and again." She nods fondly.

It doesn't take long for Rahim's family to settle or for Lileth's tablets to kick in, fortunately without the destructive mania which can prove so much harder to manage than depression.

Ana's restlessness settles after that evening out with Kai and she manages her long clinics and visits, controlling her distress until she can release it alone. She runs and revisits the exercises she was taught but cannot sum up the enthusiasm to train as her father made her, enlisting her into Krav Maga classes when she was only a child. She hated this sport that professes to be a martial art, considering it unnecessarily violent, especially the version she was taught with young army cadets wherever they found themselves based with his postings.

Rahim has become a regular feature of her day and she looks forward to their time together at least as much as he appears to. He is bright, charismatic, loyal and affectionate. He did eventually allow her to examine and treat his injuries. Horrific evidence of the terror he survived, unlike his father, at the hands of Assad's thugs, as he calls them. But still he refuses to talk about what happened. The tension in him eases and, as he regains weight, he loses years, transforming back into a beautiful child.

To start with he manages the whole family, seeing to it that all the children, including the baby, are fed and kept clean, allocating each of the girls jobs to do. She doesn't notice how he develops their roles until it is too late. When she can, she allows him to help her, encouraging his aspiration to be a doctor for clearly he could be a very good one. In turn, he takes great pride in helping her with her Arabic. Compassionate, sensitive and hard-working, he helps the children especially, with great maturity and it isn't long before his twenty second hugs have spread, becoming famous throughout the camp.

"Will you come say goodnight to me before you go to bed?" he asks her one evening. She always does and it doesn't strike her as odd at first, that he should ask. Lileth is busy tucking the girls in and Ana smiles to see how she has stepped up to her role as mother of four little children, three of whom have suffered varying degrees of trauma. All except Rahim, who will only speak with Ana about those things close to his heart, are now receiving the counselling they require and they have made friends, even renewing old acquaintances in the camp.

It is already the end of February 2013, a month after that fateful night when they first arrived. "Would you tell us a story?" Rahim asks and watches her closely as she does so, his mother feeding the baby behind him. Later, when the others are asleep, Rahim settles himself with a worn teddy someone gave him beneath his head. He holds Ana tight, his thin arms warm around her shoulders, as if he will never let her go. "The last hug has to be a right hug," he tells her, as he does every night, his fingers, soft as feathers, stroking her back. And these memories play repeatedly, his words echoing around her head for the remainder of that restless night.

Nevertheless, it comes as a complete shock to find the next morning that Rahim has disappeared. Ana tries to persuade Lileth that he is probably somewhere in the camp, but his mother is beside herself. She has already looked everywhere for he is always up first, pottering about doing the odd jobs that make the day run smoothly. Ana organises a search party and heads out herself, but though she won't acknowledge her intuition at first, deep down she knows where he has gone. "Back to Syria," she finds herself saying before them all in a daze.

"What do you mean?"

"He said he would. To get Foued." Remembering how he said goodbye, Ana looks around her in despair.

"Why didn't you stop him?"

"I didn't know. When did you last see him, Lileth?"

"I went to bed after you left."

"He can't have got far. Probably caught the last bus out."

Three to four buses leave Za'atari for Syria each day. Better a quick death there than a slow one here, being the usual explanation from those returning. Last night however, they put on an extra one. It left late. After ten o'clock. Rahim must have blagged his way onto that. Ana looks at his mother, her mind racing as she considers all options. She cannot envisage leaving him to his fate and there is no-one else to go after him. It shouldn't take long. This is the right thing to do. Her only choice. "I'll get him," she says.

"You?"

"Yes. You need to stay and look after your children. I'll go." Blinded to her own vulnerability by love of a little boy, Ana reassures herself. She has got in and out of tricky situations like this before. Foreign aid workers go into Syria all the time. MSF has hospitals over the border and Hand in Hand for Syria runs a field hospital in Homs itself. She will aim for one of those if she doesn't catch up with him before getting that far.

Kai would stop her of course and try to make her see sense. She can hear him now. One boy, Ana. Why risk your life for one boy when there are so many others who need you here? But he's wrong. Her absence will make no difference to anyone except, perhaps, Kai and she's weary of feeling hopelessly inadequate. Being swamped by need they have nowhere near the capacity to meet. To Rahim and his family she could make a real difference. Her Arabic is good enough now. She'll get by, keep out of trouble, make herself useful if need be.

INTO SYRIA

They're already queuing to get on the bus. Men, women and children, clutching plastic bags and sheets that contain all they possess. Pitiful. Ana considers what compels them back to the horrors they risked so much to escape.

"What you doing here?"

She jumps, turning instantly, her heart thumping to her throat. "Ssshh!" She checks discreetly that her disguise has not been compromised. "Please don't let on I'm not one of you."

Mohammed is here with his five young children, sitting or standing around their two black bin bags of belongings. His eyes are full of concern. "You know Rahim?" He nods, a warm smile redeeming his tragic features. "Well, he's disappeared. Back to Syria for his eight year old brother. His mother needs to stay with the children, so I'm going after him, but no-one must know who I am. Do you understand?"

When the inevitability of his wife's fate sank in, Ana stayed, supporting the family through her final hours. For this, Mohammed remains forever grateful. She could trust him with her life. "The children won't recognise you with your *niqab* on," he reassures.

"Thank you, Mohammed. Why are you going back?"

"We would rather die in dignity back home than beg in Jordan. I've spent the last of my savings here. In Syria, I had a house, a good job and enough money. Here I have nothing."

"But, it's so dangerous and you don't know what's left back home."

He smiles benignly at her. "My mind is made up. I'm not trying to change yours, am I, Ana?" She refrains from pointing out that there is no-one dependent on her.

50

They have started boarding the bus and now the mad scramble begins. Jostling and pushing, children crying, bags, even people being passed through windows to those who've already made it. Reluctant to encourage them but anxious that they shouldn't be separated, Ana takes one of their bags and positions herself obstructively behind Mohammed's children. She follows them onto the bus, paying their fares as well as her own and squeezes into the seat he saved between them and the window.

It is another warm sunny day. Soon the dust clouds will start forming, suffocating the air, covering everything and, despite best efforts to prevent it getting into the tents, settling on the food and in the water. As the bus heads off with children running and shouting behind, Ana wonders if she will see anything of Syria's former glory or even, if she will make it back to Za'atari.

She remembers Kai and feels guilty. He was on duty overnight and likely still to be asleep if he managed to get to bed at all. It won't be long until he finds her note. She tries to remember how she put it. The exact words with which she told him not to fret over her and that she'd be back before the week was out, God-willing. She told him she was off on that long overdue break he keeps telling her to take.

The bus takes them as far as a makeshift army checkpoint in the desert. They will continue the rest of the journey into Syria by foot. Already crowds of bedraggled people are waiting their turn to be taken to Za'atari. They look exhausted and worried with no sign of relief, let alone elation, at having reached the border safely. Fear gnawing at the pit of her stomach, Ana watches the first of them board their bus. Subdued, obedient, clutching all they have, those children too small to walk, the injured and the sick. Devastating evidence of the horrors she is heading into. But then she remembers a loving, innocent child, who risks his life for another despite what he has already suffered and is ashamed. She would never forgive herself if she didn't at least try. Using fear to fuel determination, Ana turns her back on Jordan.

It isn't hard to find the way into Syria for they move against the current of frightened people walking the last steps to safety. A constant stream that has been flowing under cover of darkness. Bizarrely there are many obviously middle-class people amongst them who must have left in such a hurry as to have brought not much more than the clothes on their backs. Smart suits, dresses, even some elegant handbags. Wondering at how quickly it is possible to lose everything, Ana realises she is witnessing the reality that could befall any one of us.

Inadvertently she obstructs the way and a middle-aged woman looks with despair into her eyes. "Those who didn't get out are now being killed," she says simply and, subduing the urge to run, Ana puts a trembling hand on her shoulder.

"You're nearly there." With a shake of her head, the woman continues on her way.

Cloying Jordanian mud merges with Syrian. There is nothing to indicate when they cross the border. They tramp across barren ground, coming at last, to a collection of tractors and agricultural trucks. Some of the men in their group stop to negotiate a ride and, slipping some money into his pocket, Ana helps Mohammed's children into the back of one of the trailers.

They reach a dirt road and before long, some semblance of normality. Syrians working their fields. Children playing with stones, even marbles, by the side of the road. Old tractors parked next to cinderblock houses. They appear to be skirting around areas of conflict but when they do reach a remote village, smoke is still rising from buildings that were hit by shelling overnight. It looks to Ana as if this is the work of a blind man who doesn't care what targets his ammunition finds. Bodies laid out in the streets bear testament to the lack of discrimination. Old and young, Christian and Muslim, poor and not so poor. Every house bears the evidence of trauma. Pockmarked, once white walls – some with gaping holes, windows bereft of glass, rubble hiding what were streets, great piles where buildings stood and burn't out vehicles, abandoned by the side of the road. So much misery and yet the villagers are busy making themselves useful, clearing up.

Mohammed tells her he has decided to stay with his cousin here and Ana's heart sinks, but their driver will take them no further anyway. "Do not worry," Mohammed reassures her in Arabic. "You will stay with us until we find transport to take you further. You know the buses still run in Syria?"

"Really?"

"Yes. I have a friend who drives them from Aleppo to Beirut and back. There are problems. It takes far longer due to all the checkpoints along the highways and it is dangerous of course, but he makes good money. When violence comes he simply lies down in the aisle until it is over, tidies up and carries on." Ana doubts there can be many making the journey back into Syria. "You may think his business is all one way, but there are people still working in Lebanon who return to see their families. Then there are the young men who go to military colleges outside of Syria and return to practise what they have learned.

"There are taxis too. More like small minibuses most of them, that run throughout the country. Syrian bus drivers go everywhere and are skilled in assessing risks. You take my advice Ana, travel by bus or where you see a good flow of traffic with lots of buses. Even better, heavy goods vehicles carrying valuable loads, because a driver won't risk taking precious cargo where it might get stolen or destroyed." Ana smiles. It is a relief to hear of some normality in this chaotic land. But then she worries that Rahim might have found some other means of travelling the three hundred odd kilometres to Homs.

They pass a garden which has been turned into a graveyard. A fresh hole, surrounded by grief-stricken, wailing people, waits to receive the small body laid beside it. "It is too dangerous to go to the cemetery," Mohammed explains.

"Do you think Rahim would have come this way?"

He shrugs. "I will ask."

The truck comes to a stop in what would have passed for the village centre. An open area with steps surrounding a well, piles of smoking rubble where buildings once stood and a cratered road. A handful of people are clearing up, moving bricks, slabs of concrete and wood into orderly piles, sweeping up the debris. They work quietly as if stunned, shouting occasional warning above the thunder of falling masonry, instruction through the crackle of burning wood. Restlessness agitates the air to take flight. It whispers a warning as the eyes of suspicion accuse, then drops an eery silence like a blanket around them. Ana tries to ignore it, focusing instead, on helping the little ones down.

A gentler breeze caresses her cheek but with her embrace, it crescendos to a deafening shriek then dies, rattling something like a skeleton, along the ground. Silence. The whole world waits, tension rising until the air fizzes and there can be no going back. Lightning strikes, instantaneous thunder masked by a gust of howling wind dropping that cloak of silence once more.

Wide-eyed, Ana searches, willing her thumping heart down before it gives her away. Someone shouts, "Sniper!" She hears Mohammed shoo his children into an alley but they inhabit a different world to hers. He touches her elbow, startling her out of her trance and looks at her in alarm. "Come," he says.

They pass the ruined house of an old woman, her neighbours fussing over the mess inside. A shell hit it. Through a hole that was once the front wall, Ana sees the shattered mirror of a wardrobe covered in flesh and blood and urges. She hurries the children past before they notice.

They stop at a little house further along the street. Mohammed opens the door and shouts but there is no reply. The tension in Ana peaks. She doesn't notice someone come right up behind her, only a stranger's voice suddenly so loud in her ear that she jumps, instantly ready to defend herself. A short, well-built woman looks in bemusement back at her then rushes past, her long black coat sweeping the dirty ground. Like a whirlwind, she embraces Mohammed and the children each in turn, coming to an abrupt stop before Ana. Mohammed introduces a distant cousin of his deceased wife searching for her eleven year old brother and, eyes full of pity, the woman embraces Ana with a kiss on both cheeks. She ushers them all into the house but Ana's anxiety builds to a great pressure in her chest.

"I can't stay."

Mohammed nods. "Of course. We must find out what we can about your brother."

There is no news of Rahim and, guessing that he is traveling by foot, Ana determines to do likewise, planning her route with rare gratitude to her father for teaching her to map-read. She doesn't notice how Mohammed watches, shaking his head gravely but when he insists she take a lift at least part-way, for both extremist rebels and shabiha are known to frequent this area, she reasons that Rahim is likely, anyway, to be some way ahead of her by now.

The young man watches her suspiciously from the other side of the room as Mohammed speaks with him but his demeanour softens as their discussion becomes more animated and then he smiles. They take her to his transport, a battered old, once white estate with no identifying features apart from a few strategically placed bullet holes. As Mohammed and his family bid her farewell, Ana wonders whether she should have stuck to her original plan.

She doesn't notice them at first. Not until her driver turns to look over his shoulder, cursing as he reverses his car at such speed as is bound to draw attention. Then she panics for there is no way out. He slows, reversing to the end of the road until he can turn. Paying no heed either to its one surviving wing-mirror or any remaining paintwork, he scrapes the car through an alleyway and heads in the opposite direction as she peers in terror over the back seat. There is no sign of the army patrol that blocked their way out of the village and, seeing her driver continue calmly as if nothing had happened, Ana forces herself to breath.

An ear-splitting shriek pierces the air just above them. She clutches the headrest of the seat in front, spitting out her choking niqab. A distant hill explodes in a ball of fire, triggering the rattle of gunfire all around and she dives unceremoniously into the floor well. They take a sharp turn and a door handle thrusts itself violently into her rib-cage. Her driver retrieves a mobile phone, demanding information on which routes are currently safe to use and a wave of guilty gratitude washes over Ana's terror.

At last, they come to standstill in an olive grove and he gets up to help her out, his eyes flickering as he searches her face. Mindful of the fate of so many brave young men like him, Ana is overcome by grief. She ducks back into the car for her bag before he can see the tears well up in her eyes, recomposes herself and turns to thank him but he refuses her money. With a grin that makes him look so young and vulnerable, he points out where she should head for next, jumps back into his car, reverses and leaves.

It is now mid-afternoon and, for the first time in as long as she can remember, Ana is truly alone. Beneath a cloudless sky, a winding path leads through an ancient forest of gnarled trees, no taller than she is. Apart from birdsong, the gentle rustle of the breeze tickling leaves and her footsteps, it is silent. There is no wailing, crying or shouting, no gunfire or shelling. It is almost possible to imagine the world as it was surely mean't to be – without strife or suffering.

Still, adrenaline courses through her and she feels her heart racing faster than it should. She can use this level of fear to her advantage. It will spur her on, keep her going when she should rest, alert when she needs sleep. Fear, she has learned, can be useful, motivating, even exciting. The trick is not to let it control you. I know where I'm going, she tells herself, glancing at her compass for extra reassurance. Do like Rahim. Keep away from people and, hopefully, it won't be long.

She wonders how she will persuade Rahim to leave without his brother. If need be, she'll find someone to show her to the field hospital in Homs. Perhaps, even, a friend of the family who will help her find him.

She sticks to fields and footpaths, avoiding roads where she might be discovered by government forces. Occasionally she passes others with the same ideas, except they are heading towards Jordan rather than away from it. A young man who tells her he spent two days hiding in a ditch with no food, only water and of how he raids apparently empty houses, "they're all hiding in the basements," for food. A family of four who can't understand how war has erupted in their country between civilians. Amongst neighbours. A woman with her teenage son, anxious to protect him from conscription or prison.

As dusk draws in, Ana finds an empty cinder-block hut in the middle of a field. A simple affair with a corrugated metal roof and not even a door to close off its entrance. Such as might be used by shepherds tending their flocks. Reassuring herself that she is alone, Ana decides to settle here for the night. She takes the food so gladly given by Mohammed and his family, for that needs eating before the dry rations she brought from Za'atari, and settles herself in the doorway to watch the sun set as she eats. Drinking the last from her water bottle she props it up outside to catch any rain, or at least some dew overnight then, putting on her fleece, makes as comfortable a bed as she can from her coat and backpack and lies herself down. She is under no delusion that she will sleep but she will take what rest she can.

She must have fallen deeply unconscious for the intrusion into her night takes her completely by surprise and, convinced she is dreaming, at first she does not respond.

"Ana?"

The name is familiar but the voice? She opens her eyes to pitch black, wondering where this is and, with a pang of terror, remembers.

"Ana, wake up."

For a moment she lies rigid, holding her breath, willing her pounding heart silent as well. Something touches her and she gasps.

"Sssshh, I'm a friend." He speaks Arabic. "Mohammed sent me. Said you needed help."

She takes a deep breath and sits bolt upright. "Who are you?" Forcing herself to remain calm, Ana reminds herself that, though now common in Syria, kidnappings are usually carried out by ordinary people under extreme pressure rather than fundamental jihadists. And this one knows her name.

"A friend of Mohammed's. We must be quiet, do you understand?" She nods, whispering confirmation and reaches for her torch. "No. No light."

"What are you doing here? How did you find me?"

"Mohammed was watching as you planned your route. I knew where you were dropped off and followed you from there."

"Why? Who are you?"

"First, you tell me why you risk everything to come to Syria. Are you mad or something?"

The turbulence in her stomach rises as she considers the answer to this question. She nods. There is movement behind him, a whispered voice outside. "Who's that?"

"Doesn't matter. We've come to take you back."

"Not without Rahim."

"Do you really think you can just walk into Syria and out again with a child?"

She shakes her head. It's not like that. "Leave me alone. I'm doing just fine. Thank you."

"Stubborn woman." But he doesn't say it in anger. "We can help you get to Homs."

She frowns. "Why would you do that?"

"Because Allah wills it. For extra *Baraka.*"

She senses him grinning in the darkness. "Baraka?"

"Blessing."

"So what is it you do?"

"Get people, equipment and medicines, where they are needed."

"You're smugglers?"

"Seekers of justice, freedom and democracy."

She smiles. "So, why would you help me?"

"Because you're on our side. We owe you a favour."

"You owe me nothing."

"Mohammed told me about you. He should never have let you go. We've come to take you back."

"I'm going to Homs."

"To find Rahim. Yes, I know. But what if you don't find him? What then?"

"I will. There's a field hospital in Homs. I'll head for that, maybe help out until I find him."

The intruder heaves a great sigh. "Okay, we will help you but you must do exactly as I say or you will get us all killed. Understood?" She nods. "We rest a short while, then we move out."

"How many are you?"

"It doesn't matter. The less you know the better." She frowns. "Now sleep. I will wake you when it's time."

She lies back down, feeling suddenly more secure but less settled and spends the rest of the night drifting from one nightmare to another. When he wakes her she jumps up with a start and finds him with a stunned look on his face, staring up from the floor beneath her. Mid-thirties, tall, dark and lean, he is dressed all in black. Tee-shirt, fleece, and trousers saved by a belt tightened at least two notches. Handsome and fresh-faced, he has thick hair cut short, a neatly trimmed beard and moustache and now, as he rises with a grin, a sparkle in his deep brown eyes. "Where'd you learn to do that?"

"What?" She shakes her head in agitated confusion.

"Floor me like a pro."

"Krav Maga."

He laughs warily. "Reckon we could use you in our team. Just need to master that attitude." She glares at him and makes for the door but he is up in an instant blocking her way. "Not so hasty. Few ground-rules we need to establish before I let you out," he warns and she scowls at him.

"For your information, I was doing just fine until you came along!"

"But you're not even out of the nursery yet, girlie. Trust me, you won't last five minutes once you reach the jungle. You need us a lot more than we need you."

She doesn't doubt it. She drops back to the ground beside her bag. "Okay, tell me what I need to know."

"We have made a decision. I will take you to Homs. My companions have other work to do so there is no need for you to meet them. You must understand the risk I take. If you disobey me I will abandon you to your fate. Understood?"

She nods, certain she doesn't want this extra complication to her journey but acutely aware of her naivety. "What do I call you?"

He gives her a boyish grin. "Ahmed." He moves away from the doorway and lets her out.

It is a cold, overcast day. Winter isn't over yet after all. She takes a good look around, scanning the horizon, but there is no-one else. Ahmed taps her on the shoulder and she jumps. He hands her the niqab. "Good idea." She nods, repositioning the band that controls her hair and covering her head once more with the cloth that hides all but her eyes. He grins and she wonders what he finds so amusing, then he turns and heads across the open field the way she planned to go the evening before.

Ahmed leads and Ana follows, getting her bearings from time to time to reassure herself that he doesn't lead her astray. Along dirt tracks, through muddy fields and woods. Occasionally past signs of civilisation but avoiding people whenever possible, so that it comes as a great surprise when he leads her into a village. "We eat here," he says, slowing to walk beside her.

They pass a school, a playground full of colourfully dressed, bright-eyed, energetic children and Ana stops at the gate, holding the bars as if this were the way out of her world into another, happier place. A few gather around, chatting, laughing, one at the back jumping for a better view and she smiles, recognising in them the characteristics of children all over the world. Many have brown eyes and dark hair but there are also quite a few who are strawberry blonde like she is, with green or even blue eyes. The clothes they wear are no different and they have the same loud, joyful optimism here, where they are surrounded by their friends.

In the distance, Ana sees the familiar goodie-versus-baddie war-games being played out and, remembering that these children were born into protest and war, considers that, even so, they are inquisitive and hopeful. Not indoctrinated and suffocated by the old police system as their parents were.

She feels a tap on the shoulder. With a broad smile on his face, Ahmed raises his eyebrows and flicks his head. "This way," he says and, acknowledging a chorus of good wishes with a cheerful wave, Ana follows him.

They turn into a courtyard bordered by white concrete sheds with tin roofs, and a larger double storied building at the far end to which he leads her. "This is the hospital for now." Wondering if this is Ahmed's home town, Ana considers the risk to all these people, his helping her poses should they be caught.

"The doctors here are all volunteers. This one, he is a neurosurgeon from Turkey." Ahmed waves at an overweight harassed looking bald man coming towards them and the surgeon waves back, dabbing perspiration from his face with a dirty handkerchief as he passes. Ahmed leads her past a noisy waiting room. "Quiet today," he says. "Not too many wounded. Just the usual."

He heads for a small room that apparently serves as the hospital reception. The woman sitting behind the desk rises in warm greeting and Ana examines a crude triage system scrawled into plaster-board. Three lists of names headed, "less than two hours, greater than two hours and expected to die," indicate the

61

times within which these patients should be seen and Ana cannot help but think that, for the last two unfortunates, the writing is already on the wall.

The dark haired receptionist wears a simple knee-length dress that is miraculously white, matching headscarf and elasticated belt. She looks to Ana fondly through deep brown eyes while Ahmed speaks, then makes a beeline for her with him close behind.

"Hi there," she says brightly in faintly accented English and Ana tries to shrink into the red linoleum floor. "I'm Sabeen. Hear you're on our side, so welcome! Make yourself at home." Ana nods but before she has a chance to respond, Sabeen continues, the pressure in her speech not quite enough to trip up her words. "In case you're wondering, I spent three years studying law in Seattle. Had to curtail my education. Folks at home needed me. Anyway, you're in a hurry. Eat, then be on your way and…good luck." She looks to Ana with such sweet concern, then turning without further ado, leads them out of the building to one of the outlying sheds and a temporary canteen. With a flourish of hands she tells them to help themselves, bids them farewell and heads back to her office.

There are two others in the room. An elderly man seated at one of the three tables, and a little boy in a wheelchair. "You can take off your niqab now," Ahmed tells her and when she smiles, appears to do a double take. "Eat. Drink," he commands, recomposing himself to show her the food. Flatbreads, jam of some kind and yoghurt. Ana waits for him before helping herself. She watches as he goes to the old man and how they embrace as if they have always known each other. She goes to sit beside him and the child looks up with an accusing frown on his scarred face.

"No-one here has seen an eleven year old boy headed for Homs," Ahmed informs her, "but they'll let me know if they do." He pulls a mobile phone from his back pocket and places it on the table, scrutinising it carefully for a few moments before continuing his conversation with the boy's grandfather. Ana learns that these are the only members of their family to have survived a rocket attack which took not only the little boy's left leg, but also his genitalia and, no longer hungry, fights the temptation to turn away.

The call to prayer rings out from a distant mosque. Rising solemnly to their feet, Ahmed and the old man make their way to a bowl of water in one corner of the room. They take it in turns to wash their hands, face and feet, drying them carefully on the clean towel laid out beside it then, retreating to the centre of the room, face the Kaaba and prostrate themselves to perform their prayers. Afterwards, Ahmed explains how, though he does his best to pray as he should, five times a day, this is not essential to his relationship with Allah and impossible sometimes, given the extreme circumstances imposed by the war. "It is better not to pray at all, than to pray without the right attitude of mind," he concludes.

They travel by minibus for the next leg of this journey, their driver constantly checking his mobile for up to date information on where the regime has set up checkpoints and which routes are safest to use. Unconsciously Ana shrinks into her seat, wishing she could make herself invisible to their suspicious looking companions. Watching everything through the glasses of heightened awareness, she takes it all in. The way they eye her up – the others. Ahmed's shrewd banter which makes light work of potentially serious threats. The way he gives the impression of being totally at ease whilst remaining hyper vigilant. How, though they all feel the heat in this overcrowded, confined space that throbs with testosterone and adrenaline, she is the only one bothered by the pungent stench of unwashed bodies and sweat.

Though anxious to cover as much ground as possible, for Ana their stop doesn't come a moment too soon but, to her alarm, three strangers appear to have joined them.

AHMED

They head away from the road along an overgrown footpath, past three burnt out houses, towards Damascus, aiming to skirt around it on the Lebanon side. Already the distant sound of explosions is becoming louder, more sustained and Ana tries not to think of the lives being destroyed with every single one. Injuries being inflicted on innocent civilians, like the little boy they met that morning and so many she has treated at Za'atari.

It will be pretty here in the spring. They pass olive groves, orchards of apricot and apple trees and through lanes lined with cypresses and poplars. In the distance, now that the sky has cleared, she sees that the mountains are covered in snow and what the skyline of Damascus would have looked like before the war.

Something dark ahead, blocks the way but before it has even registered on her consciousness, their companions have vanished and she lies on her back next to Ahmed on the ground. Winded, she gasps for air, staring at him in bewilderment. He looks at her thoughtfully, then consults his mobile phone. "Wait there," he hisses and with no other warning, raises his arms and stands. She rolls onto her tummy and peers through the long grass, watching him walk slowly towards the obstruction. Alone. The others remain hidden. Ana wonders why Ahmed would risk his life for them all.

Time stands still and she considers all her options. If she ran now, probably no-one would notice but what about Ahmed? He has taken more risks for her than anyone and, whatever his fate, she couldn't just leave him to it. So she waits with bated breath, motionless apart from the thumping of her racing heart and fights the urge to massage calf muscles contracting in agonising cramp.

A cool breeze rustling the fragrant grass, the occasional buzz of an insect and distant birdsong are the only sounds to break the deafening silence and Ana's eyes ache from watching. At last, she sees movement, then Ahmed walking slowly back, his arms swinging freely by his side. He seems relaxed, happy even, yet hot tears burn her cheeks and now she realises how greatly she fears for him.

It is an unofficial Free Syrian Army check-point. The suspicious men huddled around an open fire are overshadowed by a spooky figure shrouded in darkness that blends imperceptibly with that of his equally intimidating steed. Knives openly displayed in his belt, rifle laid loosely in his lap, he stares at Ana, hypnotising her with chilling black eyes and when Ahmed puts a hand on her shoulder, she jumps, her heart leaping somersaults like some wild animal that has just been netted.

"Don't worry 'bout him." He looks up irreverently, to the slit revealing all there is to see of the person within this terrifying fusion of man and horse. "Crazy fundamentalist. But for the moment, unfortunately, we need him." The black eyes flicker but the creature does not flinch and, trance broken, Ana's eyes fall to the rebel soldiers beneath him. A disparate group in age, appearance and demeanour, they could be teachers, engineers, medics. She wonders what would happen to them if the fundamentalist had his way.

They pass without challenge and after a brief exchange with a young man who can be no older than fifteen, Ahmed informs them that a local shepherd will take them over his land to where they will spend the night. Even as he speaks, an elderly man in traditional robes with checkered red and white headscarf, approaches in an open top truck. Viewing his potential clients, he speaks with one of the soldiers, nods, then ushers them forward, gesturing that they should all climb in.

They travel for many miles along routes Ana would never have considered passable for the shepherd clearly knows every track of his fields. Bringing them at last to a hut almost identical to that in which she spent the previous night, he bids them God-speed and, while the others go about the business of getting some sort of meal together, Ana watches him retrace his tracks until he disappears from view.

She remembers the food still left in her back-pack and goes to add that to what has already been laid out. Bread, cheese, even a sausage which some-one is cutting up, but Ahmed lays his hand on hers. "Save that for later." She hesitates. "The hut's yours for tonight. Put it in there." She opens her mouth to protest but he shakes his head with a smile and points the way, so she does as she was told. She places her bag in one corner of the cold damp room and heads out for a private spot to relieve her bursting bladder.

The hut is in the middle of a field sloping down to panoramic views over Damascus, behind it an olive grove and beyond this, rolling hills. Finding a dip that could only be overlooked from above, Ana satisfies herself that she is alone. Even so, an uneasiness creeps over her and she rushes back, certain she is being watched.

"You alright?" Ahmed asks in alarm and she nods. "Look like you seen a ghost. Haven't, have you?" She shakes her head. "Well,…then eat."

From nowhere, Ana finds an appetite and simple though it is, this food shared with strangers on the hills overlooking war-torn Damascus, is as delicious as any she has ever tasted. They talk about everyday things. Family, friends, homes, work, football and jobs left unfinished that will never need doing. Goosebumps ripple over her skin. These are ordinary people rendered extraordinary, set on a path of destruction by circumstances beyond their control.

She wakes with a start, dead weight bearing down on her. A hand over her mouth and that strong smell invading her nostrils. In an instant wide awake, she musters all her strength to push him off but he is immoveable. Pinning her down with her wrists above her head, his knees on either side of her thighs, he presses like a rod of iron between her legs.

She panics, her screams dying in rigid flesh and he pushes harder, forcing her chin into her neck until this must surely break before she suffocates. She feels his breath against her ear, the stench almost overpowering. Animal and liquorice. Then comes his voice, deep and guttural. He speaks slowly and succinctly but only just loud enough for her to hear. "I'm going to fuck you until you scream for more but if you make a sound, I will slit your throat."

Her terror peaks and she renews her struggle, wriggling and squirming to shake his hand off her face but it makes no difference. Her chest heaves in agony for precious air. Exhaustion overwhelms her and she knows she will die but then he relieves the pressure on her mouth just enough for her to take one breath, clamping her mouth shut even as she sucks it in. She forces herself to be still and waits, willing herself to attack as soon as she can catch him off guard.

There is a noise at the entrance to the hut, then a voice. "You alright Ana?" She calls out, the sound muffled instantly. With all her might she fights back but she is powerless in the face of a force so much stronger than hers.

"Ana?...Can I come in?"

"I swear you will be mine," the intruder growls in her ear and then he is gone. Vanished as if into thin air. Adrenaline pumping through her, Ana jumps up and waits silently for the slightest sound or movement that would give him away, but there is none. She wonders if she imagined him. A bad dream perhaps, but his smell lingers and she tastes blood in her mouth.

"Ana?"

"Yes ..." Nothing but a hoarse whisper escapes her mouth and she tries again, forcing herself to calm down. She goes to the door, startling with a shriek as an arm pins her by the neck. The barrel of a gun pushes hard against her back and she freezes, her heart in her throat, choking, but it is Ahmed and he releases her the instant he realises his mistake.

"You alright?" He kneels before her, blinding her with his torch as he peers into her face. "Sorry, I thought you were an intruder."

"Did you see him?" She makes just enough noise to be heard.

"Who?"

"He…"

"No-one came through this door and there's no other way out." Ahmed steps silently into the hut and sweeps the tiny room with his light. Damp dirty corners, corrugated metal ceiling, muddy floor. Nothing. Not even a hole for a rat to squeeze through. He looks at Ana and frowns.

"You're tired," he says. "Get some rest." She shakes her head, wondering if she really is going mad and what on earth she is doing here in Syria. Nothing would induce her to go back into that hut and she settles herself outside beside Ahmed instead.

Wide-eyed, she watches the night go by, the terrible flares that light up the sky over Damascus, shadows which wouldn't have bothered her before and her companions warming the cold night air with their comforting grunts and snores. Ahmed lies awake with her but they do not speak and when day breaks, he disappears behind the hut as she did the previous evening. She wonders if she will dare find that privacy again and determines to hold on until they are well gone from this dreadful place. Even so, as the others sleep, panic hits.

"You okay, Ana?" She jumps up, shaking from head to foot, her cheeks burning, eyes brimming. His sympathy is too much to bear. When he opens his arms, she buries her head in his chest, sobbing convulsively and he holds her tight, rubbing her back until she settles.

They travel much of the remaining eighty or so miles to Homs by foot, avoiding roads and people whenever possible, the cold speeding them on, grey skies augmenting their cover. Generally the men keep themselves to themselves and Ana is grateful for the solitude. Only Ahmed holds back to speak with her from time to time, about every day things and his family.

68

He talks of his sister, "a doctor like you," who risks her life continuing to treat the sick and injured, and of his mother still living in Aleppo. The only other surviving member of their family, he tells her, is an uncle. A surgeon now in Malta, whose wife and baby drowned when the overcrowded boat they were forced to escape in, capsized. Ana asks why anyone would risk such a perilous journey with traffickers known to extract huge sums of money for places on unseaworthy boats packed well beyond capacity. Ahmed tells her his uncle had calculated their probability of dying on the journey as three percent versus fifty if they stayed in Aleppo. "He was unlucky." Now he can neither bear to look at the photos he downloaded just before they left, nor delete them and copes by immersing himself in his work.

Ahmed speaks of his own life as a primary school teacher and what Syria was like before the war and asks Ana about her family, work and of how she came to be here. He tells her he had a brother as old as Rahim but then he falls silent and she sees that he understands her compulsion to go to the rescue of two small boys.

She asks what induces him to do this work and he tells her with pride, of the self-sufficiency and resilience of the Syrian people. Of how whole families through generations have worked the land themselves, in contrast to some Arabic countries that use cheap labour from abroad. How Syrians, unable to rely on the state, have learned instead to depend on each other, the extended family becoming a strong, tightly knit network. "Without this self-sufficiency the country would be starving by now, thanks to US and UE-imposed sanctions." He winks at her but then his smile turns to anger. "The regime wishes to divide the Syrian people but we will not fall into that trap."

He tells her of the millions in Syria stuck in the middle, deprived of a voice, silenced by fear. Fear of the consequences of speaking out, the system that was supposed to protect and the fighting armies that surround them. For most, the overriding priority is to look after family and many are too old or poor to leave. Ahmed considers Ana warmly with a smile. "But we can still tell jokes," he says. "Like the one about the man who comes home with a live chicken for dinner. His wife tells him they don't have a knife to kill it or gas to cook it. The chicken clucks, long live Bashar!"

He tells her that to be Muslim means to surrender to the will of God and the phrase she hears so often, Tawakkul 'ala Allahn – to put oneself in His hands. Ahmed considers it Baraka, to serve his people however he can, even if he must sacrifice his life by so doing. "After all," he tells her with a cheeky grin and a wink, "at least a dozen virgins wait in heaven to pleasure me, should I be martyred."

He asks if she knows the meaning of the Arab proverb, Al-sabr miftah al-faraj and she shakes her head. "It means patience is the key to happiness, Sabr being one of the cardinal Bedouin virtues of fortitude, perseverance and the ability to cope with adversity. Miftah is the key, the instrument of opening, and faraj, is release from suffering."

Ahmed's grandfather used to own a shop in one of Aleppo's medieval souks. "When I was small, I couldn't wait to get inside. I loved the glitter of gold, the smell of spices, handmade sweets and olive-oil soaps. While the men discussed business, I played amongst piles of clothes and cotton sheets. There was nothing more I wanted to do in life than carry on the family business and run that shop. We had five of them." The sparkle in his eyes is replaced by sadness. All gone.

"Did you know, Aleppo's souks were founded two thousand years before the birth of Christ? And yet they were still the beating heart of the commercial city. Twelve kilometres of winding alleys considered the finest of any in the Middle East."

"What happened to them?"

"The Free Syrian Army established a headquarter in a bathhouse nearby, so they became a target. Everything was made

70

of wood. Once the flames took hold they spread quickly. Within hours, everything was reduced to ash. A labyrinth of shops, schools, courtyards, the livelihoods of over thirty five thousand people and a way of life dating back centuries, up in smoke. Just like that."

"My great-great-grandfather opened our shop," the one Ana has come to know as Mahmoud, tells them. "D'you remember golden Thursdays?" Ahmed nods with a smile. "When the cash came flowing in from traders and we children were given money to buy cakes, nuts and clothes. My job was to check the accounting books. That was the right day to ask our fathers for things!"

Every corner of the souk held memories. Visiting a barber for a trim before meeting a girl, gathering for a feast to mark the settlement of a dispute with another trader. "My heart bleeds for Aleppo. You know, the shop-keepers are willing to pay for the restoration of the souk when peace returns, but there is no prospect of that. Most will be dead or fled by then."

"And the great Umayyed Mosque, vandalised by Assad's henchmen. That warning which is appearing everywhere now, *Assad, or we will burn it*, scrawled into its water dispenser. Then they shell it! Its unique Seljuk minaret, a thousand years of priceless heritage, as much part of Aleppo's skyline as your Big Ben in London, reduced to rubble within seconds. What effect do you think that has on morale?"

They pass an old man cutting down a tree for firewood, a truck laden with men, women and children, heading for Lebanon and a group of soldiers from the Free Syrian Army that walks with them a little way.

"Do you know much about Homs?" Ahmed asks as they get closer and, with the vision before her of an animated Rahim describing his home town, Ana nods.

"Homs is where it all started," she says. "Two years ago in April 2011, when Assad's regime responded to peaceful protests with violence." She startles as a couple of crows take to the air from the muddy field ahead of them, chastising loudly in stark reminder

71

of home. "He besieged it, cutting off all supplies including water, power and communications, claiming to be targeting armed gangs and terrorists." Ahmed nods, looking her grimly in the eye.

"In the centre of a fertile agricultural valley divided by the Orontes River, Homs links the interior cities with the Mediterranean coast and was one of Syria's most important industrial centres with its largest oil refinery. Also the central hub of its road and rail network.

"It's history goes back to a thousand years before Christ. Over one and a half million people used to live there. Sunni Muslims, Alawites and Christians, peacefully together."

"Muslims and Christians owned shops beside each other in the souk," Ahmed confirms. "Houses in the same street. During the fight for Baba Amr, where your Marie Colvin was killed, Christians fought alongside Muslims." He looks to Ana with a brief smile. "I maybe Muslim," he tells her, "but like many, I appreciate Churches as well as Mosques. They give me extra Baraka. I'm sure you agree. There is something deeply spiritual about any beautiful old place of worship, whatever faith it was built to serve." Ana nods with a fond smile and Ahmed sighs. "But nothing could prepare you for what you are about to see," he warns and they both fall silent.

"What's the difference between Shi'a and Sunni Muslims?" Ana asks at last.

Ahmed gives her a sideways glance. "Sunni and Shi'a Muslims share the most fundamental Islamic beliefs," he begins. "Their differences are based in politics rather than spirituality. They date back to the death of the Prophet Muhammad and the question of who was to take over his leadership. Sunni Muslims agree with many of the Prophet's companions, that the new leader should be elected from amongst those capable of doing the job and this is what happened. The Prophet Muhammad's close friend and advisor, Abu Bakr, became the first Caliph of the Islamic nation. Sunni comes from a word meaning one who follows the traditions of the Prophet.

"Shi'a Muslims believe, however, that following the Prophet Muhammad's death, leadership should have passed directly to his cousin and son-in-law, Ali bin Abu Talib. That it should have stayed within the Prophet's own family amongst those specifically appointed by him, or amongst Imams appointed by God Himself. Throughout history, Shi'a Muslims have not recognised the authority of elected Muslim leaders, choosing instead to follow a line of Imams who they believe have been appointed by the Prophet Muhammad or God.

"The word Shi'a means a group or supportive party of people. Shi'a Muslims believe that Imams are sinless by nature, that their authority is infallible as it comes directly from God and venerate them as saints, performing pilgrimages to their tombs and shrines in the hope of divine intercession. Sunni Muslims counter that there is no basis in Islam for a hereditary privileged class of spiritual leaders, and certainly no basis for the worship of saints. They contend that leadership of the community is not a birthright but a trust that is earned and which may be given or taken away by the people themselves.

"About eighty five per cent of the world's Muslims are Sunni but there are significant populations of Shi'a in Iran and Iraq, and large minority communities in Yemen, Bahrain, Syria, and Lebanon."

"And the Alawites?"

"They form one of our largest religious minorities at about fifteen per cent of the population and are thought to be descendants of the people who lived here at the time of Alexander the Great. The Alawites suffered centuries of oppression for heresy under our Sunni Ottoman masters, so have a deep-seated persecution complex. They lived in remote mountain communities, clinging to a highly secretive, pre-Islamic religion, which incorporates elements of Islam, Christianity and Zoroastrianism, and practised taqiyya – dissimulation. They literally concealed their Alawi identity. The perfect qualification for the secret services, don't you think?" Ana smiles.

"The Alawis drink alcohol and celebrate Christmas, Easter and Epiphany but after hundreds of years of Shi'a influence, they have moved closer to Islam. Now they worship a divine triad of Ali, Muhammad and Salman the Persian.

"You know, they don't use mosques or observe prayer times, or Ramadan?"

"Really?"

"No. When Bashar is filmed attending special prayers in mosques, it is a carefully constructed photo opportunity designed to make him look like a 'normal' Muslim. If you watch him closely, he's not even sure of the right words and movements but takes his cue from religious leaders to either side of him." Ana is unable to conceal her amusement. "Have you noticed that the back of Bashar's head is flat?" She nods. "Well, that is a typical Alawi feature."

They come to a checkpoint held by the Free Syrian Army, where they accept the offer of a lift for the remainder of the journey to Homs. "We'll get there by nightfall. Safest to do the last bit under cover of darkness," Ahmed explains. Dread strikes the pit of her stomach and once again, Ana cannot escape those terrifying intrusions. Awful images that flash through her head, of young men tortured to death in prison. She considers thanking Ahmed and telling him she'll continue by herself but apart from the stupidity of such a proposition, she would miss his company and is afraid. She hesitates. "What's up?" She shrugs awkwardly, staring at the ground. "If you're thinking of asking me to leave you to it, you can forget it, Ana. We're in this together now. I get you in, you find the boys and then we get out. Pronto. Got it?" She shakes her head.

"No. Thank you Ahmed. The deal was you got me there, not back as well."

"It's my deal Ana. I want to see you out of here alive and uninjured, then I'll set you on your merry way and find the next

74

reckless fool needing help to get in or out of Syria. That's my job now, okay?" She looks at him incredulously. "If it weren't you, it'd be someone else. Simple." A terrible sadness replaces her angst. "Don't worry, I have every intention of surviving," he says gently. "There is a whole generation of children here desperate for education and I intend to deliver it when this war is over."

"Why wait until then?" He looks at her so carefully, he can't fail to notice the tears blurring her vision of him, but he says nothing. "I have no doubt you're a very good teacher," she tells him and, distracted, he nods.

The minibus that will take them to Homs has obviously seen better days and Ana wonders that it has managed to keep going. Bare metal, twisted and dented, sides riddled and windows spattered with bullet shaped holes, it inspires little confidence. Neither does its driver, cheerful though he is. He looks at least seventy, his skin wrinkled and sallow, eyes dark and wild, crumbs of food floating in a stained white beard. Traditionally dressed, in once white pakistani style pyjamas and matching cap, he helps his passengers up, chatting away about everything and nothing. At least I'll pass unnoticed, Ana kids herself. Sure enough, his inane chatter comes, with her, to an abrupt halt. He peers at her suspiciously, confusion turning to delight and, in his eyes when he winks, Ana recognises more than a touch of madness.

Their journey is slow, for many roads are physically impassable and they have to negotiate their way through a patchwork of territories, avoiding those taken by the regime. They skirt around the city, approaching it along a highway flanked by low mountains, known as the Homs gap. Control of this route, which has been much fought over through the centuries, is the reason the Knights Hospitallers spared no expense in building the famous Krak des Chevaliers, the world's best preserved Crusader castle. "Twelfth century," Ahmed informs her and that its elegant cloister bears the inscription, *Grace, wisdom and beauty you may enjoy but beware pride which alone can tarnish all the rest.* "I wonder how long it will take Assad to destroy that."

A shaft of evening sunlight falls onto massive towers, illuminating white stones and impenetrable concentric masonry walls so that the whole scene takes on the appearance of some grand renaissance masterpiece. Ana wonders at how vulnerable, even this survivor of centuries of insurrection and war, has become to man's infinitely greater capacity for destruction.

They pass a modern part of the city called al-Wa'ar, whose tower blocks are home to a large proportion of the Sunni population of Homs and its refugees. "They are stuck," their driver informs, pointing out the oil refinery opposite which is also under blockade.

Ahmed was right, nothing could have prepared her for this. Sitting beside her, he watches as she looks with horror through the window onto the outskirts of Homs and, as they pass through this housing estate of what were once six to eight-storey blocks, Ana finds it impossible to believe that somehow, people still live here.

They come to a dead end, the road before them blocked by rubble and, stabbing his foot on the brake, their driver curses the idiot that put this obstruction in his way. Throwing his arms in the air, he rises to face his passengers. "Sorry folks, looks like its all out here, 'less you want to come back the way we came!" He shrugs, looking at them all benevolently then takes leave of them individually. Before Ana, he bows with a wink. "No place for a lady like you," he says, then to Ahmed taking her hand for she still hasn't mastered the art of seeing her feet with a niqab on, "see her safely home won't you chum?

To her dismay, their companions follow them but Ahmed is quick to reassure. "They know best how to find the hospital. We help each other."

"How?"

"As well as saving the living, the hospital does its best to identify the dead. It has an office and laptop dedicated to keeping records. Now, stay close and do as I do," he concludes as if this were explanation enough and leads them confidently down an alley.

It is impossible to imagine what here must have looked like. Sleepy tree-lined boulevards have been replaced by rubble overflowing from collapsed buildings to either side, in places almost burying burnt out vehicles and the stumps of gum trees they parked beneath. Broken household items poke through the avalanche. A mutilated red leather sofa. A rusting mangled washing machine. A toaster that looks like it exploded. Even the remains of an upright piano, its skeleton sinisterly minus every one of its strings. Shredded clothing. Trousers to a smart suit such as any executive in London might be wearing. A child's pyjamas and toys. A doll's house. A teddy-bear minus an eye and any fur, casualty to over-loving before ever the war finished him off. The paraphernalia of everyday life emerging from piles of dust, concrete and twisted metal along with a smell in places which is gut-wrenchingly appalling. Ana puts a hand to her mouth and gradually begins to see what her brain refuses to accept.

She stumbles, reaching out to save herself and her heart stops. From somewhere far away comes Ahmed's urgent voice but she is paralysed. Her heart resumes in uncomfortable race as she chokes on the overpowering stench and someone takes her by the arm. He moves her hand away but cannot avert her gaze.

Milk teeth in half a jaw are all that remain of the young child's head, lovingly cradled by a skeletal hand. Sinewy tendons connect this to an arm stripped of rotting flesh, blackened body fast melting away. She wouldn't have seen it. Covered in a light sprinkling of dust and rubble. And there beside it, the head. She stares, retching, at the face of a dead man alive with maggots and Ahmed pulls her away.

He helps her up, turning her to face him and lifts her niqab. "Ana?" He puts an arm around her as if to catch her should she fall, and wipes the perspiration tenderly from her brow. He hands her his water bottle and makes her drink then, taking her by the hand, he leads her away.

He seems to make a special effort now to distract her from the human horror they move through and slowly her focus readjusts so that she can almost ignore the signs of bodies decomposing around her. He shows her the remains of time-worn markets where people came to trade, paints pictures for her of the exquisitely detailed mosques they prayed in throughout the ages and points out blasted minarets, domes and towers lying in the rubble. Anything left of value, he explains, has been looted.

Here was a modern hospital reduced to a windowless shell and there the ruins of another, once vibrant, historic souk.

At last they come to an area relatively spared and Ana wakes as if from some horrific dream. The basement of this mosque has been turned into a food distribution centre with kitchens that produce around three thousand meals a day. Strong young men with long handled spoons that look like paddles, stir vast pots of bulgur wheat and tomato stew on giant gas-rings. One thousand calories per meal, is what they aim to provide. Enough to prevent starvation as, for most, this will be the only meal they get all day.

They meet Mariam and her nine children aged from two to fifteen. Their father was killed by a sniper. "They go both ways," Mariam says mysteriously and Ahmed explains that fighters on both sides see only two choices. Annihilation or victory. Mariam's home was destroyed by a shell, so she took her children to live in a half-built house and hides them whenever violence comes. The older ones work, only two are at school and, living on the edge of life, she has no time to consider who is to blame. Surviving the day is all that matters.

They wait for nightfall before setting out on the final leg of their journey, relying, where they can, on the deadly flares of war to light their way. Shelling and gunfire intensifies and the air grows thick with dust, the ground with rubble. Soon their eyes adjust and they fall into the rhythm of it. Jumping this, skirting that, weaving and ducking, running where the way is clear. Then Ahmed stops, killing his torch and they freeze.

Routed to the spot, they wait, every sense straining in pitch black. The sky thunders, breaking into orange flames and Ahmed makes the sign for them all to take cover. Obediently, Ana follows him to the shadows.

Darkness falls and she stumbles, landing with a dull thud on something firm, warmer than stone, sweet smelling and sticky. A hand over her mouth stifles her scream. Another helps her up. "It's me, Ahmed." The world explodes and by the fiery light, she sees. The body of a young woman, no sign visible of the injury that took her life, stares wide-eyed at the glowering sky. There is movement, the flicker of eyelids perhaps, the gush of air escaping from crushed lungs but, before she can check, a loud crack takes Ana with Ahmed to the ground. "Sniper!" he hisses, releasing her and catching his breath. "Alright?"

She nods. He peers into the darkness and they wait. Forever. Nothing but the movement of the lightening sky. "See that shop?" he whispers at last, checking that she has. "On the count of three."

The others are there already. An eternity passes, for they are trapped behind a crumbling wall, the rear of this ruined grocery store reduced to an impassable pile of rubble. Shadows fade to black then, just as her eyes acclimatise to a darker shade of night, liquid silver spills over the clouds, flooding the street. Horrified, she freezes.

It looks up from it's meal and Ana stares into the eyes of the devil. The young woman was not alone. There are bodies and body-parts strewn amongst the rubble and the dogs feast on them.

Ana turns away, dodging Ahmed and retches, her vision blurred by tears of bitterness, hatred and disgust.

"It's time to go." Ahmed waits on her again. "Keep to the shadows and follow me. No torch."

In the darkness they climb over walls, slide through muddy ditches and pass through ruins, running where they can along deserted streets. Occasionally they pass signs of life, even areas still populated where people who have come out to demonstrate against the regime, sing and chant slogans.

A group of the president's supporters waving Syrian flags, drives recklessly through the streets, songs glorifying Bashar thumping from their sound systems and Ahmed pushes Ana into a doorway. Distractions play tricks on her senses. Is that agony in his dark brown eyes? Something warm and wet sticks to her hand when he releases her and realisation dawns.

"Lucky we're going to a hospital, eh?"

"Let me see."

"Later. This way."

They turn the corner and are blasted into oblivion.

It takes precious moments for Ana to regain consciousness. Something hurts but not too badly and she can still feel her arms and legs. She gets herself to her knees, pushes herself up and peers into the darkness.

Another deafening roar and the whole awful scene lights up. Like some silent slow-motion movie, a tank bears down on them, trucks following with blazing canons. They rise like deadmen from the rubble. All except Ahmed. Desperate, she searches shadows, waxing and waning in the light of a raging fire and then she sees him, clutching what remains of his leg. Paralysed and deaf, she watches him haemorrhaging and with his life, all hope drains away.

She sees their companions find him, lift him carefully from the rubble and carry him as fast as they can away from the fire. Ana follows, compelled to be where Ahmed is whatever the consequences. She finds herself in a bare concrete room illuminated by torch and firelight, Ahmed writhing in agony against the far wall. They are doing their best but this kind, brave man who must be invincible, lies helpless, mortally wounded and Assad's forces bear down on them.

He rallies and fumbles for his mobile phone but his strength fails and Mahmoud takes it from him. Ahmed mutters something unintelligible and, touching him briefly on the shoulder with a nod, Mahmoud turns away. Ana watches in horror as they make their way to where she stands before the door.

"You can't leave him!" She runs to his side and they hesitate. She removes her niqab, pulling at it until the fabric begins to split, tears off a strip and ties it around Ahmed's leg. She tries to elevate it as if she could stop the fountain gushing from his half amputated knee but it is too slippery and she loses her grasp. She pushes her hair out of her face but before she can try again, he moves away, forcing himself to sit, one hand grasping a bloody shoulder.

"Go," he barks. "They'll get you…to the hospital." His voice fades to a rasping whisper and she shakes her head. "You promised. Do what you came here to do, then go. Get out of Syria. Go home." He pleads with her. "For me…" Someone takes her by the arm and she shakes him off. Ahmed pulls a hand-gun and points it at her but he can barely lift his hand and it shakes wildly off its mark. "Get away from me," he warns and she flinches but does not move.

With a deafening roar, the ground shakes bits of concrete and dust over them, setting one corner of the room on fire. Ana shrieks. Someone pulls her away. Ahmed puts the gun to his mouth.

"NOo…!" She reaches out but too late. He is looking at her when he pulls the trigger. Through closed eyes she sees it all as clear as day. His handsome face exploding, blood running down the wall behind him and with it, that sickening sweet smell of burning human flesh. She retches. The pain is unbearable, the horror, all consuming. There is nothing else.

The rest of their journey passes in a blur. Memories of Ahmed as she knew him, the way he died and visions of those he left behind, haunt her in a kaleidoscopic blur, rendering her oblivious to the true messages her senses relay. Places they pass through. People they meet. Sounds. Voices. Explosions. Shouting. Screaming. The smell of burning. Wet concrete. Acrid sweat. Tobacco-smoke. The discomfort of the cramped places where they hide. The wet they crawl through and the rubble they climb over. She notices neither the grazes, bruises or cuts being inflicted on her, her clothes tearing on jagged pieces of timber and twisted metal, nor the passage of time.

UNDERCOVER FIELD HOSPITAL

"Ana?" Startled, she looks around in confusion. "We're here."

From what she can see through the darkness, they stand in a relatively intact street at the door of someone's house. A rich someone, judging by the width of the road and the imposing block of wood they face. She frowns. "Where?"

"The hospital."

Of course. That's what they have to do now. Hide the hospitals and clinics, for the Syrian regime is using health care denial as a weapon of oppression. She sees Ahmed clear as day, the memory of his death flashing through her mind a thousandth time. Bitter rage rises in her and she scowls at this obstruction as if it were in some way to blame for the atrocities perpetrated against people like him. Now she understands. Once you accept you won't get out alive, you have the power to achieve extra-ordinary things.

Mahmoud knocks on the door six times, tapping a distinctive rhythm. It opens almost immediately. A young boy eyes them suspiciously, the tension in his face melting away with whatever it is the stranger whispers in his ear. He bids them enter and takes them to a room filled with cardboard boxes, medical equipment, make-do splints, walking-sticks and display cabinets which must once have held glasses and crockery rather than dressings and medicines. He tells them to wait.

Ana sinks to the ground, yawning uncontrollably, her eyes watering and eyelids flickering as she forces them to stay open. "How did you find it?" she asks Mahmoud, trying not to slur her words.

"Should have been paying attention." She closes her eyes, shaking her head free of another intrusive flashback. "But it's okay. I understand. Your first time, no? Not that it gets easier."

"Did you know him?"

"Not before you."

Exhausted, she looks around the room, her eyes returning to Mahmoud. She hasn't really noticed him before – what he looks like, what he wears. He was on the periphery of her consciousness and this is the first time she has been able to see him properly. Dark-skinned with black eyes to match his hair, he has delicate aquiline features, would be tidily groomed and wears once smart tan trousers with matching shirt under his long black djellabaya. He gives her a brief impatient smile.

"The hospitals here have been taken over by the military," he says. "If you are unfortunate enough to need them, you will be shot or handcuffed to a bed and tortured. It is now against the law to treat anyone opposed to Assad's regime, even peaceful demonstrators. Those who do, are considered to be terrorists along with their patients. A crime punishable by arrest, torture and death. Not only for the accused, but also their loved ones and colleagues." Ana shivers, her cheeks burning as she fights back tears of despair.

Mahmoud shakes his head angrily, able to look her in the eyes no longer. "I'm sorry Ana. It's just…it makes me so angry! After encouraging us to stand up for freedom and democracy, how can the world simply abandon us?" He confronts her again as if she might defend it but she is utterly defeated.

"So hospitals are set up secretly. People lend us their homes and after a few months, maybe even weeks, we move somewhere else to reduce the chance of being discovered."

"You a medic then?" Ana asks, too tired to feel surprised.

"Doctor. Couldn't risk letting you know in case …"

"I got caught?"

"We have to be very careful. Even carrying an empty blood-bag is potentially lethal. One of our ambulances delivering medical supplies, was stopped and searched at a Government checkpoint recently. The driver disappeared for two weeks, his body unrecognisable when they returned it."

"But why?" She still can't quite believe it.

"Information. A warning to those of us who try to help the sick and wounded. Punishment for so doing." Mahmoud heaves a great sigh and waves his arm around the room as if to distract her from the fresh horror he has planted in her head.

"This is a store-room. We get our supplies secretly from Lebanon but the journey is dangerous and takes three to four days. There is never enough. We use drugs that are out of date, equipment that should be condemned and blood directly from donors." Ana grimaces and he shrugs. "What should we do, let the man bleed to death or give him a chance? Often there is no anaesthetic, no painkillers and, of course, we are short of medical staff. Dead, fled or imprisoned. There were almost two hundred doctors here. Now there are three." He looks with weary hope into her eyes. "Perhaps you can help us Ana?"

She has no energy left for guilt. Rahim was who she came for and his brother. No-one else. But now she feels intimately involved in this conflict. It has bitten deep and its poison moves relentlessly through her. Until she finds them, she will do what she can to help.

The little boy returns. "Doctors come." He flicks the fringe out of his eyes. "You others, rest for now." They follow him along a hallway to what was once the kitchen. Surrounded by units, a cooker, sink, fridge freezer and a handful of onlookers, a surgical bed stands in the middle of the room and bent over the open abdomen of his patient, the surgeon.

Tall, black, thick-necked and muscular, he looks more like an African rugby player than a doctor. Unshaven, he bears the sort of head-torch you would use to go hiking in the dark, a plastic apron over a bloodied white t-shirt that looks a good few sizes too small for him, cheap rubber gloves and no mask. There is nothing sterile about his garb or his theatre that, though perhaps clean enough for minor injuries, definitely is not for surgery such as this.

Nevertheless, this patient must be one of the lucky ones, for at his head is an anaesthetic machine and a young woman operating it. Beside her, an array of surgical instruments neatly laid out on a surface that would once have borne cereal packets or kitchen utensils, is overlooked by another glass-fronted display cabinet packed to overflowing with dressings and medicines. Two buckets full of water sit on the floor beside the sink, its tap about to relinquish a precious drop of water and there is electric lighting suggesting that for now, at least, this makeshift hospital is relatively well served. But then the lights flicker, plunging them into momentary darkness and someone rushes out, cursing the damn generator.

"Marcus, this is Ana," Mahmoud tells the surgeon as if nothing had happened. "A doctor working with MSF at Za'atari. She's looking for a boy who came back for his brother in Homs. Thought we could use her help until he's found."

Marcus frowns without looking up. "You came here for what?" He addresses Ana in broad American with such frank disapproval that she feels obliged to defend herself.

"He's only eleven, his brother eight. He brought the rest of his family out of Syria to Za'atari. His mother was in labour when they arrived. She has manic depression, two little girls and the baby to care for. There was no-one else to go after him."

Marcus snorts, glancing at her over blood-spattered half-rim glasses. "You a surgeon, Ana?" He reaches for another instrument, plunging it into the gaping hole before him without waiting for an answer. "Like to give me a hand?"

"No. A physician." Aware of his eyes following, Ana goes to the sink to scrub up, takes gloves from an almost empty box and dons a dirty apron from a pile on the floor. Assuming she is being put through some kind of test but too tired to wonder at its significance, she looks expectantly at Mahmoud but he stays

86

put. Propped up by the frame of the kitchen door, arms and legs crossed, he nods sagely. It would appear he has no intention of helping.

"Ana ..." Marcus lets the word hang.

"Anais actually, but you can call me Ana." She takes the forceps holding a gauze swab someone hands her and looks into the mutilated abdominal cavity for the most useful place to press it.

"Thirty eight year old man, hit by shrapnel when a shell exploded his house, then crushed by falling masonry. Fractured right humerus, left tib. and fib. Penetrating injury to abdomen. Shrapnel removed." Marcus kicks a bucket by his feet but all she can see in it are bloody entrails. "And irretrievably damaged bowel. Sadly not enough of the rectum left to join back up so we needed to form a colostomy." He points it out, as if it weren't obvious already. "God knows how the poor bugger's going to manage that on today's rations. Probably would have been best if he'd died." He stares at Ana, wide eyes gleaming in his weary black face but she will not to be intimidated.

"You must have thought him worth giving a chance." She presses firmly on a vessel spewing blood.

"Done much trauma medicine, Ana?"

"No. Well yes, but not so acutely," she replies, awkwardly.

"Thought so. It's very simple actually. Like a bath." Ana looks at him warily but he takes no notice. "Imagine a bath full of blood Ana," and it's hard not to. "With a big plug. If someone pulls the plug, the red stuff starts emptying out. If someone turns the tap on, what's left turns pink. Pink blood's no good. So what we have to do, is put the plug back and replace the red stuff with red. Simple!" He eyes her curiously and she nods politely.

She moves her hand slightly but blood spurts into her face, pulsing from the artery with its owner's heartbeat. She replaces the swab, applying pressure to hold the bleeding in check. "Here, allow me." Marcus ties the offending vessel whilst Ana does her best to keep his field of vision dry. She sees Mahmoud move and, wondering if he will make himself useful at last, watches him wipe beads of sweat from the surgeon's brow, just in time to save them dropping into the open belly. Ana frowns.

"Damn psychiatrists," Marcus complains. "What the hell use d'you think you're doin' here anyway?" Mahmoud pretends to be offended and Ana looks at him in surprise.

"Actually, our services are at least as important as yours," Mahmoud snorts. "What's the point in you patching them up, if they're so depressed they go commit suicide anyway?"

"Too busy surviving to consider how to kill themselves." Marcus grunts. "Now where was I? Ah…yes. Problem is Ana, pain raises blood pressure, pulse and adrenaline, all of which, as you know, increase bleeding." Visions of people having major surgery without anaesthetic flash through Ana's mind. An unbearable heat comes over her and the world threatens to recede. Thankfully, Marcus appears not to notice and stepping from one foot to the other, Ana takes some deep breaths. "Sure, they pass out after a while, but that doesn't help much.

"We depend on suitable donors for the red stuff but, sadly, they're often in desperate need of it themselves." He looks to Ana. "See my problem?" She nods. "Seems like what we do's mostly a waste of time. Without proper aftercare, they'll die anyway. If not, the regime will catch up with them again. And another thing…" He's started to close up and Ana falls into a familiar rhythm, of swabbing and cutting as he stitches layer upon layer of abdominal wall.

"D'you know what the pressure wave from an explosion does to the lungs?" Ana nods, wondering why Marcus came to Syria in the first place, willing his tirade to come to an end. "It disrupts that beautifully fine membrane separating air from the tiny blood vessels that grab its oxygen. It breaks these too and the bleeding causes inflammation 'cause blood in the wrong place is one of the most irritant substances known to man. The poor old body tries to heal itself. " He appears to be speaking to his wider audience now and, with a quick glance, Ana sees two teenage boys, a man and a woman, listening and watching intently. "It pours its own medicine in, but with that comes more liquid where it shouldn't be and that's it. The victim drowns in his own fluids." Ana shifts from one foot to the other, feeling distinctly uncomfortable with Marcus's turn of phrase but there is little concern in the faces of the others. Helpers, friends or family perhaps?

"What he needs now, Ana," Marcus continues, tying the final stitch, "are antibiotics and intensive care, but guess what? We don't have either!" Ana sighs and looks on Marcus with concern. "I'm sorry." He visibly deflates. "Rant over. Welcome Ana, and thank you for your help." He tears off his apron and gloves, throwing them onto a bloody pile in a bin and, shooting her a look of despair, turns to leave the room.

"Don't mind him Ana," Mahmoud reassures, watching the anaesthetist wake the patient, whilst two of the onlookers clean him up. "That's his way of saying he's pleased to see you." She shrugs. Marcus is not the first to have made it abundantly clear she is an intruder in this terrible war and likely always to be more of a liability than a help.

She finds him in a crude courtyard carved from the remains of walls and rubble. Leaning against a doorway, he watches the smoke from his rollie wend its way to the star-studded sky and when the thunder of distant artillery breaks the stillness of the night, he does not batt an eyelid.

"Shouldn't be 'ere, Ana," he says at last. "Should 'a stayed at Za'atari. Chances of the three of you getting out'a here alive are zilch. Go back in the morning 'fore it's too late."

"I'm not leaving without Rahim and while I'm here, I'd like to make myself useful."

"Stubborn woman." He sighs deeply and looks at where she sits on a concrete block a little way from him. "If you stay, you won't leave." She smiles sweetly. "Trust me, I know. Never planned on coming this far either. This war'll kill me or spit me out, but I won't be leaving of my own accord."

"Why not?"

"You'll see. S'quiet at the moment. Go get some sleep." She makes no move. "Mahmoud!" Mahmoud melts out of the shadows. "Show 'er to her bed." Mahmoud offers Ana a hand but she declines.

"This way."

Fighting the urge to sleep on the spot, Ana forces herself to stand. For a moment the world spins and she falls against a wall. "I'm okay," she says hurriedly, shaking her head when Mahmoud tries to help. He waits patiently until she has steadied herself, then leads her through the courtyard to the building next door.

They enter it through a narrow doorway, Mahmoud placing a hand on a low beam to prevent her banging her head. A short hallway leads to a pile of rubble and beside it, a staircase. "Don't worry," he says, leading her up it without hesitation. "It's quite safe. We've been sleeping here for a week already." Ana is too tired to object. There is a landing with two doors and everything up here looks remarkably intact. She decides what she saw downstairs was an illusion and wonders at how much easier it is to accept madness than this reality.

She follows Mahmoud through one of the doors into a large drafty room. It is dark but faint blue light from the cloudless sky outside, augmented by noisy orange outbursts, pours through two glass-less windows. The ceiling is low and when she reaches up to touch it, her hands catch rough wood just above her head. She begins to see mattresses with blankets covering a wooden floor and that some of these untidy piles contain people.

The noise of shelling dies away and the room takes on a rhythm of its own, breathing in deeply of the rancid air, releasing it in guttural sighs syncopated by the occasional grunt. It smells of the unwashed, rotting apples and mildew.

"You sleep here." Mahmoud shows her to one corner of the

room and a mattress that looks more substantial than the others with a pile of blankets folded neatly on top. Next to it is a chair, the only one Ana can see in the gloom and beside that, the face of a teenage boy, illuminated by the torch he holds. He smiles brightly but just as he opens his mouth, Mahmoud speaks. The light goes out in an instant.

"What did you say?"

"It doesn't matter. He won't bother you tonight. Now sleep while you can."

"Why are you here, Mahmoud?" Ana asks resentfully.

"Because this is my home and these are my people. Now sleep. If you are to be of any use to us, you need to rest." He shakes his head but wishes her a peaceful night and retreats the way they came. Too exhausted to consider where he goes or why, Ana lays herself on the mattress and that is all she knows.

The noise is what strikes her first. People talking outside, traffic, mainly mopeds by the sound of it, and distant thunder. There is something deeply disturbing about that sound but she can't quite work out what it is. Then she remembers and braces herself.

She slips her blanket down to her chin and opens her eyes, hoping to observe before being noticed but he is there already, grinning from ear to ear, the young boy of the night. Propped up by one elbow, he watches her, brown eyes glowing, a glorious smile on his handsome face. "Morning, I'm Aadil," he says, running a hand through curly dark, blonde tinged hair.

She tries to speak but her mouth is dry and sticky and she has to clear her throat. "Hi, I'm Ana."

He nods. "Bathroom then food?"

That feeling of having lost something vital, strikes. She gasps, refocusing. Aadil is still there. "Okay, I'm ready." She throws her blanket to her feet and jumps up, hardly concealing her amusement as Aadil follows suit. "How old are you?"

"Thirteen, and you?"

"Not something a gentleman should ask a lady. What you doing here?"

"Helping the hospital." Clearly she should know better but Aadil takes pity on her. "People find us by word of mouth. I guide them in. And help the doctors. I stitch, pull fractured limbs, even resuscitate, you know?" Ana nods with deep admiration. "I help bring in supplies, with the ambulances and I lead Assad's thugs away from here."

"Oh." That dread weight settles in the pit of her stomach and she tries not to think of what would happen to him if he were caught. "Ambulances?"

"Yes. There aren't many left. They're very basic. Most of our patients are carried in but some still come by ambulance."

Ana looks around her. The room is less like a morgue by daylight and noisy sunshine floods the shattered windows. Most of the mattresses are empty but there are a few still sleeping and one, just rising, looks over to them and frowns. "Is it acceptable here then, for men and women to sleep in the same room?"

Aadil shrugs. "Why not? Allah created men and women equal."

Ana smiles. "Are there many Syrians as enlightened as you are?"

He nods. "We may be suppressed but still we are tolerant and generous."

Ana wonders if she hears his parents speak. She takes another look around her. Occasional bottles of water stand sentry between the beds. A newspaper, some paper cups, a chess set, some books, playing cards and the occasional bag or pile of clothes.

"What is this place?"

"Used to be a grain-store. Now it's where we sleep. Next to the hospital, in case we're needed in a hurry." Aadil hesitates, surveying the ground forlornly.

"What's up?" He shakes his head. "Where's your home, Aadil?" Ana asks gently.

"Here." He shrugs, looking at her sadly but then his face lights up and he rubs his belly. "Hungry?"

She nods with a smile. "Bathroom first please."

"This way."

"Your English is very good."

"Yep. Need it for London. I'm going to study music at the Royal College. You can show me around if you like."

"I'd love to. What an amazing thing to aspire to! You must tell me all about it."

"First breakfast." Ana guesses he is always hungry. Though taller than she with huge feet to grow into, he is too thin, his torn jeans and blood-stained shirt, in desperate need of a wash. His hands are strong and calloused with broken nails crowning long thin fingers but he moves them with grace and purpose.

"What do you play?"

"Piano. Used to anyway. Probably forgotten by now."

She shakes her head. "You never forget." He isn't convinced. "Music takes you to another world, doesn't it, Aadil?" He nods without looking up. "Where there is no suffering and everyone is equal. A doorway to heaven."

He smiles at her and the sun comes out. "It's like the composer is there when you play his music," he adds, "connecting you with everyone else who ever listens or plays. All over the world and all through the ages, musicians understand the same language."

Ana nods. "Where do you come from Aadil?"

"Here. We used to have a big house, like the one next door but it was bombed. My father died saving my little sister." For a moment, Aadil examines the ground again, utter devastation on his face but when he looks back, hope has returned to his eyes. "My mother and little sisters are at Za'atari. Maybe you saw them?" She hasn't. "My older sister works here," Aadil continues, undaunted. "She has learnt how to use the anaesthetic machine that makes people sleep when they need surgery."

"She's very clever. Like you."

Breakfast is in what was once the living room of the house next door and, though there is little in the way of furniture, what

93

remains has been made to look homely. There are two small tables, a few chairs and a side-board bearing jugs of water, powdered milk and plates of flat-breads laid out on a fine lace cloth. The fragrant aroma of strong Arabic coffee rises from an elaborate metal pot, beside it, a kettle, a box of teabags, a bowl of sugar and a jar of instant coffee. A few rugs and cushions strewn about a faded wooden floor, make feeble attempt to disguise the vibrant ghost of a carpet, no doubt requisitioned for some vital purpose and a couple of strategically placed lamps must break the harsh glare when it is dark, of the uncompromising light-bulb hanging from the ceiling.

Aadil leads Ana to the food and follows her to one of the tables with his own plate and mug. He hasn't taken much.

"Is that all you're having?"

He shakes his head mournfully, pointing with his eyes at the frugal table. "All there is until supplies get through," he says.

"But you need it more than most."

He shakes his head and grins at her. "I'll be alright."

"May I join you?" Ana jumps. It's been a quiet night and Marcus looks better for some sleep.

"Of course. How are you?"

"All the better for seeing you lady, though, like I said, you must go back 'fore it's too late." Ana pretends to ignore him.

"Right, Aadil?"

"Yep, thanks. You?"

"Good. Hear you bin doin some building."

"Trying to get the school going again. The older children want to teach the little ones."

"Mmm. Must 'a bin hard, dirty work."

"We managed."

Marcus hands him a piece of his bread. "No arguments." He turns on Ana.

"Finished med. school yet, Ana?"

Ana ignores him.

"Far too young, like Aadil here." Marcus shakes his head.

"You can't be much older than me."

"Good few years. So what you done since med. school, girl?"

"Surgery, medicine, Casualty, Paeds., Obs. and Gynae., Infectious diseases. All sorts."

"Mmm…" Marcus tucks into a flatbread hungrily. "Where d'you train?"

"The Royal Free, London and Derriford Hospital, Plymouth – mostly."

"Ahh… With the military?"

"No."

"Know Surgeon Commander MacLeod?"

"Yes."

"We worked together in Afghanistan. He still scanning everybody?"

"If he can get away with it."

Marcus looks through his forehead at Aadil. "In Afghanistan we put every casualty through a CT scanner called Charlie. It had a teddy-bear sitting on top of this thing like a giant donut." He glances at Ana. " Charlie found so much trauma we'd 'av missed. Not a sign on the surface of the body but there it was inside. Bits of metal, bullets, debris, fractures, trauma to internal organs. We'd 'av missed it without Charlie and they'd 'av died from their injuries without us even knowin.

"I hear he wants to scan all the old biddies who fall and re-classify their injuries as major trauma."

Ana laughs. "He's right, though. Ct scans often find fractures that have been missed. Bleeds too."

"Mmm. Worlds away from here. Give 'im my regards when you see 'im."

"Will do."

"Know Surgeon Commander Wilson?" Ana shakes her head. "Orthopaedic surgeon. Good, like MacLeod. You'll meet him later." He looks at Ana with raised eyebrows and waits.

"On annual leave, is he?"

"More'n that. Active service you might say. So, what d'you know about Homs?"

Ana takes a deep breath. "That Assad besieged it seven months ago, destroying rebel held areas and razing them to the ground. That parts of the city are controlled by a variety of armed rebels including jihadists. Assad calls them all terrorists and pursues a policy he calls, surrender or starve." She hesitates. This is happening here. Now. Not in some far away land to strangers but to these people all around her.

"This is the only field hospital left in Homs," Marcus informs her. "There are satellite first aid stations manned by nurses. Only the serious trauma comes to us. We serve a population of about seventy thousand and expect to see around three hundred a day, mainly with medical problems and in need of medication. Syria used to produce most of its drugs but now the factories and pharmacies have been destroyed or closed down. Hospitals are the only source of essential medicines for many.

"We get our supplies through charity. Hand in Hand with Syria is one of the few that dares operate within Syria's borders, using local volunteers. They send us what anaesthetics we have, the machine too and Celox. Know what that is?" Ana shakes her head. "Haemostatic gauze. You've used it, haven't you, Aadil?" Aadil nods. "A dressing that can control major haemorrhage within minutes of compression. You'll see.

"So what you doing today, Aadil?"

"Thought I'd go help Caleb." Despite herself, Ana's heart skips a beat.

"He back in town? Think you'll find him?"

"S'pect he'll find me."

"Who's Caleb?" She asks, hoping they will confirm what she knows already.

"Now there's a question! Who is he, Aadil?"

"A friend," Aadil says with pride, "who saves people. I help him take them to the hospital. Sometimes he stays but mostly he vanishes when the trouble's over. Was a fireman once and a soldier, but doesn't fight anymore because that's wrong. He's a brilliant pianist. Used to give concerts all over the world. Sometimes he teaches me. When it's quiet. There aren't many pianos left but he knows them all."

"Where's he from?"

"No-one knows," Marcus continues mysteriously. "Came back to Syria when war broke out to look for his father and never left. His mother taught ancient history at Damascus University. His father was an Irish journalist."

"Is!" Aadil exclaims. "Caleb will find him before it's too late."

Marcus nods with an impatient frown. "You keep away from Caleb, Aadil," he warns. "He's no good for you."

LIFE IN THE BALANCE

Ana's day starts relatively uneventfully. She is busy, with people waiting up to eight hours to see her but initially there is little major trauma to contend with.

She has discovered that the hospital is bigger than she had anticipated, every room of the house being used for treatment, surgery, consultations, those waiting their turn or storage. The bathrooms, divided into male and female are used by visitors, staff and patients alike and, noticing with amusement that Aadil has added her name to the cleaning rota neatly displayed on the wall of the ladies, Ana wonders how she will ever find the time to fulfil her duty here.

It is no surprise to see so many medical conditions running out of control. Most of her patients that day have had no access to medical care, including their medication, for many months. Now they present with complications, sometimes life-threatening, which could easily have been prevented and Ana has hardly any of the necessary medications or equipment that were available even at Za'atari. Far harder to deal with however, is the history behind these physical ailments, an overwhelming deluge of unbelievably harrowing stories.

Eighteen year old Ahmed was paralysed by a sniper's bullet from the waist down eight months ago. He is carried in by his father. This is the first time they have been able to access medical help. Ahmed has no control over his bowels or bladder. His legs are wasted and swollen with fluid and he is covered in sores. Ana has little to offer them but advice, which she knows, with such limited resources, they will struggle to follow.

Nineteen year old Fatima saw her husband killed by the shell that destroyed their simple one story village home. Her baby was born in the basement of a wood factory where over three hundred frightened widows and their children took refuge with nothing but the clothes on their backs. They have been living on rice, tea and tins of tuna delivered by a local sheikh who looted them from a bombed-out supermarket.

Fatima is too traumatised to breast-feed so the baby has had only sugar and water and now it is sick. Luckily there is a mother here who will breast-feed a stranger's baby as well as her own and Mahmoud to help Fatima recover herself.

Amjad is ten and was shot in the neck. "We were standing outside the school posing for a photograph. My friend Omar was standing next to me. He fell to his knees as if he were praying and then I saw that he had been shot in the head. He was dead. Everyone started screaming. There was blood everywhere. Then I felt a terrible pain, here." He shows Ana the wounds. "Luckily someone brought me here and I didn't die. But now I'm sick.

"We held a funeral for Omar. Lots of people came. We made a statue of him, dressed it in his uniform and carried it through the streets." Tears well up in his eyes and Ana puts an arm around his shoulders. "I was so sad that day."

"I'm sorry," she says, seeing already that his wound is infected.

"My biggest problem now," Amjad tells her, "is that I've been out of school for a whole year and don't know when I can go back. I want to be an engineer to help rebuild Syria but can't do that without a good education, can I?" Ana tries to reassure him, gives him some out of date antibiotics and shows him how to keep his wounds clean and dry.

Seventeen year old Raed is worried by chest pains. Ana examines him and tells him that his symptoms are brought on by stress, nothing to worry about. "In my village there was a demonstration," he says. "Some children were there but not many.

As a punishment, armed men went to the school. They selected fifty children at random from grades one to seven, some as young as six, took them out of the school and tore out their fingernails. They ripped the fingernails from six-year old children!" Ana takes a deep breath, steeling herself for she has no choice but to listen. "They kept the children. We tried to get them back but we had no weapons. There was nothing we could do. Now we have idea where they are.

"In the next village, they went from house to house. They found a shelter with fifty children hiding in it and killed them all. I don't understand how they could do this. How can anyone do this?" His despair turns to anger. "I want the whole world to know what is going on here. This is real. It is happening. The world must listen!"

So her day continues, without respite. The waiting room becomes busier, her clients ever more needy, impatient and noisy and then the trauma really starts filtering in. Ana will learn that this comes in waves, depending on where the shells and bullets land, how many survive and how long it takes to get them out. A father comes bearing an injured child and the flood-gates open. There aren't enough stretchers, beds, painkillers or medics. The sickening smell of burning flesh fills the air along with the noise of those in need. People cry out in pain, for water and yet, despite their suffering, they want to speak with the doctors so that when they go home, they can tell the world what is happening to innocent civilians in Syria.

It has been dark for several hours by the time the waiting room clears. Ana doesn't remember eating but she was thirsty and a glass of water on her desk miraculously refilled several times during the day. Now exhausted, she wants for nothing but sleep.

She meets Aadil in the courtyard and realising he too, has only just returned, resolves to go with him to what they call the canteen, after all. She wants to see him eat something and knows she should do so herself.

"Hello Aadil, how was your day?"

"Good thanks, and yours?"

Ana hesitates. "Busy. Did you get a break?"

"They offer me coffee but it's too strong, so I keep working."

"Why don't you stop with them and rest? Have a drink of water or something."

"It's alright. I stop when I need to. We worked hard but it was good. It makes me happy to know I made a difference."

Ana nods. "You certainly do that, and to those lucky enough to work with you."

Aadil gives her a glorious smile. "Did you save lots of lives today, Ana?"

"Guess so," she sighs.

"What's up?"

"You reminded me of Rahim."

Aadil considers Ana carefully. "Where do you think he might be then?"

"They used to live in the old part of the city."

"Oh." Aadil frowns.

"Hi!" Ana turns, instantly on the defence. "Sorry. Didn't mean to startle you. Man you're jumpy!" Overtaking, Marcus turns to face them. "Heard you did good today, girl. Thanks for yer help. Would've been impossible without you. Khan didn't turn up for work." He looks crestfallen and Ana's stomach rises with a familiar sense of uneasiness. "Got some news for you though," he continues, clearly reluctant to elaborate. "Bout the boys you's bin looking for. Let's grab some food."

There is nothing left but cold rice, stale flat-breads and water but, finding appetites nevertheless, from sympathetic company, animated conversation flows. There is welcome news of Rahim. He got to Homs and was seen safely into the Old City, but this is under siege and there is no news of his brother.

Days merge into weeks and, overwhelmed by the relentless need for her, Ana doesn't notice freezing winter turn to mild, wet spring. There has been no further news of Rahim, no response to the messages she sends and it is becoming as clear as the risk she would be taking, that she may need to rescue him herself. That was her plan in the beginning, of course, but now it all looks so different. Impossible.

She walks back to the hospital alone. Hiding within the abaya and niqab Aadil's sister lent her, today she managed to sneak out without being noticed. Stories of those she treated that morning rotate like a revolving door in her head. The young man who, having received treatment for injuries in another field hospital, was captured by government forces, tortured for the names and locations of those who helped him, then left to die. Somehow he survived and was brought here for treatment but he was too distressed to take anything in, his injuries too severe for them to treat. They have no choice but to move him on. Fortunately Mahmoud with a few others, is heading back to Lebanon tomorrow and they have agreed to take him with them.

Ana wonders if his was one of the hospitals she hears are deliberately targeted and what happened to the medics who treated him. She doesn't notice at first, that the two men in front of her are armed, only that they are taking bets on something. A little boy plays in the dirt further up the battered street, other children – in the alleyways, while their parents go about their daily business, taking advantage of a lull in the sustained attack that Homs has been subjected to lately.

Today wasn't the first time either, that Ana saw direct evidence of the use, not only of starvation and torture, but of rape as a weapon of war in a society where a woman's modesty is synonymous with her honour and that of her family. And it had been a child this time, the eleven year old son of one of the ambulance drivers. The regime spares no-one. Not children or even babies.

She hears a crack and jumps to attention, instantly aware of everything around her. In horror she follows the barrel of a gun to the little boy now lying injured in the road ahead of her. Everyone has run. Apart from her, the snipers and their victim writhing in agony on the ground, the street is deserted. She makes for the child, forgetting all she ever learned about ensuring a safe approach but before she has even overtaken the perpetrators of this terrible crime, she is grabbed from behind, the hand clamping her mouth shut, successfully preventing her from uttering even a sound.

"What the hell you doing out here?" He is so angry with her. Mahmoud drags her into an alleyway and twirls her round to face him, but still he holds his hand over her mouth. "Not a sound," he hisses and she nods, her eyes wide with terror. He relaxes his grip on her but doesn't release it completely. "Now you listen carefully to what I am about to say." Ana nods, her heart racing, her mouth too dry anyway, to speak. "In a minute you are going to follow me quietly back to the hospital. Do exactly what I do. Say nothing. Ignore the boy on the road, he's dead anyway. Even if we could get him to safety he would die despite our best efforts. Do you understand?" Ana shakes her head without realising, the thought of this poor boy dying alone in the dirt, too much to bear and Mahmoud tightens his grip on her.

"Look at me Ana!" She stares at him through a blur of hot tears, blinking them away for a better view. "What do you think will happen to you – to all of us, if they catch you? How long do you think you would last before you told them everything? Consider what you have seen…" He waits and she has no choice but to obey. She blinks her vision clear once more. "Are you ready?" She nods. "Don't even look in his direction. Do you understand?" She nods again.

Later, Ana will treat the mother of that little boy. He was eight. It wasn't a clean shot and it will take him hours to die. Alone on the street. His mother watching, screaming from their home only a few metres away. She will tell Ana how she tried to reach her child and how the men kept firing into the street, taunting her. "You can't get to your child, you can't get to your child!" Laughing, mocking. And those words will reverberate around Ana's head for the rest of the night.

But first there are other horrors to contend with. There is quite a commotion when they bring in thirty five year old Ayyub and the transparent plastic bag containing his fingers. He was caught delivering bread to one of the areas under siege. They chopped off his fingers and made a necklace of them which they put around his neck. "Now take this bread to wherever you are going," they said. There is nothing Ana can do with the blackening fingers and her stomach turns with the smell as she opens the bag, for she feels compelled to show the poor man that she did look at them before she throws them out.

At least the cuts were clean. As she washes the mutilated stumps and stitches them up, Ana can only wonder once more, at a regime that inflicts such cruelty on its people, that considers even delivering bread, to be a crime.

And then they bring in Khan. He was a Syrian surgeon living and working in England. One of many who couldn't sit back and watch what was happening to his people but felt compelled to act. He came here to heal, to do just what she is, helping those in need. He was targeted, as are so many who take even the slightest stand against this tyrannical regime, and now his body has been returned. A warning, they say. They found him in one of the neighbouring streets and there is talk now of moving the hospital again for fear its secret location may have been compromised. He was starved and tortured like the others. Ana won't allow herself to dwell on his injuries though they had to be documented and relayed to those collecting evidence of crimes against humanity. Everyone is afraid and an eery hush has descended on the hospital. Only Aadil remains upbeat and cheerful, for they have kept as much from him as they could.

Ana finds herself relying more and more on him, as the days

go by, to maintain some sense of perspective and normality. In asking about the world she came from, he reminds her that this isn't how it always was, always will be, or how the rest of the world is living. Even in Za'atari life was simpler. Just like the endless tents and cabins, life was ordered and regimented, the difference between right and wrong, easy to discern and there were solutions, however inadequate, to most problems. It is so easy in this chaos to forget but Aadil reminds her. Their remit is to deal with all that each day throws at them until relief comes and the war ends.

Meanwhile, President Assad continues to enforce the blockade around the city. His forces have recaptured most of it and driven the rebels into a small enclave in the city centre.

There are rumours that civilians there have little but olives to live on, that they are resorting to eating grass, leaves, domestic animals and whatever they can grow themselves. Of the remaining seventy thousand, many are living in public buildings and tents in the rest of the city, waiting for the right conditions to return to their homes.

CALEB

This day starts much the same as any other. The clinic is busy and they have to ration the few drugs left, advising many to return tomorrow. By then, they hope, fresh supplies will have got through. They hardly notice the rumble of shelling but then news of another catastrophic bombing filters through and they brace themselves for the casualties. The government is using barrel bombs against its people. Crude, often home made devices – barrels or other cylindrical objects packed with petrol, nails, shrapnel and explosives. They roll them out of helicopters as they pass over the city.

The cries of those who bear them and their screams, precede the casualties and the clinic empties. Only those in dire need remain, along with those who stay to help. The first victim lost both legs at the thigh and is bleeding profusely. He goes straight to theatre with one of the hospital's trusted band of blood donors. Chaos ensues and in the midst of it, comes Caleb. Though they have never met, Ana recognises him instantly. To her mind's eye from the distance, he is exactly as she imagined him. Tall and lean, his stained shirt, torn and covered with fresh blood, he wears coarse trousers held up by rope and worn leather boots. Waves of thick black hair fall like curtains into his face, riverlets of sweat running through a thin layer of grime along a bed of olive skin.

He carries a young girl in a pink flowery dress soaked with blood and, as they come closer, Ana sees a gaping hole where her tummy should be. He gives Ana a brief accusing look, smouldering eyes dark with anguish, the muscles of his jaw twitching as he catches his breath through clenched teeth. A few days' stubble hardly conceals the thin line of a hairlip complemented by an irregularity in his teeth and, despite his striking looks, Ana's heart warms to him.

He lays the girl down, smoothing the hair tenderly from her face, commanding her attention with his eyes. When Ana inserts the needle, the child does not flinch. "What's your name?"

"Yalda," Caleb answers for her. "Which means longest night. But soon it will be over little one. Rest in peace." Without a murmur, Yalda closes her eyes. Ana swallows, her face blazing as she fights back her tears. She removes the drip and turns to the next casualty being brought through the door. They take him to the courtyard for it is evident they will need to make use of every space available. When she returns, Caleb is gone.

They continue through the night, their hard-won experience working as a team with the scarcest of resources, paying dividends as the hours pass. A nurse triages the patients in the street, others dealing with many of them there or in the courtyard. The most seriously injured go straight to the doctors and the worst of these to theatre. Marcus and the orthopaedic surgeon operate while Ana resuscitates, administering what analgesia she can. She sees Caleb from time to time but only in the distance and then no more.

Aadil appears and makes himself useful. He seems to know what to do without being asked, never tiring or complaining, remaining calm in the worst of the chaos. Ana has had many sleepless nights already on his account, especially since Khan's return. But, despite her determination to get him out of here as well, now she understands why Aadil will refuse to come.

"Do you know where Caleb went?" she asks.

"Back to ground zero, until there's no-one left to rescue. Then he'll come help us."

By daybreak the casualties stop arriving. Their carers have cleared the street, finding somewhere for them all to rest and lined the dead up a little further away, ready for collection. The surgeons are still operating and a few of Ana's wards hover precariously on the brink of death, but there are many still alive who wouldn't be without medical care. Those that are stable enough to be moved and for whom the hospital has nothing more to offer, will be taken to wherever now serves as home. Perhaps they'll return later for further treatment or review. Caleb didn't come back and dismissing any concern for him, Ana takes comfort from Aadil's reassurance instead. "He's done this many times before."

By mid-morning the clinic is filling up again. Deprived of sleep and food now for over twenty-four hours, Ana is reduced to zombie mode as they jokingly call it, and waits without thought or feeling, for that second wind to kick in. She would have missed him had she not needed supplies from theatre.

"Hey, Caleb!" Marcus looks up from an open abdomen and peers over half-rim glasses, to where Caleb sits, pale and dazed, in one corner of the room. The right sleeve of his mutilated shirt is missing from the shoulder down, a black hole gaping ominously in his upper arm with fresh bleeding from a wound at his wrist and his hands shake uncontrollably.

His hands. Ana cringes, wondering at how desperate he must have been to reach those suffocating beneath the rubble. Swollen and calloused they are covered in blood coagulated grime and every nail is either broken or missing, exposing sensitive beds rendered raw. Yet, strong and shapely, these hands would once have graced the piano with elegance and style. Ana's heart sinks and she looks through tears into his thoughtful eyes.

"Caleb?" No response. She reaches for the pulse at his wrist. It is strong but rapid. She pulls a tourniquet from her pocket, applying it above the hole as she raises his arm. "Caleb."

This time, he looks at her and smiles. "Hello Anais."

Her heart skips a beat and she blushes, feeling suddenly exposed.

"Utility room's free," Marcus calls out, referring to what has temporarily become a second operating theatre and, wishing

Surgeon Commander Wilson would come to her rescue, Ana wonders why she feels anxious about treating this patient when she has had so much worse to deal with in the preceding twenty-four hours. She leads Caleb to the room next door and he lies himself down on the table, extending his arm onto the arm-rest conveniently left attached to it.

"I'm afraid we have no anaesthetics or painkillers left."

"It's okay, Ana. I know the score. Just make it quick, eh?"

She looks at him in surprise and nods. "I'll do my best." Now that he's stretched out on the bed, she notices his lower abdomen exposed where part of his shirt is missing. It looks likes it's been torn away deliberately.

"Tourniquets and bandages," Caleb tells her. "Doesn't look very hygienic, does it? Must remember not to wear white next time."

"You tore strips off to…?" Obvious, when you think about it. Ana smiles.

"Yes. The rope comes in useful too."

"Oh?"

"You didn't think it was just there to hold my trousers up?"

"Well, it looks like you've lost a lot of weight." Caleb's face lights up with a glorious smile and, stunned, Ana stares unconsciously into his dirt-stained face. She returns to cleaning his arm, acutely aware of how he watches as she removes the tourniquet and does her best to pretend he can't see the blush rising from her neck to her face.

Thankfully the bleeding has stopped. She considers putting up a drip but rendering the red stuff pink, as Marcus so eloquently put it an age ago, won't help. She inserts a venthlon into the other arm anyway, just in case, warning Caleb without thinking, that this will hurt. "Sharp prick coming…now." He laughs and, realising the absurdity of what she has just said, Ana shakes her head.

The orthopaedic surgeon enters the room, reminding her that she has a job to do and looks at them both in surprise. "Came to help but looks like you've got things covered. Shout if you need me." He walks out again and Ana flushes the venthlon with water.

"So what do you use the rope for, Caleb?" she asks, gathering a tray of surgical instruments, swabs, a kidney bowl, some disinfectant, stitches and scalpel blades.

"Lots of things." He winks at her and she ignores him but blushes again. "It's good for hoisting people out of awkward places, moving things, climbing. You can make a lasso with it and catch things or use it to bind things together. People sometimes." Ana frowns disapprovingly. "Only the bad ones, of course," he hastens to add and she can't restrain the glimmer of a smile. "And it's good for holding up trousers that are a little too big." Ana looks involuntarily at Caleb's flat stomach, finely honed muscles bulging as he holds himself in the best position to watch her without moving his arm. She notices how the rope wraps itself several times around his waist.

"It's longer than I thought then," she says without thinking, feeling herself reddening as soon as the words leave her mouth. He laughs and she cannot resist looking into his face. She wants to tell him how beautiful he is. "You need to stop doing that," she says. "It's very distracting." He blesses her with a glorious smile and for a moment she is paralysed, caught in some wonderful trance. She shakes herself out of it. "And that," she adds, considering how she should, but won't, ask him to stop using that mesmerising voice on her as well.

A bit of pressure and a few strategically placed stitches are all she needs to stop the bleeding from the cut in his wrist. She bandages it firmly and moves up to his shoulder. She'll have to deal with his hands last. He's lain himself down now, the effort of raising himself to see her, too much to maintain in his exhausted state. "Are you hurt anywhere else?"

"No, but you're welcome to check."

She smiles. "So what went in here?" She peers into the cavity in his arm.

"A sniper's bullet. Luckily for me, not a fragmentation one." Ana stares at him. "Would probably have cost me my arm," he elaborates and she shakes her head with a frown.

"They were shooting at you while you rescued the victims of their bombs?"

"I don't know who it was Ana," Caleb replies wearily. "It's become so complicated. Most likely a government bullet though. It didn't come out the other side, so you'll need to remove it, I'm afraid." Having done this so often before, now she is even more acutely aware of their lack of x-ray facilities, let alone CT scanning. They have to rely on clinical acumen, a fair bit of digging around to remove all the debris that gets sucked in with any projectile, and luck. She probes the hole and Caleb closes his eyes. He grits his teeth and moans when she locates the bullet and tries to prize it free. It has lodged itself in bone and will take some force to remove. She considers asking the orthopaedic surgeon for help but Caleb stops her. "It's okay. Just grab hold of it and pull really hard, I'll try not to move."

"I was thinking of getting help."

"You can do it Ana." He raises his head to look directly into her eyes and, in that instant, she knows she could do anything he asked her to.

She takes a pair of pliers from the tray and braces herself. Caleb studies the ceiling. "Are you ready?" He nods.

Fortunately, for he, too, appears to be holding his breath, it doesn't take her long to remove the bullet and she drops it with a satisfying clang into the metal kidney bowl. It takes a good while longer, however, to clear the wound of debris and Ana finds herself flinching in anticipation of what he must be feeling. Concentrating too hard to make distracting conversation, she hardly notices him taking on that role, only how musical the lilt in his slight accent makes his deep voice sound and his occasional lisp.

"What are you doing here Ana?"

With a sigh, she pauses, dripping scalpel in mid-air and he rolls his eyes back up to the ceiling. "Sorry." She gets back to work.

"Well …" She reassures herself that he is no longer watching then puts her head down again. "I came here by accident really and haven't been able to tear myself away."

"Has that effect on you, doesn't it?"

A dozen memories wash over her, enormous sadness welling up inside and she applies herself with fresh determination to the task in hand. Caleb cries out and she stops abruptly. "I'm so sorry." He smiles reassuringly and, taking a deep breath, she peers back into his arm.

"So, what accident brought you here?" he persists.

"I was working at Za'atari, the refugee camp in Jordan. There was a boy. Rahim. He came with his little sisters and their mother in labour. Rahim is eleven. He'd seen his father die in prison. They're from the old quarter of Homs. Had to leave in a hurry. There wasn't time to find his eight year old brother." Ana hesitates, looking to Caleb as if he could absolve her of some sin. "Rahim often talked about going back for him." She swallows and refocuses on his arm. "Should've taken him more seriously." She takes a last good look at her handiwork then proceeds to pack and dress it.

"So you came after him?"

"I felt responsible. He trusted me. His mother too. I couldn't bear to do nothing and there was no-one else. He got under my skin, see?" Caleb nods. "Despite everything he'd been through, he had the courage to go back for the sake of his little brother." She considers Caleb listening intently. "He told me once, how he saved his brother's life. Surrounded by shelling and snipers, Foued was trapped. He had seen his best friend torn to pieces by shrapnel." Overwhelmed, Ana hangs her head and turns away. There is movement behind her, something touches her shoulder and with a start, she remembers. "Your hands!" She blinks away the tears and turns back. "I'll get clean water. Please don't move."

"What happened next?" Mesmerising eyes catch hers and she hesitates. He nods.

"Rahim rescued his little brother and promised never to let anyone hurt him." Ana stands motionless, looking through mist into bottomless pools of black and feels something magical happen inside. Warm and comforting. She remembers how quietly Yalda lay in Caleb's arms and briefly, she too, knows he was always here, that time and everything around them, is an illusion. But then the moment passes, chased away by a feeling of impending doom. "Stay there," she blurts, as if he might suddenly disappear again, and he nods with a smile.

"You okay, girl?" Marcus is closing his patient's abdomen and Ana sees his next client lying in the hallway outside. "Caleb?"

Ana nods. "Nearly done, thanks."

She feels Caleb's eyes on her as she returns and great relief that he didn't go, after all. She puts the water on the floor to move a stool in front of him, then places the bowl where he can comfortably reach it. "I'm sorry Caleb, this is going to hurt." He smiles reassuringly and, taking a deep breath, puts his hands into the water.

It takes forever to scour out what debris she can and Ana hates herself for every moment but, at last, the job is done. She paints Caleb's raw nail beds with iodine, covers this with a medicated netting and begins to dress each finger.

"Not too thick."

She eyes him suspiciously. "You need to rest," she tells him in no uncertain terms and he sighs. "Caleb?"

"Yes?"

"Does Yalda really mean endless night?"

"Yes." He looks away, a different kind of pain in his face. "And I need to find her brother."

"What do you mean?"

"Yalda saw her parents die. She knew they wouldn't be able to save him."

"Save who?"

"Her little brother…was buried in what remains of their home yesterday. We couldn't find him." Caleb lifts his hands, contorting them into claws and stares at them angrily through wet eyes.

Ana's indignation disintegrates. "Please don't use them to dig," she pleads and helps him up.

"You shouldn't be here." Caleb's eyes are full of concern. "Go home before it's too late." She shakes her head with a frown and he sighs. Raising a bandaged hand to her forehead, he thanks her and turns to leave. Ana's heart sinks.

"Something we said?" Marcus calls after him.

"You need to move this hospital!" And, with that, Caleb is gone.

Ana returns to the waiting room and wonders again how such a small space can possibly hold so many people. She is getting used to it now – the sheer volume of need they aspire to meet, her usual answer to this challenge, that every day comes to an end, long rendered obsolete. She has made it a habit before she sleeps, to reflect on anything positive about her day, however small, and derives much satisfaction from the knowledge that she has done a good job as well as anyone could have with the tools at her disposal.

However, there are some things she will never get used to, that she battles with to preserve her resilience. The cancer patients for whom they can do nothing come into this group. She can't even offer them simple painkillers to cover their often dreadful demise. The fatal respiratory tract infections that could so easily be cured with simple antibiotics, even in a population whose susceptibility to them increases through malnutrition, trauma and disease. And then there is the trauma. Words cannot describe the awfulness of what she witnesses. These people are so brave. Often Ana wonders how they do it, how they live with what they endure. She feels certain she would have given up long ago and yet, their suffering seems to ignite a camaraderie which is inspiring, uplifting, infectious, and Ana knows this to be one of the reasons she stays. In the face of overwhelming adversity she witnesses the power of the human spirit and that love really does conquer all.

Ana is in the middle of an argument when Caleb returns. She is trying to persuade the head of this family, a man in his fifties, that his grandson is not crazy. Rather than hallucinations, he is having flashbacks and what he needs is understanding, time and counselling which, sadly, is currently lacking. The man wants her to give the boy drugs but she doesn't have any even if she thought that might help and his grandfather thinks she is being obstructive. Ana doesn't have time for this, though she fears there is a lot more to his story and that the man has much to answer for that he will never admit to. His daughter seems to have more sense but little power and Ana struggles to understand what she says. They have been without an interpreter now for weeks. Another casualty they fear, of Assad's monstrous killing machine.

Ignoring the torrent of abuse she is getting from her father, the woman pushes the boy out of the room. "Can't tell some-one that don't wanna listen," she mutters in English with a wink as she passes Ana.

Caleb watches this altercation in amusement, patiently bearing his load until Ana is ready to receive them but when she freezes at the sight of him, he cannot help himself. She had expected him to return distraught or with a casualty in urgent need of medical attention but here he stands in the doorway, evidently enjoying the show. The bundle in his arms shakes a parting through a shock of blonde curls and piercing green eyes lock onto hers. At only two or three, like his sister before, he seems hypnotically calm. Ana is puzzled. Even if he wasn't injured, he was buried alive, alone for twenty-four hours and now he lies in the arms of a complete stranger.

"Unhurt," Caleb says simply, "but I thought you should check him over, just in case. Then we need to think what to do with him."

"Does he know?" Caleb raises his eyebrows. "What happened to the others?" He shakes his head. "Oh." Ana regrets being so tactless. "This way."

She leads them to her consulting room and offers them water. The little boy drinks thirstily. She offers him a biscuit and he shrinks into Caleb's arms, shaking his head warily. She starts to talk in soft monotonous tones, feeling his forehead gently, touching his hair and stroking his back until, curious, he turns to watch what she is doing.

She takes one hand, looking at it with him then smiling into his eyes, feeling gently as she goes. He does not flinch. She moves his fingers and his wrist, running her hands up his forearm and now he allows her to move his elbow.

"Can I look under here?" Without him noticing, Caleb removes his top. A few scratches and bruises but nothing serious. Everything moves normally without bothering him. "Can I feel your tummy?" Unflinchingly, he stares at her, the hypnotic trance unbroken and Caleb lays him flatter in his lap. Soft, non-tender. No lumps that shouldn't be there. "Now I need to listen to your chest." She brings out her stethoscope and he doesn't complain when she puts it on his chest and, finally, mindful of Rahim's reaction, a torch to check his eyes. Physically at least, the child appears to have come to no harm.

They decide to keep him with them at the hospital overnight. Caleb will stay with him for Ana still has patients to see.

She finds them later in the canteen. Caleb drives a car made from wood and bottle tops, along a street carved into the dusty floor. Whenever he places something alongside – an empty cup or a box, the little boy knocks it over angrily and Ana witnesses in miniature, the devastation of his homeland. Her foot strikes a can and he jumps, his eyes wide, face pale, then he buries himself in Caleb's chest rocking them both from side to side. Ana goes to sit beside them. The little boy peeks out at her and she smiles back.

"What's your name?" He frowns, blinking long ginger eyelashes and looks as if he is about to cry.

"Saad," Caleb answers.

"Saad." She says it softly and his ears prick up, his eyes fixing on hers. Ana wonders what his mother was like, at the thoughts that ran through her head as she died and if Saad saw what happened. The heaviness in her heart becomes unbearable. Piercing green eyes stare unblinkingly despite the tears gathering in them, from a face that has no expression otherwise and Ana cannot help herself. She closes her eyes and looks away. Caleb puts an arm around her and she buries her face in her knees.

A little hand comes to rest on her back, a thin arm around her neck and soft lips touch her forehead. She lifts her head and opens brimming eyes. Little Saad stands silently before her, waiting, then he takes her hand and pulls. She smiles at him and he helps her up. He takes the car and hands it to her expectantly, clearing a way for it on the dusty road then, picking up a box and the can, he places them carefully along its verge.

Tantalising smells hit. Fried onions, tomatoes, peppers and strong spicy coffee. Ana's stomach grumbles and Caleb laughs. "Ana's tummy says she's hungry. Shall we go eat with her?" Saad nods. Taking his hand, Caleb leads him to the food. Cookies shaped like rings. That cheese they call ka'ak. A spicy stew. Flatbreads and yoghurt. It's someone's birthday and they've gone to extra trouble with the meal tonight. There are days when food is more plentiful. A store that was raided perhaps. Fruit and vegetables someone grew. Aid that managed to get through. There are many reasons supplies fluctuate.

They find an empty table and settle down, pretending not to notice what Saad does, anxious that he should eat, nevertheless. He looks at the food suspiciously then at Ana and watches as she puts a spoonful into her mouth. She holds some up to him with a smile and nods, waiting patiently for his hunger to get the better of him and all the time, his eyes never leave her.

They rest together in the dormitory that night, Saad with his back pressed against Caleb's chest, clutching a freshly dressed hand and Ana facing them both. Neither moves but whenever she wakes, Caleb's eyes are on her and she knows he watches over them both.

Caleb is in no rush to move on over the next few days whilst Saad finds his feet. A rare opportunity he wouldn't have taken otherwise, Ana learns, to rest and allow his injuries to heal. She checks and redresses his wounds daily, relieved beyond measure to find no sign of infection. Fresh supplies still haven't got through and they have no antibiotics left, not even those that were long out of date.

Saad continues to weave his magic, captivating the hearts of those he meets and the dark fog that seemed to have descended on the hospital, lifts. He is eating well now, enjoying playing with the older children who come to help out each day and the little ones that are brought in to be seen. Saad has become the hospital mascot and no-one is in any hurry to move him on, using his continued silence and physical response to their administrations, as excuses to keep him. Attempts are being made to find relatives, friends or simply a suitable family that will have him and all visitors are scrutinised carefully but nothing has, so far, turned up.

Ana is busy but makes the most of every second she can get with Caleb. "There just aren't enough hours in the day," she finds herself confessing one night as they lie in the dormitory, Saad sleeping peacefully between them. "So much to discover and so little time." Caleb raises his eyebrows but does not help her out. Once more, she is burning to interrogate him. She wants to know everything there is to know and, though she senses that the feelings she has for him are mutual, something is holding him back. Perhaps, she reasons, she doesn't want to find out what that is.

"Tell me about yourself, Ana." Caleb takes the initiative and Ana looks to Saad in confusion.

"You know most of it already," she answers defensively and he shakes his head.

"I think not. Why did you go to Za'atari?"

Might as well start there then. "Because my father didn't want me to," she answers flippantly. Caleb raises his eyebrows, transfixing her with eyes full of passion and she wonders if there is anything she could keep from him. "What about you?" she asks.

"I'm sure your story is far more interesting." He heaves a great sigh, shakes his head and smiles in resignation.

He tells her then, of how he grew up in Ma'aloula, one of the oldest Christian villages in Syria, built into a rugged mountainside about sixty kilometres northeast of Damascus, where his grandparents still live. Of how his parents worked away. His mother at the university in Damascus, his father all over the world. Of how they spent long periods of time, therefore, with various members of her large close-knit family until they were old enough to look after themselves.

He waxes lyrical about the barren beauty of the place he has considered more than any other, to be his home, sunsets over distant hills and surrounding desert and the freedom of the rugged mountains that protect the village itself. Of how they learned to climb, run and cave in the local gorges and ravines and of how these flood in the winter, powerful currents carving great bowls to make the water boil like a devil's cauldron.

He tells her that Ma'aloula, considered a symbol of Christianity in Syria, is one of only a few places where the Aramaic language, believed to have been spoken by Jesus Christ, is still used by both Muslim and Christian residents, that there are usually about two thousand of these and of the visitors that swell these numbers to eight thousand or so, during holidays. Of the two monasteries, the shrines and grottos, the beautiful historic paintings, frescoes, mosaics and byzantine windows. Of the religious festivals and a valley illuminated at night by a thousand candles and of the giant statues of Mary and Jesus that stand high above the village watching over them.

As he recounts his memories, Ana inhales the yeasty smell of freshly baked breads laid out by women on low walls in the sunshine, scans the colourful array of aromatic food presented in a dozen baskets at the back of a pick-up truck and tastes sweet pomegranate juice freshly squeezed from a mountain of fruit set out by the side of the road. She basks in the warmth of the early morning sun as they wander through narrow streets, feels the breeze against her face as they climb time-worn steps between houses that seem to have clung to the hillsides forever, and glides through the cool silk of pools that appear in the gorges after the rains.

Caleb falls silent and, waking from the spell he has cast, Ana becomes aware of him watching her. "Go on," she pleads.

"My mother, Ishtar, taught ancient history at the University of Damascus. She resigned at Assad's brutal response to the protests that started this war." He hesitates. "Strange how things turn out don't you think?"

"What do you mean?"

"We knew Bashar al-Assad when he was a child. Even went to the same school for a while. He wasn't that different to the rest of us. Not born, you see, to the position he assumes above us. He comes from a minority sect in Syria, called the Alawites. Down the ages, the Alawites have been persecuted, subservient. In the 1940's and 50's, they were the only ones that didn't consider serving in the military, beneath them.

"Like many, Assad's father worked his way up through the ranks, in his case, to defence minister and commander of the airforce."

"How did he become president?"

"When Syria gained independence from the French in 1946, the Alawites were in a good position to form an alliance with the favoured political party at that time, the Ba'ath party. Like most Arab countries, people here were used to authoritarian rule and accepted that needed strengthening to stabilise our fragile country.

"Hafiz al-Assad was made president of Syria and ruled for thirty years until his death in 2000. Bashar's older brother, Basil, had been groomed to replace him but died in a car crash six years before this. Bashar, as you probably know, was an opthalmologist, training in London at the time." Caleb sighs. "How could he have guessed that eleven years later he would become one of the world's most hated tyrants?"

Ana shakes her head angrily. "How is he capable of inflicting such atrocities on his own people?"

"Well," Caleb considers her carefully. "The Alawites had worked long and hard for their positions of authority, as had leading, mostly Sunni businessmen who jumped onto the bandwagon. They were not going to give up their privilege easily. They rushed Bashar through all the positions needed to prevent serious opposition to his succession and on his father's death, the son became president. He was seen then, as the hope for the future of Syria. A breath of fresh air who would lead his country into the modern world. He even criticised some of his father's policies, suggesting that economic progress had been compromised by the state's control. Believe it or not, in his inaugural speech he stated that authority without responsibility is the cause of chaos and called for a democracy specific to Syria that takes its roots from its history and respects its society. "

"Vile hypocrite!"

"Maybe, but it can't have been easy. Bashar had inherited a mukhabarat state. Do you know what that is?"

She nods. "One in which security services control the population, using informants and the military to defend the regime against perceived threats. Internal as well as external."

"Well put. The economy was stagnant, there was chronic political instability, pervasive corruption and war on Syria's borders in Lebanon and Iraq. The first few months of Bashar's rule came to be known as the Damascus Spring. Political prisoners of all persuasions were released, forums encouraged where open criticism and dissent were tolerated and control of the media was relaxed. But the number of prodemocracy organisations that rose up and the scale of criticism of it, took the regime by surprise and the old guard took Bashar to one side to tell him that this was not the way things were done around here. Pro-democracy laws were repealed, released prisoners re-imprisoned and Syria continued its dependency on the ruling regime.

"The Americans didn't help. They ran Assad down, doing their best to belittle and humiliate him, particularly to the Arab world. Syria's position became even less stable and Assad's need to assert himself, grew. Then came the assassination of Lebanon's former Prime Minister – Rafiq Hariri, Nine-Eleven and the Iraq war. Syria was made to look like a terrorist state when, perhaps, all it was trying to do, was antagonise as few of its neighbours as possible." Caleb gives Ana a wry smile.

"Assad felt his political insecurity personally. He was under tremendous pressure to get it right, especially when it came to peace negotiations with Israel and was desperate to get the Jolan, which his father had lost, back for Syria."

"What's so special about the Golan Heights?"

"It's the mountain range with Syria's highest peak. Jabal Ash-Sheikh as we call it for the white beard it wears six months a year. Mountain of the Wise Old Man. Its snow-melt feeds the Jolan's rich volcanic soil and Israel's largest reservoir, Lake Tiberius, the biblical Sea of Galilee. The region is famous for its orchards, apple farms and wine.

"Today, Israel controls over two thirds of the Jolan, depriving Syria of access to mountain villages, gorges and spectacular historical sites like Baniyas, City of Pan. When you look back to Syria, the contrast is striking. The countryside around Majdal Shams, the largest town on the Jolan, is green, well-irrigated and organised into farms and fields, compared to Syria's neglected villages. Syria could have made a significant income from tourism in the Jolan but now Israel takes it all. It has turned it into a year-round weekend getaway with its own ski resort and established Jewish settlements there. Over forty of them now.

"From its highest points you can see Damascus," Caleb tells her and that, in response to Israeli initiated firing, Syria launched bomb attacks from the Jolan onto northern Israel for nearly twenty years. "So now Israel will never give it up. Forgotten by the rest of the world, the Jolan is in political stalemate. So much so, that

Israel has started to exploit the region for oil and gas, and has built a security barrier to protect itself from Syria's civil war.

"It is home to Druze, who, like so many, have tried to remain neutral. With the regime summoning extra reserves from both Druze and Christian areas and threatening to execute their families if they refuse, this becomes increasingly difficult, however. Some of the Jolan Druze, desperate to avoid having to make the choice between the regime and the rebels, seek Israeli citizenship and, to complicate matters further, the superior Israeli hospitals have been treating emergency cases from Syria. Taken to the security fence, they are collected, treated and discretely returned. Israel, it would seem, is trying to win the hearts and minds of the people of the Jolan, to form a buffer between itself and its war torn neighbour.

"Along with Syria's silent majority, unable to choose between the regime or the rebels, the Druze say they are like the donkey between two carrots. The donkey agonises over which carrot might be juicier or bigger for so long that it ends up dying of starvation in the middle. You see, indecision is a form of decision, its consequences potentially deadly. As was Obama's, on whether to strike against the Assad regime or not." Ana smiles but her heart weighs heavy.

"To many Syrians it seemed that Assad sacrificed his vocation to be president even though he had not been traditionally groomed for this responsibility. They were patient with him as he did his best under the constant pressure of conflicting expectations.

"In early 2011, Syria seemed a fairly stable place, the Assads cosmopolitan. The President was complacent about the Arab Spring, even hailing it as a new era in the Middle East, where the rulers would need to meet the rising political and economic demands of the people. Assad backed the Palestinians in the face of Israeli brutality and supportive US policies, so felt he was on the side of the Arab people. But he hadn't reckoned on a growing young population with expectations of its government to build it a country with a future in the 21st century.

"The global economic downturn of late 2008 had stunted Syria's slow economic growth and unemployment rates were high, especially amongst the young. Of the twenty two million people in Syria before the uprising, about sixty percent were under the age of twenty five. The agricultural sector accounted for about a quarter of Syria's GDP and workforce but with the droughts of the 2000's, food production fell, prices rose. Three million farmers, pushed into extreme poverty, fled the countryside and were squatting in shanty towns on the outskirts of the cities. Oil reserves dwindled. Market orientated reforms increased inequality in the distribution of the country's wealth, enriching the privileged few with connections to the regime. Some thirty percent of Syrians lived below the poverty line, eleven percent below subsistence level. A million or so refugees had settled in Syria following the US invasion of Iraq. Added to this, Syrians faced arbitrary violent repression by the state on a daily basis. Most Syrians know someone who has been arrested, tortured or interrogated by the mukhabarat."

The flame from their oil-lamp flickers as its light begins to fade and, careful not to disturb Saad, Caleb rises to adjust it. With a warm smile as he settles back down, he asks Ana to tell him something about herself.

"How did the Arab Spring go so disastrously wrong?" she asks.

He searches her eyes, a weariness settling back into his as the shadows behind him grow. An explosion outside breaks the still darkness with a ghastly orange and Ana startles, her heart beating uncomfortably against her ribs.

"The Arab Spring, as you know, was sparked by Mohammad Bou Azizi, a twenty-six year old Tunisian university graduate humbly working on his fruit and vegetable cart. Police confiscated his produce because he lacked the proper permit. One, no doubt, that he needed to bribe someone to get. In despair at the humiliation he felt under the forces of oppression, Bou Azizi committed suicide by setting himself on fire.

"Now, you have to understand. The Quran states that after

death, a body must be washed gently in lukewarm water as we don't know it doesn't feel anything after the soul has left it. Then it must be wrapped in a white shroud, placed into a simple grave and buried, within twenty-four hours. There should be no extravagant banquets or lavish funerals which are false vanity and a waste of money. The Quran prohibits the use of fire on Allah's creation, so cremation is forbidden.

"So you see, there was nothing worse Bou Azizi could have done to himself. It was the ultimate despair. An act which resonated with his generation and ignited the flames that spread throughout the Arab world.

"This is a world full of young men who cannot afford to provide for their families and have been led, through education, to expect more from life than they have any prospect of achieving unless there are radical changes in the way their countries are governed. These young people are angry and frustrated. They want to be heard – for progress to be made and yet, they find themselves enslaved to systems stunted by pervasive corruption and decades of political repression.

"Bou Azizi was humiliated and suffered unimaginable pain for the two weeks before he died on 4 January 2011, a fate he did not deserve. The protest this sparked, spread from his home town to his country and then, via Facebook and mobile phone feeds, to the extended Arab world, and it was effective. Regimes toppled, longstanding entrenched rulers were overthrown and, despite the overwhelming military power that repressive regimes were able to use against their people, the technologically savvy young had the advantage of social media.

"But the differences between Syria and other Arab countries made it less likely to get caught up in the Arab Spring and its people more reluctant to do anything that would risk instability. From Syria's turbulent development since independence, to the sectarian violence fuelled by political upheaval in neighbouring Lebanon and Iraq, we have seen the consequences of getting it wrong. Of course, the Assads have played on such fears over the years, the President claiming to be all that stands in the way of all out civil war. He and his family were generally not disliked by the people, who saw them as one of them, devoid of the extravagant lifestyles displayed by leaders of other Arab countries. Also, the Syrian regime has done a good job over the years, of ensuring its opposition is uncoordinated and divided with no clear leadership. Exiled opposition are considered illegitimate by the regime and out of touch with the reality of day to day life, by people living in Syria itself.

"To start with, the protests in Syria didn't amount to much but then, in Daraa, one of its poorest regions, ten children aged from nine to fifteen did what children do the world over. They misbehaved. They wrote 'Down with the Regime' on a wall of their school and for that they were arrested, interrogated and tortured. At first, only a few hundred came out to support family and friends in protesting for the release of their children but once again, security forces reacted with unnecessary violence, killing four protestors. By the next day their numbers had swollen to thousands.

"Daraa epitomized everything that troubled Syria. Poverty, a failed economy, population explosion, a bad governor and overbearing security forces. The government tried to contain the protests there and cut basic services – electricity, water, mobile phone networks. Even funerals were banned as they became focal points for protests but the apathy of the young had turned to anger. There was too much unemployment, too little freedom and modern media had given them a powerful weapon to fight authority.

"There were protests in other places as well but to start with, these were isolated, focussing on local issues, not co-ordinated national affairs. It was Assad's delayed response and then his assertion that these were all part of some conspiracy against Syria by terrorists with his ensuing violent crackdown, that caused the people to unite against him. Suddenly they had a shared mission. No longer disconnected from each other, they felt able to speak about that of which they had always lived in fear, for now they dared hope for a better and democratic future."

"His rhetoric was paranoid," Ana recalls.

"And he set a precedent in his response to the protests, when he clearly stated his intention not to give in, that any reforms he announced were merely restating what the Ba'ath party had declared six years earlier."

"He used the word 'sedition', repeatedly in that speech."

"And delivered a chilling warning to any opposition when he quoted the Holy Quran as saying that sedition is worse than killing."

"Interesting isn't it, that though so ponderous in its response to any challenge, the state's reaction to dissent is immediate violent repression? And now that this ball has been set in motion, there can be no going back."

Caleb nods. "Neither the people of Syria nor the world will forgive Assad the atrocities he has committed. He is literally fighting for his life and the people for theirs for, whatever it may say, the state will never forget or forgive. From peaceful protests they were forced to protect their families and now they are willing to sacrifice everything in a fight to the end. What's more, they know they fight an army that serves a person and his family, not a country and its citizens. Like most dictators," Caleb adds bitterly, "Assad lives in a world of his own, his ego inflated by a brainwashed population and the propaganda of sycophants. As they say, absolute power corrupts absolutely."

"And yet, he could have been defeated, don't you think?" Ana asks regretfully for it all seems so unjust. "Before the jihadists came. If Russia and China hadn't opposed international pressure on Syria, the United Nations might have intervened and given the legitimate opposition the support it so desperately needed. Now it's too late."

"Neither the Russians nor the Chinese are likely to support the deposition of a regime on humanitarian grounds and, consider what Russia, especially, stands to lose should Assad's regime fall."

"What does it stand to lose?"

"Influence in the Middle East and access to a mediterranean port."

"So now Syria must die a slow death with the mass exodus of refugees transferring unrest to countries with limited capacity to cope."

"It will take at least a generation to replace the drain of Syrian talent."

Ana shakes her head with a frown and they consider Saad in silence. "So what happened after Assad's speech?" she asks, at last.

"It was seen as too little, too late, threatening and insincere. Protests broke out across the country and were followed, as you say, by almost reflex, violent crackdowns by government forces. By April 2011, most journalists had been expelled from a country in which access to true information had been severely limited from the start. That was when my father disappeared." Ana takes a deep breath but Caleb doesn't give her the chance to ask.

"There were reports, then videos of Syrian soldiers wounded by government security forces for refusing to fire on protestors, often their own people. By the summer, defectors had formed the fighting force that became the Free Syrian Army. They tended to operate near the border with sympathetic Turkey, Lebanon and Jordan, in order to evade government forces when necessary and more easily resupply. So here the regime laid minefields. It continued to paint the uprising as a foreign conspiracy using armed gangs, terrorists, criminals and thugs, so denying the real socioeconomic and political roots of the crisis and the legitimate needs of protestors. Already, by June 2011, a paper had been published by Human Rights Watch entitled, *We've never seen such horror : Crimes against humanity by Syrian security forces.*

On the first of August, the Muslim world entered the holy

month of Ramadan, marking, the demonstrators hoped, what would be a turning point in their revolution. Instead, it became clear, not only that the regime was too powerful to be overthrown peacefully, but that it was determined to wipe out its opposition. Taking up arms was simply a matter of self-defence. The regime's use of the shabiha to terrorise its people and escalate sectarian hostility, only served to strengthen their determination."

"Shabiha?"

"Ghosts. So called for the way they seem to appear from nowhere and disappear into thin air. Mafiosa-like criminals used by a number of prominent Syrian business-men over the years, to protect their lucrative privileges. They fanatically support the regime and deliberately carry out the most gruesome atrocities in the wake of government led attacks. Mostly Alawite, they are paid vast sums of money for their sadistic work though it could be argued that they fight also for survival, given that extremist Sunni elements would wipe them out should Assad's regime fall."

Saad stirs, crying out in his sleep and Caleb strokes his back. "It's okay Saad, you're safe." They watch him settle, smiling at the soft unintelligible noises he makes as he falls more deeply unconscious again.

"What about the rest of your family?" Ana asks, hesitating to enquire directly about his father.

"My father is Irish. A journalist. I came back to find him."

"And did you?"

Caleb shakes his head. "He's most probably in one of Assad's jails. My older brother, Baltasar, is a policeman but has been unable to find out much. They have three children. He has to be careful. And we have a younger sister, Fadia. She and her husband teach at the local school. They are expecting their first child."

"So where did you come from?" Ana asks. "What did you do before the war?"

"Kenya, and nothing much. I played piano, wrote articles for newspapers like my father and did other things I'm not at liberty to tell." He winks and the warmth of his gaze melts the chill that has descended on the room.

"You're a musician?"

He nods. "I was quite good once. Billed as a virtuoso, even. Gave concerts all over the world. I was particularly sought after for my interpretations of Chopin and Rachmaninov." The shadows flicker across his handsome face, highlighting his hairlip. "I travelled a lot. Got in and out of trouble from time to time. Saved some, caused the demise of others."

Ana frowns, unconsciously shaking her head for she cannot believe him capable of doing harm and they fall into a silence broken only by the gentle breathing of Saad.

"Tell me about your childhood."

An uncomfortable heat rises from the pit of Ana's stomach and she breaks the hold of those mesmerising eyes. "Why did you travel a lot?" she asks, ignoring his concern.

He heaves a great sigh. "Never really felt I fitted in, belonged anywhere, if you know what I mean." She nods. "I was looking for an answer."

"And what did you find?"

"Suffering and heartache."

She frowns, the tension in her growing as he waits. "Have you ever killed a man?" Caleb glances at Saad sleeping peacefully between them and when he looks back at her, there is an intensity to his gaze that seems to penetrate deep into Ana's soul. "No man has the right to take the life of another," he says, "but on occasion, that is the lesser of two evils." He watches as she considers the possibility that she was wrong about him after all.

"How does a good man become a killer?"

"Out of necessity. Fear perhaps." He searches her eyes. "I was young. Had spent much time in an Iranian prison or recovering from it. That made me restless so I travelled the world, like I said. To places you should never go without knowing how to defend yourself. And those you love." He falls silent, watching as she assimilates what he has just told her.

"How did you learn to do it?"

"Military service is compulsory in Syria. They allowed me to postpone mine until I was nineteen but I still had to do the full two and a half years. I was still a bit mad from what had happened. Took it all very seriously." That far away look returns to his eyes and something else – terrible, haunting. "I imagined going to war against those who had committed the most terrible atrocities," he says. "I was young, foolish, bitter and angry."

"What happened to you Caleb, when you were a teenager?"

For a moment, he looks away. "I'd rather not talk about that right now." He looks back at her defiantly. "Yes, I have killed, but only when I had no choice."

"But there is always a choice."

"Not when the toss up is between sadistic killers and the innocents they persecute. Besides, when it comes down to it, there isn't time to consider what you're doing too carefully. They were the right choices Ana, believe me."

And she does. Remembering the people she has treated, the stories she has heard and the evidence she has seen. When she thinks of what may be happening to Rahim and his little brother, the fate that may await Aadil – what could she be capable of if ever she found grown men raping or torturing them? She believes him.

"Now tell me about you."

But her head is full to bursting. "Why did your parents give you a Jewish name?" she asks, wondering if he was bullied as a child.

"She didn't, my friends did. It's a nickname. My real name is Sargon and, in case you're wondering, my mother made us all learn a martial art as children. If ever we were bullied, it wasn't for long."

"Which martial art?"

"Krav Maga."

"Really? My father made us learn that too!"

"You?" He can't quite see it.

"Yes, and believe it or not, I was good." She can't help but consider what drove her to excel at such a brutally effective sport which aims to neutralise threat, targeting the most vulnerable parts of the body with no attempt to avoid permanent injury or death.

Caleb nods. "I'll need to be careful with you then."

"Don't worry. I haven't trained in ages."

"Did you think of your father when you fought, Ana?" He couldn't have hit her harder if he had struck her physically. She takes a deep breath, willing her heart-rate back down, the dryness in her mouth to abate.

"I'm sorry." He frowns and makes to come closer but she shakes her head and he stops. "D'you know how it started?" he asks instead.

Ana nods. "With Hungarian-Israeli martial artist Imi Lichtenfield, who used it to defend the Jewish Quarter against facist groups in Bratislava. It was developed and is used by the military in Israel."

"Do you want to work-out with me some time Ana?"

Her heart races, the heat in her rising with the colour of her face and, wondering if she will survive this roller-coaster, she looks to Caleb as if to say, you must be joking. "Yes, okay, that would be good," is all her mouth can come out with however, and she closes her eyes, shaking her head as if to ground herself again.

"Look at me," Caleb implores and she stares into turbulent pools, dark with desire. She feels no urge to speak and it is so easy to let him in. "You need to sleep," he tells her, coming round to lie beside her and, this time, she makes no attempt to resist him.

THE WALK TO
PARADISE GARDEN

She lies awake in the eery silence of the night, waiting for the familiar sound of shelling but it does not come and the suspense of waiting is as unbearable as the inevitable insult. Though she has been here lifetimes, the sound of destruction still makes her jump in terror and she wonders if she will ever get used to it. Perhaps it is as well that she doesn't. Fear prevents her from taking unnecessary risks. Unlike those whose lives the onslaught destroys along with our legacy of thousands of years of civilisation, at the end of the day she can still leave and go home to peace and security.

The explosions are constant when they come. Sometimes they sound like they are next door and sometimes she is convinced they are in her room, that she has finally been hit. She has become used to listening in the dark to the different sounds of death. She has learned that the shells are the ones that boom with a much deeper sound than anything else. An all encompassing kind of sound that seems to swallow the ground itself. Tank rockets on the other hand, give off a much hollower sound leaving more of an echo in the air without rocking the ground so much and a bomb dropped from the sky will make the whole street sway so that you feel compelled to jump out of a window before the building collapses.

Her tummy tightens itself into knots. Her head throbs with her racing heart and her swollen eyes still sting from when she cried herself to sleep in the early hours. She tosses and turns, welding her thin mattress to the dips of the uneven floor, her anxiety building as she frets about how she will cope with the pressure of another day with so little rest. She wants so much, to do her best for these poor victims of man's inhumanity to his own but she is close to exhaustion. Not so long ago she lay here with Caleb and Saad and wanted for nothing more, but now they are gone and she is sure to suffocate for her lungs can no longer expand enough to take the air she needs.

She tries to distract herself from the memories that sparked her insomnia tonight, to run through the positive events of these terrible days and focus on those for which she can be grateful. The kindness of strangers and the generosity of those who have lost everything. Moments to be treasured when what is to be celebrated in mankind, shines through. She forces herself to think of the young man who brought her flowers and of how he must have scrabbled through the rubble to find them. It is of some comfort to consider that these little plants, no more than weeds really, beautiful as they are in their own way, have survived the destruction that falls from the sky. That some of its victims still have the energy to appreciate beauty where they find it. She is touched by the thoughtfulness of this simple gesture and the young man, no older than eighteen at most, who thought to thank her for taking care of his brother.

The old lady who made biscuits, goodness knows how, to bring to the children. The ones they saved. But then those images return to assail her tired mind and she hasn't the energy to fight them off. Her eyes fire up again but there is no water left in them. She feels her heart constrict in her chest and sees the little boy once more.

Small for his age at thirteen, he sits, as any boy of his age might, on the edge of the wooden bench. But he is naked, his clothes burned off with his skin. He looks like he's been covered in white powder, his pink face blistered and raw, his hair melting into his scalp. He holds his hands loosely in his lap and looks with them up to the sky, terror in his eyes, shaking from head to foot. There must have been chemicals in those devices. Napalm, she heard someone say. The incendiary bombs they dropped onto the school playground.

There were so many of them, mostly teenagers but the youngest – only seven months old. They had writhed in agony on the floor as the disfiguring blisters grew and the smell of their burn't flesh had been overwhelming. She will never forget how hopelessly inadequate she felt ripping open sachets of normal saline to pour over the victims and applying what little cream was left to their charred bodies. The hospital had been inundated with parents desperate to find their children, cursing their president for what he had inflicted on them again, whilst a fighter-jet circled above looking for fresh targets.

The headmaster had come, wailing inconsolably, telling anyone who would listen how terrible it was to see the children dying before his eyes, people burning in front of him, running. "But where to? Where is there to run to?" Of the thick fog and the terrible smell. Chemicals and burning flesh. Of all the horrific things Ana has witnessed since her arrival here, this was the worst. A day that will always stay with her, faces she will never forget.

Two weeks have passed since. Over sixty made it to the hospital, many of these with greater than fifty percent burns and most have already perished but the boy, Asu, is still alive. He was one of the smartest in his class, his teacher tells them and always had a smile on his face. Now, though they do what they can to ease his pain, he pleads every day for it to be over and Ana is haunted in the night by memories of his screams when they change his dressings.

He is so brave. Thirteen year old boys don't want to be seen crying. It is embarrassing. He didn't cry when he told her how his neck hurts and his back and his face. Fortunately he can't see the disfiguring contractures that restrict their movement and have altered his appearance for ever. Ana tried so hard to keep it from him. How his suffering affects her and her fears for his future, but then he hit her once more with his innocence and she lost control of her emotions. "Why did they bomb us when we were at school?" he asked, as if she might be able to explain it. She shook

135

her head, unable to speak or hold back the tears and they wept together.

A little boy, she thinks to herself now in the lonely dark hours of the night. How could they do these things to the children? She curls herself into the foetal position, her mind tormenting her with countless horrific memories and waits for the pain to pass, forcing it to abate with thoughts of the day ahead. They were innocent children who had gone to school and yet, in other parts of Syria – controlled by Assad's forces, there is no sign of the devastation he has wreaked on his people. She knows because one of the defectors described it to her. Buildings stand unscathed. People meet, eat and drink, visit the parks and public baths, go to work and school... Ana feels her anger rise and decides to get up. She will not sleep again tonight and there is always work to be done. Her agitation needs to be channeled into something useful.

She takes a quick cold shower for they rarely have hot water, dresses without thought in shabby brown leggings and a blouse which was once white, ties her unruly curls behind her head with a piece of string and heads for what now serves as a ward. Asu sleeps restlessly, his mother wrapped in a blanket on the floor beside him. They share the room with four other casualties of that attack and their families, each here to provide for its child's basic needs.

She returns a smile to an old man who waves at her from one corner of the room, his grand-daughter sleeping peacefully in his lap. Ana is not needed here tonight. She turns to the waiting room. It is dark and empty now but it won't be long before it starts to fill again and she wonders what will emerge from its bustling crowds today.

A chink of light falls onto the floor and she hears subdued voices from the closed door of the operating theatre. It is no surprise that she's not the only one who couldn't sleep. Ana knocks gently on the door. The voices fall silent and Marcus appears, a heartwarming smile breaking the anxious lines on his face. "Ana! We were just talking about you." He opens the door and she sees three others standing before a pile of boxes on the table. Two are strangers to her but the third is Caleb.

Her heart leaps for joy as he captures her with pools of molten black. That is all she needs. Her relief at seeing him alive and well, outweighing any consideration for the others, she runs to him and, as he lifts her into his arms, throws hers around his neck. Without warning, her eyes fill with tears and she is covering his face with wet kisses. He responds by taking her lips with his and someone cracks a joke about having to send in the resuscitation team. "Ana is the resus. team," he says, placing her carefully on her feet and then he introduces them as his closest friends.

Both also probably in their early thirties, they look total opposites otherwise. Bearded, dark skinned and black-eyed, Ahmed, not much taller than she, with thick hair that falls untidily about his face, has the shifty appearance of some-one on the run. Blue-eyed, clean shaven Tuan, on the other hand, his blonde hair neatly cropped, has the bearing of ex-military, softened by crows-feet which touch the edges of his handsome face with a heart-warming smile.

Ana blushes, going to shake each of them by hand, but it seems that protocol has already been breached and the men take it in turn to gather her in their arms instead.

"Never told me she was a looker, nor 'bout her amazing hair!" Tuan accuses and, cursing herself once more for not having it all cut off before ever she came here, Ana wonders what draws an Irishman to conflict in Syria.

"Hands off, she's mine, d'you hear?" Caleb replies, light-heartedly. "Too good for you anyway."

His friend snorts indignation. "Not for you then?"

Feeling distinctly uncomfortable, Ana turns to Marcus watching the whole scene with amusement. Ahmed returns to the pile on the table and she sees that, though the cardboard boxes declare contents of rice, flour, oil and water, they are full of little packets. She looks at him shyly, hoping she hasn't offended with her overt display of affection towards Caleb but it would seem that he hasn't noticed her inappropriate behaviour after all. "We've brought medicines," he tells her, "and some food. You have a little boy to evacuate?"

"We can take only one this time," Caleb adds. "Of those who could survive the journey, Asu is most needy, is that right?"

She and Marcus nod. "Where will you take him?" Butterflies rise in her stomach.

"Beirut," Ahmed replies. "My uncle is one of the best plastic surgeons in Lebanon. The boy will be in good hands there."

"Can his mother come too?" Ahmed looks to Caleb. Caleb nods and Ana heaves a sigh of relief. Though this is Asu's only chance, he will be afraid, the journey – painful and perilous. "When do you need to leave?" she asks reluctantly, the thought of losing Caleb so soon after he was returned to her, becoming more unbearable by the second.

"Today." Ana's heart sinks. Caleb glances at Marcus. "Marcus thinks you should have the day off and there is something I need to show you." He doesn't look pleased at the prospect.

"What's wrong?"

"We've found Rahim and Foued and formulated a plan to get them out, but its success depends on you." Ana's heart lurches. "It's okay." Caleb's voice is calm and reassuring. "You can do it. I'll show you how. But first, do you want to go talk with Asu and his mother?" Ana nods and heads for the door before she can give too much away.

"Are you sure?" His friend speaks so softly. Feeling Caleb's eyes on her, Ana cannot resist the temptation to look back.

"There's no-one else Rahim would trust. He'll starve with his brother rather than risk them being caught."

Tuan throws him a bundle of cloth from one of the boxes. "Think it'll fit?"

"Perfectly."

He leads her by the hand through the ruined streets of Homs. They left what passed as the habitable part of this district some time ago and now they move through no-man's land. This rubble is all that remains of what were once people's homes and businesses, a graveyard to those that remain buried where they fell. The occasional building stands defiantly, lifting pock-marked walls to the sky, jagged holes at the higher levels bearing testament to rockets that passed through and amongst these, they sometimes see signs of life. People still live here, Ana realises and wonders how. They have skirted districts controlled by the government or jihadists and are headed for the old part of Homs.

Ana wears the clothes Caleb gave her – the perfect disguise, and is pleasantly surprised by how comfortable she feels in them despite the heat of this beautiful August day. A brown niqab reveals nothing but her eyes, the matching jilbab doing its best to conceal the curves of her now, over-slim body. Beneath these nondescript formless garments, exquisite silk pyjamas of the same deep green as her eyes, hug and caress her skin. They fit perfectly, leaving her midriff bare from the bottom of her bra to the top of her knickers and Ana wonders at the audacity of this man who appears to have sized her up so well.

She senses they are close though she has never been to these parts of Homs before. They are having to duck, weave, hide and wait to avoid the military presence here and there is more evidence of fresh damage than they have passed so far. The rubble is littered with explosives, bullets and shrapnel and, as she looks more closely at the collapsed buildings, Ana sees shredded clothing, bedding, toys and mangled furniture.

A terrible pain clutches at her chest stealing her breath and bringing her out in a cold sweat. Paralysed, she recalls the last time she passed through such a landscape and images flash through her mind of people being torn apart, everything about them smashed to smithereens. Unspeakable violence being perpetrated on innocent people while the world simply looks on.

She doesn't hear his voice but when Caleb takes her by the hand, she jumps, her heart doing somersaults into her throat.

His frown melts into an encouraging smile. He pulls her gently onwards and she follows.

He takes her to the ruins of a mosque, carefully checking that they are alone before leading her to its one remaining tower and Ana wonders at how beautiful this place would once have been. Gold gleams from the domed roof of a minaret lying broken on the ground. Blue and white ceramic tiles, intricately decorated with geometrical black, cling precariously to damaged walls. Cracked marble – white, yellow, pink and grey, still covers parts of the courtyard floor. Vibrant purple and red flowers sprout from lush green in the corners, damaged stone and piles of rubble. The remains of a fountain signposts the once clear pool it served. "There hasn't been much looting here yet," Caleb explains. "Probably too close to the frontline."

It is brighter inside the tower than Ana had anticipated, the worn stones of its narrow spiral staircase illuminated by frequent unsightly holes and occasional glass-less windows. The platform at the top is almost intact though the dome that should have risen behind them has been replaced by an ugly jagged hole. "Here." Caleb pulls her down and she realises with a start, how exposed they were.

On splintered wood, they lie peering through a hole in the parapet that encircles them and he points towards old Homs. "That's were the children are," he says. "They've been befriended by a Dutch Jesuit priest. He'll help you find them." He pulls a map from a trouser pocket and unfolds it carefully. "He's lived here most of his life. Syria is his home. He can't leave his flock, so stays and suffers with the few that remain." Caleb points to the map. "This is where we are now. That's where the old man lives and this is our way in and out of old Homs." He marks a point on the map with his thumbnail, looks briefly to the ruins of the old city and pulls binoculars out of another pocket, leaving the lens covers on until the last moment. "Be careful that the sun doesn't reflect off the glass. If a sniper sees it, we're dead." He shades them with his hands, looking through and focusing them, then shifts sideways so that she can take his place behind the eyepieces.

"Look straight ahead, past the block that still stands." Hardly. The top several floors have collapsed like a pack of cards. "Beyond that – to the left, do you see a tower rising above the ruins? Grey brick with a white diamond half-way up and a bell-tower?" Ana nods. "That's where the priest will meet you."

She wonders how she will get there and Caleb considers her grimly. "This part of the city has been under siege for many months now," he says. "The government cut off water, electricity and supply routes. People trapped inside rely on wells and generators where they can. They have neither food nor anything to treat injury or disease." His face dark with emotion, he hesitates and Ana looks at his trembling hands. "I saw them picking weeds and grass from cracks in the concrete to make soup. Children stop you in the streets, begging for food." Caleb searches Ana's eyes.

"I have no choice," she mumbles and he shakes his head.

"There is always a choice. You told me, remember?"

"But they'll die if I don't go."

"And you might die with them if you do."

"I know."

He watches her and her heart feels as if it might break. "Okay," he says at last. "There are some tunnels leading to neighbouring districts and, though these are controlled by Assad's forces, some of the officers are susceptible to bribes. We have negotiated safe passage for a Syrian woman to go in alone and out with her two children, but the timing is crucial. This passage will be safe only while our contact is on duty. We're waiting for final confirmation of when that will be but it is likely you'll need to spend two to three days in Old Homs. Our friend, the priest, will accommodate you with the children.

"You should know," Caleb considers her thoughtfully "that the priest looks after all in need, regardless of religion or allegiance. He sees the human being first."

Ana nods. "Of course."

"Starvation is the cruelest torture," Caleb adds, his eyes dark with fear. "If I could go in your place, I would, but Rahim will trust only you. Do you think you can do it?"

Ana remembers a compassionate, brave little boy in need of a comforting cuddle, who held her so tightly, making her count to twenty before letting her go. She sees Ahmed standing before her as he has done countless times already, urging her for his sake, to get on with what she came here to do and out, then taking his life to make her go. Bitter anger fuels determination, strangling crippling fear and feeds the belief somewhere deep inside, that she is immune to it all. The horrors of this war, the misery of its victims, the deaths, the grief, the lives destroyed. For though these all have an impact and she will never be the same because of them, naively there is still part of her that believes she is somehow exempt.

"I can do it and I will," she says with conviction, remembering how particular Rahim had been that last night. How tightly he held on, telling her that the last hug has to be a right hug. He knew what she did not. She cannot bear to think of what he suffers now, of how he hides his fear for the sake of his little brother. Consoling herself with thoughts of the kind priest who has taken them under his wing, she looks back to Caleb watching her silently.

"A brave man," she murmurs and he nods.

"I have something else to show you," he says and, putting the binoculars and map back into his pockets, helps her up.

He leads her carefully down the damaged staircase and out into the courtyard, stopping regularly to reassure himself that they have not been compromised. Once, he pulls her back into the shadows and they hold their breath beneath the throb of a helicopter, the draft from its blades sucking at the cloth of her jilbab so that Ana has to pull it back in terror for giving them away. But death passes them by for now.

They leave by a different way. Though clearly heading back, this route is far more circuitous, taking them to the edge of the city where suburbia blends with fertile countryside. After so much time cooped up in the overcrowded hospital, Ana begins to enjoy the exercise and, as she relaxes, to see how here used to be. Trees still standing unscathed. Cypresses and poplars marking minor roads. Lanes that lead to neglected orchards of apple and apricot. Olive groves and vineyards. Distant purple mountains shimmering above the sparkling water at their dusty feet.

They come to what must once have been a pleasant tree-lined boulevard, piles of overgrown rubble all that remain of the spacious homes it once fronted, except for a few which still stand relatively intact. The fractured, pot-holed road is covered with rubbish left by looters, fallen lamp-posts and hopelessly damaged vehicles, abandoned where their owners gave up on them. Caleb continues undeterred.

They round a corner and he stops dead in his tracks, raising a hand to keep her back. Silence. Only birdsong and the occasional sound of something fluttering in the breeze, then the distant roar of a shell and thunder as it hits but too far away to feel its vibrations rock the ground. Caleb relaxes, rising to his full height and turns to give her a reassuring smile.

The wall must once have been magnificent and it is still barely possible to see what lies beyond. He takes her to one side and a door she would have missed, leaning precariously off its bottom hinge. "Looks like we've had visitors again," he says, lifting it back into place and leads her into an airy hall.

Clearly also victim to looters, a lonely wooden side-board, doors wide open, leans against a pebble dashed wall, its feet resting on an island of beautifully decorated floor. Intricate geometrical patterns of pale marble and black volcanic basalt peep from piles of rubble, glowing through footprints in a thick layer of dust. A thousand specks of gold dance in a shaft of sunlight beaming through a hole in the roof. Closing the door carefully, Caleb drives the barrel of its bolt home and locks it with a key on a bunch he takes from his pocket.

They follow the footsteps into a gloomy passageway, stubbing their toes where fallen masonry lies hidden in the dark places and emerge, without warning, into the dazzling sunlight of another world. A lovely courtyard, warm, comforting and peaceful, "designed," Caleb confirms, "to shield us from the outside world."

"It's beautiful." She lifts her niqab and, smiling into her eyes, he takes it from her. She looks around on arcades of soft golden limestone crowned by flowering climbers, a pastel pink marble floor, orange trees, vines and bougainvillea. The sweet smell of jasmine and musky rosemary waft on a gentle breeze and birdsong fills the air. In the centre, an elaborate fountain runs sadly dry, its large basin empty but for dirt and leaves, and a crumpled towel lies on a lounger beneath one of the arches.

"Belonged to my uncle," Caleb explains as Ana wonders if this is where he disappears to. "He was an architect. He designed it in the fashion of the old Ottoman Palaces. Look, I'll show you." He takes her by the hand. "There are three courtyards. This for the men, nearest the front door, kept in readiness for visitors. Another, far more elaborate, for the women and children, further into the house so that business should not interfere with family life and a third, far simpler, for the servants." He leads her through dusty corridors and lofty, empty rooms and she sees that the first is the only to have survived in anything like its original state.

"Those Ottomans were so clever," he says distractedly as he watches her.

"What do you mean?"

"The way they designed their palaces. My uncle adapted their plans slightly. The rooms all around us interconnect but originally, they were individual living areas open only to the courtyards, so that extended family units could live independently of each other. This," he says, waving at it, "is the *iwan,* where the family would sit in the shade on cushions with the breeze from the courtyard and the coolness of the fountain wafting over them."

Ana seats herself in the large covered alcove and he tells her that, because it faces north, the sun never shines on it. "To either side, would have been the main indoor reception areas with ceilings six metres high and windows on two levels that caught the breezes during the day and trapped the cooler air by night." He sits beside her and looks around. "I take care of it as best I can, but each time I come back there's fresh damage." He shrugs. "Looting more than anything for the time being. Assad's forces are thinly spread and this area is largely deserted. So long as it stays that way, they'll leave us alone."

"Do you think your uncle will come back one day?"

"His family, maybe. They're in Germany. But he stayed…and paid for his compassion with his life."

"I'm sorry."

"Come, I'll show you the rest." Caleb helps her up and leads her by the hand through an open doorway.

High, bright and airy, the elegance of this room is marred by a huge concrete ulcer in the middle of an elaborate red carpet and, above that, a gaping hole in the ceiling, mirrored by another in the roof above it. "Rocket. Luckily, it didn't start a fire. Haven't had time to clear up the mess yet." Except in one corner. There, protected perhaps, by the mezzanine floor above, stands a grand-piano, the sheet over it devoid even of the fine layer of dust that covers everything else. Caleb smiles into Ana's eyes. "Miracle, isn't it?"

She nods. "Do you play it?"

"Sometimes."

"Will you?" She hesitates. "For me?"

"Later, perhaps. This way."

He leads her up a flight of stairs and she feels the temperature rise. "The roof is covered in tiles that absorb heat. It can get very cold here in the winter so we go upstairs for warmth, downstairs to cool off. Careful now." He helps her over a hole where a step

145

should be, onto a landing, and shows her into one of the upstairs rooms. "Usually I sleep in the courtyard," he tells her. "Sometimes here. It's the only bedroom still habitable." He watches as she walks over to the freshly made double bed and looks around. This room is far smaller than the ones downstairs, the ceiling lower. "Designed to retain heat in the winter."

"The ultimate eco-house," she replies, wondering if he can read her mind and he laughs.

"Indeed. Thought we could rest here for a while. What do you think?" She nods, emotion momentarily overwhelming her ability to speak and wishes time would stand still.

She sees a photograph on the wall behind him and goes to take a closer look. A beautiful woman, her fair wavy hair tided into a bun behind her head, smiles down on two young children. The girl, absorbed in the small ball she holds, must be less than a year old and has a shock of dark frizzy hair. Ana sympathises and hopes she won't be bullied for it when she's older. She wonders if the boy watching over her, a little older and presumably her brother, will try to protect her as her own brothers did. It is an intimate, informal portrait that could grace a family room anywhere in the world.

"My grandmother, mother and uncle." Caleb searches her eyes and Ana wonders if he sees into her soul. She looks away, struggling to control the smile starting to play on her lips but the attraction is irresistible and, fighting the temptation to take his face in her hands and smother it with kisses, she examines it instead, consciously avoiding those hypnotic eyes. She wants to smooth away the dark shadows that have formed beneath them, the lines that wrinkle his handsome brow, to run her fingers through his thick wavy hair and skim her thumbs over his sculptured lips and then she wants, so much, to feel those lips on her own, those strong hands all over her.

He comes closer. Enchanted, she closes her eyes. He lifts her jilbab. Without thought, she raises her arms. She feels his lips skim her breast-bone and gasps, her knees threatening to give way so that she feels the need to excuse herself with thoughts of how little sleep and food she has had lately. He throws the jilbab behind her, his breathing accelerating with hers. "Look at me Ana," he pleads, gathering her curls to place them behind her shoulders. He describes a soft cloud of bronze-tinged gold crowning a beautiful angel and she laughs, opening her eyes to molten pools dark with want. Something delicious tightens deep inside. A deep breath escapes her parted lips, the heat in her rising. This feels so right. What can possibly be wrong with following through what they have both tried so hard to resist?

His hands skim beneath her thick hair over her shoulder-blades and she shivers. She wills him on and they wander to the fastenings of her top, undoing them and those of her bra slowly, surely. Her hands find their way to his chest, one sliding beneath his shirt over bare skin and rippling muscle, the other deftly undoing him. She pushes the redundant garment off his shoulders onto the floor. The need to be close overcomes them simultaneously and they throw themselves at each other, skin against burning skin, mouth on hungry mouth. His hands move over her as if they just can't get enough and the electricity that sparks between them makes her skin fizz, the hairs rise on the back of her neck.

They come up for air and he buries his face in her hair, tickling her ear with his breath. "I love you, Ana. I've waited my whole life for you." He hesitates and she wills him on. "But now you're here, all I can offer you is a future of uncertainty and pain."

She pulls away, shaking her head with a frown. "Love is all I need from you Caleb," she tells him, "and now may be all the time we have." She blushes, anxious not to be too forward but he blesses her with a glorious smile. A delicious warmth sets her heart racing so that she has to catch her breath. She cannot imagine anything more beautiful. Those uneven top teeth that seem to have turned slightly to look at his left ear, the fine line that breaks the perfect symmetry of his upper lip, the passion in eyes like liquid chocolate, spilling over to soften the lines of his roman nose. Black stubble that perfectly compliments the thick hair falling in waves about his forehead and the way his breath labours, deep and wanting through his parted lips.

He lifts her from the floor and lays her on the bed, one hand caressing the nape of her neck as the other finds her breasts and the wanting ache inside her grows. He trails kisses down to her naval, the soft fall of his hair, tantalising hypersensitive skin as he renders her naked and then he goes lower, deeper and that delicious pressure builds to an exquisite tension deep inside. "You are so beautiful…wonderful…delicious," he tells her between kisses, "and I love you." With that he kisses her again and, crying out, she loses herself to him.

He holds her tight, watching her, kissing and caressing, and then he begins again. Covering her face, engaging her tongue with his, simulating the most sensitive parts of her from her forehead to her toes until she writhes and moans with pleasure. "Perfect," he says and his words as he adores her, take her to the brink again.

He holds her tight. Totally spent, she thinks she might melt in his arms but then he kisses her again, she feels him hard against her belly and her desire for him becomes overwhelming. "Caleb, I love you," she tells him, " and I want you. All of you." She sits up to unbuckle his belt and helps him remove his trousers and pants. Lean and muscular, he kneels naked, straddled over her.

She reaches down to kiss him but he pushes her gently back onto the bed with a shake of his head and she sees doubt, guilt even, in the light that shines from his eyes. She pulls him close, her breathing coming in short wanting gasps but still, he hesitates and she takes his mouth with hers. "It's what I want," she whispers and, at last, the tension in him dissipates.

It has never felt like this before. So right. Exquisite. Nothing else exists. Neither the world around them nor time. Just the two of them. "Open your eyes Ana," he pleads and the sight of him in the throes of this passion for her, tips her over the edge. She cries out and he stills, waiting and then he takes her higher, falling into a rhythm with her that comes as naturally as the tides. She watches, this vision of him making heartfelt love to her reducing her to tears as the delicious tension in her mounts. When they climax, he extends his neck and roars, looking back to her with such adoring gratitude as to make her wonder at the terrible prison she must have released him from.

For an age he watches her, balancing on his elbows and stroking her hair. No trace left of the tension that haunted his beautiful face, only a perfect reflection of the overwhelming love she has for him. Gently, he rolls her over to lie on top of him, his hands skimming her back, triggering waves of ecstasy that ripple up and down her spine. "Will you marry me?" he asks and, though she wants nothing more, Ana laughs for it is all so sudden and unexpected.

"I've died and gone to heaven!"

"So, is that a yes?" Blissfully, she nods, for words fail her and when he kisses her, the passion in them both, rises again.

They make love and sleep until the sun begins to sink, drawing out the shadows as cooing palm-doves return to roost. When he takes her hand to lead her out, bats swoop silently in the dusk to catch mosquitoes in the courtyard. "We need to eat," he tells her and, with a sigh, Ana recalls that they are mortal after all.

"I need the bathroom," she tells him shyly but his smile banishes any regret.

"This way. I'm afraid we have to make do with rain-water, candle-light and my old trangia stove, but that'll suffice," he tells her cheerfully, leading her through the rubble to what would once have been an elegant bathroom. There is a bowl already full of water and a bucket with a toilet seat on it. "The loo for now. Will take a while to sort out the plumbing. I'll empty it into the river later." He hesitates, gazing at her like an awe-struck teenager but rather than backing off when she laughs, he comes closer. "I'll go get you a clean towel," he says but puts his arms around her, kissing her on the lips instead and, once more, she is unable to resist.

He returns barefoot in nothing but his trousers, with a faded pink bathrobe and towel and watches as she dries herself. The water was cold and, though the air still carries the warmth of the day, she is grateful. "You've sized me up so well," she tells him and he smiles smugly.

"Of course. From the moment I first saw you, I haven't been able to get you out of my head," he confesses.

"Well, I'm glad you didn't."

He leads her by candlelight down to the cellar. The kitchen stands mostly intact above them but nothing works and the cupboards are bare. This store-room too, has been emptied by looters "but not completely," he reassures. "My uncle's secret hiding place has yet to be compromised and there are edible plants in the garden they missed. Tonight Ana, we feast!"

Arches supported by columns, all of brick, span the low roof and she wonders if this was once a wine-cellar. Her eyes begin to adjust and she sees empty shelves, boxes, piles of books, journals, suitcases and stacked furniture. Caleb makes straight for a chest of drawers against a stone wall but the drawers hang open and she is sure they must be empty. He smiles and hands her the candle. "Take this." Putting his back to one end, he pushes the chest to one side. Ana peers into the gloom but there is no secret door. Nothing in this flickering light, to distinguish one stone from another. No cracks, levers or handles. He takes the candle and fixes it into a holder on the chest. Removing something from the top drawer, he drops to his knees and scrapes it along the uneven line connecting wall to ground. With a grating noise, the wall begins to move.

Slowly but surely, it opens, revealing a small metal door with a keyhole. Resisting the temptation to ask if his uncle was a secret agent or something, Ana watches Caleb take another key from his pocket. "My uncle was a bit paranoid," he explains as he inserts it into the lock. "With good reason. A bit outspoken you could say. Often found himself in trouble with the authorities." He opens the door, takes the candle-holder and ushers Ana through.

It isn't a vast space. Big enough to hide a family with enough food and water for a few days, and incriminating documents – in that filing cabinet discretely tucked into one corner, perhaps. An empty desk is overhung by a whiteboard covered in writing and photos. Beside it, a wooden chair and a mattress covered in blankets. Rows of bottled water line one of two, otherwise barren shelves and neatly stacked beneath these, is a pile of cardboard boxes for which Caleb makes a beeline. He opens one up, finding carrier bags and proceeds to fill these with tins, packets and tubes of food, "for us and the priest."

He locks the door behind them, carefully replacing everything as it was and leads Ana back up to the kitchen. In the distance, a mournful call to prayer rings tunefully out and she wonders if there is anybody left to respond to it. Caleb drops the food onto the table beside a small backpack and she follows him into the courtyard.

The musky scent of rosemary and thyme wafts tantalisingly on a slight breeze, along with sweet jasmine and something else, equally lovely. Pausing to take her fill, Ana watches Caleb kneel by a border of greenery and flowers. "Beautiful and edible but, fortunately for us, few people know that," he tells her, proceeding to pick a handful, then some rosemary. She feels something catch, freeing itself as quickly with an agitated squeak and, combing her fingers through just to be sure, tucks her hair into the neck of her bathrobe. Another bat swoops and, laughing, she ducks to avoid it hitting.

"Nearly got one then," Caleb laughs. "Not much meat on them though."

She watches him heat oil in a pan on his trangia, fry the meat she spooned out of the tin so carefully in order not to miss a single bit and finally, add the fresh greenery and rosemary. She drains the rice, saving the water it cooked in and shares it out. Caleb has cleared the table and laid it with cutlery, glasses of water and another candle. "We do have a generator but not much fuel and this is far more romantic." Now he divides the contents of his pan between the two plates and she cannot take her eyes off him. Still wearing nothing but his trousers, his unruly hair falling almost as far as his shoulders, he looks happy and relaxed in a way she has never seen him and she struggles to recall the Caleb she knew before.

"What's the matter?"

"Nothing. This is perfect." Unconsciously she bites her lower lip and, dropping his pan and spatula into a bowl of sizzling water in the sink, he comes to sit beside her.

"Something's wrong, but before you tell me what that is, eat up or it'll get cold."

They feast, as much on the view as the food, for they are unable to take their eyes off each other. "What do you want in life, Caleb?" Ana asks him at last.

"The same as you do."

"Oh?"

"I want you, Ana." He smiles, taking each of her hands in turn to kiss them. "To be my wife and the mother of my children. I want them to grow up in a different world. One where I won't wake up thinking how lucky I am to be able to feed them. I want to share their childhood and your motherhood, to earn a living from making music and for no-one to need me to be anything other than a husband, father, friend, son, grandson, brother or uncle.

"I want democracy, freedom, fairness and respect for everyone. An end to poverty, and I want love to be the motive behind every man's actions." Ana laughs at this grand speech but her heart swells and she wonders if she could possibly love anyone more.

"I want those things for us, too," she confirms. "And for our children."

Even before the words are out of her mouth, the image of

Rahim flashes before her. With a frown, Caleb gives her hands a gentle squeeze and peers into her eyes.

"I don't want you to do this."

"Neither do I but we both know I have to. It's why I came here. What Ahmed died for." A shudder runs through her. Shaking images of Ahmed dying, out of her head, Ana trembles before Caleb. "But I wish I wasn't such a coward."

"Do you know what Nelson Mandela said about courage?" Ana shakes her head. "I learned that courage was not the absence of fear, but the triumph over it. The brave man is not he who does not feel afraid, but he who conquers that fear." She smiles but butterflies are playing havoc with her stomach. "You can do this and you will – bring Rahim and Foued safely back to their family." He says it with such certainty that Ana is convinced and in that moment she knows, with Caleb she can do anything.

"Is there anything you're afraid of?" she asks him at last.

"Many things." His eyes fill with pain and he frowns with a shrug. "Man's inhumanity, anarchy and civil war. Global warming. Being disabled. Mostly I fear for those I love and endangering them by what I do." He hesitates and she senses a fear in him that has never been so great. "And what I could be capable of," he concludes.

"Who's important in your life, Ana?" he asks, watching her carefully.

"My father is a general in the British army. He told me not to come here. Za'atari, that is. He doesn't know I'm in Syria. Which is partly why I did." She looks to Caleb for disapproval but finds none. "I don't see much of my mother. She left him when I was eight. I have two brothers – Daniel who is twenty-nine and Chris, thirty-two. They're both in the SAS. Don't see much of them either. My best friend, Lina, is busy raising kids and, well, there isn't really anyone else. Apart from here. Kai at Za'atari," a pang of guilt catches, "Rahim, Aadil, Marcus." She smiles into Caleb's eyes. "And you."

"Boyfriends?"

"There was one I nearly married. A medical student, a year above me at Guy's Hospital in London where we trained. He was very sweet, besotted with me, and I loved him dearly. But like a brother, not the way I love you. And I had been in love once, so knew the difference."

"You refused him?" She nods. "And the one you fell in love with?"

"I was fourteen, he...seventeen. He played oboe in our youth orchestra. It was a whirlwind holiday romance on tour in Austria and Bavaria." She blushes and feels awkward. "It just felt right. Like we do, Caleb. I didn't know there was anything wrong in it. We loved each other, that was all."

Caleb frowns. "Why do you feel the need to excuse yourself?"

"My father was furious when he found out. Threatened to have him locked away and worse. But what we did was out of love, not lust. There can't be anything wrong in that, can there?" He shakes his head. "There was no-one else of significance," Ana concludes, "until you came along." She reaches up to push the hair out of his eyes.

"Who was there for you before me?"

He takes a deep breath, letting it out on a sigh and a shadow falls over his face. "Only one that mattered," he answers at last. "Her name was Selideh. She was twenty-one, an Iranian student of my mother's at Damascus University. I was seventeen. We fell in love. Selideh was a modern educated woman with a mind of her own but she came from a fundamental Islamic family that was vocal in its disapproval of our relationship. She was safe while she was in Syria." His eyes drop to Ana's hands, defocusing as his breathing accelerates. Clearly he stares at something else. She comes round to sit on his lap and puts her arms around his neck.

"Caleb? I'm sorry. I shouldn't have asked."

He shakes his head with a smile but something has returned to haunt his beautiful eyes. "There should be no secrets between us," he tells her then falls silent. She waits, certain that whatever he chooses to tell her or not, will make no difference to how she feels about him.

"They died because of me." Ana searches his eyes, the shiver running through her, intensifying. "She was pregnant, you see." He looks at her and she nods. "Selideh insisted on going home as she usually did at the end of the academic year. I knew something was wrong when she didn't call. I couldn't get through so I went after her. They were waiting for me at the airport." Caleb shakes his head angrily. "I should have known."

"You were only seventeen."

"They put something over my head and beat me unconscious. When I came to I was lying on the ground, bound hand and foot and she was standing before me." He stares at the table, reluctant to continue. "They had buried her to the knees and tied her hands behind her back. We were somewhere remote. A field near a small dusty village. There was a pile of stones and a crowd of men determined to vent their rage." Caleb closes tortured eyes but the dreadful vision follows him there as it must have done countless times already. "There was nothing I could do. I watched them stone her to death, Selideh and our unborn child."

Able only to comprehend the horror of what he has just told her and powerless to do anything more, Ana puts her arms around him and Caleb surrenders to his grief. "I'm so sorry." At last, the convulsions that wrack his powerful body subside but Ana does not move until he relaxes his hold on her.

"You alright?" he asks and she nods, feeling far from alright.

"I wish I could take that pain away from you."

"I've not been able to love anyone since then, until you came along. You are my salvation, Ana."

They clear up together with the intention of leaving the kitchen tidy and clean. There is little conversation at first for, though anxious to lift Caleb out of his sombre mood, Ana can think of nothing to say that won't either reinforce his loss or trivialise what he has just told her.

While she dries the dishes he fills the daypack. "You can hide it under your jilbab," he says, "and give it to the Jesuit priest." Ana frowns, the prospect of what lies ahead, looming and he comes over to give her a reassuring hug.

"When?"

"Probably tomorrow. The plan is to aim for dusk if it's on. We'll stay here tonight." She chews her lower lip and he eyes her gravely, undoing the belt around her waist then the bathrobe. "Come here." He pulls her close and she snuggles in, closing her eyes and breathing deeply of the smell of him. With his strong arms around her and the steady beating of his heart against her skin, for a moment she is aware of nothing else. No past or future, only here and now and together they are invincible, eternal.

They make love by the light of a moon that bathes everything in liquid silver and, entranced, find that healing rest that has eluded them for so long. As morning breaks and she drifts in and out of consciousness, she becomes aware of his hands on her body, massaging aching muscles with gentle tenderness and the touch of his lips on her tingling skin.

"Morning, beautiful!" A warm glow rises from the pit of her belly and she stretches dreamily, her hands coming to rest on his back as he balances over her. Shamelessly she runs her eyes over him, from his thick muscular legs to his handsome face and the vision stokes a fire inside. He brings his face close, rubbing his nose gently against hers so that his breath falls gently onto her lips and she opens them in anticipation.

The sun is high above them by the time he wakes her fully with a kiss and, though he says nothing, she knows it is nearly time. Naked, he straddles her and she smiles. "I want to wake up to this view every morning!"

"Then marry me."

She rises to face him. "When?"

"How about, as soon as this is over?"

She smiles but her joy is superseded by dread. "Have you heard?" He nods and the butterflies somersault in her stomach. "Today?"

"Our man comes on duty at three. We'll aim for dusk." Her mind races and she turns away, struggling to recompose herself. "Look at me Ana." He takes her chin and lifts her face to his, capturing her with eyes full of resolve. "Soon it will be over and we'll be free to live the rest of our lives together." She nods, forcing herself to look beyond today, to feel the joy and relief of bringing the children out to safety with Caleb by her side. She imagines the expression on Rahim's face when he sees her and remembers the feel of his small body warm against her in his hug. She sees herself walking hand in hand with Caleb through Za'atari and the joy on Lileth's face as the children run into her arms. She dreams of Caleb on their wedding day, a little cottage somewhere safe and peaceful, children playing happily in a pretty garden and his arms around her as they stand watching from the patio. With a nod, she smiles into Caleb's eyes and he helps her up.

"We need to talk through the plan," he tells her, "but first breakfast."

"First bathroom." Oblivious to her own nakedness, she watches as he leads her on, collecting their clothes on the way and giving her a hand over the gaping hole in the stairs. She wonders if she could ever get used to seeing him like this or if it will ever fail to excite her.

There is fresh water in the bowl in the bathroom and the toilet has been emptied. Ana wonders how she didn't notice Caleb's absence and how he managed to get there and back so quickly. It must be really close. She has heard that the regime dumps the bodies of its victims in the river as a warning to their families and neighbours, and shudders, guessing that he wouldn't tell her if he had come across anything so gruesome. She hears him whistling in the kitchen and relaxes a little herself.

"There's shampoo in the cupboard if you want it," he calls out. "And soap next to the bowl. Take as long as you like."

He's made a batter from flour, the rice water she saved last night and reconstituted egg and when she's ready, he'll cook pancakes. Until then he'll play the piano for her as promised. Anxious not to miss a second of that, Ana hurries, washing herself carefully to avoid wasting any of their precious water. She'll leave her hair for now.

He starts with Chopin, sweet, tender and romantic, moving onto Rachmaninov with the same stirring passion as carried them through that magical night and she sits still as a statue, bewitched as much by the music as this vision of him lost to another world free of fear and pain. "Had enough yet?" She shakes her head and he moves onto Beethoven and Liszt, his face a picture as it passes through every emotion. Sensitive and vulnerable, one minute, full of a powerful joy the next. "And now we must eat," he says, finishing with a flourish and rising with a flamboyant bow to her applause before setting about closing the piano back up. She heaves a great sigh, wishing it could be like this forever, just the two of them in this bubble that protects them from the rest of the world and rises to help him with the dust sheet.

"That was so beautiful!" Unexpectedly filled with great sadness, she looks to his fingers, the traumatised nail beds supporting tender new growth, the fresh scar on his shoulder and other reminders of insult past, which seem to multiply with the rising light, then his eyes so full of determination and passion. "Will you come away with me and the children?" she pleads and he shakes his head, taking her hands in his. "I can't leave without you Caleb. I would rather die with you than live with the agony of waiting, fearing the worst."

"I'll finish what I came here for, then I'll join you. Promise. I'll take you to the tunnel. Look, you can have this." He pulls a satellite phone from the back-pack and she frowns over their empty plates. "Don't worry, no-one knows they want me yet. It's perfectly safe.

"It stinks in there and it'll be dark. You'll need this torch but don't switch it on until you have to. Focus on where you're headed and getting there as quickly as possible. Half-way along is a staging post with a ladder and above it, kind of a manhole cover. You need to get out through that. It should be half-open, not too heavy for you to push to one side. You'll find yourself in a covered alleyway. Head for the light. There might be snipers." He peers with consternation into her eyes. "Stop and check for anything obvious, then run, fast as you can for the shadows." He draws a pencil over the map he has fashioned from a creased piece of paper. "Look, here. Into this alleyway towards the tower – the one we saw, remember?" He checks that she understands. "The priest will meet you there."

He tells her of the huge ditch that has been dug around the old town, everything in its way razed to the ground and where Assad's forces are positioned. "But you shouldn't get any trouble from them. Our contact is in charge of the units controlling that area. The deal is half the money upfront, the rest when you come out safely with the kids. I'll meet you at the exit to the tunnel. At seven, Thursday evening." Three days later. Ana looks on him in horror and he shakes his head. "That's when our man comes back on duty."

BESIEGED OLD HOMS

They bypass the mosque, skirting the Khalidiya district, a stronghold of the Free Syrian Army. This is the place of Moath's story and as she recalls it, bitter anger strengthens Ana's resolve. "Children in Syria live in the worst circumstances in the world," he told her as they sat in his tent watching his injured brother sleep. "Instead of balls, now they play with fragments of shells, guns and bullets."

He had been there when almost two hundred of them were murdered. "We call it the forgotten massacre because no-one knows about it. There was no media, no outrage. Many people came to the funeral as a sort of peaceful protest. Perhaps a thousand. Half of them were children. And then they dropped a bomb. A powerful one. We recovered two hundred and twenty bodies. Nearly five hundred were severely injured. I tried to help. I took someone's hand to pull them out of the rubble, but it was only a hand. People were panicking. Looking for their loved ones, their children. We took the injured and dead to the mosque and then they bombed that too. I thought, surely after this, there will be no more shelling. But I was wrong. And then they sent the snipers in."

Moath was arrested and crammed with seventy others into a room perhaps four metres by four that had one small window and a tiny door through which they shoved new prisoners. He told Ana of the children who were tortured. "What was their crime? Where else in the world does this happen? These children were eleven, twelve, thirteen! The guards did not hesitate. They used electricity on their hands, their legs, their genitals. They beat them until they bled. Many died. They tied their hands tight together and when they begged for them to be loosened, they tightened them more instead. The veins in their wrists would start to bleed. I saw so many die this way.

"Sometimes they put children into isolation rooms. They were completely alone in the dark. Children as young as eleven. Why do this? What harm were they doing? Now, if they survive, they will always be afraid of the dark."

He described how children were being used to fight as well. Given guns and put on the borders or forced to march ahead of armed men. "I thought Syria was a safe place to live." A student at university, he used to watch dvds, go on Facebook, play football and hang out with his friends. Now he sits hopeless at Za'atari refugee camp.

They move through the shadows of twilight. Over the rubble of a ghost town. Past rows of buildings collapsed like packs of cards, around burnt out vehicles, towards a military check-point on the main road into the old city of Homs. The barrels of two guns rise to greet them. They stop dead in their tracks, raising their arms high in the air and wait. One of the soldiers shouts something and, telling Ana to stay, Caleb walks slowly towards the make-shift cabin by the side of the road.

He says something. With a contemptuous look, the guard speaks into a walkie-talkie. It crackles and he barks a command. The guns drop. Ana waits, hardly daring to breath, unable to look away. Silence descends. The wind crescendoes to an eery wail then falls back, making the guns rattle, Ana's jilbab flap. It takes forever. The sickening ache in her stomach rises with the violent beating of her heart and the world begins to recede. Back and forth, like waves on a shore. Someone approaches. The soldiers shift and the unbearable tension cracks.

He is a portly man, clean shaven apart from a small moustache, with beady eyes of the same midnight black as the scant hairs on his head. From his bearing, uniform and the way the others salute him, he appears to be an officer of superior rank. There is little else about him to inspire such respect, Ana concludes, for he is shorter than she and, in a plethoric face that betrays a tendency to overindulge, she detects pitiful weakness.

He beckons Caleb closer and, briefly, they converse. The officer nods, pocketing the envelope with a discrete glance to ensure his comrades haven't noticed and the soldiers stand back to let them through. Profound relief washes over her but, as she approaches, they draw Caleb to one side and usher Ana forward alone. "It's okay," he says. "Trust yourself and don't look back." Blinding tears burn her cheeks and she hesitates. "I'll be with you every step of the way."

Her foot sends something scuttling along the ground. It smashes into a block of concrete and she startles. Clenching her fists, she forces herself to breath and takes a good look around to get her bearings. Caleb stands beside the wind-swept check-point, watching but now he is a world away. Beside the pockmarked road, a pile of rubble reminds her to take cover. She considers the others out here unaware of her ticket through no-man's land and searches mutilated landscape, her eyes flicking from one landmark to another. She understands now why the children do this. Those who have survived the gruesome destruction that lurks around every corner. Eyes that never rest, staring from faces prematurely aged.

She sees the tower and orientates herself. Now left. The instruction comes to her with Caleb's voice and she feels less alone. Fearful shadows wax and wane but she forces herself to chase away the monsters they conceal, to seek them out as shelter. She searches the gloom for the bushes that mark the end of the pipe and braces herself but as she takes the first step, a deafening crack takes her to her knees, spitting earth into her face. Paralysed, she waits for her pounding heart to betray her and the eery silence growing out of the shadows becomes more appalling by the second.

It's okay. She swallows and looks around, half expecting Caleb to be there but she is alone. That one wasn't for you. Now go. She rises gingerly from the ground and, gathering the skirts of her jilbab, runs for her life towards the pipe. Full pelt. Deep into slippery, stinking, pitch black. Just as she believes herself safe from snipers, something grabs her by the throat, winding her so that she doubles over, gasping for air. Toxic fumes burn her airways, making her cough and now she has no choice. Holding her breath she sprints back the way she came, gulping in sweet fresh air when she reaches it, oblivious to how she exposes herself. Then she turns and heads back into pitch black.

Something brushes against her legs with a squeal. She grabs the torch from her pocket and switches it on. Curved walls close in, the awful stench of sewage and death rising to meet a low ceiling and something vile scuttles about the debris looming out of the darkness.

It doesn't take long to find the ladder. The pipe has swollen here into some sort of staging post and, just as Caleb said, its cover only partially blocks the man-hole at the top. She peers out, assuring herself that she is alone and climbs into an alleyway, adrenaline driving her towards a lighter shade of black.

A crack of thunder shatters the darkness, propelling her through burning air to crash into splintered concrete. Everything fades away.

She wakes with a splitting headache, for a moment certain only of her need to sleep. Distant rumblings shoot orange flares into a sickly sky and remembrance flashes back. She picks herself up, gathers her skirts and runs.

She has come quite a long way down this narrow street by the time she stops to catch her breath and her eyes have readjusted to the gloom. Above, dirty grey sheets hung between the remains of buildings, flap in the breeze and she is grateful for the cover from snipers they afford. She looks back at the path she took, turning the one hundred and eighty degrees to where the tower should be. The clothes tease, revealing then concealing in windblown dance. It takes seconds to be sure, but there it is. The white diamond gleaming in the dark. Something else appears and she freezes, willing herself into the pockmarked wall behind her.

The bent ghost of a man manoeuvres himself clumsily like some giant crab, an injured leg swinging between crutches that push uncomfortably into his armpits. Behind him, two teenage boys, gaunt and sallow, follow like shadows lost to another world. They pass her by.

She turns to the tower standing proud amongst the ruins and wonders if she has stepped back into some medieval time warp. This is Rahim's home-town. A place where modern convenience rubbed shoulders with ancient history. Here, at the end of a hard day's work, friends met to relax and socialise. Youths congregated on motor-bikes and scooters. Children played hide and seek and tag in the alleyways. Women met girlfriends for coffee and couples wandered hand in hand, just as they do all over the world.

Here, the oldest of the city's mosques and churches boasted frescoes and relics dating back to the earliest centuries, that were of significance to Christians and Muslims alike. St John the Baptist's head, they say, was discovered nearby in 452. When five hundred of Muhammad's companions conquered Homs and settled in, they transformed half of St. John's Church into the city's Friday Mosque, a place for Christians and Muslims to worship alongside each other. Like every mosque in Syria, not only a place to go and pray, but somewhere to meet, picnic and nap, where children could run around playing on soft carpets or worn flagstones outside. A timeless place of calm and serenity where generations, people of all races, nationalities and religion, mingled. Until now.

Lost to her thoughts, Ana doesn't notice the doorway, only the priest emerging from it as she passes. "I'm sorry. Didn't mean to startle you." He speaks English and taking a moment to recompose herself, Ana looks up to warm brown eyes in a deeply lined boyish face.

"Father Hans?"

The black garments of a priest hang off his skeletal frame and he wears a brown leather jacket with a hat, almost a beret, that wouldn't look out of place on some fashionable Parisian Boulevard. "Hans van deRijke, at your service." He takes the hand she offers, puts an arm around her and gives her a warm hug. "Come," he adds hastily, "we're not safe here."

"Is anywhere?"

"Relatively." A warm smile exaggerates his worn features and she notices cracks like spiders legs, radiating from a small hole in one lens of his glasses. "This way."

They come to a low grey stone building set slightly apart from the others, a crucifix and colourful sign declaring a welcome to the monastery. "This is where I live, though we have to move from time to time to where the power is." He leads Ana to the door, opens it and stands back to let her pass. "Welcome," he says, startling to the crash of something falling as the sharp tap of footsteps follow. "Here is Liliane."

A homely woman, brown eyes sparkling from a once round face, folded in crepe-paper skin and a head-scarf sprouting wispy grey hair, bustles towards them. A dirty apron tied tight around her shrunken waist, protects a faded summer dress and she wears plain wooden clogs that clatter along the stone floor. She smiles, lifting Ana's niqab to kiss her on both cheeks before drawing her into a comforting hug with mutterings of, "face of an angel, such hair," and "so thin!"

Hans laughs. "Sadly, Lili was widowed and has been reduced

to looking after me. She is an efficient housekeeper and an amazing cook. Can even make grass taste delicious!"

Ana screws up her face. "I've got something for you. From Caleb." She removes her niqab, jilbab and then the backpack. It is surprisingly heavy and, wondering how she didn't notice that before, Ana recalls Caleb carefully fastening the straps that held it close and secure.

The priest nods. "Caleb is a good man," he says, taking it off her. "He loves you, you know?" Ana smiles but her thoughts are elsewhere. "This way." He leads them through the stone corridor to a large kitchen, placing the bag on one of a half dozen trestle tables. Without hesitation, Liliane proceeds to unpack. Tins of vegetables and meat, bags of rice and flour and a bottle of oil. She lines them neatly up and crowns them with a pile of that delicious greenery. "I've known him since he was a small boy."

Ana nods, able to contain herself no longer. "Hans, where are the children?"

"I don't know but we will find them when it is safe to do so."

"Why not now?"

Hans turns to face her and looks earnestly into her eyes. "There are times when it is best to stay hidden and times when we dare take risks. The children have learned. They are survivors. We will find them in the morning if the shelling has stopped but there is no point in risking it now. Don't worry. They have been here all this time, one more night will make no difference."

"But where are they?"

"In Dua's apartment I expect, but it depends."

"Who is Dua?"

"You'll see. Trust me. They are as safe there as we are here. Now Caleb," he smiles at her kindly, as if to distract her, "was a quiet boy. Even so, he stood up for the weak and injured and stuck his neck out for what he thought was right. He worked hard. A talented pianist, I recall." Ana stares at the table, a yawning chasm opening in her chest. "Three days will pass quickly," Hans reassures.

"This food is very welcome. Thank you. Tonight we must make do but tomorrow we feast like kings!"

Though simple – bread, water and olive oil, this meal, eaten in good company on an empty stomach, is as delicious as any Ana could have wished for and she feasts as hungrily of her meagre share of it, as of the eloquent conversation that flows between the priest, his housekeeper and the handful of guests who will stay the night at the monastery.

Inevitably, conversation turns to strife in Syria and civil war, "anarchy with no accountability, no punishment, no limits," as Hans describes it. "It is said that the tyranny of a sultan for a hundred years causes less damage than one year's tyranny perpetrated by his subjects against one another.

"Any kind of order is better than anarchy. But even worse for Syria, she has become a pawn in a proxy war. If the west had intervened as it did in Libya, early enough to back the legitimate opposition, this could all have been over by now. Instead, we see a power vacuum for militarised
fundamentalists to fill."

"Lebanon's civil war lasted fifteen years," a journalist who lived many of those years in the country, tells them. "The solution to that crisis was the creation of a buffer from the Christian heartland of Mount Lebanon between the Shi'ite south, Hezbollah and the Sunni north, with most of the Druze retreating to their own mountain strongholds. So, these rival groups were prevented from destroying each other. But it took almost one hundred and fifty thousand deaths for this compromise to be reached, out of a population of three million. Syria's equivalent would be to seven hundred and fifty thousand!"

"Maher al-Assad has threatened to kill a million if need be." Ana shakes her head. "Bahar's violent younger brother. History repeats itself. The Assad regime appears to believe that past methods will succeed in the modern world and perhaps, with its clever manipulation of sectarian differences, they will."

"What do you mean?"

"Well Ana, the West has a lot to answer for so far as politics in the Middle East are concerned." There is no doubting that. "When Syria's borders were arbitrarily drawn up by the British and French after World War One, Syrians rose up against their French oppressors. That was the Great Revolt of 1925. The French response, like Assad's, was uncompromising. An artillery bombardment flattened much of the Old City of Damascus – a quarter now known as al-Hariqa, the Conflagration. They killed thousands, hanging bodies and carrying out public executions in the central Marja Square as a warning to the rebels. Their 'divide and rule' policy fuelled sectarian divisions, whilst they made themselves out to be the noble guarantors of peace. It worked. After two years of fighting, the rebellion was crushed and the French went on to control Syria for another twenty years.

"Hafez al-Assad, Bashar's father, grew up resenting the privileged and arrogant land-owning families of the ruling class. He was one of eleven children born into poverty but, through hard work and natural ability, became the first person from his village get to secondary school. Though poor, his father was respected, known for his resistance to the French and before him, his grandfather resisted the Ottomans, refusing to pay taxes. His grandfather, a great personality, became known as the wild beast, Al-Wahhish, also for his size and strength, and this became the family surname until Hafez's father changed it to Al-Assad, which means lion.

"Young Hafez wanted to train as a doctor but his father couldn't afford the fees so he joined the Homs Military Academy instead, training here and in Russia as an Air Force pilot and winning many distinctions and awards. At the same time he learn't how to manipulate the ruling Arab Nationalist Ba'ath Party ideology.

"Within the Air Force, he created a highly efficient security system that specialised in uncompromising torture methods. He became Defence Minister in 1966 and, in 1970, took the presidency in an almost bloodless military coup. He went on' to rule Syria with a rod of iron for three decades.

"In 1982, the Assad regime led by Rif 'at, Hafez's younger brother, crushed the Hama Muslim Brotherhood uprising in a four week bombardment. Just like his nephew, Maher, known as the Butcher of Daraa, for his unpredictability and violence. Said to enjoy the act of killing, Maher leads the savage fourth Armoured Division.

"Rif 'at, now exiled and living a life of luxury in London's Mayfair, flattened the Old City of Hama with his pink-uniformed special forces, destroying centuries-old buildings, just as Maher now flattens the Old City of Homs. A business man once accused Rif 'at of killing seven thousand people there, to which he is alleged to have replied, 'what are you taking about, seven thousand? No, no. We killed thirty eight thousand!'

"They say Rif 'at has built himself a fortune of several billion pounds and his investments include the Arab News Network with one of his sons chairing the television station.

"Both Homs and Hama, by the way, are of great strategic importance as corridors to the coast.

"To Iran, this revolution, like that of 1982, is simply another battle against the supremacy of Sunni Islam. So, when it looks like the current regime might lose, it sends in its own militias and Hezbollah fighters to support Assad. For him, however, this has nothing to do with religion. It is simply about retaining power."

"Violence is the way of Bashar's regime," the journalist confirms. "It simply does not know how to cope with peaceful protests."

Hans nods. "Indeed. Its method of punishing areas of opposition is always the same. Cut off water supplies and electricity so that residents are forced to evacuate, shops to shut, then pulverise from the sky using fighter jets, helicopter gunships or

169

fixed artillery. Finally, after weeks or months of shelling from a safe distance, with no risk to pilots given the rebels' lack of antiaircraft guns, shabiha and regime soldiers are sent in to search house to house, flat to flat, looting, slitting throats or raping anyone left behind."

"Shabiha?"

"Government thugs, paid by the regime, who roam the streets carrying out hideous acts of brutality just as they did centuries ago. Armed gangs, paid to do the dirty work of the ruling class, go back a long way in this part of the world. The scum that rises to the top in times of war. The shabiha are often big men with beards and wild eyes, sometimes dressed in black, sometimes, ordinary clothes. Mostly Alawis, they first started appearing in the 1970's in the Lattakia region after Hafez-al-Assad came to power, probably the result of patronage from some of Hafez's own Alawi clan. Considering themselves to be above the law, the shabiha ran various smuggling and protection rackets often involving drugs and weapons. Their daily rate is now equivalent to at least six times the average monthly wage. Sometimes they work with Iranian Hezbollah militia from Lebanon – doing Assad's dirty work together, carrying out a deliberate policy of ethnic cleansing. Religion is not stated on secular Ba'ath ID cards but a person's name and birthplace indicate which sect the holder belongs to.

"Similar networks of patronage have been practised through the ages. When the Ottomans succeeded the Mamluks in the 16th century, they continued to use the so-called zu'ar gangs of thugs and robbers to control popular resistance. Highly organised groups of young men, described as wild beasts, who enjoyed terrorising the local population into submission."

"Unbelievable, isn't it?" the journalist agrees, noticing Ana shiver.

"Did you know," an academic in her thirties, here with her one remaining son, elaborates, "that the Assad family has a mausoleum approached by a specially built four-lane road? It lies on wooded slopes bearing fine new villas with views across the Mediterranean coastal plain, out to sea. Yes, the Alawites have come a long way since their former lot as housemaids and labourers!"

"So you see," Hans explains, "Bashar has followed the French example, calling peaceful protestors – sectarian extremists and foreign terrorists who want to destroy the Syrian motherland and need to be taught a lesson. Otherwise all hell will break loose. A fanatical Islamist government will take over and Syria's precious minorities will be wiped out. Assad, with his powerful security apparatus and tightly controlled armed forces has declared himself to be the only possible saviour of Syria's future."

Ana learns that thirty-five Christian families still live in the besieged Old City and of how they are supported financially by Muslims, their families intertwined for generations. There were two main churches, each a beautifully kept oasis of calm. The larger of these was part of a complex of buildings serving the Syrian Orthodox Archbishopric. Today it is on the front line, its windows blown out, its priceless frescoes guarded by Muslims.

Homsi humour has helped the people cope with tragedy. Hans shows them spoof Facebook pages such as the 'Homs Tank Wash Services' which offers to wash and service tanks cracking down on protesters; posters making fun of the regime, Bashar with his paternally raised hand, saying "I am free," or, "I am with Syria," and images of Homsis with aubergines, zucchini and potatoes hanging from their belts like mock grenades. "After all, we are armed gangs with sophisticated weapons."

Ana sleeps badly that night. Her tummy aches and her racing mind will not let her rest. She finds the priest meditating in his simple chapel despite the earliness of the hour and settles on her knees beside him, closing her eyes in earnest prayer. When she opens them again, he is waiting, watching her thoughtfully. "When you're ready, we'll go," he says. "Rahim longs to see you but his brother will not leave the little one."

"Little one?" Alarm agitates the butterflies in Ana's stomach for they have only secured safe passage for three but Hans is already on his feet. He looks her over then takes off his leather jacket.

"Put this on," he says. "It'll do for now."

DESCENT TO HELL

They leave the monastery through another entrance, moving deeper into Old Homs as the sun rises. Already there is the occasional sign of life, cold and subdued like the dying embers of a fire but, despite the hopelessness emanating from their depleted frames, all have some kind of greeting for the priest.

Sheets crossing the street flap above them in the breeze. "It may be early but still we must be careful," Hans warns. A rifle cracks and he pulls Ana deeper into the shadows, searching the levels above them.

"Where are they?"

"Anywhere. They hide on the rooftops, in abandoned apartments, ..."

"Assad's forces?"

"Jihadists also."

"But why do they target innocent civilians?"

"Because Ana, they are not here to serve the people, only themselves. They blame the murders they commit on Assad and he tells the world we harbour terrorists as though this justifies his actions. "Now it would be safer to go this way please."

She follows him into a passageway and through the entrance to what was once a store of some kind. Shards of glass litter piles of twisted metal and splintered wood and, in one corner, the black shadow of a fire still taints the air with acrid smoke. "This was a food store, but as you can see, it is all gone." Hans shrugs, turning to the wall and a ragged hole that looks like the handiwork of a giant rodent. Through it, opposite, Ana sees another, almost identical. "We build passageways between the buildings to avoid the streets," Hans explains.

He leads her through deserted, decimated homes and businesses. A living room, its floor laid in readiness for a meal but food long gone. Stolen by some starving creature that licked every plate and bowel clean. Deformed remains of chairs and a desk in a charred office. A once beautiful hand-made carpet, shredded by twisted metal that fell from the sky. A side-board loaded with broken crockery. A newspaper, empty cans, a mobile phone, a wheelchair minus any wheels. An exposed cracked toilet. Rooms and passageways illuminated by holes in walls and ceilings. Everything covered in dust and debris.

At last they come to the foyer of a block of flats and Hans leads her up a flight of stairs. "This is most likely where they are." They go up to the third floor and a spacious hallway with a large wooden door. Hans puts a hand gently on the handle and opens it quietly. "Hello. Rahim? Foued? Is anybody there?" Silence. He puts a finger to his lips and Ana nods.

It is like walking back into the normal world. Evidently home to a family of good income, the rooms are spacious and light. Lavish rugs cover a wooden floor. Solid, well built furniture lines the walls. Two sideboards, overflowing bookcases, comfortable chairs and a sofa. There is a coffee table with a pile of newspapers and magazines crowned by a copy of Time with a photograph of Syria's conflict on the front page. The adjoining kitchen is furnished with modern appliances. A cooker, microwave, fridge-freezer, washing machine and television. Empty food-bags, cardboard boxes and wrappers have been crammed into an overfull bin, glass jars and bottles neatly lined up beside it and cupboard doors standing wide open, proudly reveal nothing. The shelves are bare.

Hans begins to speak in Arabic. Quietly. Slowly. Still there is no reply. They come to a bedroom and the delusion of normality vanishes. The back wall is missing, affording them views far across the devastated city and the strong breeze, free access. There is a bunk-bed, beside it, a double and beyond these, looking about to fall out of the gaping hole beyond, a substantial wooden wardrobe. The bedding is shredded and everything is covered in fine grey dust but the sheets have been straightened and someone has evidently slept in the lower bunk along with an armful of stuffed toys. Three bears, a doll, a lion and a lamb, neatly lined up against the wall, shelter from the violence. Between them, the happy faces of a young couple smile from a framed photograph, in their arms a baby, it's green eyes piercing a shock of ginger hair.

Hans makes his way to the wardrobe, peers behind it, then drops to his knees. "Hello Dua,…Asalan," he says gently. "Are you alright?"

He can be no older than three. Orange hair protruding at all angles, crowns a pale, hungry face with haunting green eyes and cracked swollen lips. Wearing a once white, adult t-shirt, he sits in the corner behind the wardrobe, chin resting on knees pinned tightly to his chest and looks with desolation over the destruction laid out below. Before him sits a dog. A bedraggled starved creature, it is huge nevertheless, with thick pale fur that comes in tufts around inflamed bald patches. One ear stands stiffly to attention, the other flopping into unearthly pale blue eyes. It bares its teeth and growls at Ana, then looks in confusion to the priest, whining tunefully. "It's alright," Hans reassures. "Ana is a friend." He beckons her closer and she puts her hand out for the animal to sniff.

"Dua, this is Ana. She's a friend of Rahim's. And this is Asalan," Hans says, glancing at Ana as he strokes the dog. "Asalan has looked after Dua since his family went away. Hasn't he, Dua? In fact you look after each other."

No response.

"Asalan brings you food and you keep him safe from the others. Now will you come back into the bedroom?"

Nothing.

"Dua used to hide here," Hans continues undaunted, "when the shelling started, but the wall disappeared, then his parents. Now he waits for them to return."

Apparently satisfied that she poses no threat, Asalan returns to his ward. Whining, he laps at the boy's face and arms as if to wake him from a deep sleep but Dua does not flinch. The dog startles with a loud bark, its head flicking round, ears bolt upright. Eyes suddenly wide, Dua begins to wail. He grabs the dog and pulls it close to bury his face in its scraggy mane. The sound of excited children erupts and Dua stills.

"Dua, Dua, we're back!" Rahim bursts through the door and freezes, his eyes flicking from person to person. Ana sees that they are silhouetted against the bright sky and moves into the shadow of the wardrobe.

"It's me! Ana. And Hans, the priest."

Realisation dawns. Shaking his head with a smile, Rahim rushes into her arms and they hold each other tight. "You came," he says at last, pulling back to get a good look at her and follows her gaze to blood trailing from a tear in his trouser-leg. "It's nothing. There was glass."

He looks over to Hans and Asalan waiting patiently, his whole body wagging a tuneful welcome and proceeds to deposit treasure on the double bed. "Look, we've brought food." Some leaves that could be dandelion, grass, a few crusts of mouldy bread, a half empty soiled bag of rice and a tin of some kind of stew. He lays them out, exposing his arms and Ana sees the scars of fresh cuts, grazes and burns. "It's okay," Rahim reassures. "I didn't die, and here is Foued."

Apparently emboldened by his brother's enthusiasm, a younger version of Rahim creeps out from his hiding place. With dark hair that someone must have cut recently, he wears dirty jeans, a checkered red shirt, sandals and, though they carry the woes of the world, there is a glint of hope in his deep brown eyes. He looks to Rahim with awe then up to Ana. "Do you know, it takes only five breaths of smoke to kill you?" he says. "It's the smoke that gets you before the flames." He nods knowingly, then holds up his bounty for the room to see. "Look what I got!" A jar of olives, a tube of apricot paste and a tin of chick-peas.

"Where did you find all that?" Hans is genuinely amazed.

"Oh, you know," Rahim replies. "Here and there. All over the place really. You just have to look really hard in the places no-one thought of. That's all."

"Except you. Well done!" Kneeling to stroke the skeletal hound, the priest looks anxiously at Dua then back to the others. "Ana brought food too and later, Yalda will be cooking us a feast. We know you're anxious not to be away for too long, but we were hoping you boys, Asalan too, of course, would join us and stay the night at the monastery. You could leave a note for your parents Dua, just in case but I'm sure they won't be back tonight." He waits for his message to sink in. "What do you think?

The brothers' faces light up and the dog barks excitedly but Dua remains silent. "He doesn't speak," Rahim explains. "Probably did once though. Understands alright." He crouches before him and puts a hand on Dua's shoulder then, looking him purposefully in the eye, Rahim begins to speak but there is no response. He calls Foued over and they continue in conversation together. Rahim says something about going to find Dua's parents rather than waiting for them to return. Still nothing. At last Rahim gives up. "I'm sorry," he says, "but we cannot leave."

Ana frowns. "Rahim," she says. "I've come for you and Foued. We have a ticket out through a secret tunnel in two days time. That's our only chance of escape. Please come with us."

He gives her a look of utter devastation. "Foued won't leave Dua and I can't leave Foued."

"Dua can come with us."

"Dua won't go anywhere without Asalan."

"Then we take Asalan too!" Right on cue, the scabby mongrel trots up to Dua, settles back on his haunches and barks. The little boy startles, sees the crowd gathered around him and launches himself at Asalan and the dog covers his face with its enormous tongue, whining and barking as if giving him a good talking to. That seems to do the trick. Taking Foued's hand, Dua allows himself to be led from behind the wardrobe, but at the centre of the room, he stops abruptly. Drawn lips quivering, fat tears rolling down his cheeks, he looks around and Foued whispers something into his ear. The little boy nods and the two of them head for the bunk bed. They gather all of the stuffed toys and the photograph, placing them carefully in a backpack Rahim found, then the food and, when he offers, hand it to the priest to carry. With one last devastating look around him, Dua takes Foued's hand and follows the children out of his home.

They stick to the tunnels wherever they can but sometimes they have to cross the streets, keeping as low as possible, even crawling along the ground to avoid gunfire that snaps around them, spitting dirt into their eyes and mouths. And sometimes they run for their lives, checking each other for injury after each crossing, hearts pounding, lungs burning, faces red with fear and exertion.

It is late morning by they time they reach the monastery and life stirs its corridors. Delicious smells waft from the kitchen and an unbearable ache grips Ana's stomach. She thinks of Caleb, certain that the wait is at least as agonising for him and fingers the phone in her pocket. He warned her to use it only out of dire necessity. She wonders why anyone would bother with a woman and two young children and assumes it to be Caleb's life she would be risking. With a heavy heart, she watches the children, apparently quite at home here, run ahead with Asalan.

"You know they've been eating their pets here in Homs?" She nods with a frown. "Asalan is lucky to have survived this long," Hans elaborates. "A tribute to the children's ability to keep him hidden. He is fortunate that you will take him also." Ana's heart skips a beat. "Ahh, don't worry, you'll be fine. What is an extra child, a tiny one at that, and a dog, anyway? Nothing. No-one will notice. They're just waiting for the money to line their pockets. That's all they want.

"Do you think you can deal with that gash on Rahim's leg? We have no medical supplies left but Yalda has needles and thread."

They eat at four, the meal anticipated with much excitement for this is their first of the day. Yalda has done wonders with what little she had though, with eighteen mouths to feed, it doesn't go far. Flatbreads, rice and a spicy stew. Ana doesn't ask what the meat is. Tinned tomatoes, the greenery from Paradise Garden and, for the children, a kind of biscuit made with Foued's apricot paste that looks almost like a giant jam-tart. "Don't think we eat like this every day," Hans warns before saying grace. "But today we are doubly blessed. I'm sure too, you will agree. Better a glass of water in good company than a glass of wine in bad. Alhamdulillah. Praise be to God!"

Two of the trestle tables have been pushed together for the adults and, to Ana's disappointment, they sit just out of earshot of the children. She watches them suss each other out. How Dua, now wide awake, flinches with the slightest movement or sound, wanting to be part of it all but unable to accept attention except from his two closest friends.

When they have all finished, the little ones take their plates and cups to the sink then come for permission to go play. The tension in Ana rises. With his precious load on his back, Dua stands before her, forehead creased, eyes full of anxious expectation, by his side, his guardian angel. One ear standing to attention, the other flopping into his face, with top teeth just showing above his lower lip to form a comical smile, Asalan clearly considers himself one of the pack.

"We'll come say goodnight when we're ready for bed, okay?" Foued reassures.

A hush settles on the room once the children are gone and, looking around her, Ana wonders at the stories waiting here to be told.

Ordinary people in extra-ordinary circumstances, trying to live their lives minute by minute, day to day.

Like Ana, the Arab journalist has come far and risked his life to get into this part of old Homs. The others are trapped or have chosen to stay. Some don't trust their president's promises not to harm them, others are too poor or old to leave and some will not abandon loved ones who fight for freedom and democracy.

A former successful businessman explains how they all knew the price they would pay because of what their facist government is capable of. Through his work he met many of the Syrian elite, including members of President Bashar al-Assad's family. "I saw their true nature. They act as if they are Gods, regarding everyone else as slaves. We do this for freedom," he tells Ana. "I have no regrets."

The main topic of conversation is the lack of food for they are always hungry and malnutrition is rife, particularly amongst the children. "I lost over seventeen kilos in four months," a twenty eight year old who used to work in a five-star hotel, exclaims.

"You are our voice," Hans tells the outsiders. "You must tell everyone what is happening here and make them listen. We feel abandoned by the world. Assad's military machine was on the verge of defeat. If we had had help, this could all be over but now he is propped up by Iran and its Hezbollah proxy, and the jihadists have arrived. We have done nothing wrong and we love life. We don't want to die! Tell them that dying of starvation is more painful than dying from chemical weapons. I am a trained psychologist, tell them, and I see people going crazy with hunger!"

They say they have been able to hold out for so long because of their comrades in the Free Syrian Army, who steal ammunition and weapons from Assad's forces, and because of the teamwork of the community – sharing food, wood for fuel and encouragement. They say it is this spirit that keeps them going and that, though the price is so high, they don't regret the revolution. But Ana thinks of the children and wonders what choices they would have made.

There is a soldier here who used to fight for the President but couldn't fire on his people as he was ordered to do. He is a deserter. The price for his head is very high as will be the cost to those who conceal him. "When a person is injured here," he says, "all we can do is pray to God to alleviate his pain."

A young woman with the scars of terrible facial burns, explains how her stove blew up because the cooking oil is of such poor quality, how she fears now she will never marry and of how, in Syrian society, a woman's awrah, her modesty, is so important. She has heard that rape has become a weapon of war and considers this to be the greatest violation.

A radiologist has been sitting quietly listening to the conversation but now she too, has something to say. "Families in my city are being starved to death she tells the reporter. Tell the world that it has allowed a peaceful, popular revolution to be turned into a nightmare proxy war hijacked by radicals. My home is their battlefield and my people its victims." Looking at the anxious faces gathered around the table, she hesitates. "I have something else for you to show the world." She picks a large brown folder off the floor beneath her chair, removes the black and white x-ray films it contains, placing them with the packet on the table before her and holds one up to the light above them. "You'll need to come closer. Perhaps just you Ana, and you," she nods at the journalist. "The others don't need to see this." She picks each picture up in turn, holding it to the light to point out the most signifiant features.

Ghostly images of children with horrendous injuries. Crushed skulls, chests, and smashed bones, shrapnel and bullets clearly lodged in vulnerable bodies and, an image Ana will never forget, of a woman's heavily pregnant belly, a bullet lodged in the brain of her unborn baby.

Ana's night is restless. Full of nightmares that blur the distinction between her imagination and reality. Even Caleb seems a world away though so little time has passed since they were as one and she weeps bitter tears from the depths of her heart, certain she will never see him again. She is so weary, yet cannot rest. At last she can bear it no longer and rises from her bed just before dawn.

The others in the room sleep on as she dresses. She takes a towel, closing the door quietly behind her and heads for the courtyard. A trough that passes for a bath, lies half-full of rainwater, perfectly reflecting a cloudless sky and she looks with wonder beyond the infinite twinkling stars, to the dust they emerge from in the dawn of time. She slips off her clothes and steps into the abyss, turning her eyes to eternity when its image shatters in a cascade of ripples then, oblivious to how she shivers with cold, she seats herself and watches. Time flows before her. Past, present and future blur with her identity until she is in everything, everything in her and because Ana has ceased to exist, she doesn't notice, until it is too late, how she slips ever deeper.

Icy hands grip her by the throat, forcing her under and, suddenly aware, she fights for her life, gasping for breath as she breaches the surface. Coughing and spluttering in the eery silence of the night. She grabs the sides of the trough and looks around, half expecting Qassem to emerge from the sinister shadows but she is alone. It was all in her head and the stars are already fading, their magic lost to desolate emptiness.

A bar of soap balances precariously on the edge of the trough. Careful not to push it over the edge, she picks it up, forcing herself to focus on the simple task of cleaning herself as if everything could be ordinary again. The moon bathes the world in ethereal silver and she smiles, breathing deeply of that peaceful moment. And then it comes. Ripping the sky apart and shattering the earth. Thunderous bursts of red and yellow push her heart into overdrive and she scowls as if this outrage would take her disgust personally. Shivering, she rises into the fading night, wraps herself into the voluminous towel and sits on the ground to watch a new day dawn.

She wakes with a start, to warm sunshine and fear weighing heavily in her stomach. Dressing hurriedly, she runs her fingers as far as she can through her hair, ties it loosely behind her and heads for the kitchen. She finds Hans in the living room, lost to a trance of his own and settles herself quietly into a seat beside him.

"What will become of us Ana?" he asks at last. "We can't hold out much longer. Unless salvation comes, we'll starve to death and it'll all have been for nothing." She hesitates and the journalist appears with Asalan whining a mournful answer as he dumps his boney body unceremoniously on the floor beside their host. Ana doesn't know whether to laugh or cry.

"You can shut your furry face!" The priest pats its mangy head fondly. "Should've eaten you long ago." Asalan jumps up, his ears flat against his head, happy ending stilled and barks. "Don't worry, I was only joking." Hans laughs. "The children would never forgive me, would they?"

He kneels before the dog, narrowly avoiding its wet tongue and strokes it vigorously until it loses its balance, falling gracefully to one side and rolling onto its back. Legs waving inelegantly in the air, naked pink flesh exposed, it waits and when the priest begins to rub its tummy, purrs like a cat, the back leg it holds aloft, twitching, out of control. They have to laugh and, as the priest continues the belly rub, Asalan's purr turns to an appreciative low-pitched growl.

"I'm afraid there's nothing left for breakfast," Hans apologises, "but we hope to provide supper." He stands to consider them, scratching his chin thoughtfully. "There's something else I want you to take back to the outside world. I didn't want to speak of it while the others were around.

"It's about Assad's policy – surrender or starve. I believe it to be more than a paranoid attempt to wipe out any opposition. You may have noticed how he systematically empties Homs and all the cities, towns and villages that border the Alawite lands. The reason for some of the worst ethnic cleansing and for razing these communities to the ground, is to give better protection to the Alawites. If Syria is eventually partitioned, he will have a country of his own, heavily fortified and isolated from the rest of the country.

"Assad has always said he's all that stands in the way of civil war and anarchy. He'll make damn sure, if he doesn't prevail, that his prediction comes true. He's carving an Alawite conclave out of the flesh and blood of his people. Raising all that stands in his way to the ground and, with the help of North Korea and Iran, stockpiling the most sophisticated weaponry including biological and chemical." Hans pauses and Asalan barks, his tail wagging as he heads for the door.

Ana guesses the children are on the way. "Will you show me how to get to the hospital?" She asks hurriedly.

With a shake of his head, Hans tells her not to get involved. "You need to be at the end of that tunnel tomorrow evening," he adds.

But she'll go mad if she has to wait all that time with nothing to do. "Don't you think I'd be able to get away?"

"Is it worth taking the risk? You can make yourself as useful here as anywhere, trust me. Now you must excuse me, I have prayers to lead." He says it as if he expects to have a congregation. "You're welcome to join me if you want."

They pick their way through rubble, tangled cables, rubbish and overgrown shrubs. Past burnt out vehicles, collapsed buildings and surreal blue signs directing them to districts which can no longer exist, the roar of shelling and the crack of gunfire, a constant companion. Though they did their best to dissuade him, Dua is determined to go home one last time. "He thinks his parents may be looking for him," Foued explains. "Just wants to make sure they haven't come back before we go."

Rahim leads, Dua and Asalan close on his heels while Foued falls behind to speak with Ana privately. "I think Dua's parents were killed and that he'll never see them again. Or they would have been back for him by now, wouldn't they Ana?" He doesn't wait for her reply. "I think he's lost. He and Asalan must come with us or they'll die. Like all the others."

Dua's home is just as they left it. There is no sign of life but Asalan sniffs his way slowly around the apartment anyway, returning to report to his master when his inspection is done. The little boy stares into the dog's face then, tears welling up in his eyes, he takes Foued's hand and heads for the door, turning in the middle of the room for one last look.

Ana realises nothing but the horror in his face until it is too late. Knocked to her feet by the impact, she falls onto the children, a deafening howl and blinding light, robbing her momentarily of her senses. Enveloped in searing heat, she struggles to breath for there is nothing but acrid suffocating smoke.

She hears Asalan barking and struggles to her feet. Rahim is already at the door and when he opens it, for a brief moment they gulp in sweet life-saving air but this fans the roaring flames. "Everyone out!" She waits until she has counted them all, then follows, slamming the door shut behind them.

They run down the stairs but their escape route is blocked. They will have to risk the open street. The shriek of a missile falls to deafening explosion before them, a ball of flame sending a billowing tower of thick black smoke up from the quaking ground. Great chunks of hot shrapnel fly through the air, decapitating one man instantly. Sick with horror, Ana turns away, impulsively covering the children where they cower in a huddle behind her. Someone shouts a warning but still they wait, hugging the ground as if they could be invisible to the forces that rage around them.

At last the noise of terror from the skies gives way to that of anguish and destruction. Agonised wailing, desperate shouting. The sinister rumble and crash of avalanching rubble and the crackle of flames. Still Ana waits with the children, unable to move.

Then one of them stirs. "It's okay. It's over." Coughing up choking dust, she rises to her knees as the children, recover themselves. She doesn't notice Rahim take her shaking hands in his. "We go now, yes?"

She looks around. Someone lies injured on the ground only a few metres away. He cries for attention but the able are busy tending to others in need and, torn between the compulsion to help and the instinct to get the children to safety, Ana looks to Rahim in despair.

"Can you get them safely back to the monastery?"

He nods, gravely. "Yes, I've done it many times already but you should come too. He will probably die anyway. You cannot save them all."

Ana is overwhelmed, and then the injured person cries out again. She pulls herself together, ignoring her raw heart and trembling body, for she will force them to obey her mind. "Go," she tells Rahim. "I won't be long."

She watches the children disappear, Asalan running rings around them to ensure they stay together then turns to the victim in the road. For a moment her heart stops, its gallop resuming in her throat only just in time to prevent all her blood rushing to her feet but now she cannot breath. How can it be? Everything starts to spin and, wondering if this is all some ghoulish nightmare, she wills herself awake.

He is young, fourteen perhaps but, though he looks so familiar, this is not Aadil after all. Blood gushes from an ugly wound where his leg should be and now Ana sees why no-one is stopping to help him. But she has made a decision and adrenaline spurs her on. She kneels beside him. "*As salam alaykum,*" she says earnestly, fixing his brown eyes with hers. She asks him his name and puts a hand on his shoulder, nodding with a smile as if she could reassure him, her back deliberately shielding them from that which strikes terror into the hearts of them both.

She looks around for someone to help and an elderly man

followed by a young woman, hobbles towards her. "Can you help me get him to the hospital?" she pleads, refusing to believe that there is no point. The old man nods and the woman runs off. Together they turn to consider that which pins this poor boy to the shattered ground.

Gleaming in the midday sun like a tower looming over them, the rocket seems to tease. If I hadn't chosen to wait, it seems to be saying, you would all be dead by now. She shakes the thought out of her head. They are going to have to move it or... She takes a deep breath. Unwrapping a scarf that once belonged to Dua's mother, she ties it tightly around the top of the injured leg then presses with all her strength on the major blood vessels beneath. And now she waits, diverting all her willpower to engage her patient's attention as she stares into his eyes and talks.

At last the woman returns and with her, two young men – gaunt, sallow, with dark hollows beneath their eyes, swarthy beards and *keffiyeh* covering their heads. Ana hardly notices the weapons they bear, registering their status as fighters at some deeply unconscious level instead. When gentle hands pull her away, she finds herself shaking violently and, though she turns to bury her head in the old man's chest, it is already too late. What happens next will haunt her for the rest of her days. She will never forget the evil glint of metal against a deep blue sky, that piercing scream as the machete detaches its victim from certain death, or the agonised wailing that follows. She retches, but when the old man draws her closer, rubbing her back in sympathy, pulls herself together and turns to confront this image of hell that adds itself to her growing collection.

The tourniquet holds, the cut clean just below it. The boy looks with shock into her weary eyes and replacing her fingers in his groin, Ana elevates his stump. They have brought a stretcher and now as she holds on tight, they place him onto it and lift. "Hospital?" she asks, knowing there must be something that passes for one here somewhere, and they nod.

Hidden in a basement, the entrance to the hospital is a hole in a wall just like those they passed through to get here. They had to run across exposed streets between buildings and each time, they were deliberately targeted, the bullets of snipers raising clouds of dust from the ground around them. There is a door to this building but, though protected by a wall of empty barrels and sandbags, snipers target it from both sides and it is too dangerous to use.

They are greeted by the sound of screaming and the barked instructions of the doctor to those assisting him. Most of his helpers are children, some probably no older than ten but the bearers of these casualties are staying too and doing what they can. The small room is already overflowing and they are told to lay their patient with the others in the building next door. There is one operating table, several mattresses and people lying on the bare floor. Ana introduces herself hastily and the doctor stops in surprise, to look her over. He points to a unit next to a sink. "What we have is over there," he says, "ask the children for anything else."

She sets to work, blocking images of little ones dealing with injuries they should not even have to bear witness to, focusing instead on their skill and bravery. There are no painkillers, anaesthetics or antibiotics and they have to use old rags, sheets and towels as dressings. The supply of water is intermittent and dirty, electricity – unreliable. The injuries they treat range from catastrophic chest, head and abdominal trauma which the victims have no chance of surviving, to open fractures and burns.

By night-fall they are still busy. Some have died already, others play the waiting game, their destiny now down to fate. A few remain to be operated on, their bearers waiting patiently to hold them down when their turn comes. Now that the volume of work has reached a manageable level, the doctor begins to talk. He asks Ana where she comes from and why she is here and she learns that he is the only medic left. All of twenty five years old and called Mo'amin, he tells her how he has to rely on people with no medical training to assist him. Of how they do the best they can. "You must tell the outside world," he says with passion "what's happening here, the circumstances in which I'm having to treat the wounded and their injuries. Tell them that we are like them. Imagine if this was to happen to their loved ones – how would that be? And tell them that we are dying, still waiting for their help."

They talk of politics and she asks about the foreigners. "Ah, the jihadists. Some welcome them," he tells her. "They see heroes come to help fight their cause when the rest of the world has abandoned them. Can you blame them?" She shakes her head with absolute conviction for anything must be better than the existence these poor people have been reduced to. "Most Syrians have never raised a stone before, let alone a gun. The jihadists are teaching them to defend themselves." But there are radicals, the doctor agrees, who inflict as much harm as Assad does.

He tells her of a man caught trying to connect a cable to a power line. " He was considered a thief by the Islamists. They cut off his arm." A girl shot dead because her dress was too short and of how music and smoking have been banned in some areas. Many of those from the Free Syrian Army complain about the brutality of the Islamic factions, especially those from the al-Qaeda linked groups: the Islamic State of Iraq and the Levant, known as ISIS which seeks to crush anyone who opposes them, and the al-Nusra Front known as JAN which aims to overthrow Assad and create a pan-Islamic state.

By morning, the injured have stopped arriving and the sick have started. One of the first is a fourteen month old girl who looks less than half that age. She is starving and, fighting back bitter tears, Ana watches as Mo'amin examines her. Brown, unseeing saucers flit about a veiny eggshell head, stick like limbs protruding from a swollen abdomen but though in obvious distress, the girl is too weak even to cry out. The doctor explains how, because they have no milk for the babies, they have to feed them sugar dissolved in contaminated water. By midday she will be dead.

"They have a saying here: the lucky can choose their fate. Much better to be killed quickly than to die slowly." People are reduced to eating shrubs and grass that cause illnesses such as indigestion, fever, diarrhoea and sickness. The elderly and the young are particularly vulnerable and several have already died as a result. "These people haven't been used to living without sanitation," Mo'amin explains. "Or a regular supply of food. Large parts of Syria were very sophisticated and have not seen hunger before. Also, with the vaccination programmes no longer running, there is the risk of illnesses we haven't seen in decades. Most of those born during the conflict have had no vaccinations at all," and there are growing concerns about polio outbreaks, measles and other diseases. "It's like a terrifying nightmare that just keeps going on and on. You live every day as if it's your last because you might die any second."

By mid-morning, Ana manages to catch up with the boy who brought her here. Trying so hard to be brave, he thanks her for helping him but, even as she utters words of encouragement, she can't help wishing he hadn't survived after all. He tells her that his parents, brothers and sisters are all dead. He lives with his grandmother now. She is all he has left but she is sick and needs him. He must get well again to look after her or she will die. Ana will never forget what they had to do to him and that he never lost consciousness. He shows her a crutch someone made him and she smiles, mindful once more, not only of the ingenuity of those left with so little, but also their resilience.

"Here you are. You must go!" Mo'amin exclaims. "But there is one last thing I want to show you before you do." He takes her to the main entrance of the hospital. "Look outside." She sees utter devastation. It is as if a bomb has fallen, destroying everything in its wake. "The rockets and shells did this. I've made a film for you to take with you Ana. Post it on the internet for me then give it to the media. Tell the world we are waiting for its help." She stares at the memory stick, certain this will be a memorial to Mo'amin, his helpers and those they treat then, taking it with a tearful nod, tucks it carefully into her trouser pocket.

At around midday, an old woman emerges from the hole in the wall, her dark eyes almost submerged in a field of wrinkles, body in a black jilbab and white hair covered by a simple black scarf. The doctor waves an enthusiastic welcome. "Sabeen, how good to see you! Come and meet Ana, a beautiful angel like yourself, sent by God to help us." The old woman blesses Ana with a toothless grin and reaches deep into her voluminous folds. "Sabeen brings us food," the doctor says, gratefully accepting the parcel. "Without her we would starve because we don't have time to find it for ourselves. How she does, I do not know."

"God provides, *Alhamdulillah!*" the old woman replies. "Now get on with you, you skinny wretch – eat!" The doctor heads with the bundle to his office.

"Come join us," he invites then calls out to the hospital in general. "Dinner's ready kids."

A host of them descend on the small room, some armed with jugs of water, others with plastic cups and plates and, as they lay everything out on the office table – bread, olive oil, tomatoes which Sabeen grew herself and a dish made from hibiscus and cactus leaves, Ana wonders how there can possibly be enough to feed them all.

They have hardly swallowed the last crumbs before chaos descends on them again. Mo'amin looks to Ana and shakes his head. "You must go," he tells her with a despairing shrug and once more she is torn. There is still a little time. But she has come all this way and risked everything, including Caleb, to get the children out and of one thing she is certain. That if she fails they will die a miserable death. Their fate depends on her.

"One of the children will show you the way." Mo'amin takes her hands in his and looks earnestly into her eyes. "Thank you Ana.

You are an inspiration and you give us fresh hope. Remember my memory stick. You are our voice Ana, speak for us to the outside world. Tell everyone that we are waiting for their help. We will all die if they don't come soon."

She looks at him, tears clouding her vision. They wait for salvation which will not come and she is part of that world which is leaving them to it. That greedy world which is too worried about politics to consider the men, women and children caught up in this terrible drama. It will leave them to their fate at the hands of their arrogant, brutal president and the inhuman monsters who invade in the name of Allah.

"Go!" he commands urgently and they both jump as a shell explodes in the street outside. She nods, throwing her arms around him then, stopping only to pass her saved lunch to the patient that brought her here, follows her young guide back through the tunnels to the monastery.

Asalan's bark is the first sign of life to greet them, the dog closely followed by a horde of excited children and Hans, his sparse grey hair in a state of disarray that betrays anxious hours spent pacing the corridors. "At last! We thought you were never coming back!" He hugs her then steps back for a better view. "You look terrible Ana." She smiles wearily. "What happened?" Everything blurs and she shrugs, Mo'amin's voice ringing in her ears. She remembers the memory stick and clasps it to the palm of her hand as if welding the two might brand it into her memory, then she turns to her little guide and smiles.

"This is Khalil, without whom, I would never have made it back." The children crowd round, taking it in turns to introduce themselves but Khalil struggles to keep up and, when Foued touches his arm, he jumps back, staring at him in wide-eyed terror.

"It's okay, I'm not going to hurt you! I was just wondering if you're coming with us, that's all."

Khalil shakes his head with a nervous smile. "I must get back to the hospital."

"How old are you Khalil?" Hans asks.

"Eight. I can find my own way, thank you." An unbearable ache gnaws at Ana's chest.

"I'll come with you." Hans tells him then turns on her. "You stay here with the children please."

She is too exhausted to argue. Falling to her knees before Khalil, she tells him that he did a fantastic job and thanks him for helping her and all his patients. "You are so brave," she says and Khalil beams with pride then, looking shyly up at the priest, takes his hand and leads him out of the monastery.

She doesn't notice the children disperse, only that hers and the dog remain and then she feels Rahim's hand on her face. "We were so worried about you."

"I'm sorry. They needed help." Strangling emotion erupts within her and she looks away but when Rahim puts his arms around her, she cannot help herself. Burying her face in his chest, she weeps bitter tears, for him and all the others. The lost generation of Syria who have been robbed of their childhood and future, yet accept their fate, making the best of it despite the most terrible adversity.

"What this?" Liliane finds them in a huddle, Asalan howling a pitiful tune in sympathy. "Feeling sorry for yerselves?" she admonishes. "You gone soon – out'a here. We's the ones 'as gotta stay!" The knot of children unravels and, wiping her wet face with her hands, Ana raises her eyes to Liliane in shame. She looks so funny trying to be angry with them and, as the children fall about giggling, Ana cannot help but smile. "You kids need to be getting ya stuff together," Liliane continues undaunted. "Not long now. And you," she takes Ana's hand to help her up, "got two hours to sleep." Then, without further ado, Liliane puts her arms around Ana and holds her tight.

She wakes with a start, disorientated and blind, nausea rising from the pit of her stomach. The voice comes again and she realises it was no dream. "Ana, it's time to go. Wake up." She screws up her eyes, opens them again and the fading face of the priest returns to stabilise before her. She tries to sit but dizziness overcomes her. "Ana, Caleb will be waiting for you. We have to go." There is urgency in his voice and he mentioned Caleb. Butterflies waken in her stomach and excitement stirs her.

"Caleb?"

"Yes, Caleb. It's time to go. He's meeting you at the end of the tunnel, remember?" Instantly awake, she trembles in anticipation.

"My jilbab."

"It's here and I've put your phone in your backpack for now. The children are waiting for you in the kitchen. I'll take you as far as I can, then it's down to you." She nods but stares at Hans wide-eyed. "You can do it," he tells her confidently." He hands her the jilbab and she pulls it on. Then the niqab. Finally, she takes his hand and he helps her up.

The excited chatter of children spills into the corridor and amusement calms her nerves. They look so comical with Asalan seated in their midst, whining and barking away as if he were holding court. "Ana!" Rahim sees her first. "Are you feeling better?"

"Yes, good thanks." She nods with a smile. "Are we ready?" The children all shout at once and Rahim pats the backpack beside him. It seems to have grown since she saw it last.

"We went to what's left of our home," he explains "and brought a few things. Is that okay?"

Ana shakes her head disapprovingly, wondering why the priest let them go. "Yes, that's fine," she says.

"And I found us each a torch."

She would have forgotten that. "Well done but please, don't any of you run off again!"

"We won't," he replies sheepishly.

Ana glances at the kitchen wall and the clock still ticking away time. She takes a deep breath. "Shall we go?" The little ones jump up, Rahim looks at her gravely and Ana turns to their hosts. Hans the priest who won't leave without his flock and Liliane, the widow who mothers them all. "Thank you." She hugs each in turn knowing that she will never see them again. "Look after each other." As they bid their farewells to each of the children, the dog heads for the door.

Somehow the ruined street looks different now. More familiar. Relatively safe, even and it feels like three months, rather than three days, since she left that uncertain world outside. It doesn't take long to pass through the shadows and by the edge of besieged Old Homs, Ana hesitates, deep foreboding doing its worst. "You must go," Hans tells her quietly. "Stay safe. God go with you all and tell Caleb from me Ana, that you have my blessing."

From the safety of the shadows she shows them where they need to run to next. "See that building over there?" They nod, looking to where her finger points over the sunny street to the ruins beyond. "The one that used to be a bakery – see the sign?" She waits until she is certain they all understand. The dog too, listening intently, sits to attention, its floppy ears remarkably erect for once, its wet nose and eyebrows twitching as its pale blue eyes fix on her. "Behind that sign is an alley-way and halfway down that, an open manhole with a ladder leading down to a tunnel. You all have your torches?" They fumble in their pockets and bring them out to show her.

"You're coming with us, aren't you?" Rahim looks on her in dismay.

"Yes, of course. I'm only telling you this in case we get separated. Whatever happens from now on, you must keep going until you get to the end of the tunnel. Caleb will be waiting for you there. Go with him. Do whatever he tells you to. Do you understand?" They nod in unison and Asalan opens his jaws to bark. "NO!" She mouths the word, shaking her head sternly as she grabs his snout and closes it firmly with her hand. "Shush!" The dog looks at her in surprise, wagging end frozen, ears laid flat against its head. "Good boy." She relaxes her grip.

"Okay, everyone. This is sniper alley so we need to be quick. Understood?" They nod and the dog stares sullenly at her from beneath fidgeting eyebrows. "I'll go last. Don't look back, just run. On the count of three, okay?" They look at her earnestly and she feels sick. This is it. They leave or die here, it's that simple.

"Well done everyone. Now here goes. Three, two, one, GO!" They run. Full-speed exactly where she told them to, without faltering, the dog leading the way but coming back to check on his ward whenever he falls too far behind. Ana takes up the rear. They are almost there. Her heart feels like it will explode from her ears, her chest burns for more air. So close and yet, a world away.

The crack comes simultaneously with the pain in her ankle. The dog looks back but continues to usher the children forward. Good dog.

She sees what is coming though it happens so fast. Reflexly her hand goes out to break her fall, landing in soft wet mud. The pain that shot through her is superseded by waves of nausea. She is about to pass out. She rests on her knees, one hand in the mud, the other on shattered concrete and gasps for breath, listening to herself moan as the feeling returns to her leg. She has been hit. A sniper's bullet, no doubt. So sudden and unexpected, though this was her greatest fear. She hopes the children didn't look back and have kept going like she told them to. Keep them safe, she prays. Don't let them come back for me.

At that moment there is nothing more she can do. She is paralysed, helpless. A sitting target in the fading light. Yet there are no further shots.

She pushes herself off the ground, gasping with the pain of moving her foot, forces herself to stand and tries to balance on her good leg. Faintness overcomes her and she leans on a pile of rubble, willing it not to collapse further under her weight. She hears the distant sound of men's voices and footsteps closing in but is powerless even to turn and face them.

Rough hands grab her from behind, forcing her arms behind her back and she loses her balance. She tries to save herself but her good leg won't hold and she cries out as the injured one hits the ground. She feels her hands being bound and panics, screaming hysterically as they turn her round to face them. Three men, one pointing a gun at her. She catches her breath and the constriction around her chest, tightens.

Muscle-bound with steroid induced madness in their eyes, they are dressed in combat trousers and black T-shirts, the unofficial uniform of the Shabiha. At that moment Ana knows she will die, that she has nothing to lose. Then something extra-ordinary happens.

It is as if she detaches from her body and watches what happens to it from a safe distance. With terror no longer clouding her judgment she notices how ridiculous they look – these pumped up monsters loaded with their trade-mark AK-47's and machetes, and laughs. Evidently surprised, they hesitate, then the closest removes her niqab and grabs her jilbab. Reflexly, she pulls away, wrapping herself more tightly into it and it is their turn to laugh.

Dispassionately, for she has no feelings from this vantage point, she wonders if information about her nationality or the status of her father in the political arena, would afford her any protection. Knowledge of her vocation, she is certain, will have the opposite effect. Deep down, however, she knows nothing will save her now. She views herself as these thugs do. An imposter. A wisp of a woman with piercing green eyes, a fair complexion and wavy blonde hair. From the lust they do nothing to conceal, it is clear there will be no concessions. Forcing her mind back to the children, she prays that Caleb is taking them to safety and, shaking from head to foot, resigns herself to her fate.

Then she sees him. Qassem. Striding towards her in the same uniform as the officer Caleb bribed to get her here. Dumbfounded, she scowls at him and he comes right up to her. He lifts her chin to make her look full on his arrogant face and she shrinks back in confusion. There is something terribly familiar about him. A cold shiver runs through her but she shakes it off. "You're with ISIS," she hisses, as if she might have some advantage over him and he laughs.

"Am I?" Evil glints from those chilling eyes and there is no reaction to her accusation from his minders. "It is for me know and you to guess who, or what I am," he smirks. "I know the answers already to all the questions you won't answer. Except, of course, you will. How long will it take? Minutes? Hours? The toughest last a day or two at most. I trust your hospital will have moved already. That was the plan anyway, when Caleb took you.

"Ahh...!" He eyes her hungrily. " Where did he take you Anais? What did he do to you before he gave you to me?"

"What plan?" Dread confusion overrides terror and Qassem gloats over her. Ana determines to entertain him no further. "Cowardly traitor!" His eyes light up but as he waits, she has the satisfaction of feeling his impatience grow. At last he can contain himself no longer.

"Why did he give you to me Anais, do you think?"

"How do you know my name?"

"How do you think?"

"You're playing games with me." Deep down, Ana knows now that the devil does exist for he stands here, before her and there will be no escaping him this time. Hot tears burn her cheeks but she shivers with icy cold.

"His company will give me so much pleasure!" Qassem runs his tongue over his lips, staring at her intently. "And to return the favour he did me all those years ago. Of course, you know he is my brother?"

"Who?"

"Caleb."

Ana gasps for breath and shakes her head, refusing to accept the likeness. His eyes are Caleb's but not as she has ever seen them before. "No. Liar!"

Qassem laughs. "We shall see." He says it with unnerving calm. "And the children. Shame about them. Sweet little things." He waits for her to respond and she cannot help herself. "Don't you dare touch the children!" He smirks at her avariciously. "Please," she begs. "Please, don't hurt them…"

The world begins to recede, spots before her eyes coalescing. The sound of her racing heart, the sniggers of those around her, the disgusting smell of them – fading but, just as she falls into merciful oblivion, a sharp pain on her cheek, snaps her back to consciousness. Instinctively she tries to put a hand up to it, losing her balance and falls to her knees before him.

"Don't think you're getting away from me that easily." He snaps his fingers and two of his thugs come towards her. She considers taking a defensive stance but those evil, confusing eyes steal any focus of concentration she might have been able to muster and she has no energy to rise from the aching dead weight that holds her like a shackle, to the ground. And still he watches, his gaze boring into her. Threatening, possessive and full of sadistic primeval lust.

"Of course, I have you to thank for bringing Caleb to my attention. I must admit, I'd lost track of him. How do you say… bigger fish to fry? Though I would have caught up with him eventually, even without your help. I knew he'd be up to no good somewhere but in my very own back yard?" Qassem's face contorts into something resembling one being poisoned, passing through a grimace to a traitorous smile. "Of course, I made his step-father pay. You should have heard him scream! Squealed like a pig. Just like the children."

Ana retches, cursing her weak body for betraying her, for complying with her persecutor's every whim. Qassem snaps his fingers and her abductors approach. They stand beside her and she waits, screwing up her eyes and tensing herself but nothing happens. He laughs. They pick her up by the arms, carrying her that way to a truck that draws up at the end of the road and drop her to the ground beside it. She hears doors opening, footsteps and then it starts.

MERCIFUL OBLIVION

"Ana!"

Caleb? Something soft touches her forehead.

Breath catches in her throat. Fire consumes her body. She tries to block it out but the heat intensifies and she moans.

"We need to move on."

Caleb?…Qassem? No!

Panic strikes. She can't make her body move and the pain is unbearable.

What is that sound? Mustn't give anything away…

She feels herself drifting, willing the darkness on.

Something pushes its way beneath her, slicing daggers, pulling her back to awareness. She screws her face up in disgust.

"Relax, Ana." She opens her eyes but someone has glued their lids together and now they roll in agonising spasm. "Keep them shut for now." She tries to speak but everything in her mouth is dry and stuck. She retches. The pain is all consuming.

A whimper rises to an eery wail and something terrible intrudes on her consciousness. Her chest tightens and she gasps for air. The wailing is replaced by panting.

"Ana, it's me, Caleb. It's over. We're taking you to a hospital." She shivers and the fever in her rises. "Not much further."

Caleb?

So tired. She feels herself falling, everything fading away but then his arm beneath her moves and those daggers jolt her awake. "Caleb?" She grimaces but he kisses her on the forehead. "Leave me be…"

"We're nearly there," he whispers. There is something in his voice but she cannot see how he fights back the tears or feel his despair.

There are some things she doesn't need to know. That they will only make it so far as a field hospital still operating secretly in a dead district of the city is one of them, or of how it struggles to cope with the scarcest of resources. It will be a staging post to stabilise her condition enough to move her on for Caleb will get her the medical expertise she needs if it's the last thing he ever does.

She doesn't need to know what he found himself capable of when they found her in that Damascus death-cell. That something within him died when he saw what those sadistic brutes had done. And she doesn't need to know that he would shoot her rather than leave her to die of her injuries. He could leave no-one to that fate, least of all, Ana.

"I can't lose you, Ana."

Her eyes scald. Hot tears tickle her cheeks. She feels his arm beneath her tense and how carefully he raises hers to wrap it around his neck, but shocks like the electricity, shoot through her and she cries out. He lifts her into himself and, mustering everything she can, she snuggles into him.

"Can we rest?" she whispers but hears neither his answer nor the tension in Tuan as he urges them on.

It is the longest moment but she is unaware of most of it. She knows nothing of the ruins they run through, how often they have to stop to take cover from falling shells, shrapnel and crumbling masonry or when they hide to avoid being discovered. She doesn't notice how they weave and duck, the flames or thick black smoke that engulfs them at times, the foul stench of rotting corpses and body parts that no-one has been able to collect or the deafening roar of warfare.

They reach the hospital shortly after nightfall. It is some way back from the front-line and they have begun to encounter signs of life.

People are living here and doing their best to maintain some kind of normality.

They passed a parade of maybe fifty. Men and boys, chanting and dancing, led by one who looked no older than twelve with a microphone and a voice like an angel. They were chanting anti-government slogans regardless of the consequences. It is the protestors and their loved ones who disappear first.

Some come to help, leading them to where the hospital lies hidden in the basement of a grand old house. They pass through what were once corridors, wires dangling freely from the stumps of walls. A portrait still hangs, apparently unharmed, the surreal face of an old man beaming benevolently down on them. He looks well fed and happy, as if he led an untroubled life.

Here is a bunk-bed, toys peeking out of the rubble. Movement in the shadows. For a moment beneath the half-light of the cloudless night, Caleb sees a child sleeping peacefully but then the body disintegrates into a pack of rats and he freezes. "This way." The knowing voice of concern spurs him on.

A chandelier dangles precariously above them, sparkling in the silver moonlight. A polished sideboard hosts a lace cloth beneath a silver platter, the shattered remains of its glasses, the only sign of the violence it witnessed.

Ceilings and walls disappear, the cold wind of the bleak night attacking them as they stumble over what once stood here. On into the remains of another room. A broken sink. Empty cupboards and a fridge balancing precariously over a hole in the floor, the sudden burst of light and noise from an opening door, threatening to tip it over. Tuan steps back, catching his friend's eye with a grim nod as he passes. He will stay and guard this entrance. With his life if need be.

The hubbub of an acute hospital in hiding, rises with the rank odour of sweat, decay and disinfectant. For a moment, Caleb hesitates at the top of the narrow staircase. They talk quietly but with urgency, these people who work so diligently to save the dead of this crazy war and now he can clearly hear the groans of its victims. He regrets bringing Ana here, but he had no choice. She will die if she isn't treated now.

"What have we here?" The pale face of exhaustion emerges from the gloom. Like Ana, he looks far too young and naive to be a doctor, let alone working in a place like this.

"Who are you?"

"Khalid. Surgeon."

Caleb nods. "This is Ana. A doctor like yourself. From England. She was caught rescuing some children…" He falters, the horror of it all threatening to overwhelm him at last as he struggles to remember what he has done countless times already. M.I.S.T. Mechanism of injury, Injuries, Symptoms and Treatment so far. "She was shot in the left ankle and tortured. For three days and nights."

The surgeon frowns, touching him with gentle encouragement. "Bring her over here." He leads Caleb to an empty mattress on the floor, clicking his fingers as he passes his young helpers. Like bees to a honey pot, they swarm around her. "What are her injuries?" the surgeon asks and, as he places her gently on the filthy mattress, Caleb completes his handover.

"When you've stabilised her, we'll take her on, across the border."

The doctor shakes his head. They have already inserted tubes into her arms though there is nothing but polluted water to run into them. She stirs and the surgeon speaks to her in English. "Ana, I'm Khalid, a surgeon. You're safe now. We'll do what we can for you here and move you on when you're ready. Do you understand?"

Nothing.

"I'm going to feel around. Let me know where it hurts, okay?"

He starts with her tummy and she moans. He watches her face, his hand moving downwards as it presses gently into her and she cries out. The surgeon removes his hand. "Ana, I need to examine you internally, then we'll put this right. Meanwhile Fadia here is going to do what she can for your eyes, okay?"

Caleb kneels on the floor beside her, stroking her forehead. The nurse takes a bowl of water from a stove, some cotton wool from an untidy table on the side and the surgeon draws Ana's knees up to her chest. "Hold on to me Ana," Caleb whispers and leans over to pin her to the mattress.

Tormented by what they inflict, they struggle to do what they must to save her. At last she loses consciousness. Pale, wet with perspiration, blood and tears, at first she clings to life but then the abnormal heat in her dissipates with her breath and Caleb knows she is gone. They don't seem to notice, for there is no anaesthetist to monitor her state. Only one, no more than a child, with a finger on her pulse, who startles when Caleb cries out.

"Ana!" He holds her shoulders and shakes her. "Ana, come back."

Someone calls out. "She's flatlined!"

They administer mouth-to mouth resuscitation and Caleb calls her name, stroking her hair, begging her to come back. At last she responds.

They have done all they can for her and she lies unconscious before them, fighting for her life. "Where do you plan to take her?" The surgeon tries so hard to distract him, to be upbeat about her prospects.

"Jerusalem."

"How will you get into Israel?…Caleb?" He startles. "They'll think you're a terrorist."

"I know what they think of me but they're wrong. I'll take my chances," Caleb replies angrily but then he sees the concern on the surgeon's face. "She has an uncle in Shabak, her father is a General in the British army and her brothers are special forces."

"Well, at least she'll be alright." The surgeon pauses. "But what about you?"

Caleb shakes his head. "I know the score," he says quietly.

"And what the hell is an Israeli doing in Syria, for God's sake?"

"She's British."

"What?"

"Her father's Scottish, her mother French. The uncle shared a mother with her father."

The surgeon shakes his head. "What about Lebanon?" he asks. "It's closer and sympathetic to our cause."

Caleb frowns. "The best hospitals are in Jerusalem and I have a friend who can get us in."

"Really?"

"Yes, really." Caleb looks at the surgeon with angry disdain but the poor man, beyond exhaustion, only has their best interests at heart. "A pilot who owes me a favour."

"Will he get you out as well?"

"No."

"But Ana will be safe." Caleb nods. "I'm sure they could deal with her injuries just as well in Lebanon," the surgeon persists but there is no response. "Well," he concedes at last, "Israel is probably better placed than any country in the world, to deal with injuries such as these." He considers Caleb carefully and heaves a great sigh. "Now will you let me see to your arm?"

She whimpers as she regains consciousness for she hasn't the strength to scream. She has fought this moment a lifetime but can evade it no longer. Death was not her destiny after all. She hears a distant voice and strains to see where it comes from, then remembers why her world is so dark. The black void is pierced by two scorching suns and she recognises Caleb. The voice appears to come closer and she hears him calling her.

"Ana? Ana! Can you hear me?" He waits but, though she answers, her body fails and she remains silently immobile. "You're in hospital in Damascus. When it's safe, we'll move you on."

She feels his hand stroking her hair. "Can you see me Ana?" She nods. Her body this time, makes a feeble effort to obey and she hears Caleb heave a sigh of relief. Waves of excruciating pain surge through her accompanied by an eery wail and she wonders what could have made such a dreadful sound. "Look into my eyes, Ana." She tries to keep still. Perhaps it will ease if she doesn't move, but suffocating pressure forces her to breath and she cries out again, panting for it hurts too much to satisfy her lungs. Her heart races and she shivers with cold though the heat in her rises.

"Ana, listen to me."

Caleb? Though she speaks, nothing happens. She feels so tired. All she wants is to sleep. Please let me be. She sees his eyes burning a path in the darkness. So bright, demanding. They spin around, rendering her sick and dizzy. She cannot make them disappear so tries instead to focus and, as she succeeds in stilling them, they draw her into themselves. She feels herself sinking.

"That's it, let go …" The agony subsides, giving way to a lesser, more tolerable pain and the pressure on her lungs eases.

She remembers the children. Did they get away?

"The children are safe." She sees his hands coming towards her and feels the heat of him bore into her dead eyes. She cries out. "It's okay Ana, trust me." She begins to see flashing lights, then shapes, then colours. Hexagons in blues, purples, yellows, oranges and reds, whirl until they blur. He takes his hands away and when she opens her eyes the view has altered. Inky blackness gives way to a grey haze and his burning eyes. "What do you see Ana?"

"Shadows moving through the fog and…two suns."

"You will see again!" He sounds so happy.

She tries to touch him but her hands are blocks of lead and her arms ignore her. Electric shocks shoot through them and she gasps. She wriggles her toes. They move freely but the same pain wracks her body and she whimpers.

"It's okay Ana. It'll take time but you're healing already."

Terrifying visions flash through her head and she becomes aware of an unbearable ache intensifying deep inside. Her breath catches in her throat and she holds it there to stifle any movement in her chest. She breaks out into a cold sweat augmented by waves of nausea and tries to bring her knees up but her legs will not move.

"Ana," Caleb chooses his words carefully, "you were bleeding internally. They did what they could to stop it but then," he falters, unable to give voice to that which will haunt him for the rest of his life. "They had to get your blood pressure up," he concludes instead. She doesn't need to know how they did that. That they transfused his blood directly into her with no way of checking beforehand that it was compatible. "We don't know for sure that the bleeding has stopped," he tells her reluctantly, but not that they might have to operate again.

She can hold it no longer. She gasps for breath, the agony of movement making her retch and wishes for it all to end. Now.

But it doesn't. In a timeless void, she drifts in and out of agonising consciousness. Only Caleb remains, her feelings for him deepening as all else fades away and from somewhere she finds the strength to keep going for his sake.

Bombs fall like rain. Thunder and lightning. Searing heat. Choking smoke.

His arms around her. Slipping, falling. Blissful sleep.

The rhythmic pounding of his feet on the ground. Jolting agony. His lips against her forehead. His reassuring voice...

Tuan?

Excruciating pain. Nausea. So cold. So tired ...

A motorbike? Men's voices. Strangers. A child screaming. Noooo!

A tunnel?

"It's blocked. Those bastards have sealed it. We're trapped!"

Panic...Caleb.

"We'll dig our way out."

Desolation. Agony. Oblivion.

The steady roar of an engine. Turbulence.

No shelling?

Sirens. The beeping of monitors. Urgent voices. Hands from everywhere. The smell of disinfectant. Something sharp...

Caleb? ...

THE GENERAL

She drifts in and out of merciful oblivion. Strange faces – blurred, unformed – loom and fade away with the noise. So much noise. Always there when she wakes. Beeping, buzzing. Voices. Intrusive yet never quite clear enough to make out what they say and bright light. Blinding white light. She cannot open her eyes. It hurts too much but they persist in forcing them.

What do they want with her anyway?

Terrifying flashbacks. Don't tell them anything. Mustn't give anything away… Leave me alone!

The children. Her heart bleeds for them. They don't deserve this. No-one does, but the children have no choice. Did Caleb take them somewhere safe?

Where is Caleb? Didn't he rescue her?

Why is there still so much pain? What are they doing to her? To him? Fear tightens its grip on her. "Where have they taken him?"

A face looms closer.

"It's alright Ana, you're in hospital. You're safe."

He doesn't understand.

"Caleb. Where's Caleb?"

"He's safe too."

Panic. "No, you're wrong. They're hurting him. We have to stop them!"

She tries to get up but nothing happens. There are two faces now. Something sharp – and it all fades away.

Ruth.

Who's Ruth?

A friendly face smiles down on her. Blurred. Emerging from the fog. It's peaceful now. No noise, no blinding lights, hardly any pain.

"Ana?"

She sounds surprised. What is that on her head?

"Ana, can you hear me?"

Should she answer?

"Ana, I'm Ruth. I'm looking after you for your stay here."

Stay? Where? Where is "Caleb?"

"Caleb?"

She heard her thoughts. How did she do that?

"I need to see him. Where is he?"

"I don't know where he is but I'll see to it that he's found. Is that okay, Ana?"

"But it's urgent. Do you understand?"

"Yes, I know who Caleb is Ana. The young man who rescued you. Your uncle is looking after him."

"No!" Panic really sets in but as Ana sits, the world starts to spin, flashing lights and black holes appearing in the fog and she falls back onto her soft pillow.

"Not so fast Ana, take it easy. There's no rush."

Ana's voice fails and she weeps tears of bitter frustration. The nurse sits on her bed, brushes hair out of her face and takes her hands. "It's okay. Everything is fine. You're safe here." Ruth seems kind and homely. Her warm hands caress gently. Ana relaxes a little.

"It's so good to see you after all this time. I was beginning to think you would never wake up."

"Where am I?"

"Jerusalem. In a private hospital attached to a convent. Your father brought you here to convalesce."

"Father? How long have I been here?"

"A few days. Before that you were in the Intensive Care Unit of Hadassah Hospital, in an induced coma for six weeks."

Six weeks! Panic. Ana sits, fighting the faintness. "Please let me see Caleb," she pleads.

"Ana, I can't do that but if you lie down, I promise to bring you someone who can."

She waits for ever but, when at last the door opens, it is a pale, dark haired, bearded stranger in a white coat who approaches. "Hello Ana, I'm Doctor Levi." She nods, unable to conceal her disappointment. "It's good to see you awake. How are you?"

"Okay, I guess… and you?"

"Well, thank you." He looks her over and takes a clip-board from the end of her bed. She notices now that she is alone in the room. There are no patients here but her. "I just need to take a quick look at you. The nurse tells me you were getting distressed. I'll give you something to make you feel better."

"No, thank you. I'm fine."

The doctor eyes her suspiciously. "It's a miracle you're alive you know?" he informs her and she nods. "Do you know what happened?" She shakes her head. It's all so confusing and, though she wants to know, already she is aware of a great force she is struggling to hold back. "Don't worry, it'll come back to you."

"I'm not sure I want it to."

Looking her directly in the eyes, Dr Levi nods, knowingly and Ana gets the distinct impression he's after something. "Do you remember what happened before you went into Old Homs?"

How? Well she supposes he would know that much. Her hands find their way to her temples and a pressure that seems to be building there. Unconsciously she begins to rub, and memories of her time with Caleb make her smile. She opens her eyes to the doctor watching intently and startles for he suddenly seems so close.

"Some of it."

He takes her wrist and looks at his watch. "How did you come to meet Caleb?"

What has that got to do with him? She shakes her head.

"Pulse is down. Just check your blood pressure."

"It's fine. Ruth recorded it on my chart." She points to the clipboard. "Look, there is only one thing I need right now and that is to see Caleb. I don't suppose you can help me with that?"

The doctor frowns and she sees something disturbing in his eyes. "What is he to you?"

"The man who saved my life." For some reason it seems wise to give no more away right now.

"Why do you think he helped you, Ana?"

"Because he's a good man and that's what he does – help people."

"Mmm ..."

"Do you have a problem with that?" What is it to you anyway and what sort of a doctor initiates such a conversation with a patient who's just woken from a coma?

"I'm just trying to understand how a nice girl like you gets involved with a terrorist."

"What?" The heat in her rises, confusion turning to anger. "What the hell are you talking about? Caleb is no terrorist!" The doctor raises his eyebrows but says nothing. "You know nothing about him! He saved my life and countless others."

"Well, I can see why he might want to save you." Ana does her best to calm herself. There is obviously no point in trying to converse with this arrogant fool. He brings the chart closer and she thinks he will show it to her but he puts it on the bedside cabinet instead, takes a stethoscope out of his pocket and looks down on her. "So, how are you feeling?"

"Fine," she repeats.

"Do you have pain anywhere?"

"No," she lies.

"Any shortness of breath, cough or tummy pain?"

"No, thank you."

"Ana, I'm afraid there is something we have to tell you." He doesn't seem too upset to be the bearer of bad news.

"Oh?"

"I'll leave it to the boss."

Arse-hole.

"Any bleeding?"

"No." She hasn't had the chance to look yet. "Actually, could you tell me where the bathroom is, I need a wee," she adds, hoping this will get rid of him. The doctor points to a door and she dangles her legs over the side of the bed opposite to where he stands. She takes her time and moves with careful deliberation, determined not to let him see her falter.

"So, you can see alright?"

"Amazing isn't it?" She stands for a moment, steadying herself against a world that seems determined to topple her, then makes her way to the bathroom. No catheter? How strange, but what a relief.

"You pulled the catheter out, in case you were wondering," the doctor informs her helpfully and she closes the door on his fresh face.

She looks around on a bright, spacious room with a huge cast-iron bath perched on four ornate feet, a deep sink, the toilet and a magnificent view framed by pretty flowery curtains, over rolling hills to Old Jerusalem below. Rows of laden olive trees stretch in neat rows away from her and in the distance, the golden Dome of the Rock gleams in the midday sun. The pain in her bladder intensifies but, as she turns back to the toilet, something catches her eye and she freezes, panic-stricken.

The stranger stands motionless, staring. She has mad hair and… Ana's heart skips a beat, the hairs rising on the back of her neck. Her hair is shorter than she remembers and someone must have washed it. She closes her eyes in vain and cries out as her nostrils fill with the rank odour of fear, the foul stench of rotting flesh. Consumed by the deep ache of smashed bones, a fire that rages in her belly and the stabbing suffocation of every breath, she hears the crack of a whip cut the air and relives the excruciating pain of it slicing through her. He leers at her – Qassem, for his lust feeds on her agony and she dreads what comes next even more than the lashes.

But why? Why does he play with me like this? What does he want from me? He knows the answer to every question they ask.

She assumes it is for her defiance. That he seeks to break her spirit. Never in her wildest dreams does it occur to her that it could be someone else he intends to destroy.

And why does he prevent the others from raping her as he does but give them free rein to do anything else?

Wailing disintegrates to a pitiful whimper and there is a knock on the door. "Ana, are you alright?"

The handle turns and suddenly aware, Ana prays she remembered to lock it. "I'm fine." Trembling, she takes herself closer to the full-length mirror on the wall. The stranger fades into the shadows and peering into them, Ana reaches for the ghost that remains. She touches it with pitiful tenderness and it reappears in a sudden blaze of sunshine as if it was waiting to pounce. She startles but holds her ground, her heart racing, her breath coming short and fast. She puts a hand up to its gaunt face and feels the brush of its fingers against hers. Haunting green eyes pierce a mass of strawberry blonde curls and an eery chill settles in Ana's bones.

She wears a white gown – this tormented stranger, that is open at the back. As she turns to look, Ana blushes with the realisation of how she exposed herself. Physical scars have begun to fade but not the memory of how they were inflicted and she falls to her knees, a prisoner to her flashbacks once more.

It is her ankle that frees her, begging for release so that she has to stretch her legs. She reaches down to touch it, her fingers skimming gingerly over ugly scar tissue and soft new skin but when she tries to massage the pain away, they are resisted by unyielding metal. She winces and her breath catches in her throat.

Bound hand and foot to that chair, she struggles to free herself despite the injury she aggravates by so doing for they are turning the dial on that evil machine and she knows what will happen next. She will lose the last shred of control she has over herself for there is nothing to compare with the excruciating pain inflicted by electricity.

She forces her eyes to open and look through the window onto Old Jerusalem. Taking deep breaths to slow her pounding heart, she examines her hands and wrists. They have plated the one that was broken as well and she still has ten normal looking digits. She lifts her gown, ignoring the sound of those who would intrude on her privacy, and looks at the fading scar that runs the length of her panty line. Taught, like her shrunken belly, between the prominent bones of her pelvis.

The voice of genuine concern rises above the noise in her head and she recognises Ruth. "Ana, my love, please open the door."

She picks herself off the floor. "I need the toilet. Please stay there Ruth," she pleads, anxious not to be left alone with the doctor. She takes a deep breath, letting it out with one last look at the more familiar stranger in the mirror and turns away.

It stings to pass urine but then she pulled the catheter out. It's a miracle that she can pee at all and hasn't been rendered incontinent by what they did to her, like so many of the wretches she treated with similar injuries. And then she remembers Caleb risking his life for her and closes tired eyes to bitter tears for what he suffers now.

"Hello Anais." The voice that wakes her is so familiar yet she can't quite place it.

Where? In bed again.

Was it all a dream? Ruth? The creepy doctor?

Her father beams down at her and she smiles back, hesitating to rise to his embrace.

"Thank God you're alright!"

"Hi. How are you?"

He nods curtly. "Well, thank you and you?"

"Good, thanks. Where's Caleb?"

"Caleb?" Her father looks stunned. "Where he should be."

Ana forces herself to stay calm. How does her father still command this effect on her? "Can I see him?"

"What?"

The General looks on her with disdain and she shrinks away from him, the terror of her childhood taking her by the throat again. She takes a deep breath. "I want to see him father. Where is he?"

"Anais, the bastard's where he should be for now and getting his just desserts, I hope."

"Father!" Ana rises with her anger. "What have you done?" She falls back to the bed, what little strength she has, almost spent and he looks on her in furious disbelief.

"What have I done? I'll tell you what I've done. Ensured you get the best medical care in the world and protected you from further harm. And you want to see that dog? A terrorist who betrays his country and puts you at the mercy of sadistic thugs?"

"No, you're wrong. He saved my life. He risked his life to bring me here. I saw it with my own eyes – how he brought the wounded to the hospital." She doesn't understand. Why does her father speak about him in this way?

"He's a terrorist Anais, and he deserves to hang with the others."

"No!" She shakes her head in despair. "Caleb is a good man and he's on our side. You have to believe me. Please let me see him." She musters all the energy she can, to push herself up and off the bed.

"Stay!" he barks but his efforts to restrain her are wasted. She falls back exhausted. In an instant she is a child again, helpless in the face of a power so much greater than her own, bewitched, for what seems an eternity, by ice blue eyes full of malice.

"Please father. Listen to what he has to say," she begs, recovering herself at last. "He's a good man. Please don't let them hurt him."

But it is already too late. Over six weeks have passed since Caleb sacrificed his freedom for her, placing himself at the mercy of her father's psychopathic whims and his violent half-brother, now a senior officer in Yamas, the special operations unit of the secretive Shin Bet. With its motto, 'Defender that shall not be seen,' and purpose to safeguard state security, her uncle's responsibility to it lies primarily in Arab-related counterterrorism and includes the interrogation of suspects, at which, she has every reason to believe, he excels.

There is a sharp tap at the door, followed immediately by a flustered looking Ruth. Probably in her early sixties, her hair neatly wound into a bun behind a starched linen hat, perfectly complements her tidy grey dress and she wears a bountiful apron such as Ana has only ever seen before on hospital wards staffed by the armed forces. Ruth marches over to sit beside her, tenderly brushing the hair out of her face, and puts an arm around her shoulders then turns to the intimidating soldier standing before them.

"I'm sorry sir, but I must ask you to leave. This is a hospital. A place for the sick and injured to find peace and healing."

"And you are?"

"We have met before. My name is Ruth. I am in charge here and respectfully request that you restrain yourself whilst under my jurisdiction as I would under yours. I will not have you, nor anyone else, upsetting my patients." She turns to Ana, her voice softening with the expression on her face. "How are you my dear?" Ana frowns. "You're quite safe here. No-one is going to hurt you." Ruth speaks gently as if to reassure a young child. "And you're doing really well." She shoots the General an angry look. "Do you want your father to leave now?"

"I want to see Caleb," Ana says quietly. "Please father." Ruth looks at him expectantly and he ignores her.

"Now listen to me carefully, Ana. There are answers to be had. Believe it or not, I came here to help you. Do you think that was easy? That it's usual for a General in the British army to be seconded to the Israeli Defence Forces? You can speak with me first and I will relay what you tell me. Perhaps then they will leave you in peace."

Ana shakes her head in utter confusion. "What are you talking about?"

"The last thing you want is for them to believe you're in this together."

"In what together?"

The General stares at her coldly but says nothing.

"I don't understand. Father, Caleb is an innocent man who sacrificed his freedom for my life."

"Now you're awake they won't be long. I suggest we talk it through before they come to question you."

"Who?"

"Your uncle and his cronies." She cannot believe what she is hearing. "And so far as seeing Caleb is concerned, your only chance will be to visit him in prison."

Ana takes a deep breath. "Then, would you organise that for me please?"

He takes his time to look her over. "I don't think you're in any fit state…"

"Please father! He saved my life."

"Alright. I'll do what I can… But don't get your hopes up too high. You must understand that he is guilty of the gravest of crimes. He will be brought to trial and sentenced. You can say your goodbyes and be done with him." And with that, showing no remorse, despite the way his daughter flinches, the General salutes the room and turns to leave.

There is movement in one corner. Startled, Ana sees the creepy doctor rise from a stool where he has obviously witnessed the whole scene.

"What are you doing here?"

"My job."

She shakes her head, watching with disbelief as he follows her father out, then turns to Ruth. "What was he doing here?"

"Snooping, I'd say."

"He gives me the creeps."

"Me too, but the powers that be, have allocated him to your case and there doesn't seem to be anything anyone can do about it."

"Has anyone tried?"

"Your father doesn't like him either but..." She is interrupted by the door opening and to Ana's astonishment, her father hurries back in, closing it quietly behind him. He looks around then brings a chair up to sit before them.

"Look Ana, I'm sorry. It's difficult to talk. I need to be careful." Ana looks to Ruth in confusion. "It's okay," her father reassures. "She's on our side."

Ana shakes her head. "Why are you here?"

"Because I'm useful to them and you need me, but for this to work to your advantage, you need to co-operate."

"With who?"

"Mossad. Institute for intelligence and special operations." Ana flinches. "There is information it wants from Caleb but so far, he has been unforthcoming. Caleb has been in an isolation cell from the time he dropped you off. The only way I can think of enabling you to see him, is by persuading his minders that he might talk to you. Even so, you must understand, this would be highly unusual. He is allowed no visitors."

Ana's heart lurches but her father doesn't give her the chance to interrupt.

"They've been watching you and waiting. Perhaps they think you know something." He holds his hand up to silence her. "Or perhaps they're just waiting for the opportunity to use you. I have influence still over my half-brother. We harbour a mutual respect, shall we say. If you agree, I will talk with him about how we might make this work to everyone's advantage." He looks behind him as if to check they are not being listened in to.

"What's going on father?" Ana is desperate now.

"Not sure. Something to do with Operation Cast Lead and Caleb being in Gaza at the time. Look, I need to go before I'm missed."

"Why are you doing this?"

"Because, believe it or not, I have always loved you. I may not have been blessed with the best parenting skills but I did the best I could. I didn't know any better." Ana shudders, her mind full of images she has only just learned to control. "I had the benefit of a confession, as well as hindsight," her father goes on to explain and suddenly his eyes fill with tears. "I'm so sorry." He takes her hands in his. "I would have killed him if I'd known."

It is as if her father has flicked a switch in her head. Transported back through all those years that separate them, she sits once more on his best friend's lap. A little girl, desperate to get away but terrified of the consequences should she tell.

"Ana?"

Ruth?

"But by then it was too late," her father continues as if she hadn't just been dragged to hell and back. "He was dying anyway." He searches her eyes, a plea for forgiveness written all over his face and Ana stares back speechless. "Were there others?" Ana closes her eyes. For a moment, there is a pause in her father's heavy breathing and then he heaves a great sigh. "Do you want to do anything about it?" Overwhelmed, she shakes her head, refusing to acknowledge that guilt. Not only for what she became but for the others she left at risk because, too terrified of the consequences, she did not tell. One day, it whispers, you will have no choice. But not today.

"I'm sorry." He sounds devastated and she is hopelessly lost. "I have to go. Ruth?"

"I'll take care of her."

It doesn't take long, though she finds the wait unbearable. The General returns with the creepy doctor who, she is told, has been tasked with accompanying them, "just in case."

Ana has eaten now. Her first meal for many weeks – rice, fish, salad and juice. It was delicious and she feels much better. Still a bit shaky on her feet and unbelievably weak, but that is not surprising. She has no need of a chaperone and definitely not that creepy doctor but it appears that she has no choice.

They are driven to the prison in a black volvo limo by a man in military uniform who salutes her father and opens the door to help her in. Ana is grateful because she doesn't want to let on how she would have struggled with even this simple task. She wanted to bring Ruth but they wouldn't let her. "You'll have forty-five minutes with him at most, anyway, and no contact except by telephone or the holes in the glass between you." To aggravate her distress, they brought a wheelchair which she flatly refuses to use.

The prison is everything she imagined. A stark, barren place surrounded by high walls, razor wire and observation towers. They have to go through several checkpoints and revolving doors to get in but, though she sees other visitors being body-searched, thankfully, this is a humiliation she is spared. She suspects that has something to do with the company she keeps but is too angry, now that she realises the extent of Caleb's predicament, to consider it too carefully.

They usher her into a bare white room divided by a partition, the upper half of which is a transparent screen with three holes at face height when she sits on the chair before it. Much to her relief, the doctor has disappeared and she wonders why he bothered to come at all. Her father props himself up against the wall behind her and now she waits. For an eternity. Watching the faint outline of a door in the wall opposite.

When at last it opens, for a moment she thinks there has been a mistake. In a brown jumpsuit, tall but hunched, with one shoulder at an awkward angle, hands cuffed before him and masses of unkempt hair falling about his face, this man is not someone she recognises. But then he looks up and, despite the wildness in his eyes, she knows it is him. Dirty, gaunt and pale, with dark shadows beneath his eyes, his bare feet covered in sores, Caleb is led, limping, from the door behind the screen.

He doesn't see her at first but when he does, in an instant, he is transformed and, as he rises to his full height, that indomitable spirit returns to shine through his passionate eyes.

"They didn't tell me it would be you. Hey, don't cry." He lifts his hands to the glass between them as if he could wipe her tears away and she cannot resist his glorious smile.

"What are they doing to you Caleb?"

He shakes his head. "Doesn't matter. You're here. Are they treating you well?"

Overcome, she nods. "Why, Caleb?"

He searches her eyes and that warmth she had almost forgotten, washes through her. "You have to trust me. Everything is going to be alright." He hesitates and a shadow passes over his face.

Able to bear it no longer, Ana turns on no-one in particular. "What has he done to deserve this?"

"Ana, come here. Look at me." Caleb reaches out, touching the screen between them and she puts her hands up to meet his. "There is nothing anyone can do to hurt me so long as you're safe. All I need is for you to get well again. Will you do that for me?"

Overshadowing this image of him full of the joy of seeing her, the reflection of her father grows. "We need to go." He takes her by the arm and she shakes herself free. "We can't leave him like this! I need to see his lawyer."

"Understand this. So far as the law is concerned, you are nothing to this man. Not related to him in any way. By blood or marriage. You have no power to influence what happens to him." Goosebumps prick her skin and Ana looks to the General in despair. "I'll speak with my brother but remember, what can be done depends on your co-operation. Understood?"

"Ana, I'm doing okay," Caleb reassures and with that, one of his guards ushers him with a gun towards the door. "Your place next time?"

She paces her room, unable to rest. It is so unfair. Bullies and thugs always seem to prevail. But then she remembers the children and is ashamed of her weakness.

There is a knock at the door and, without invitation, the doctor enters followed by a much older man, also in a white coat. "Hi Ana. This is Professor Liebonitz."

Ana shivers, feeling distinctly uneasy but determines not to allow herself to be riled. "Hello Professor," she says brightly.

"Hello Ana, how are you?"

"Fine, thank you and you?"

He smiles at her kindly. "Do you mind if I sit?" She shakes her head and smooths a place for him on the bed beside her. The professor makes himself comfortable and looks around the room. "Where is Ruth?"

"She went to do something for me. But it's okay." So long as he doesn't leave her alone with that creepy doctor.

"I've some news for you Ana, which might come as a shock given what you've been through."

Ana frowns. Resigned already to the probability of having been rendered infertile, she has consoled herself with thoughts of countless orphans in need of a good home and she knows her doctors will have checked for venereal disease. There is treatment for them all, even AIDS. She believes herself to be prepared for the worst he could tell her. "What is it?" she asks cautiously, nevertheless.

The professor looks upon her with paternal concern. "You are pregnant, Ana."

"What?" She is completely dumbfounded. The professor has succeeded in shocking her and she cannot believe him. Nothing could have have survived what she's been through. It isn't possible. She shakes her head. "You must be mistaken."

"I'm afraid not Ana. It's a miracle, I know, but you've had three positive pregnancy tests and an ultrasound."

Ana wishes Ruth was with her and that the Professor had come alone. "How far?"

"Nine or ten weeks by now."

It makes no difference. There can be only one way of telling if it is Caleb's. "Have I had anything that could harm it?"

The professor sighs. "Probably. Our priority was to save your life. The scan you had didn't reveal any abnormality but we will do another in a few weeks to be sure." He hesitates. "It's not too late for an abortion – if that's what you want."

"It's a miracle it survived," she murmurs.

"Indeed."

"And this might be the only chance I ever get," of a baby of her own. The professor nods. "Could you do genetic tests to determine if Caleb is the father?" She ignores his colleague's obvious disdain.

"Yes, but amniocentesis, as you know, is not without risk. It carries a one percent chance of miscarriage. Of course we could test the baby, but it will be too late by then for…"

"I couldn't abort," she interrupts. "This baby, whoever it came from, is as innocent a victim as I am, of this ghastly war and has clung to life despite the worst possible insults. It's a survivor and deserves every chance. I will love it whoever the father is." But she hopes he is Caleb.

"Do you have any influence over Caleb's fate?"

"I'm afraid not."

"I need to see him. In private," Ana persists. "Can you facilitate that for me?" He shakes his head. "Please?"

"I'll see what I can do but don't get your hopes up."

The professor takes her hand, kisses it and smiles at her. "You are a remarkable woman, do you know that?" She frowns. "To have survived what you did and come out fighting. I believe you saved the lives of the children you rescued… and their dog, not to mention those who were lucky enough to encounter you in their need for medical attention while you were in Syria."

She shakes her head. "I did nothing you, or anyone else wouldn't have done in the same circumstances." She searches the professor's eyes. "How can the world just sit back and watch what's happening to those poor people?"

"It's complicated," he replies. "No longer simply a dispute between an oppressed people and their autocratic president, Syria has become a battle ground for the world. We hesitate to help the opposition because Assad has the backing of Iran, Russia and China, as well as North Korea, and whilst he defends his stance as all that stands between peace and the civil war he fuels, nobody sees the real threat to world stability. The rise, not only of fundamental Islamists, but of the influence of Iran and Russia in the region." While the professor speaks, his protege frowns.

"Now Ana, I need to speak with you about your condition." Butterflies wake in the pit of her stomach and Ana wonders if she really wants to know. "I'm sorry, I didn't introduce myself properly. I am professor of Obstetrics and Gynaecology at Hadassah medical school and responsible for the majority of your abdominal surgery."

"And to be congratulated on the quality of his workmanship," the obsequious young doctor pipes up. "You wouldn't believe the mess you were in!"

Ana scowls at him.

"I apologise for my over enthusiastic friend here," the professor says awkwardly.

"It's okay. I'm sure he's right. Thank you for doing such a good job for me."

"Yes, well. If the repairs hold out, which they have done so far, you should soon be as good as new. The only thing I would say is that further trauma, through delivering a baby vaginally, especially if instrumental intervention was required, for example, could lead to irreparable damage." He looks to see if she has understood and she nods. "Also, the treatment you had for infection was inadequate and too late. There will probably be adhesions. To be frank, I would say the chances of you conceiving naturally in the future are slim at best." He's already confirmed that, though she hasn't had a chance for it all to sink in. "Luckily, however, you were free of venereal disease.

"I expect the orthopods and chest physicians will be along to speak with you later." His voice fades away as Ana fights another flashback. She gasps for air, every breath generating waves of excruciating pain and her tormentors watch over her, gloating as she drowns in her own blood.

The wail of a tormented beast, rough hands shaking her, shouting, then a sharp pain on her face.

"Ana, wake up!" She opens her eyes to the doctor and puts a hand on her burning cheek. Disorientated, she hesitates. The present re-asserts itself, igniting her anger and she turns it on her attacker.

"Get your hands off me!"

He relaxes his grip on her shoulders.

"That wasn't necessary," the professor admonishes. "Ana, I'm sorry. Are you alright?" She nods, looking into eyes full of concern. "How would you feel about me examining you?"

She frowns, resenting him not waiting for her to calm down. "That would be okay." He must have done so countless times already, she reassures herself. Just pretend his protege is a nurse. She lies on the bed and wishes Ruth was with her.

"All is well. You're healing remarkably quickly," the professor tells her when it is over and she smiles politely.

"May I speak with you privately?"

He turns to his companion, dismissing him with the shake of an arm.

"And frankly?" she continues when they are alone. He nods. "I'm sorry professor but there's something about that doctor. I don't want to be rude but I don't trust him. Could you assign someone else to my case or deal with me yourself, perhaps?"

ISHTAR

Nothing could have prepared her for her next visitor and, though they have never met Ana could not fail to recognise the beautiful doe-eyed woman who must have been waiting for the professor to leave. She comes alone with a grievance to bear against those responsible for her son's unenviable predicament and, though anticipated with much joy, Ana realises this meeting will be far from easy.

"So you are Ana."

She nods, longing to embrace Caleb's mother but it is clear that would be highly inappropriate. Strikingly elegant, in a fitted grey suit, heeled black court shoes and a simple pink scarf that covers her cropped dark hair, Ishtar bristles with anger born of fear.

"I am Ishtar."

"Hello Ishtar. It's a pleasure to meet you." Holding nothing back, Ana looks deep into the timeless eyes of the universe but Ishtar is angry.

"Why is it Ana, that, though he risked his life to save yours, my son is held prisoner by your uncle and treated worse than a criminal?"

Ana shakes her head. "I'm so sorry."

"What is your father doing to secure his release?"

"What he can."

The world starts to sway. Worms of light flash a warning and Ana steps back, seating herself when the bed presses hard behind her knees. Ishtar braces herself then, reassured that Ana isn't about to faint after all, turns to fetch a chair and sits to face her. "All I can say is that I hope you're worth it," she continues severely, as if nothing had happened. "It won't be the first time he risked his life for the sake of a woman."

Perhaps she really doesn't know what he does for a living then. Ana raises her eyebrows but says nothing.

"Has he told you about Selideh?"

Ana nods.

"And what happened to him afterwards?"

Actually he hasn't. A sharp pain catches in her chest.

"I thought not." Ishtar considers Ana carefully. "After they had made him watch Selideh stoned to death, they arrested him as a spy. It took seven months for us to get him out." Ana gasps, rising with her agitation to pace the room but waves of nausea overcome her and, dumping herself unceremoniously back onto the bed, she draws her knees up to her chest to hide her face.

"Did he tell you why he hates rats?"

"No."

"For seven months they kept him a filthy, rat-infested hole, starved and tortured. He was only seventeen. We didn't think he'd pull through and when his physical wounds began to heal, the nightmares began." Ishtar hesitates then drives her message home. "His treatment here will be little better."

Ana weeps tears of bitter grief. Relenting, Ishtar puts an arm around her. "Have you seen him?" Ana nods. "How is he?" She shakes her head but all she can say is that she loves him. She feels Ishtar's eyes boring into her. "You're pregnant, aren't you?"

"What?" Ana shakes her head. Gently at first but, when her defences are down, the flashbacks hit and, try as she might, she cannot rid herself of them now.

That stench poisons the air. Rough hands pin her down as her body is invaded, torn apart again. She hears screaming, feels herself being shaken and tries so hard to sink. Into the darkness. Nothingness.

"Ana. It's me, Ruth. Ana, look at me, please!"

Ruth's eyes are full of concern but she is smiling.

"It's over. Your mind is playing tricks on you. It's not real, okay? You're safe. I've got good news for you. About Caleb."

Ana remembers Ishtar and panics. "Don't tell him," she begs.

Ishtar shakes her head. "I'll leave that for you to do. Forgive me for being so unkind." She hesitates. "He's special, you know?" Ana nods but words fail her. "Did he tell you the meaning of his name?"

"Caleb?"

"Sargon. Only king. True."

It has caused him more trouble than she will ever know but the General has secured some time for Ana with Caleb alone. "He's coming here, can you believe it?" Ana shakes her head, "but on condition," Ruth adds, ominously. Ana frowns. "They intend to bug your rooms before he comes and there is certain information they expect you to extract from him."

"What information?"

"I don't know but you need to co-operate. You'll be briefed beforehand. There'll be guards posted outside your room and in the hospital grounds. They have orders to shoot if he tries to escape."

"He won't. Ana's all that keeps him here." Ana stares incredulously at her but Ishtar does not elaborate.

"D'you think he has any choice in the matter?" Ruth's patience clearly wears thin. Ishtar shrugs.

"That's crazy! No way he could he get out of there!" Ana counters.

Ishtar raises her eyebrows. "The two of them defy belief."

"Who?"

"Sargon and Tuan."

"Are you saying that Caleb could just walk out of there?"

"With Tuan's help."

"How?"

"I don't know but it won't be the first time they've got themselves out of an impossible situation."

"What do they want from Caleb?"

"Sargon. How should I know? The first I ever hear of his shenanigan's, is when he needs my help." Ana frowns. "Now, if you'll excuse me, there are papers I need to draft, people I need to consult. Perhaps your uncle will allow my son a visit from his mother." She takes a good look at Ana standing before her. "I'm sorry," she says abruptly but her demeanour clearly softens. "I can see you love him. Get well and look after my precious grandchild, okay?"

"You told her?" Ruth asks when Ishtar has gone.

"No. Ruth when can I see Caleb?"

"I don't know. Soon. Now eat. You must be famished."

Until she was starving, food was never high on Ana's agenda and even now, though her body craves nourishment, the thought of it turns her stomach.

"What would you like?"

She shrugs. "You knew I was pregnant?"

Ruth nods.

"How did it survive?"

"A miracle. This baby clings to life just as its mother did."

Ana smiles. "I'll eat whatever you want me to Ruth. How did it go?"

"My husband will have a word with the mayor and we've left a message with a lawyer in the city. An Israeli married to a Palestinian, famous for upholding human rights. If anyone can help Caleb, it'll be him." She searches Ana's face. "Are you alright?"

"I need Caleb."

"I know."

Unbearable time drags, endless days turn into weeks and sleepless nights blur reality with illusion, nauseating flashbacks morphing with terror for Caleb.

Ana is alone when at last they come. Her father with Ruth beaming a reassuring smile to counteract his scowl and an entourage which fans out, spilling into the bathroom to examine everything. Windows, doors, the cupboard, her bedside cabinet, under the bed, even the lights and chairs. She doesn't see it but they will be laying bugs, removing anything that could be used as a weapon and securing escape routes.

Then they come to her. Two of them pull up chairs to face her sitting on the edge of the bed. The General stands to attention behind them.

"This arrangement is exceptional," the one that looks like an eagle in a soldier's uniform informs with no introduction. "For it to be successful, we need your co-operation. Do you understand?" Ana nods, resentful of the way he speaks to her and the implication that she is guilty of something she knows nothing about.

"We need information from Caleb and believe you can help us get it."

She scowls. "What the hell is going on and why do you think he'll tell me what you've failed to extract in all this time?" Her father shakes his head, glaring at her and, though she tries to ignore him, the tension in her peaks.

"Because he cares what happens to you and this is his last chance." The officer doesn't give her the chance to express her outrage. "Caleb was in Gaza between late December 2008 to January 2009. We need to know why, what he did and the names of those he met up with. That is all."

"What happens if you get that information?"

"His detention will be over."

"He'll be free to go?"

Looking straight into her eyes and without hesitation, the officer nods. "Of course," he lies.

Ana glares at him but he does not flinch and her agitation gets the better of her. "What guarantee can you give me that Caleb will come to no harm?" The officer smiles but says nothing.

"We'll make sure he doesn't," her father adds impatiently.

"And that he'll be free to go?" She is desperate now.

"That too."

"And those he names?"

"What happens to them is none of your concern," eagle face returns.

"So, he's guilty of being in the wrong place at the wrong time, nothing more?"

"That, I'm afraid, is classified information. As you may have realised, he has suffered not inconsiderably as a result of his non-compliance. We believe you to be in the position to put an end to that."

Dread sinks to the pit of Ana's stomach. "And we'll both be free to leave when this is over?"

"Yes. Your father, the nurse and the doctor pay witness to this meeting."

"What if he won't tell me what you want to know?"

"Then nothing changes."

"But what you're doing is wrong and illegal!"

"What are we doing?"

"Holding him prisoner on false charges. Not giving him access to proper legal representation. Torturing him!"

"You must be mistaken."

Ana closes her eyes, waves of exhaustion overwhelming her capacity to focus. "When can I see him?"

"Tomorrow. Four p.m."

"You have an hour. Not a moment longer. If the prisoner leaves the room before then, he will be shot. Do you understand?" Ana flinches and closes her eyes with a reluctant nod.

Her father returns with four guards flanking Caleb, no longer wearing the brown jumpsuit but still in handcuffs. He looks dazed and squints in the bright sunlight flooding the room. Ruth heads for the blinds. Ana turns to Caleb instead, desperate to be close, to feel the warmth of his body against hers, but wary also. She is no longer the woman he knew. She watches as they release him, wondering at how loud the keys are, turning so slowly as the tension in the room mounts.

Without a word, his minders retreat and, rolling her eyes at the General's curt order not to let the prisoner out of her sight, Ruth slams the door loudly behind them. She leans heavily against it as if to keep them out then, with a shake of her head, goes to the bathroom, closing this door also, discretely behind her. They hear the splutter of water as she turns the bath-taps on and Ana stands frozen before Caleb.

"Hi. How are you?" Tears prick and she stifles a sob, speechless in the face of his suffering. He opens his arms with a smile and his eyes are full of joy. He kisses her gently on the forehead, pulling her close and, as he rubs her back, unable to help herself, Ana sobs into his chest.

The bathroom door opens and for a brief moment until it closes again, the sound of running water drowns out all else. Ashamed of her weakness, Ana pulls herself together. She hears Ruth go to the bedside cabinet, tap a number into the phone and order food. "You have just under an hour," she tells them. "You could do with a wash Caleb and I suggest you let me take a good look at you. I'll record your injuries. My husband can pass that information on to your lawyer. Now be quick, you also need to eat.

"Can't believe they can get away with this," she mutters as she busies herself organising them both.

Caleb raises an eyebrow. "Thanks, but I've survived far worse and I'm here to see Ana."

"We must document any evidence. Ana can help. Now go. Forget I'm here for a minute."

Caleb smiles fondly. "Would you like a bath?" he asks and Ana shakes her head. She feels hot, sick and the world is beginning to recede. She feels Caleb's arms tense and finds herself leaning into them. He lifts her and she snuggles into him.

The sound of running water. Warm humidity hitting as the

bathroom door swings open and the soothing touch of cold tiles as he places her carefully on her feet. Waves of faintness threaten, he helps her to the ground and she sits, her head between her knees until they pass.

The sun plays games with fleeting white clouds, shimmering reflections from the water, rotating on the white walls around them. Ruth calls from outside. "Remember to turn the taps off."

Caleb peers into Ana's face. "Okay now?" She nods. "Don't go anywhere." He stands, turning to test the water and, suddenly bereft, she follows, leaning over to help. His shirt hangs open at the neck, flashes of light revealing bruises and scars on his bare chest and she is so sorry.

He follows her eyes. "I'm fine," he reassures, "and it won't be much longer, promise." She remembers the intruders in her room. Wide-eyed, she puts a finger to her lips. "They've bugged the rooms," he says. "I know. What have they told you?"

"They want information for your freedom."

He glances at the water, his eyes ablaze. "And they expect you to get it from me? Nothing will buy my freedom, Ana. It is for me to take what is rightfully mine." He smiles at her. "Trust me." He turns the hot tap full on and whispers into her ear. "I'm an expert at escaping impossible situations." He kisses her on the ear, turns both taps off and returns to kiss her forehead. "Now let's make the most of our time together. Ruth thinks I should wash and to be honest…"

"It's okay. Don't mind me."

"Don't suppose you'd like to join me?" She shakes her head. "Another time. I'll be quick."

He strips, throwing his clothes in an untidy pile onto the floor. With a wink, he steps into the bath and immerses himself and she watches, blushing, unable to take her eyes off him. He too, has changed so much since they last saw each other. A lifetime ago. A world away. But none of what has passed makes any difference to how she feels about him.

He sits, searching her eyes and she hands him the soap. He lathers himself and she watches a shadow pass over his handsome face. He rises to his knees, leaning over to place a wet hand on her belly and she loses herself. Trembling, she falls back to her haunches and stares at something visible only to her, struggling to discern now from then.

"Ana, look at me."

Splash of water. Rush of displaced air. Strong arms wrapping around her, wet against her skin. Thick, unkempt hair dripping onto her back and his breath tickling as he whispers into her ear. "It's alright, we're safe." He holds her tight until she relaxes then, resting back on his heels, peers into her face. "Look at me," he entreats for she remains lost somewhere between the past and the present.

She becomes aware of him on his knees before her, dripping wet. Naked. It is surreal. She laughs. "I love you," he says. "Will you marry me?"

Dread does its worst and she hesitates. "There's something I have to tell you," she says and he raises his eyebrows. "I'm pregnant." She waits fearfully but nothing changes. Caleb still kneels before her, his eyes full of adoration and love.

"I know." He looks down and places a hand on her belly. Delicious coolness quenches the fire inside and she looks on him in confusion. "And they're mine."

He must have misunderstood. "What do you mean?"

"Twins. Yours and mine."

She dismisses the probability that they have driven him mad. "Were you there when they did the scan?"

"They wouldn't let me anywhere near you."

"Then how do you know?"

"I just do." The turbulence in his eyes increases. "I'm a twin too. But I never knew my brother. He was taken when we were babies."

Ana stares at him, dumbfounded, something elusive threatening her sanity. "By who?"

236

"I don't know. Baltasar used to say the devil stormed out of the desert. The devil demanded one of the twins in return for everyone's lives, he'd say, and mother chose to keep you."

"Baltasar? Your brother?"

"Yes. He was only small but he never forgot. Drove everyone mad hiding me when our parents were away. So the devil couldn't find me."

"What happened to your twin?"

Caleb shakes his head. "Our parents wouldn't talk about it. Mum got angry if ever we mentioned him but we could see that really she was scared and sometimes she'd sink into a deep depression. So we stopped asking.

"I'd dream I was him sometimes. Scared witless, lonely, starved. Beaten half to death when I disobeyed. Savaged until I became a monster to rival the one who stole me."

Ana shivers. "Do you think he's still alive?"

Caleb nods. "I saw him once. By chance. We never spoke but we recognised each other. Twin thing, I guess. I could have rescued him but there were others and I thought he could save himself. They were trapped in a burning building. The floor was disintegrating beneath my feet, the walls about to collapse. The others were closest, easiest to get to, so I got them out first. By the time I came back for him it was too late." Caleb hangs his head and the lines in his face deepen.

"But you said he was still alive."

"Something in him died." Caleb puts a hand gently on Ana's belly. "But now it comes full circle."

She shakes her head. "How does this change anything?"

"I had no control over what happened to us but now… This is a fresh start. I won't let anyone harm our babies. They'll grow up knowing they were wanted, loved and treasured."

As raw and vulnerable as it is possible to be, with all the odds stacked against him, Caleb is so confident and, despite herself, Ana's hope revives. "Couldn't you have got me here without giving yourself to the Israelis?" she whispers.

"There isn't anywhere I'd rather be," Caleb replies, "than as close to you as possible and nothing can hurt me so long as you are safe."

There is a knock at the door then Ruth's voice. "There are clean clothes on the chair and Ana's mobile. Could you get some photos of your injuries Caleb?"

He smiles at Ana. "Okay."

Mouth-watering smells waft into the bathroom as they open the door. Roasted onions, fried meat, garlic, tomatoes and herbs. Cardamom scented chickpeas, fresh bread and salad. "Now eat," Ruth orders, making herself discrete and Caleb draws up a chair to face Ana sitting on the edge of the bed.

He eats ravenously, watching her with a contented smile. Now and again, he brings a forkful to her lips but she is mindful of why he is here and cannot be tempted. "Fifteen minutes left," Ruth calls out. Caleb washes down the last few scraps and Ana pours herself too, water laced with lemon, mint and ice.

"There are questions," she starts but he shakes his head.

"Not now." Placing the tray on the floor beneath the bed, he pushes his chair away and falls to his knees. "Ana," he says, "I need to know before they come. Will you marry me?"

She gasps for this time she has truly heard him and there is so much otherwise to distract. "Yes, of course," she says hurriedly. "I love you Caleb and we belong together, but…"

"Indeed!" He rises as she gets to her feet, takes her face in his hands and touches her lips with his. She cannot resist.

"I wish we could do it now," she breathes when they come up for air.

"Maybe we can," he says as if there was nothing in the world to hinder them. He calls to Ruth and she hurries out of the bathroom, certain something is wrong.

"What is it? Are you alright, my dears?" She looks anxiously from one to the other.

"We wanted you to be the first to know. We're engaged to be married!" Caleb informs her, "and we wondered if you could help us."

"Congratulations!" Ruth looks happy but confused.

"This is a convent, yes?" She nods. "So it has a church. People can be married here."

She shakes her head. "Your father would never allow it," she tells Ana. "You may not even be allowed to see each other again. Until Caleb is cleared of those trumped up charges, of course."

"But if I could get myself there could you arrange for someone to marry us?"

Ruth hesitates. "Perhaps."

"Tomorrow?"

"No!"

"The next day then," Caleb pleads. "How about three o'clock."

There is a sharp knock at the door. "Wait!" Ruth shouts. "I don't know if I can arrange it that quickly and how on earth would you get here? Do you think they'll just let you walk out?"

"They won't be able to stop me," he says with such conviction that Ana almost believes him. "Three o'clock in the chapel, the day after tomorrow. You'll be there Ruth?"

"Caleb are you mad?" Ana demands looking around with an exasperated shrug.

"I'm afraid you're going to have to trust me. Please Ruth. Be there, okay?"

"Have you seen your mother yet?"

Caleb shakes his head in dismay. "What's she doing here?"

"Looking for you." The knock comes again, and tutting at them to hurry, Ruth rushes to the door. Caleb pulls Ana close and the door flings open.

"That's it. Time's up. Get your bloody hands off my daughter, you scoundrel!" But even as he speaks, the General winks at them.

Ana straightens her clothes and scowls furiously at the young doctor standing beside him. "He's no scoundrel father. Caleb is an innocent man who has been wronged, my husband to be and the father of your grandchildren." Stunned, her father hesitates and Ana takes the advantage. "I love him and he loves me."

"What are you talking about girl?"

"I'm pregnant. Caleb is the father and we're going to be married."

"Over my dead body! You have no idea who the father is. He could be any one of the thugs who raped you. It should have been aborted before you even knew about it."

Gritting his teeth, Caleb clenches his fists and Ana puts a hand over his. "Then you would have been guilty of murdering your grandchildren," she tells them all coolly.

The General turns to the door, clicking his fingers at the guards and, as they approach the prisoner, turns on him in anger. "You may think you can seduce my daughter with your fancy fuckery but I will not be moved. You will pay for your treachery!"

"Father, please! Why are you so angry with us? What has Caleb done to deserve this?" Her father looks to the floor and shakes his head.

"Take him away," he orders but Caleb stands his ground.

"General, may I say something?" he asks and without waiting for a reply, "I love Ana with all that I am. I know that you love her too and want what's best for her. I promise you that I will always care of her, love, honour and protect her and that I will do everything in my power to see that our children grow into happy, confident, considerate people.

"I know we have our grievances and there is information I cannot divulge for fear of endangering innocent men, women and children, but I mean you no harm.

"I will go with you and endure whatever your brother chooses to inflict on me but I must ask one favour of you." He turns to the young doctor gloating over him. "This man is not who you think he is. He is dangerous. Please don't let him near your daughter." The General scowls, snapping his fingers and when the guards apprehend him, Caleb does not resist. He looks the General earnestly in the eyes but, though they flicker, there is no response. Caleb turns to Ruth. "Don't let him go near her," he pleads and Ruth nods, watching as the doctor turns first to the General to perform an obsequious bow, then to Caleb.

"So what gives you the right to use her as the others did?" he demands.

Eyes ablaze, Caleb clenches his fists but handcuffed, he is easily overpowered by the guards. "How dare you! Of all the men in this room, Caleb is the only one who hasn't abused me in some way. He's the innocent one here! We love each other. So far as we're concerned, we're already married and I'm pregnant with my husband's children."

The doctor smiles vindictively. "There was only one foetus on the scan." He sounds so smug.

"You'll see." Ana turns to Caleb. "I'll be alright," she smiles, coming closer. "Promise. I'll take good care of our babies." Quick as a flash, she dodges the nearest guard, putting her arms around Caleb for one last time until they pull her away. I will not give them the satisfaction of knowing I'm afraid, she tells herself and watches calmly as they lead him out.

"Caleb is a terrorist and a murderer," her father tells the room but, as his entourage leaves, he hesitates, waiting until Ruth has shooed the last of them away before closing the door discretely behind them. He motions for them to follow him into the bathroom and, without a word, turns the bath-taps on full blast.

"I have to make this look convincing," he says into Ana's ear and she shakes her head in astonishment.

"So...what is he supposed to be guilty of?"

"The murder of an officer with the Israeli Defence Forces. On the 27th of December 2008, the Israelis started an offensive they called Operation Cast Lead, its stated goal – to stop rocket attacks into Israel from, and the smuggling of weapons into, Gaza. On

3rd January, 2009, after attacking what it considered to be military targets and administrative organisations, despite these being in densely populated cities, Israeli Defence Forces started a ground invasion which resulted in over a thousand Palestinian deaths.

"For some reason we have yet to establish, Caleb was in Gaza city at the time. He claims to have been helping a friend rebuild his home. The officer in question, was a little too enthusiastic, shall we say, in taking revenge for the casualties inflicted by Palestinian militants on Israeli citizens. Also, for his best friend who died under interrogation in one of their detention cells.

"He took a young boy as a human shield then ordered the child's home to be bulldozed with his mother and younger sister still inside. Caleb witnessed this and saw that the troops were heading for his friend's house next. He rescued the boy and the officer was shot dead."

"But Caleb didn't shoot him?"

"So he alleges. He says he was unarmed."

"My husband and I have instructed a solicitor to act on Caleb's behalf," Ruth interrupts. "We trust he will be granted full and private access to his client and that his captors co-operate with all investigations."

The General shakes his head. "You have no idea, lady." He heaves a great sigh. "I would suggest his solicitor contacts General Cohen directly, because my getting involved in Caleb's defence will compromise any potential I may have to help him." He looks with a perplexed frown at Ana. "Grandchildren?" he asks. "Are you sure you know what you're doing Ana?"

"Absolutely positive father. Caleb and I belong to each other."

"They can be very persuasive these MacEoins, I must say."

"You've met his mother?"

"Yes, and now I must go."

"Father?" He nods. "I had a memory stick. Did that make it out with me?"

"Nothing made it out with you."

242

ESCAPE

She perches restlessly on the edge of the front pew, Ruth beside her, doing her best to calm them both. Her husband paces the isle.

"Jacob, will you sit down! Look, the poor girl is beside herself yet manages to sit still."

Suddenly aware of her legs twitching against the unforgiving wood, Ana stills them and looks at Ruth. "This is madness. What were we thinking?"

"Having second thoughts are we?"

"No..." Ana shakes her head. "But how can he possibly get away from there?"

"He said he'd be here and neither hell nor high water will keep him." Ana's heart resumes its race as she imagines the worst. "Anyway, the priest isn't here yet. P'raps they're on the same bus." Ruth laughs nervously and Ishtar puts a comforting hand on Ana's knee.

"He's on the way," she informs her and Ana's nerves settle a little. It means so much to her, that Caleb's mother came but there is sadness in her eyes and it falls on Ana like a soft blanket of snow. If only he could be here too. Caleb's father, whose fate she cannot bring herself to contemplate.

"Is he still alive?" Ishtar shakes her head, excusing herself to make her way to the altar and when she bows her head in prayer before a simple crucifix, Ana does likewise.

A gush of cool sweet air, the chirruping of cicadas and birdsong flood the chapel as one of its great doors swings open and Ana jumps up. She gasps, for the afternoon sun casts a glow around him and, as he rushes towards her, his cheeks flushed, his eyes are bright with anticipation and love. Defying the band that would hold it back, thick dark hair falls untidily into his handsome face but, clean shaven, he wears a spotless white shirt that billows about him and new black trousers.

"You are so beautiful!" He takes her in his arms, relinquishing her, at last, for the others and, hardly able to bear his absence, Ana watches as he greets them one by one. "D'you remember Tuan?" Caleb looks on her with concern but now is not the time for nightmares and with his best friend's embrace, they shrink into the shadows of her joy.

"Thank you Tuan."

"No worries." He says it softly, taking her to arm's length for a good look at her and his grin dispels a world of pain.

Clearly their efforts were not wasted. The cream dress Ruth found is simple but flattering, the beauty of the flowers, enhanced by special memories of the hours spent collecting and arranging them in her hair. Freshly washed, Ruth has managed to pile this onto her head, pinning it so that only a few wayward locks fall onto her shoulders, these laid bare to reveal her neck. She wears a simple necklace. A gold chain with a green stone that reflects the colour of her eyes. Malachite or jade perhaps. With matching earrings and pale, high heeled sandals borrowed from one of the nuns.

"Lucky bastard!"

Ruth tuts. "Remember where you are now, boys!"

"Hi Ruth." Tuan turns his charm on her, kissing her hand with an extravagant bow. "Heard so much 'bout you, and this must be ya husband." They shake hands, embracing briefly and then he turns to Ishtar.

"Why aren't you in prison like Caleb?"

"S'good to see you too Ishtar. As you can see, currently neither of us are in prison, though, I grant you, that circumstance is likely very soon to change. Fortunately for me, however, I am not bound to my chains by love as is poor Caleb here and someone has to take care of him as well ya know." He bows ostentatiously before her and she shakes her head with a smile.

"You are incorrigible!" She tells him and surrenders to his embrace.

"I'm afraid the priest isn't here yet. Can't imagine what might have happened to him." Ruth is really worried now.

"It's alright Ruth, he'll be here. Besides, if you don't mind, I could do with a few private moments with my bride."

Her every sense heightened as he leads her to the back of the Church, Ana takes it all in. The sunlight that pores through coloured glass, laying a bright carpet before their feet to rise up the plain block walls. Glittering dust motes swimming in the beams it throws between thick stone columns and how these hold the roof so far above them. Row upon row of dark wooden benches, empty now but for their handful of guests. The central isle leading to the understated alter and the crucifix that is such a vivid reminder of every agony inflicted on mankind. The sound of peace and the smells of incense, wood, old books and polish. She feels his hand around hers – warm and strong. The calluses, soft hairs and firm give of the veins that run along the back.

He seats them beside each other, placing a gentle hand over her belly and something stirs deep inside. "We need to get out of here while you can."

He shakes his head. "When you're well enough and it's safe, then we'll go. Trust me Ana, we're nearly there." But she is filled with dread. "Look I'm here. Fit and well. Nothing's going to happen.

"So, where do you want to go?"

A cold chill blows through her and she shivers in the warm afternoon sun. "To see the children."

Caleb nods, unhappily. "Za'atari then."

She has to go. At least once.

"They're all there," he reassures. "Rahim, Foued, Dua and Saad. Asalan too. Safe with Rahim's mother. Apparently they were not short of offers but the big boys are managing it all perfectly well."

245

Ana remembers with a smile. "And Aadil?"

"We'll get him out. His sister too." Caleb looks at her thoughtfully. "Where do you want to have our babies Ana?" Sunlight, noise and wind blow in behind them and she startles. The priest is here at last, already fully robed. He closes the massive door behind him, running its thick bolt home and turns to face them.

"Sorry I'm late. Got held up." He surveys his handiwork then looks at Caleb. "That should keep them out for a while. Now shall we get on?" He hurries to the altar, depositing some paperwork there, bows his head in brief prayer and with the sign of the cross, turns, beckoning his audience closer. "May I have the betrothed?"

It is a simple ceremony. Though obviously anxious about what may interrupt them at any moment, the priest does not seem rushed. Caleb has learn't his marriage vows by heart and when he looks into her eyes, promising "to love and to cherish, till death do us part, according to God's holy law," Ana feels something momentous stir within her. The priest declares them man and wife, inviting Caleb to kiss the bride but, as he does this, there is a thunderous banging on the door.

"Ignore it," the priest commands. "Do you have the rings?" From nowhere Tuan spirits two simple gold bands. Ana holds her breath. They fit perfectly for now. The priest beckons them all to the altar to witness the newlyweds sign the marriage register and, when thunder resounds through the chapel once more, apologises for the noise with a frown. Ensuring everyone has made his or her mark correctly, he waves them back to their seats and proceeds to read to them about Love from 1 Corinthians, 13.

A nun appears from the vestry, followed closely by another clergyman. They go to unbolt the door, opening it a fraction to speak with the hooligans outside but there is no holding them back. The priest continues his address undaunted. A troop of armed soldiers led by the General, bursts into the church but when he realises what he is witnessing, with one hand he silences the clatter of boots echoing off ancient stone walls and takes a seat.

The service continues regardless. After his address, the priest leads the congregation in prayer with the newlyweds kneeling before him at the altar. When that is done, he raises them, turning them to face each other, brings their hands together and congratulates them. Once more, he tells Caleb he may kiss the bride and they lose themselves in each other to clapping, cheering and whistling. From somewhere, someone pulls a camera and the priest turns to the newcomers.

"You are welcome to this holy place," he says, "and we are happy for you to share this joyous occasion. As you know, the joining of a man and woman in holy matrimony is a holy sacrament, through which they are united and become one. For, as the Lord Jesus said, for this reason a man shall leave his father and mother and be joined to his wife and the two shall become one flesh. So then, they are no longer two but one flesh. Therefore, what God has joined together, let not man separate. Matthew 19 verses 5 and 6."

The General rises with due anger but his eyes sparkle despite the gravity of his words. "The prisoner must be returned at once."

"Would you allow the newly wedded couple a few moments before your son-in-law comes with you?" the priest implores.

The General shakes his head, angrily. "We'll be outside. Ten minutes." He nods at the soldiers. "If he leaves the church without us, he will be shot." He starts to follow them out but as the last of them passes through the door, closes it behind him and turns back. "I need to speak with you both," he says urgently, leaning against it. "Caleb, they're planning to move you on. To another unit where I have absolutely no influence. I don't know how much longer I can put them off but they've given me two weeks at most. I would suggest you make your escape before then."

"Thanks for the warning General. I'll see to it," Caleb says curtly and Ana panics.

"Caleb, you must go. Without me if need be. Please, before it's too late! I'll get them to bring my scan forward. Could he come to that now we're married?"

Her father shakes his head grimly. "Impossible."

"Why? He's here now, isn't he?"

"Yes and I'd like to know how you did that Caleb. Fortunately for you, these are my men and will take orders from no-one but me. I trust you'll make the exchange back, as discretely." Ana looks at them both in confusion and her father smiles grimly. "So far as his guards are concerned, Caleb is still in prison. If he can get his imposter out before the next cell check, they may be none the wiser.

"That young sycophant, the doctor, by the way, is watching my every move. He believes me still to be the psychopathic, controlling father you grew up with." The General clears his throat. "Who hates Caleb with a vengeance. For reasons I have yet to establish, he has it in for you, Caleb and is reporting everything back to his father who, incidentally, is a general in the Israeli Defence Forces."

"He was there."

"Who was where, Caleb?"

"The doctor in the white coat. Doing his national service no doubt, for he was no soldier. He took a child as a human shield. I put my hands in the air and walked slowly towards him, pleading with him to let the boy go, to take me instead. But he panicked and in the commotion that followed, shot his commanding officer."

"And they think it was you?" Caleb shrugs.

"Trouble is," the General explains, "you saw something you shouldn't have. Correct me if I'm wrong. Terrible atrocities committed that day, were witnessed by you and those you protect." Caleb says nothing. "Unfortunately, it was never going to be a simple matter of making you disappear. The security services want them all. I hoped they would bring you to trial but that's looking increasingly unlikely."

"His name is Michael."

"That creepy doctor?"

Caleb nods, considering Ana with a frown. "He burned innocent people to death that day. Men, women and children. He ordered them to be barricaded into their houses, torched and any who tried to escape, shot. Then he had the evidence bulldozed. He wasn't the only one. I couldn't stop it. No-one could. We couldn't match their fire power." Caleb hesitates, his eyes dark and turbulent. "How the hell did he ever become a doctor? He mustn't be allowed to get to Ana. Do you understand?"

The General nods. "I'll see to it and if I can persuade them to let you attend the ultrasound now that you're married, though that'll take some explaining. " He clears his throat. "Go from there. I'll do my best to clear the way for you." He looks at Ishtar and Tuan standing behind them now. "They should head for Jordan via the Sheikh Hussain Bridge at Beit She'an," he tells them. "I'll divert the search to the Allenby Bridge. Now Caleb, we must go."

They race north towards Beit She'an in a seven seater sheroot. Ruth and her husband insisted on coming too, so far as the border to see them safely into Jordan. "Just in case there're any more complications." Exhausted and injured, Caleb languishes in the back seat for he was moved out of the General's jurisdiction over a week ago. Ana snuggles into him, elation vying with the ache in her heart and when he touches her face with a blood-stained hand, she takes it and kisses it tenderly.

Deep inside something flutters, catching her unawares for she has only just learned to recognise what this is. So faint, like wind moving in her belly, that she wouldn't have noticed had they not seen it on the scan. Joy overcame his pain and she had been overwhelmed for, though unaware of any doubt, here lay the confirmation she had been waiting for.

That was the first time she really felt them move, as if they had been waiting to reveal their secret. As she remembers, Ana turns unconsciously to Tuan and smiles gratefully, for without his strength, wit and courage she would have witnessed it alone. Caleb would never have made it. How he did that, got him out of prison without anyone noticing, she has yet to learn and then to the hospital without attracting attention.

She feels his hand heavy on her belly – the hand of her husband, and considers that they have committed themselves to each other forever. Such a strange, bitter-sweet feeling comes over her. Elation shackled by harsh reality and she struggles to convince herself that soon they will be free.

A smile relaxes the lines of pain etched into his face and with his eyes closed, Ana sees that he recalls it too. The moment their baby lifted its arm to reveal his little sister. Two of them indeed. Truly a miracle. She hasn't allowed herself yet, to consider what this means, the physical effect carrying twins will have on her, the risks to them all of inadequate antenatal care and the implications for all of their futures. For now there can be only one priority and to that end they speed into the shimmering dust.

The heat rises despite air gushing through open windows and she closes her eyes as the world flies past. Over the roar of the engine, their driver sings loudly to a radio blasting Arab pop-music, reassuring her of how well they blend into the local scene. They pass without interruption through the one checkpoint that could hinder their two hour journey towards the Sea of Galilee. Sheikh Hussain Bridge will be the real testing point however. Though Jacob has procured the necessary paperwork, they came into Israel illegally. None of them had reckoned with the Israelis moving Caleb on so soon and it remains to be seen whether the General's influence still reaches far enough to get them over the border safely.

She must have drifted in the stifling heat and it is the lack of something that wakes her though she is hardly aware until the significance of it hits home. The taxi-driver has stopped singing and now, as the soldiers approach, the radio dies with his engine.

So this is it. Suddenly wide-awake, Ana looks at Caleb, discretely covering all but his face with the long white robes they have dressed him in. She smiles nervously and he nods confident reassurance, a glimmer of hope in his tired eyes. It is time.

There is a commotion outside. Thankfully, they are not the only ones trying to pass over. Jacob gets out to deal with the paperwork. If asked, he will say that the injured man fell and that he is going to relatives to convalesce. They will be waiting on the other side should anyone wish to check, he will say. He will do his best to prevent the border officials stamping their passports for many Arab countries, including Syria will deny entry to anyone who has visited Israel and he will pay their departure tax. Hopefully that will be enough to get them through the Israeli check-point and onto the shuttle that will take them across the bridge. They anticipate no problems passing through the immigration process into Jordan.

Ishtar pays the taxi while they disembark, carefully helping the injured man as inconspicuously as they can. Already it is clear that all is not as it should be and, as Ana watches without looking directly at the animated scene unfolding nearby, a flustered Jacob returns with an exasperated shrug of his shoulders. She prepares herself for the worst. She will stay with Caleb come what may. There is nothing that matters to her more than him, not even their tiny perfectly formed babies.

Terrifying emotion rises in her, making her gasp for breath as hot tears spring to her eyes but then she feels the comforting touch of his hand. So brief. She longs to hold it. To stroke the back of it with her fingers. To feel its sturdy veins, the tendons that tighten as he gives her an affectionate squeeze and the warmth of those calloused palms that can convey such magic. But she has been instructed to deny all knowledge of them – Caleb, Tuan and Istar. For now she must pretend to be a young English doctor taking a well-earned break to explore the Middle East.

Jacob returns without the papers. Visibly struggling to control his agitation, he tells them to follow him. "Just a formality," he mutters and Ana shrinks beneath the suspicious eyes of hyper-alert guards. One speaks into a walkie-talkie. A phone rings from the little office that serves border control and she is sure they are being watched.

"This way." Jacob goes first. Alone into a cubicle with two Israeli soldiers – both men, and the fear in Ana rises. Surely they aren't going to interrogate them all, individually? Her heart pounds so that they must see it shaking her whole body. Her tongue sticks to the roof of her dry mouth but, anxious not to draw attention, she denies herself any of the water still left in her bottle. She presses her clammy hands into her cotton dress, fighting the urge to wriggle her toes for there is nowhere to hide them in these elegant sandals and steps forward, forcing herself once more, to do what needs doing regardless of what it will cost her.

The cubicle is bare apart from a grey formica topped table and two plastic chairs facing each other. One of the two border guards motions her to sit, seating himself opposite, watching her carefully as he does so.

"Why are you so anxious Dr Strachan?" he asks with a casual glance at her passport. "Anyone would think you had something to hide. You don't, do you?" Certain they speak Arabic to catch her out, Ana shakes her head in terror.

"Okay, I need to ask you a few questions." The other sounds more menacing and her mind tripping her up again, she trembles in anticipation of what they will do if she disobeys. The soldier examines her passport. "Strachan... as in General Strachan, currently on secondment to Shin Bet? Strange arrangement that. Never heard of it before." He looks at her but speechless, she is helplessly trapped. "Perhaps we should give them a ring."

A sharp tap at the door. "Ana, it's me, Ruth."

Someone pulls Ruth away. "Look, you can't just come barging in here!"

"No, you look and listen up! I am a sister at the Intensive Care Unit of Hadassah Hospital, Jerusalem. Here is my ID card and a number to call for confirmation, should you require it. Ana was gravely injured when she arrived. She survived a death cell in Damascus. Do you understand what that means?" Suddenly aware again, Ana wonders why Ruth tells the truth. Surely their alibi was safer?

"She is suffering from post traumatic distress. You, of all people, should be able to recognise that." The anger in her rises. "She was tortured and raped by men and you think it acceptable to interrogate her without even a chaperone?"

"And you are?"

"I've told you who I am. Weren't you listening to me? Here are my papers." She hands him her passport and after a careful look the soldier puts it with Ana's.

"Why is she travelling to Jordan?"

"She was working at Za'atari refugee camp with MSF."

"How did she get to Damascus?" Ruth heaves a great sigh and returns to her ward.

"Ana, it's me, Ruth. Look at me darling. You're safe. No-one is going to hurt you." She takes a firm hold of Ana by the shoulders and peers into her eyes. "We're nearly done here. I just need to clarify a few things with these border-guards, then you can be on your way, okay?" Ana nods. Ruth turns back to the soldiers. "One of the children Ana helped at Za'atari went back into Syria for his younger brother. Ana went to their rescue."

"Is she the daughter of General Strachan?"

"Indeed she is, and I doubt he would be happy with the way his daughter is being treated. I suggest you do what you need to in my presence and let that be an end to this."

There is silence in the little room but for Ana's pounding heart. At last, the soldiers give Ruth their papers and usher them out. "Without so much as an apology?" Ruth is incensed. As she fusses over Ana, doing her best to embarrass them, the officers return the rest of the paperwork to Jacob now standing at the doorway, and wave them all through.

A loud beeping makes Ana jump and she looks in bewilderment at a yellow coach revving its engine impatiently. "This is your lift, Ana," Ruth says. "Goodbye my darling. Remember us. Come see us one day, and take care of those babies. They're very special, you know?" Ruth looks on her with such tender kindness. Ana is unable to help herself. Regardless of prying eyes, she holds her long and tight. Ever constant and loyal, Ruth has accompanied her to hell and back.

"We will," she says, choking back the tears. With a reassuring smile, Ruth takes Ana's face in her hands.

"This isn't like you Ana. You've been so brave. Now your freedom and the rest of your life is just across that bridge. Go get it girl!"

The curse lifts and Ana laughs. "Thank you so much Ruth. I couldn't have done it without you. Visit us in London. We'll have such fun together!"

"We will Ana and that's a promise." They embrace one last time and while the others board behind them, Ana bids Jacob farewell.

BEDOUIN HOSPITALITY –
THE RWALA TRIBE

Two dark-skinned, black-eyed, hairy men, one the younger version of the other, are there to meet them at the checkpoint into Jordan. Their all covering, loose fitting djellabaya, flap in a welcome breeze, the keffiyeh draped over their heads, saved only by the thick black cord that holds them in place. They greet Ishtar, her son and his friend, like long-lost family, fussing over the injured man until he introduces them to Ana but he is failing fast and she wastes no time with pleasantries.

"He needs a hospital," she tells them urgently but Caleb disagrees.

"We need to go to the desert. Trust them."

She shakes her head in exasperation, looking to their hosts for support which isn't forthcoming and then it dawns. "They wouldn't follow us into Jordan?"

"They will Ana," the father informs her. "Sayetet Matkal. Famed for kidnappings and assassinations that defy belief, anywhere in the world. So long as Caleb is a danger to Michael, there is nowhere he will be safer than in the desert with us. There are a million Bedouin in Jordan alone, nearly two million if you add our Syrian and Israeli brethren and we wander. They will never find him amongst us."

"And, so long as we don't cross 'em," Tuan winks as he struggles to hold his best friend up, "they won't betray us, for Bedouin are fiercely loyal to their own." He gives Ana one of his boyish grins. "Don't worry, he's survived far worse. And 'is mum's 'ere. What could possibly go wrong?"

"Besides, which," the older Bedouin adds, "there is almost nothing we can't do in the desert. The hospital, if needed, can come to us. Certainly we have better facilities than you had in Syria. Now this way please." His son leads them to an open pick-up truck and they lay Caleb gently in the back, Tuan making himself comfortable beside him, Ana on the back seat, as close as she can get.

The journey seems to take forever and, despite her concern for Caleb, Ana begins already to feel the warmth of Bedouin hospitality. Each family will take its turn to host a party in their honour, Ishtar explains, for guests are considered to come from Allah.

Sheikh Ahmed Hussein and his son are members of the Rwala tribe. The largest, with more than seventy five thousand members, of a confederation of tribes called the Anazah, in the north of the Arabian peninsula. The Rwala tribe migrates among the deserts of Syria, Jordan and northern Saudi Arabia. Ishtar's family has been close to them for many generations. Originally, she explains, the home of the Bedouin was the Arabian desert, Syria one of the first lands they moved to from there, but now there are Bedouin communities in many countries. Sheikh Hussain's clan specialises in camels and still makes its tents the traditional way, weaving them out of camel hair, "but, as you will soon see, they are luxurious nonetheless."

With their rich oral poetic tradition, herding lifestyle, traditional code of honour and extensive kinship networks, the Bedouin are seen as Arab culture's purest representatives. The first converts to Islam came from amongst the Bedouin and their host has a daughter married to a man from the Qaraysh tribe, which considers itself to be directly descended from the prophet Muhammad. Sunni Islam is deeply embedded in Bedouin culture and prayer is an integral part of life. "Even though there are no mosques in the desert, the Bedouin pray wherever they are, facing the Ka'aba in Mecca and performing their ritual washing in sand if there is no water."

They head ever further away from anything Ana would recognise as civilisation, higher into a shimmering desert landscape punctuated by rocky outcrops and strangely beautiful sculptures carved by centuries of wind-blown sand. It is a wonder that anyone can survive such desolation let alone thrive in it. "You know Ana, that Arabia is almost completely desert with only a narrow strip of habitable land round the periphery?" Ana shakes her head. "Well, the Bedouin say that in the fertile crescent empires have come and gone, but in the barren wastes the Bedouin remain forever the same."

At last they reach their destination. In the middle of the desert with no sign of other life for hundreds of miles. Invisible to within a hundred meters, the camp lies tucked into a sheltered valley between dune and cliff. A collection of round "Saudi" tents and the traditional black ones woven out of camel or goat hair. "Which shrinks when wet, becoming water-tight in the winter and sags when dry, separating into holes which allow any breeze to circulate in the hot summers. Feel the surface," the Sheik's son encourages. "It is hot, yes?" Indeed. Reflexly she withdraws her hand. "But inside, very cool."

A couple of dogs run up, their slim muscular bodies wagging enthusiastically with their tails and, as her host bends to pet them, cover him with wet kisses. Tall, elegant, not that dissimilar to greyhounds back in England but with fluffy drop ears, they have narrow intelligent faces with large brown eyes and soft silky fur. "Saluki hounds" the young Sheikh, who calls himself M'hammed, tells her. "One of the oldest breeds of domesticated dog. Known as sight-hounds for the way they hunt by speed and sight rather than scent. They have always been with the Bedouin though few of us can afford to keep them now. They need lots of space to run, careful training with love rather than discipline, and make beautiful companions. Ana, a Saluki hunting is a wonderful sight. Perhaps you would like to see?" Ana is embarrassed and distracted. "I'm sorry. Very rude of me. Come let us go to your husband."

A crowd has gathered to greet them. Women in *abaya* – long, thin, intricately embroidered black cloaks hardly concealing their brightly coloured dresses and black shawls that cover their heads, the men in djellabaya with head covers of white and red. Carefully, they lift Caleb from the back of the truck and carry him into one of the Saudi tents, closing the entrance behind him. "They'll let us in, when he's ready," Ishtar reassures. Ana tries to distract herself. She takes a closer look at the camp around her. It appears to be well organised. Many of the black tents have sections open to the desert and M'hammed points out areas for guests, family, cooking and how the water-tank sits mid-way between the living quarters and where the animals are penned. Ana sees camels and goats. A tent-pole with a rubbish bag tied to it. A few chickens scratching around. A suave looking young man dressed traditionally but with expensive-looking sunglasses, playing with a group of children. Saluki wandering freely. Various vehicles now neatly parked beside each other and, closer to the tents, a handful of the most beautiful Arabian horses.

"You'll be impressed by where we get our water," M'hammed boasts. "There are few springs here but we build dams in the hollows of rock formations to collect rain-water in the winter. Interior reservoirs that are protected from the heat of the summer day and can provide water all year round."

At last there is movement and the flap to Caleb's tent opens. Sheikh Ahmed Hussein is the first to emerge, closely followed by his entourage. Beaming as he approaches, he informs them that, "Caleb is comfortably settled and ready to see you." Ana frowns. "These will be your quarters Ana, for as long as you want them. Everything you need will be provided. We look forward to entertaining you when you are ready." She thanks him, smiling politely as she removes her shoes at the entrance and heads into the gloom.

Nothing could have prepared her for the sumptuous decor within. The plain, rough exterior of the tent is completely hidden beneath extravagant carpets, tapestries and throws, hanging from the roof and covering the floors. Caleb lies on a king-sized mattress at the back of the tent, large cushions strewn across the floor to one side of him, a low long table to the other. On this, neatly laid out before her is an array of surgical instruments, dressings, towels, a bowl of steaming water, two glasses, a transparent jug of water, and a basket of fresh fruit. She gasps, taken aback by the trouble their hosts have evidently gone to and turns to thank them, but only Ishtar remains.

"Impressed?" Caleb raises his eyebrows with a smile. Pale and haggard, he looks truly spent.

"How are you feeling?" He shrugs, putting a hand on his chest as if to brace it, then tries to raise himself for a better view. He falls back gasping for breath, his face contorted with pain. Ana tells him not to move. "Show me where it hurts."

She begins gently to feel around, watching his face which will give far more away than he would ever tell and is alarmed to find him maximally tender over the liver. "Just need time and rest. I'll be fine," he reassures.

"But you can lose so much blood from the liver," Ana says, sick with the realisation of how such injury might have been caused.

Caleb shakes his head, flinching as he tries to make himself more comfortable. "Promise, I won't move."

"No point trying to help. He makes a bad patient," Ishtar warns.

"Ana lie with me," Caleb pleads. "Mother leave us, please."

She lays herself next to him, taking care to avoid his injuries and he puts an arm around her. "This is not what I had planned for our wedding night," he says.

Ana smiles. "I love you, Caleb." He takes her hand to kiss her fingers one by one and, touching his forehead with her lips, she tells him he needs to sleep. But he cannot rest. She looks to the table, searching in vain for painkillers and considers calling out, for she cannot contemplate extricating herself.

"It's okay. Please stay…" Caleb closes his eyes and she curls into him, watching his face, the rise and fall of his broken chest restricted by the agony of each breath and the stillness of his belly as he struggles to control the pain here also. Why isn't there more she can do for him? She wonders when he last ate or drank. Not in the last twenty four hours to be sure but he seems to be on the brink of consciousness and she lies motionless, reluctant to do anything that might deprive him of merciful oblivion.

Aware only of waking terrors, Caleb's torturous rest, descending darkness, voices, the sounds of contented animals and the heat of the rising sun, Ana does not remember sleeping but when she wakes, two bowls of water, towels and a clean set of clothes for each of them, have been placed on the floor at the foot of their bed. Caleb is still unconscious and she extricates herself with care not to disturb him, quenches her thirst with two glasses of water from the jug, peels off her clothes and heads for one of the bowls.

With great care not to spill water onto the luxurious carpet, she washes and dries herself bit by bit then dips her head into the water as well. She feels for a towel to wrap up her hair and her hand falls onto a wide-toothed comb. She smiles. Their hosts have thought of almost everything.

Caleb groans and she jumps, reverie shattered. He lies motionless, deathly pale. She rushes to his side and feels for his pulse. It is strong and regular. His eyelids flicker open but his look is glazed, far away. She takes a deep breath and lies down beside him, waiting.

"You are so beautiful." His voice is clear and strong, his face full of emotion but then he squeezes his eyes tight shut and grimaces. She leans over and kisses his forehead, running her fingers gently over his face and he smiles. He tries to swallow but he is parched.

"Don't move," she commands. "I'll get you some water." She waits a moment, watching, then fetches a glass from the table and helps him raise his head enough to drink from it as she holds it to his lips. She refills the glass three times before he has had enough. "Do you want something to eat?"

He shakes his head and looks her over. "All mine."

Ana laughs, suddenly aware that she is naked. "Better put something on before anyone comes."

"Don't worry, it'll only be my mother."

"And how appropriate would that be, for your mother to find her wounded son being tended by a naked woman?"

"My wife. Seems totally appropriate to me."

She laughs. "Later I'll help you wash but now sleep, okay?"

"Okay boss."

She lies beside him and waits until he seems to have drifted then rises to dress. Someone has left her silk trousers and she puts them on with a grateful smile but as she pulls the matching top over her neck, she remembers the last time she wore such an outfit and terror strikes. She shakes the images out of her head. Now I am in Jordan, she tells herself sternly, willing herself calm as she falls to her knees.

"Look at me." She startles, trembling and opens her eyes to Caleb kneeling before her. "We're safe. No-one is going to hurt you." He leans forward to put his arms around her and she flinches in anticipation of how this must hurt, wondering at the horrors he has learnt to live with.

"I should be looking after you," she tells him and he shakes his head.

"We look after each other." She helps him up and he pulls her close. She feels his heart beat strong and regular, his body warm against hers and, as she soaks in the smell of him, tranquility returns. In his arms she feels safe and secure. Time stands still.

There is a commotion outside, the sound of a tent-flap opening and Ishtar's voice, loud and intrusive. "Good morning! May I come in?"

"Good morning mother. Could you come back in an hour or so?"

"Is everything alright?"

"Yes. In fact we'll come out to you, okay?"

"Okay." She sounds bright and breezy. "See you in a bit."

Ana heaves a great sigh and Caleb lets her go. She smiles into his eyes. "While I help you wash, you'd better enlighten me on Bedouin etiquette."

"All things in good time." He falls to his knees on the thick red carpet, his shirt drenched with the effort of movement and shakes his head to her frown. "No, it's not your fault." She helps him out of his clothes, throwing them in a pile onto the bed and begins gently to sponge away sweat and grime, grimacing at what she sees beneath it all, wincing whenever she hurts him. At last the job is done and he takes her hand to kiss it. "Thank you." He tries to stand but his strength fails and he lies himself naked on the carpet instead, closing his eyes and screwing up his face.

"What is it?"

"Nothing," but his hand reaches for his broken ribs, holding them against his damaged liver, the veins and muscles in his neck standing out with the effort of willing himself well again. "I can't open my eyes right now because everything's spinning," he says. "Ana, lie with me."

She cannot tell how many days have passed, but it is gone midday by the time she wakes. Though it remains cool in their tent, the angle of the sun has altered dramatically. Caleb is asleep and she cuddles up, nuzzling her face into his soft hair and breathing in the scent of him. She thinks she could lie like this forever, watching his breathing slow and deepen, his bruises change colour and fade and the lines on his face disappear as he heals. It is so peaceful here. Hidden away from the rest of the world. So close to, and yet so far from war, starvation, cruelty and trauma. She heaves a sigh of contentment and closes her eyes, drifting back towards blissful sleep and then it comes again.

Instantly wide awake she lies motionless, holding her breath as if she could make herself invisible, waiting for the intruder to betray his whereabouts before she does. She hears the flap of their tent close and turns towards it but they are alone. She sits herself up and looks around. Their dirty clothes have disappeared and a pile of fresh towels has replaced their used ones. The jug of water has been refilled and next to it is another with two matching earthenware mugs. The smell of freshly baked bread wakens her stomach and doing its bidding, she rises to her feet, following it to a wooden board loaded with loaves of varying sizes, shapes, colours and textures. One of the balls is more symmetrical than the others. She picks it up. It is heavy, hard and smells like cheese. Beside it is something that looks like a hammer and she guesses that with this, they are supposed to smash it open. She looks into the jug, smiling as she pours two cups of milk that smells strongly of ginger. Then it strikes.

In her hurry to replace the jug, she misjudges its distance from the table and it crashes onto the surface spilling. Regardless, she sinks to her knees, resting her head on the floor and waits for the faintness to dissipate, the nausea to pass. She takes some deep breaths, closing her eyes tightly against the outside world, then falls onto her side and, as the pain builds, curls herself into the foetal position, clutching her belly.

She doesn't notice him at first, the way he folds himself around her, his hard body against her back, an arm holding her tight but, as the heat in her builds and he unravels himself, she becomes aware of his absence and then of him touching her face with a cool wet cloth. There is nothing she can do but wait for it to pass. She feels his hands on her head and pelvis and, though the pain and nausea ease, is too afraid to open her eyes or move. He lies down in front of her but does not take his hands away and that is all she knows.

She has no idea how long she was out for but Caleb is still there watching her. He kisses her first on her forehead then beneath the belly-button. "You okay?" he asks, anxiously and she nods.

"And you?"

He blesses her with a glorious smile, full of tender love and she feels an unearthly calm descend upon her. "You need to eat. Our babies are taking everything they can from you but there is nothing left." Ana frowns, at once puzzled and guilty. She sees her wonder reflected in his eyes and smiles.

She was so worried about him at the time that it hardly registered. As if it was someone else being examined, not her. The Professor had only been able to find one baby at first and, if it hadn't been for Caleb's insistence, would have given up long before the second revealed itself. He had been so concerned. Despite his injuries, her husband had declined any help, shrugging off the Professor's shameful apology for what had been done to him and thanking him instead, for making him the happiest man alive.

The Professor had warned them that the first sixteen weeks were likely to be the most risky. That the chance of miscarriage was high given the poor condition of the mother. That being twins and her first pregnancy, she was likely to deliver them early. That this should certainly be by caesarean section at a hospital with good neonatal intensive care facilities and that their estimated due date, when the babies would be expected if this were a normal pregnancy going to term, was the 21st of May 2014. Caleb had looked so smug, as if he had known all along that their babies would be born on his Birthday.

"Our babies are fine Ana." He radiates joy and confidence. "Just wanting to make themselves felt, that's all. Do you think we could feed them now?"

They feast on goat's cheese, bread, fruit and ginger milk and Caleb tells her of how he kept himself going in his prison cell by focusing on her, willing her better, reliving their good times together and imagining what they might do with their children. Then, taking her by the hand before she has a chance to think, he gives her a reassuring smile and leads her out into the sunshine.

There is a welcome committee waiting for them. Children, dogs, a couple of women and Ishtar, augmented, as the cry goes up that the guests have woken at last, by Tuan, and Sheik Hussain. Caleb smiles fondly. *"As-salamu alaykum Abu M'hammed!"*

"Wa alaykum s-salamu wa rahmatu l-lahi wa barakatuh" the old man replies, taking Caleb's outstretched hand and putting his arms around him "We are old friends, let's be done with formality. It is good to see you looking so much better." He turns then to Ana, greeting her in the same way. *May peace, mercy and blessings of Allah be upon you.* Pretending to be embarrassed, Caleb puts a hand to his mouth and coughs and with their giggling, Ana notices the ladies blush beneath their black shawls.

"Of course, this way please." One of them holds a slender arm out to his wife and, taking her hand, Ana allows herself to be led, along with all the women and children, away from the living quarters, to a long low tent behind the animal pens. It is divided into two – for men and women, and inside, she is pleasantly surprised to find two proper wooden toilets which open into a hole dug deep into the ground, a bowel of water, soap and a clean towel.

The men are fussing over the horses when she returns, M'hammed expounding, with what appears to be characteristic enthusiasm, the magnificent features of Arabians, of which they have such beautiful specimens. "Ana, do you ride?" he asks her without so much as a hello, and she nods.

"Since I was a baby, I'm told."

"Have you ever ridden a pure Arab horse?"

"Not sure I have." She gives him a disarming smile. "Hello Sheikh M'hammed, how are you today?"

"Good thank you, and you Ana?"

"Very well thank you."

"You can call me M'hammed by the way and please forgive my rudeness." He waves an arm in front of Caleb and Tuan as if he were about to bow before them but turns back to Ana instead. "You see, we practically grew up together, have no secrets – or very few at least, and have saved each others' butts many a time. Am I right?" Caleb nods while Tuan casts his eyes to the sky and shakes his head in mock exasperation. "Formality is unnecessary. Not that these two rascals would ever worry about that. Anyway, I was wondering Ana, whether you and Caleb here, if he's feeling up to it, would like to come for a ride with us later. Sunset is the best time. Nice and cool. The horses love it. We'll take the Salukis too. What do you say?" Ana shakes her head, reluctant to disappoint but no longer worried about being rude.

"I'm pregnant," she tells M'hammed. He appears to do a double-take, congratulates them both warmly, then continues undaunted.

"That isn't a problem. These horses don't mind who rides them. They are sound and sure-footed. Nothing would make them throw you Ana. You can't be far enough into this pregnancy for there to be any other risk to your baby. What do you think Caleb? She would love it, no?"

"Yes, she would love it. Another time perhaps."

M'hammed looks disappointed. "Why not just trot around the campsite and see how it feels?" Ana shakes her head but someone else has other ideas. A handsome bay, big for an Arabian at about sixteen hands, seems to have taken a shine to her and, unconsciously, she rubs the nose it thrusts over her shoulder, longing to get onto its back. But it is a long time since she rode, she is weak and unfit, there is no way she would allow Caleb onto the back of a horse with his injuries and it wouldn't be fair to leave him, so reluctantly, her answer has to be no.

"Thank you M'hammed. I would really love to ride one of your magnificent horses,…" Interrupted by a frustrated whinny, she turns as her new friend scrapes its hoof along the ground, its black eyes staring directly into hers. "Another time perhaps?" Even as the words pass her lips, laughter erupts within her. The horse starts to neigh and before they can help themselves, the others too, have caught the infection. At last she can bear it no longer and, gasping for breath, her hands on her aching sides, Ana straightens herself, wipes the tears from her eyes and turns back to the horse watching indignantly. "I'm sorry…"

"Sargan," M'hammed informs her helpfully and she frowns. "His master took his time and he needed a name. Seemed appropriate."

"So you …"

"Yes, I know. But of the two of them, the horse is by far the worthier king."

"And anyway, his name isn't the same as mine," Caleb interjects.

"By one letter only. There had to be something to distinguish his above yours!" Caleb gasps, a look of mock horror on his face and the horse neighs a warning.

"Sargan. That is a beautiful name and very fitting." With a soft whinny, the horse makes a show of what can only be appreciation, its intelligent brown eyes watching Ana's every facial expression as she talks. Then it begins a conversation with her, modulating its neighing, grunting and whinnying in answer as she speaks with it. "You understand why we can't ride you yet, don't you Sargan?" The horse shakes its head. "Your master is injured. Being jolted about is likely to tear his liver open again for it is only just healing." Heaving a great sigh, Sargan stares at Caleb in agitation but when his master takes his nose, searching his great dark eyes, the magnificent creature stills.

Silently they commune then, giving Caleb a wet kiss that encompasses so much of his face that he has to wipe it dry, the horse turns back to Ana, scrapes a hoof impatiently in the dust and looks at her expectantly.

"Sargan will make sure no harm comes to our babies. He would like to take you for a ride, Ana."

"But …"

"You'll be in the safest of hands, hooves even. Sargan is an expert. He'll respond to your strengths and weaknesses, taking you as far as you want to go and no further than your limitations. Trust him and enjoy yourselves." Excited anticipation vies with doubt and Ana looks to Caleb in confusion. "Come, I'll help you up," he says with a reassuring smile.

She doesn't notice that there is no saddle, for her preference has always been to ride bare-back, but neither does Sargan have collar or bridle and she has never ridden in a long coat. "Well Sargan," she whispers into his ear. "Shall we see how much fun we can have together?" The horse turns his head for a good look at her, his eyes widening in apparent delight and for a moment they lose themselves to each other. Then, seating herself just behind his shoulders, Ana begins with both hands, to stroke his mane.

"I'll show you around," M'hammed offers, beaming at her from the back of a handsome chestnut.

They skirt around the tents to an area where women are preparing food, stopping to watch one roasting coffee beans at the end of a long shovel in an open fire. Mysterious, almond eyes peer from an apricot scarf, an open abaya revealing a long orange dress to match. When they are done, she crushes the beans with a mortar, drops them into hot water and, with a smile for Ana, adds Cardamon with a flourish. "She will leave it standing now to infuse," M'hammed explains.

Nearby, an old woman rolls paste made by boiling goat's milk down, into balls, covering them in flour before leaving them to dry in the open air and Ana recognises the cheese she shared with Caleb for breakfast. A walnut face flashes a toothless grin and says something unintelligible. "Can be kept indefinitely," M'hammed translates "and either soaked in water to soften, ready for eating or sucked as it is."

They head next up a steep track into the hills behind the camp, for its water supply. A series of dams built into the hollows of natural rock formations, have formed reservoirs soon, hopefully, to refill with winter rain up to three meters deep. There are footholds and rungs by which the water can be reached when its levels are low, places where it can be covered to prevent animals and children from falling in and plastic pipes which bring water down under the force of gravity to the water-tank.

They come to a place where they can look over the camp and M'hammed explains how it is organised, every tent representing a family, the encampment – a clan and a number of kindred clans – the tribe. The tent and all within it, belongs to the family but water and land is common property of the tribe. "Bedouins, being born democrats," he concludes, "meet their sheikh on an equal footing.

"Now, if you wish to ride, I suggest you go this way." He points back down the track towards open desert. "Sargan knows the way."

'Thank you, M'hammed.' Ana thinks of Caleb and hesitates.

"Do not worry about Caleb, I will take good care of him."

It hurts at first, truly to ride but, as with any skill acquired in childhood, once the memory of it revives, Ana's body begins to respond automatically and she relaxes into it. Sargan leads her gently, responding intuitively to the cues she imparts. The slight shift in her balance when she looks the way she wants to go next, the subtle way she leans forward when she wants to go faster, how she strokes his mane as if she is speaking to him with her hands and the tension in her when he pushes her too far.

Woman and horse meld, their union shifting to unconsciousness and then something magical happens. To Ana, it is as if they flow with a great surge of energy that frees her from the limitations of her physical manifestation, rendering insignificant, the horrors that so cruelly floored her.

She doesn't notice how far they have come, only the breathless joy of the ride as the sand-dunes and cloudless sky fly past but as she tires, Sargan slows to a canter and turns back towards camp. She adjusts her position, anxious not to hurt him with her boney bottom and wonders if he might be more comfortable with a saddle for whatever M'hammed has planned later on.

Caleb waits where they left him, lines of worry etched into his face. Though Sargan neighs in apparent indignation, Ana is sorry for she understands. Full of the joy of the ride, she jumps down eager to hold him but something catches and she freezes. She hesitates then, taking his hand into the dark folds of her abaya, places it over the hard swelling rising from her pelvis and watches his face. "I can feel them moving," he says in wonder and, unable to resist, with Sargan neighing quietly behind them, they kiss.

Ana is not disappointed to learn that their communal ride must be delayed but, though business steals precious time from their hosts, this does not hinder preparations for a great feast. Tonight, the visitors will be guests of honour. She worries about Caleb but he seems unfazed. "I'll rest when I need to and we can leave whenever. These people are family. They understand."

They are taken to Sheikh Hussain's quarters. A lavish communal area, thick with elaborate carpets, tapestries and cushions, it is open on one side to the desert and already alive to the animated chatter of a good number of guests. Low-lying tables bear jugs of ginger milk and water, spoons, silver platters and bowls of sliced melons and figs, served by traditionally dressed young men and women, all relatives of the Sheikh, Ana is informed.

Dodging well-wishers with a friendly grin, M'hammed makes his way towards them and they follow him to his father smiling benevolently down on everyone. "Be seated!" He waves at the empty spaces beside him and, as his son disappears, his guests do his bidding. M'hammed returns, first with a basin which he sets before them, then a large jug of water. He waits for Caleb to explain this ritual to Ana then pours water over their outstretched hands, throws him a towel and moves on to their neighbours.

There is a commotion at the entrance and Ana startles. "It's okay. Come see." Caleb takes her hand and brings them both to their feet. He finds their shoes and leads her to a group of men watching the flames of an enormous fire settle. Hanging over it, three giant pots of rice bubble vigorously, their lids positioned to prevent them boiling over, nearby, an enormous metal contraption, its central pillar supporting three circular trays laden with meat, balls of dough and vegetables. Three of the men lift the barbecue over the embers while a stream of women and children carry bowls of food into the tent. Ana wonders if she should offer to help. "Our duty is to eat, drink and appreciate," Caleb reassures, with an affectionate squeeze of her hand. "Come." He pulls her away. "Just quickly." He leads her to a narrow path carved into the sheltering cliff and together they climb high above camp.

He points to the horizon and she follows his finger to shimmering mirage. "Syria," he says, "and just before it, Za'atari. No more than half a day's drive away." She shivers and he pulls her close. "We don't have to go back," he says. "The children are safe. We can send word that we'll meet them later. I have relatives in Canada, your father has a flat in London. Or we could go to your house in Cornwall."

"Cottage." He laughs. "There is a difference," she tells him in all seriousness. "My cottage has history. Hundreds of years of it. Lots of character, open fire-places, flag-stone floors, beamed ceilings, beautiful views and a quaint little garden. Also, it has a ghost, but a nice one." Fighting back images of shabiha, she looks to Caleb with dread but she must know. "How did you get me out?"

A deep frown creases his forehead, a storm rising in his eyes. "It took us three days to find you," he says and takes a deep breath. Three days. It took them three whole days to track her to that Damascus hell-hole. For three days and nights she suffered unimaginable cruelty at the hands of those sadistic thugs.

"That's not so long," Ana whispers, trembling in his arms.

He shakes his head and looks with tears into her eyes. "You were on an airforce base. We highjacked one of their supply trucks, uniforms and ID cards. Somehow we got away with it."

"Who?"

"Tuan, Ahmed and me. Just the three of us. Ahmed created a diversion as we headed off base. Quite a riot, actually. He found his brother and freed a few others as well. So far as we know, most of them got out alive." Caleb shakes his head. "Miracle we got away with it."

Ana nods. "Thank you." He draws her closer, kissing her tenderly on the forehead. "I think we should have our babies in London," she says. "But first I need to see the children."

Tuan has made himself at home with the women by the time they return and, though she shakes her head, Ana cannot conceal her amusement when he catches her eye and winks.

M'hammed asks about her ride and the conversation turns to the Arabian horse. Like their Saluki hounds, these are one of the oldest breeds. "A creature of luxury," she is informed, whose feeding and care constitute a problem to the man of the desert. For centuries, the Arabian horse has been celebrated for its physical beauty, endurance, intelligence, spirit, devotion to its master and for providing the speed necessary for successful raids. A prized possession, it was kept in the tent with its owner to protect it from predators and thieves. "It would have been given the last of any precious water before the thirsty human child."

But now it is used mainly for sport and hunting. "The camel on the other hand," one of his clansmen teases, "is a true creature of the desert, without which, life here would be inconceivable. The Bedouin's constant companion, his nourisher, his vehicle of transportation, his wealth. We drink its milk and sometimes of necessity, its water, eat its flesh, clothe ourselves in its skin and make our tents from its hair. We use its dung for fuel, its urine as hair tonic and medicine ..."

"Actually Zeydan, some of us have different tastes." Laughter ripples through the tent.

"So, what do you do when you're sick?" Ana asks.

"Well, it is true that some of our medicines come from the camel, also the plants we find around us, but here in Jordan, we are well provided for by the Kingdom, for we Bedouin make up to forty per cent of the population and have always supported the monarchy. In return it provides us with education, housing and health care and, though some of us prefer the nomadic way of life, others have settled."

"Even Syria has made an effort to support our way of life though officially it disapproves. The Bedouin assisted the al-Assad government, you see, during the Muslim Brotherhood uprising of 1982."

"But also, we took part in the Arab Spring demonstrations."

"Yes, but society here is too divided to make a stand against the government and our King is clever. He maintains a distance from complaints, allowing the blame to fall on his ministers, whom he replaces at will."

Their host considers his guests with concern. "What of your homeland Ishtar, and Ma'aloula?" Ishtar looks to Caleb in alarm. He and Ana must be ignorant of events during their absence from Syria and she had no intention of enlightening them now but he watches her with quiet consternation.

"Jihadists have taken over Ma'aloula," Ishtar informs him reluctantly. "They have murdered some of its residents and hold others hostage. Many have fled to safety in Damascus."

"Damascus?"

"Yes, Ana. Christians have tried hard not to take sides in this conflict," Ishtar explains, "but now we see atrocities committed by jihadists attempting to create an Islamic Emirate in all of the Middle East. We hear of massacres, with Christians being buried in mass graves, torture and beheadings for wearing a crucifix or refusing to convert to Islam. The desecration of our religious institutions, vandalism of businesses and homes. Bans, punishable by death, on practising Christianity and taxes for the right to continue to do so. You pay or die, it's as simple as that.

"The population of Christians in the Middle East is declining rapidly as a direct result of intimidation and violence against it by Islamic extremists. After the fall of Saddam Hussein's regime, horrific acts of violence were perpetrated against Iraqi Christians by both Sunni and Shiite extremists. We are expecting the same to happen in Syria if Assad is overthrown."

"How are our family and friends, mother?"

"All safe so far as I know."

Caleb stares into an invisible distance, the muscles of his jaw twitching and Ana wonders if she will ever be free of her fear for him.

"Son, you have other responsibilities now. A wife with child. Don't go back to Syria. You were invisible but no more. Now they know who you are and you are a wanted man." She omits to add what he must inevitably be considering as he shakes his head, clenching his fists and closing his eyes. That so too, therefore, is his family.

I HAD A HOUSE
IN DAMASCUS

"I had a house in Damascus," Ishtar tells them. "An old house, in the Christian Quarter. We renovated it together, Sean and I, with the children running riot around us. Those were the happiest days of my life.

"It was a beautiful house. It belonged once to a doctor who practised the enlightened holistic medicine – using nature, music, architecture and art, that has been handed down through generations of Syrian healers. Garlic for hypertension, valerian for nervous diseases, parsley as a diuretic. Nervous illnesses were treated with calming teas, a simple diet and beautiful courtyards where patients would sit surrounded by plants, listening to the sounds of fountains and gentle lutes. Nature, water and music were used to heal in Syria at a time when people classed as having mental illnesses in Europe, were being imprisoned and abused, even tortured.

"It had a courtyard within it, designed to protect you from the outside world. A space of total tranquillity, built of golden limestone, pink marble and black volcanic basalt. In the centre was a marble fountain with bronze dragon heads that splashed cool water into a sparkling octagonal pool. Beneath the surface of this bahra, little sea, a pair of terrapins glided in care-free abandon. All around the courtyard, intensely coloured orange trees, vines, bougainvillea and jasmine rising from exquisitely crafted pots, filled the air with intoxicating scents which a cool breeze carried through the cleverly ventilated house. It was a kind of paradise.

"When I came back to my house in Damascus and sat in the courtyard, a feeling of total peace would come over me. I would listen to birdsong and the buzz of insects, watch the stalks fly over the city and the light change everything around me as the sun dropped, hear the call to prayer, the choir singing from the Umayyad Mosque and, at dusk, the doves returning, the bats swooping to catch insects.

"You know, Ana, to the Arab way of thinking, beauty has the power to release us from sorrows and so this is cherished and reflected in Islamic art."

Though she falls silent, Ishtar has cast her spell. At last someone asks what happened to the house. "I was a lecturer of ancient history at Damascus University with responsibility for the pastoral care of our students. I couldn't reconcile my work on my conscience with the politics that engulfed even student life.

"Right from the beginning, I frequently found myself in conflict with the authorities. I was vocal in my condemnation of the regime's violence towards peaceful protestors, so it confiscated my house."

"In what way does politics affect student life?" a young man asks.

"The students' Union at Damascus University, which has to give permission before any event can take place on campus, has been run for a long time by the Ba'ath Party. Though membership is not compulsory, the rewards for joining it are considerable. The Ba'ath Party MP responsible for the Student's Union is reported to be a close friend of Maher-al-Assad, Bashar's violent younger brother and the activities of students are closely monitored. Even before the uprising, dozens were arrested simply for speaking out against the regime. Plainclothes secret police patrol the campus and students are encouraged, through a system of rewards like better rooms or money, to report others."

"Our lives begin to end the day we become silent about things that matter," Caleb tells no-one in particular.

Ana frowns. "How do ordinary people become monsters?"

"I'd say it has something to do with the selfish gene," M'hammed replies and someone laughs. "No, I'm serious."

"Well, you keep ya genes for ya wife," Tuan advises but his friend will not be so easily put down.

"What do you think Ana? Is it primitive evolutionary forces that make us so selfish that we put ourselves above all others, regardless of the hurt we inflict by so doing?"

Ana nods but she is distracted. "Teamwork pays but yes, when the chips are down, perhaps it is our selfish genes that drive us to do the things we do.

"Once, in Za'atari, a twelve year old boy was describing what it was like to be a child in Syria. He had been living with the remains of his extended family, four generations of them, in a tiny flat close to the frontline amongst the ruins of Aleppo. With the constant sound of gunshot and shelling, no running water and sporadic power.

"He talked of how the children played. Only war-games. Of how they formed gangs and defended their territory. He said that if they caught a member of the opposition, they would torture him to find out where his soldiers were hidden, weapons and warehouses. He laughed and joked about it but then he fell silent, any semblance of childhood in him gone and at last, in all seriousness he said, I want to torture Assad. Not kill him, but torture him like he has tortured us." Ana looks around at them all watching her. "I understand that now. Assad deserves to share the suffering he inflicts on his people. He can't be allowed to get away with it. I want to hurt him the way he hurt me and every one of his victims. I would never have believed myself capable of behaving like he does, but now I know I could. Perhaps his ultimate tyranny is in making monsters of ordinary people."

"No." Taking her hands, Ishtar searches Ana's eyes. "You could never harm someone deliberately. When we're angry, wild thoughts attack us that bear no relation to what we are actually capable of."

"But monsters rise from ordinary people."

"So do heroes, Ana. I have seen this far more often…and so have you."

There is a commotion outside and a horde of children appear, laughing and shouting as they lead three men bringing the hot food in. They have lifted the whole contraption off the fire and now a space is cleared in the middle of the tent for them to place it in the sand. Their host rubs his hands together with glee. "Time to eat," he tells everyone. "I'm sure we all deserve this delicious feast, so beautifully prepared and presented to us. *Alhamdulillah!* Thank you, thank you!"

"Are you planning to return to Za'atari?" M'hammed asks quietly as the others prepare to eat. Ana nods. "You know, it's changed a bit since you were there last. It has become one of Jordan's largest cities with all the problems generated by so many people trying to get along. Over one hundred and twenty thousand refugees of an intolerable crisis, essentially being held prisoner in one of the biggest camps in the world." Before she can reply, a young girl takes her hand and, bidding her with a big smile, to rise, leads her to the hot food.

They feast like kings and then the entertainment begins. Men, women and children recite traditional poetry, dance and sing along with a spiked instrument – a bit like a primitive violin, called a *rebab*. There are wooden flutes and pipes, hide hand drums, a primitive lute, a *Santur* or hammer dulcimer with metal strings that comes from Iraq and what looks like a long decorated mortar and pestle which doubles as a symbol of affluence and hospitality. "The songs were passed down from our grandparents," one of the women explains, "to make us feel strong in the desert and the loneliness disappear. There are also songs for the camels to make them happy and strong."

Beautiful bejewelled women in elaborately decorated, brightly coloured costumes, perform traditional belly-dances and then the young men show off their sword-skills, their lethal weapons flashing in the fire, torch and candle-light now that darkness has fallen, to the clapping and singing of those who dare face them. An exciting and elaborate display of traditional skills and customs during which the guests continue to be plied with richly spiced sweet arabic coffee, dates, milk and dried camel flesh.

The conversation afterwards continues well into the night, inevitably reverting to the war in Syria which has so deeply affected them all. Ana is horrified to hear how the government attacked the Ghouta agricultural belt around Damascus, using rockets filled with Sarin that killed over a thousand and realises that this happened just before she went into besieged Old Homs. "Assad was on the offensive against rebel held territory," Caleb explains. "His use of chemical weapons against his own people, made it clear there were no depths to which he would not sink and time was running out. I had to get you in and out of Old Homs before it was too late. I'm sorry Ana." He looks defeated and so tired.

"I would have stayed until the job was done whether you helped me or not." She searches his troubled eyes, "and would most certainly have failed if you hadn't. You saved my life." Her current predicament makes itself felt and, distracted, she gasps.

"They're moving?" He smiles, placing a hand on her belly, but she is lost.

"Oh my...!" She sits up, struggling to breath and he rises in alarm to his knees before her.

"What is it?"

"I'm pregnant with twins!" Caleb shakes his head in amusement but she is serious. "What are we going to do?"

"Stay here until we're strong again, see the children at Za'atari, then go to London to deliver our babies." But there is something else in his eyes and Ana's agitation rises.

"Can you get him out without going into Syria?"

"Aadil?" She nods and Caleb shakes his head.

"I'm working on it." The light plays tricks with the lines on his face and he looks exhausted.

"Bed?"

"Soon." He sinks back into the cushions, adjusting his position so that his arm hangs properly in its sling, then beckons her to settle back down with him. "We'll go to bed soon," he whispers, tickling her ear as she nestles her back carefully into him and she heaves a sigh of contentment.

The discussion turns to the many disparate groups that collectively form the opposition and Ana does her best to understand. There are hundreds of groups affiliated to the Supreme Military Council of the Free Syrian Army, she is told, but these don't always agree with one another. The Islamic Front was created only a few weeks ago when seven Islamist groups came together forming, with an estimated forty five thousand fighters, the largest rebel alliance. Then there is the Syrian Islamic Liberation Front consisting of about twenty rebel groups; at least six independent groups; the Popular Protection Units representing the Kurds who have sought to stay out of the conflict, focusing instead on consolidating their territorial gains since the withdrawal of the Syrian Army; and, finally, the jihadists. These include the Islamic State of Iraq and the Levant, known as ISIS. Formed in April with about five thousand fighters, this is a group that crucifies and beheads its opponents, that subjugates women and girls and kills anyone who gets in its way, including Muslims.

"A perverted militant cult presenting itself as a religious movement," Caleb calls it with venom.

"Whose singular bloodlust for power, eclipses all those Islamic teachings relating to the beauty of the Creator and his creation," Hussein adds, "and whose acquisition of religious 'authority' through violent territorial control, even by mugging other extremist groups with the same worldview, exposes as myth its claim to be a brotherhood and aim to create a united Ummah."

"Community of believers," Ishtar translates for Ana's benefit.

"Considered so extreme, as even to have been disavowed by al-Qaeda," Hussein continues angrily. "Full of foreigners! Saudi Arabians, Libyans and Tunisians. Chechens, Kuwaitis, Jordanians, Iraqis, Pakistani Taliban, even Chinese. And led by an Iraqi! Terrorists that bristle with weapons in their Pakistani-style tunics and menacing balaclavas in stark contrast to the indigenous moderate Sunni Muslims of Syria."

"Then there is the force from which ISIS spawned – the Al-Nusra Front for the People of Levant created in 2011. A militant group that includes al-Qaeda in Iraq and has disciplined, well armed fighters regularly taking part in rebel offensives. Most of its fighters are from Syria," someone else adds.

"And, finally, there is Jaysh al-Muhajiran wa al-Ansar, the Army of the Emigrants and Helpers, a group comprising hundreds of mainly foreign fighters, formed in March and led by the Chechen Jihadist Omar al-Shishani."

"This is the problem now, of course," Sheikh Hussein explains. "The reason for Obama's indecisiveness, or ploy as some call it, to keep Assad in power despite the atrocities he commits against his people."

"What do you mean?"

"The last thing anyone wants, is a jihadist state bordering Israel."

Well-fed, pleasantly exhausted from the days activities and desperate for the bathroom, Ana struggles to keep up as the discussion becomes more heated. "I'm going for some fresh air," she tells Caleb, declining his offer of company for he looks so comfortable and sleepy.

A full moon hanging like a lantern in the sky, bathes everything in liquid silver, contriving with the crisp night air to take her breath away. Spellbound, Ana stops to take it all in. This is the same moon as looked down on Cleopatra...Shakespeare... Beethoven and it will be the same when all she recognises, ceases to exist. Steadfast and cratered with imperfections. Companion to a million twinkling stars that join it now and beckon, as if to say, this is your home. Of stardust you were made and to the stars eventually, you will all return.

OASIS

Ana's rest is fitful again that night. Though Caleb sleeps peacefully, her mind is full of horrors and nightmares of orphan twins. A boy and a girl, bewildered and frightened as they struggle to survive a world of hunger and pain. By the time she falls into a deep sleep, the sun is rising with the temperature of the tent and her husband is drifting in and out of consciousness.

He wakes her with a kiss, a glorious smile, a few days stubble and eyes full of promise. "How are you?"

"Really good Ana, and you?" He strokes her forehead tenderly but the dis-ease of her nightmares haunts her still. "What were you dreaming about?"

She shakes her head reluctantly. "What happened between you and your twin?"

Caleb frowns. "It's complicated," he says, looking with resignation into her eyes. "Let's just say, he wasn't what I expected and we never had the opportunity to reconcile our differences."

"Did you ever see him again after the fire?" Caleb shakes his head. "Or hear of him?"

"No."

"Do you think you will one day?"

"No doubt." He doesn't sound too enamoured of the idea.

"What's he like?"

Caleb shrugs. "He's what I fear I could've become."

"What do you mean?"

"You said once, right, that monsters are made, not born?"

Ana nods but Caleb looks so desolate, she hasn't the heart to pursue him further.

"Do you think there will ever be peace in Syria?" she asks instead.

"Mandela once said, people must learn to hate, and if they can learn to hate, they can be taught to love, for love comes more naturally to the human heart than its opposite.

"Yes, I think so. One day. He may be an arrogant butcher but Assad has learnt the price he'll pay for getting it wrong a second time."

"If he gets a second chance."

"He's made quite sure the alternative will be worse." Caleb strokes her hair but is clearly troubled.

"Do you ever speak of what they did to you?" He frowns. "I can't imagine going back to my normal world. How can anything be the same, ever again? How is it possible to speak about such terrible things…as we've …? And if we do, what are the chances of being believed?

"Is that how it is Caleb? Do you just hold on to it and drift through a world that no longer seems real, a prisoner somewhere far worse?"

He closes his eyes as if to shield her from what she has just inflicted on him and she regrets her words. Then, taking a deep breath, he searches her soul. "Ana, there is one thing I want you to realise before all else." He hesitates. "You're not a victim but a survivor." He waits for what he has said to sink in. "Do you understand?" He strokes her hair back so that his hands frame her face and waits for confirmation. "I want you to tell me everything. Your mind has buried the worst of it so deep. But I already know. The truth can't hurt me more than it has already. I understand."

"Have you talked with anyone about what happened to you?" He shakes his head. "Will you? To me?"

He sighs. "Maybe. But if I don't, it's not because you're not strong enough to bear it." Lying on top of her now, resting on his elbows, he seems invincible and yet, so vulnerable.

"Maybe it's better not to remember?"

He nods. "If you stare into the abyss for too long, the abyss stares back at you." He kisses her forehead. "Sometimes, however, it surfaces despite your best efforts to keep it back. Then it's good to be with someone who truly understands."

"I'm so sorry." She can't bear to think of how he suffered.

"I know. But it's over. Death has taught me the value of small things and for that I am grateful. Now all that matters is us. We're what's real. The rest is an illusion." He waits but what he has disclosed is sufficient. Ana smiles. "How are our babies today?" Shifting onto his good arm, Caleb places the other low on her belly.

"They're fine, thanks."

He moves down to them, putting a hand on either side of her pelvis and she touches the skin over his fractured humerus. "Mended," he says and she shakes her head.

"Can't be!"

"Just needs to harden now, that's all."

He kisses their babies softly, reverently, then her pubis. Waves of pleasure wash through her, making everything tingle and something delicious tighten deep inside. He kisses her again and, taking on a life of its own, her body rises from the bed. "I'd like to ride with you tonight," Caleb tells her and she is in no position to argue. "You can have Sargan, I'll take one of the other horses. I ride well. It'll be perfectly safe. I've ridden for my life before with injuries far worse." She frowns and he kisses her again, lower this time so that she gasps, grabbing his hair as if to stop him. His hands skim hyper-sensitive skin amplifying the thrill pulsing through her and she moans, wondering how she can already be so close to losing control.

Slowly, carefully, with sensitivity to her every need and fear, both conscious and unconscious, he takes her to the heights of ecstasy and gently down again. When she lies helplessly exhausted before him, every dread of what was done to her, dispelled, he tells her that she is beautiful and he loves her more than words could ever say.

It is past midday by the time they emerge from their tent but their welcome committee remains undaunted, full of the joy of seeing them again. Embarrassed, Ana takes Caleb's hand and he squeezes it gently. "We thought you'd never wake up!" M'hammed tells them and reassured that they haven't compromised themselves, Ana returns his greeting with equal warmth and sincerity.

"How are you M'hammed?"

"Wonderful, thank you Ana. All the better for seeing you! Might I say that you look absolutely radiant this good morning?" She blushes as if the reason for her utter contentment might have been discovered after all, and looks with helpless adoration at her husband.

"Good morning M'hammed. We are indebted to you and your family for entertaining us so lavishly and for the luxury in which you keep us. Thank you, *Alhamdulillah!*" M'hammed bows graciously. "We are both healing at a rate that could only be possible in the refuge of your wonderful hospitality and are eternally in your debt."

"Okay Caleb, that's enough, you obsequious scoundrel!" Caleb pretends to be offended and M'hammed turns to Ana for support. "You know, we are only repaying a debt?" She shakes her head. "Caleb saved me from a fate worse than death. As well as that a few times, if the truth be told. This is the least we could do for you, though I would do it a thousand times with no dream of recompense other than the happiness in your beautiful face."

Momentarily lost for words, Ana hesitates. "So what was the fate worse than death?" she hardly dares but cannot resist asking.

M'hammed coughs in fake embarrassment. "It grieves me so to speak of the fairer sex. Suffice it to say that I was saved from the clutches of one of devious intent with but a shadow of the charms so radiantly displayed by present company."

"Thank you M'hammed. It's good to have one's virtues at long last, recognised and extolled!" Caleb retorts. His friend snorts in derision and ignoring him, addresses himself instead, to she who inspires his compliments.

"So, why were you at the mercy of a woman intent on taking advantage of an innocent such as yourself?" Ana asks mischievously.

"What makes you think it was a she?"

Again his friend feigns to ignore him. "She cast a spell on me. I had no choice but to submit," he complains and Caleb laughs out loud.

"And did you derive any benefit from this uneven relationship?" Ana teases.

M'hammed shakes his head sadly. "I was shamelessly taken advantage of. Misused and cast aside when I had served my purpose. Luckily this rascal was at hand to save me."

"Why? What would have happened otherwise?" M'hammed appears to be genuinely embarrassed and, blushing as he makes his reply, proceeds to recount a tale of brotherly retribution. An honour killing that saw him as something other than the innocent he was. Looking in consternation to her husband, Ana waits for his explanation of their, presumably disrespectful, behaviour and he shrugs.

"What else could I have done? Whether he deserved it or not, I couldn't have stood by and let them murder him."

"But I thought the woman was usually the victim of an honour killing."

"Yes, you're right. Unfortunately for us on this occasion though, said victim was the one wearing the trousers, so to speak. The men of her family towed her line rather than vice versa."

"So how did you ...?" Ana is beginning to lose the will to pursue this line of banter any further.

"It's a long story. Suffice it to say that a man has needs ..." Ana frowns. "Women have needs too, of course," he adds, hastily, "but on this occasion, I was led, saw the light when the love of my life entered it and beat a hasty retreat which the former recipient of my attentions did not appreciate. Despite her being the first to reject me. I am now, of course, happily married to my love and like you, expecting our first child."

Ana is taken aback. "Congratulations! How exciting!"

"Indeed. I will introduce you to my beautiful Laila …"

"Dark beauty of the night," Caleb interjects and Ana scowls at him, "… later today. Thank you Caleb for explaining the meaning of her name, which I must say, fails to do her justice." Caleb smiles graciously and M'hammed proceeds to clear a path for them through the crowd. Ushering them onwards with mutterings of plans for another glorious day, he expresses the need at some point, for a private word with Caleb.

"Another secret?" Ana whispers but M'hammed hears.

"Some things, Ana," he says, gravely, "you do not want to know. Ah, here is father. Ana can I leave you in the hands of these beautiful women?" Looking beyond her, he waves his arms before him, bowing ostentatiously and she turns to see a dozen or so women and children watching in excited anticipation.

The women take it in turns to look after her. Over the course of the day Ana finds herself at a loom, weaving camel hair into a strip of material that will be used to make a tent, grinding and cooking coffee, kneading bread and rolling balls of cheese. Then, with baskets full of dirty clothing, they take her to one of the reservoirs. "This water is not for drinking, only washing," she is informed then, with fits of giggles, "and swimming!" The men seldom come this way.

They drop the dirty clothes onto the water, the baskets by the side and, without hesitation, their outer robes. Elaborately decorated, brightly coloured silk and cotton, accentuate sylph-like figures, beautiful refined faces and those mesmerising eyes – varying from black, through Caleb's chocolate brown to Ana's piercing green. Even the unearthly pale blue of the northern fox. Chatting away, giggling and laughing like girls of their age anywhere in the world, they begin to peel this layer off also, goading Ana to do likewise and when they all stand naked before the reservoir, count down from the three that signals them to jump in together.

It feels like silk against her skin. Refreshingly cool, soft and buoyant. Liberating. As she floats on her back looking up at warm blue sky to the sound of happiness, splashing and bubbling around her, Ana begins to drift peacefully away.

A chilling shriek startles her, agitating the calm water and, though it was a false alarm, she dives, desperate to subdue her frantic heart. She swims the circumference of the reservoir, estimating it to be about a metre deep, twenty five by ten at its widest and finds a man-made dam. She imagines this overwhelmed by the winter rains, completely submerged in a magnificent pool at least twice this size and, stretching herself as far as she can, glides blissfully, her mind wandering with her body.

When she emerges, she sees that the others are not so sure of themselves. She offers to teach them to swim and they line up eagerly at the water's edge, laughing and giggling as if freed from the very discretion so many describe as liberating. This, Ana will never fully understand. Though she has learned the benefits of being able to hide under the customary concealing clothing, one of the many means by which women are controlled in the Arab world, she has yet to reconcile these with the freedom of expression and movement it denies. "Ahh…," her beautiful companion, exclaims, "but it is equality with men and the freedom of choice women want, not freedom from the niqab!"

Temporarily lost to a world of injustice and oppression, Ana does not notice until it is too late. Though the hands are soft, the touch gentle, when she feels it on the now distinct bump rising from her otherwise flat tummy, she jumps, startling all around her as the water amplifies her shock. Adrenaline sets her heart racing, restricting her breathing to short shallow pants and Ana fights off the terrors once more. All else fades away so that she hardly registers the alarm on Caleb's face or how Tuan pulls his best friend back. But that is enough to bring her to her senses and she rallies.

She sees the pain in the young girl's face and sorrow chases away fear. Taking her hands in her own, Ana wills them both calm. "It's okay," she says. "I'm sorry. It's okay." The girl looks at Ana sadly, swallowing hard as she barely touches the scars on her back. "It's over," Ana tells her. "I'm here now. Safe and happy. Sometimes the memories catch me out, that's all. Okay?" The girl nods and, taking her hand, Ana places it on her belly. "Two babies," she says. "Twins."

"Twins?" Their concern turns to joy and, as the women fuss over her, Ana sinks into the cool water, submerging every visible reminder of the brutal treatment she received at the hands of Syria's elite. She wonders if the vision she had of her husband was a delusion and if not, what she should do about it. The Rwala tribe seems very tolerant in its outlook and these girls didn't hesitate to strip off, though they must surely realise how easily they could be discovered. Ana settles herself with the suspicion that excitement of possible discovery outweighs prospect of shame and in the sure knowledge that neither Caleb nor Tuan would do anything to compromise their honour.

"Are you ready to swim?" she asks and the girls jump about, splashing each other, laughing and shrieking. "Then do what I do." Ana lies herself on her back, floating effortlessly in the water with her arms and legs spread out like a starfish then rights herself to watch the others do the same. Most succeed and she shows them how to support those who struggle until they all float in the tranquil water, looking up to deep blue sky. Next, she encourages them to float face down and when they have mastered that, lines them up at the side of the reservoir ready to push themselves away and glide.

So the lesson progresses. By the time they return to their washing, all of them have succeeded in getting from one end of the pool to the other and Ana has convinced them of their ability to become proficient swimmers. There has been no sign of intruders. As they wonder happily back, Ana relegates her vision to the same place as her flashbacks. Hallucinations. All in the mind.

A reddening sun drops from a pale pink sky into fiery orange, setting the desert ablaze. She feels utterly contented here in this oasis yet, deep inside, an uneasiness takes root. Unconsciously she puts a hand over her babies and with that, he takes the other. Tall, handsome, strong and reassuring, Caleb walks beside her, his eyes full of love, a knowing smile on his lips and neither of them say a word.

"Hungry?" he asks at last and she shakes her head. "Feel up to a ride then, before supper?" She had forgotten about the night ride. Though the days here are eleven hours long, the sun rises early, setting by six, so there is time to ride the night before the celebrations of the evening begin. She nods warily but he seems so recovered now.

"You shouldn't," she tells him nevertheless.

"Don't worry, I know how to look after myself."

Before them, the shadows lengthen and a bloated moon glows a subtle shade of pink.

They ride hard and far into the darkening night, away from camp through inhospitable desert. The horses, excited to stretch their legs in the rapidly cooling night, place their feet fearlessly, ignoring dark shadows that threaten and recede all around them and Saluki hounds that turn to silver streaks in the moonlight. Every now and again one of these alters direction and they follow, chasing some creature visible only to the dogs. A hare perhaps, jerboa, gazelle, ibex or Arabian oryx, startled from sleep by the dangerous intrusion. But for Ana's sake, tonight they will not kill.

Caleb did not boast when he said he rode well. There is no sign of injury in the way he moves with his horse and Sargan, despite his determination to prove himself, is clearly conscious of the responsibility he bears. They all ride bareback tonight, high on adrenaline of a different kind to that Ana has become accustomed to and she uses this to push her excitement to the limit of fear. Tonight she will be the one in control.

They have ridden a good hour, their path constantly changing so that she is totally disorientated, when they arrive at the foothills of a mountain range. While the others dismount to rest and water their horses from camel skin bags, Caleb bids her follow him. The dry bed of a valley fast becomes a deep ravine, ominous walls looming to either side. A gentle breeze dances around them, touching her face and filling her nostrils. Moist. Full of the scent of sweet flowers, rosemary and thyme. Ana wonders if she is dreaming and then they turn the corner.

Silver tinged moonlight illuminates this heavenly garden. Date-palms. Anemones of rare white. Oleander and dark mountain tulips – blood red by daylight. All flower out of season as if this oasis were untainted by time. From high in the mountains, water gushes over glistening rocks through a series of pools. As she wonders where it disappears too, Caleb takes Ana to a window onto an underground river. "There's something I want to show you," he says, dismounting and she follows, taking his hand as the horses make their way to the water to drink.

He leads her to a flat stone surrounded by glowing anemones, that projects like a spring-board over a large tranquil pool. Just close enough to catch the spray from the water-fall. Ana searches for the magic that keeps this piece of heaven alive but Caleb's thoughts are elsewhere. She follows his gaze to their feet and there, perfectly formed, like an elegant white ribbon, lies a verse of Arabic carved into the pale grey stone.

Selideh and Laila. Lost but never forgotten...Listen, as the wind blows.

The translation comes to her in a whisper on the breeze. Releasing her hand, Caleb drops to his haunches, brushing the words lightly as if he could reveal them more clearly and she falls to her knees beside him. The fragrant air plays a tune, rustling leaves, stirring tinkling water. Perfect harmony. Peaceful. Forgiving. Full of the joy of life. The sound of infinite eternity encompassed by nature.

"How did you know your baby was a girl?"

Glancing at her swollen belly, Caleb smiles. "I just did." They seat themselves beside each other on the stone and he takes her hand. "She would have been eleven." He pauses to listen to the music of the wind.

"My uncle found Selideh. Retrieved her body, for they had buried her according to Islamic law. It took far longer to find me and she was a Christian, so he had her cremated. And waited for me to decide what to do with the ashes. This place was like heaven to us." He falls into contemplative silence, watching as Sargan ambles up to them and strokes his nose tenderly. "Of course she loved you too, Sargan. Only three years old, you were a young man in your prime. Though Selideh didn't ride as well as Ana, you took good care of her even then."

Caleb heaves a great sigh and looks to Ana with brimming eyes. "Funny how things turn out, isn't it? Never quite as we expect …" He touches her cheek gently with the back of his hand and she leans in with a heavy heart. "It means so much to me that you're here."

They hold each other for a lifetime in that place that time forgot. Remembering. Making fresh memories and nurturing hopes for their future. But the moon lives for the present, shifting shadows as if to remind them that others wait and, at last, Caleb tells Sargan to go get them. "When they're done, we'll head for camp."

Another lavish meal later, provided once more by Sheikh Hussein, his brother insisting on taking the honour the following day, conversation returns to politics with a general attempt to make sense of the mad world. Here in the desert, it all seems so simple. A matter not only of surviving from day to day but of living life to the full. A pursuit which both demands and rewards with team-work, loyalty and love.

They ask Ana about Medecin Sans Frontieres. "Without borders – what does that mean?" She explains how this organisation responds to need regardless of political allegiance, ethnicity or religion. "As we live without borders? To us these artificial boundaries created to turn our land into a commodity, do not exist. We should be free to go wherever we wish. Whose right is it anyway, to say the land belongs to him, or to this person or to that? We are all born with the equal right to live on this planet. No-one has a greater claim than another to any piece of it. It all belongs to us all." She couldn't agree more and they go on to discuss not only physical but spiritual borders as well.

"So what do we think of the concept," Caleb asks, "of us all belonging to one infinite and eternal spiritual being? Of our physical existence being merely an extension of our true selves?"

"Or as the Buddhist would say," Tuan elaborates. "I am in everything and everything is in me?"

"I would say that is an interesting concept young man and each to his own," Hussain replies.

"No, seriously man. He may be a bit way out but he has ideas ya know…that are worthy of consideration."

Caleb appears to choke on his drink and laughs out loud. "Emm, actually I'm serious," he says, recovering himself. "It kind of puts things into perspective for me, anyway. Islam teaches, does it not, that our physical lives are very brief. We should not think twice about sacrificing ourselves and others in the service of Allah because of the rewards awaiting us for an eternity in heaven. If you believe your spiritual life to be eternal, then inevitably your physical life must be negligible and, if I am everything and everything is in me, whatever harm I suffer at the hands of another, is actually inflicted by myself. Blinded by ego of course. That does lend a different perspective."

"Do you think the parents of Hamza al-Khateeb would be happy to consider your idea?" a young lady asks angrily from the centre of the tent.

Caleb shakes his head with a frown. "No, I'm seeking neither to excuse unacceptable behaviour nor belittle suffering, but to come to terms with destructive forces within us which we seem unable to control." He looks around, realising that an explanation of what has just passed, is in order. "Hamza was thirteen years old when he was imprisoned and tortured by Assad's regime, his body returned to his family shortly after the start of the uprising."

"Tell them what they did to him, these monsters you want me to identify with!"

Caleb looks to the young woman with compassion. "Yes, I agree with you. It is hard, maybe impossible. Best not to inflict the details of what he suffered on our companions tonight though, don't you think?"

"What did they do?" the young man next to her asks and she looks first on him in confusion, then the others.

Hussain shrugs. "It's okay, most of us know and perhaps those that don't, should. All the children have gone to bed, have they not?" He makes a show of looking round the tent but there are no children. Ana shrinks into Caleb, knowing she does not want to hear what is coming next. Only thirteen years old. The same age as Aadil.

"He was detained during a protest in Daraa in April 2011, this boy, and returned a month later covered in bruises and cigarette burns. He had a fractured jaw, smashed kneecaps and three bullet wounds. There was evidence that he had been electrocuted, whipped with cable and… they had cut off his penis." A gasp of horror echoes around the tent and her neighbour tries to console the woman delivering this atrocious news, but she hasn't finished. "He was only thirteen, the same age as my brother. A generous gentle boy, who walked the twelve kilometres with his family and friends because everyone seemed to be going to the protest. It was just a family outing. He wasn't political – just a kid! And you Christians turn to the perpetrator of such atrocities for protection?"

She is beside herself but refuses to be comforted and Ishtar looks to her son as if to say, now look what you started. "Assad and his forces are guilty of the most terrible crimes against humanity," she tells them, "but so too, are those who have hijacked a legitimate opposition to depose him. We are more afraid of them than we are of him. To us, he is the lesser of two evils."

"Also, many Christians in Syria have been horribly tortured and murdered by muslim rebels," a young woman dressed, like Ishtar in a smart trouser-suit, adds. "And we know this persecution will continue if the Islamists topple Assad. He is at least tolerant of religious diversity and has a history of defending Christians in his land."

"Isn't it interesting," one of the elders pipes up, "that whilst the United States, Saudi Arabia and other Gulf Arab states supported protests in Syria, they turned a blind eye to those in Bahrain? There medics, including doctors like yourself Ana, are being held and subjected to similar brutality simply for treating injured protestors. Even Turkey treats its people in this unjust way. With no respect for medical neutrality. It doesn't seem likely to me, that what the Arab Spring has succeeded in removing will be replaced by anything more tolerant or democratic. There is no ideological consistency to all of this."

"Indeed. See how the West sits back and watches the Palestinians suffer under Israeli occupation...and Washington's hypocrisy, as the Russians point out, when it pressures Syria because of human rights abuses whilst lifting a ban on military aid to Uzbekistan, a country ruled by a repressive authoritarian regime that just happens to be important in supplying NATO troops to Afghanistan."

"And, there should be more concern about Iran," Ishtar adds. "With a non-combatant American president fast losing the respect of world leaders, there is little standing in the way of any despot and no-one to prevent Iran developing its Shia nuclear bomb. Iran is very clever. Like most of the world it seems, it will hedge its bets. Even in Syria, it is reported to have made contact with opposition leaders when there seemed a real chance Assad might fall.

"Despite Iran's claims to be the champion of Shia Muslims,

western governments make themselves vulnerable to these Persian masters of deception for Mr Rouhani's rhetoric has become more sophisticated over the years. The West fails to see that he is merely tolerated by the Revolutionary Guard who would see the abandonment of its nuclear dream as humiliation. It costs to fund Iran's military intervention in Syria, Lebanon, Iraq and Gaza and, with its economy in a mess, there is little to spare for its nuclear programme. That will all change once economic sanctions are lifted. Iran will rise to a prominent position regionally and there will be no going back.

"Imagine how that will fuel this new Sunni revolution. How it will drive recruits anxious about a Shia backlash, into the arms of ISIS. We cannot seriously expect the gulf states to sit back and watch a Shia power rise from the ashes of this chaos. They'll be clamouring for their nuclear bomb as well, with a willing partner in Pakistan. Can you imagine? Nuclear proliferation in an unstable middle east with Islamic fundamentalists cashing in on ethnic tensions raised by Maliki's policies in Iraq and Assad's megalomania in Syria." There is stunned silence from the audience.

"Meanwhile, Tehran expands its ballistic missile programme under cover of UN talks!"

Ana turns to Caleb with a frown. "Where do Hamas and Hizbullah fit into all this?"

"Hamas was founded to liberate Palestine from Israeli occupation," he tells her, "and to establish an Islamic state in the area that is now Israel, the West Bank, and the Gaza Strip. It has governed the Gaza Strip since June 2007 and been supported by the Syrian regime but it is an organisation born of the Muslim Brotherhood which is Sunni, along the majority of protestors against Assad. From the start of the civil war, Hamas stated that, whilst being grateful for the support it received from the Syrian regime, it also admired the people's aspirations for freedom, reform and prosperity. It tried to advise Bashar al-Assad on reform but when all attempts at mediation failed, cut its ties with him. Unlike Hizbullah which would likely collapse without him, Hamas has the support of the people.

"Hizbullah – which means, Party of God, on the other hand, is a Shi'a Islamic militant group and political party based in Lebanon. Its paramilitary wing, regarded as a resistance movement throughout much of the Arab world is considered more powerful than the Lebanese Army. It was conceived by Muslim clerics, funded by Iran following the Israeli invasion of Lebanon in 1982, and formed primarily to offer resistance to the Israeli occupation. It receives military training, weapons, and financial support from Iran, and political support from Syria. Since 2012, Hizbullah has helped the Syrian government fight its opposition, describing the protests as a zionist plot to destroy its alliance with al-Assad against Israel. Its involvement in the civil war has been key in turning Assad's possible defeat into his probable victory."

"And if Assad does survive, what will happen to the refugees?" Nobody seems to have an answer.

"We don't have the resources to support so many here indefinitely. None of the host countries do. But the refugees have no choice but to stay. Unemployment, poverty, unrest and hostility towards them will grow. That is how it is if you are a refugee. See your country Ana. It is rich compared to ours and yet it limits the number of refugees it takes far more than ever we have." Ana nods shamefully.

"Of course, so many people living in unsanitary conditions increase the risk of disease and now we hear that polio has returned to Syria. Did you see this Ana while you were there?" a young woman asks.

Ana nods. "I saw children who had been paralysed by a viral illness," she replies, "but officials won't admit to cases that aren't proven by laboratory testing. And to think, Syria had been free of polio for fifteen years!"

"Another weapon Assad uses against his people."

"What do you mean?" Hussein asks but when Caleb shakes his head, the Sheikh turns to Ana instead.

"They believe it came from Pakistan. You know polio is endemic now in only three countries?" she tells him and he shakes his head. "Afghanistan, Pakistan and Nigeria, in all of which, vaccination programmes have been disrupted by conflict. In Syria now it is the same. Sanitation and government vaccination programmes have collapsed in rebel held areas and the children are weakened by starvation, stress and sickness. Perfect conditions for polio to make a come-back. Terrible isn't it? How do you tell a desperately poor labourer that the one son he put all his hopes into, will never walk though he is not yet five months old?"

"Denying the population basic health-care is one of the strategies the Syrian regime uses against its people," Caleb tells them bitterly. "Attacking anyone who helps the vulnerable, destroying the health-care system and denying vaccines to areas considered politically unsympathetic or that are outside government control. This is a man-made outbreak and Assad is responsible!"

"Suddenly we find a very old disease affecting the children again. A silent killer that rises from the water rather than blasting us from the skies," an old woman warns.

"How many children are likely to be affected then?"

"The problem is that for every affected child, there may be hundreds carrying the virus and spreading it undetected. In ninety percent, symptoms are mild but in some, the virus goes on to destroy nerve cells. I heard that up to ninety thousand are likely to be infected within the next few months."

"Ninety thousand?" Ana nods. "Then its spread throughout the region is inevitable!"

"Intensive vaccination campaigns are under way but this is dangerous work. Health-care workers are targeted and six doses of vaccine do not guarantee protection for every child. Good sanitation is also key."

"We see a mass exodus…how many?"

"Two and a half million have fled, a further six and a half million are internally displaced. Nearly half the population of Syria."

"So many people forced to live in shelters made of whatever they can find, often with no sanitation. Even, as I've seen, drawing water for washing, cooking and drinking from unlined wells downstream of temporary latrines."

BACK TO ZA'ATARI

Her eyes follow his finger to shimmering haze where land morphs with sky and she sees hills, mountains even and at their feet, a glimmering streak. The Dead Sea. She shakes her head in wonder, wishing for that time but with Caleb instead, when they were free to float in water too buoyant to swim, that fizzed with exotic minerals they had to shower off before it dried into the same crystalline crust as cakes its shores. When they read with ease, the paper he wrote for, floating on their backs as if reclining in some giant armchair before wandering hand in hand through the skeletons of Roman encampments and up the rocky slopes of once besieged Masada. A snatched romance and another world now so close and alien.

"Eight times saltier than the ocean." She hears her voice and grounds herself.

"And the lowest spot on earth. I'll take you there one day Ana, and show you the wonders of the Wadi Rum."

"Petra ..."

"You'll see it as no-one ever has before. I promise."

She'd no idea they were so close. They must have headed South from Sheik Hussain Bridge all those weeks ago, for that is nearly on the border with Syria.

Comforting arms enfold her and she snuggles in, relishing the warmth of Caleb's body against her back, the touch of his lips on the nape of her neck. She closes her eyes. "We have to go," he whispers and though the words pain her, his breath in her ear makes her smile. He turns her to face him and, reluctant to lose even a moment of contact she frowns petulantly into his radiant face. "You are so lovely," he tells her, his eyes sparkling and when her lips hunger for his, he meets their passion with soothing, calming love.

They left early that morning, when the sand felt cool and creamy underfoot, the air so cold and crisp that you could see far into the future. "At least twenty kilometres," their host had beamed. It was hard to leave an Oasis whose people have become family and with whom they shared so much, but their departure was necessary. Time passes and the babies inside her make their needs ever more keenly felt. The whole clan came out to see them off, full of promises and gifts and, somehow, they found room for these too, in their already bulging panniers.

So now they follow this ancient road of sand and stone, iridescent cliffs rising to either side of them, the cool air rushing past, laden with exotic smells. Salt, green, heavenly blossom, and where they pass the occasional Bedouin, spiced coffee, burning wood and cooking food.

Here whole cities, like Petra, have been lost and found, Caleb tells her, hidden in Earth's clefts and cracks. He stops the bike from time to time, killing its engine and they sit in silence, breathing in the spirit of sacred places where nature harmonises with man-made structures in flowing shapes of glowing colours. Reds, oranges, pinks and purples.

Sheik Hussein spoke with her, sitting late into this last night before glowing embers that had cooked them a feast of chicken.

"For most, the light is hidden," he said, "behind a series of veils. Layers of ignorance. As we progress through various stages of understanding to higher levels of perception, the veils begin to lift and become more translucent, bringing us closer to God. Every life, whether realised or not, is a voyage of discovery towards what unity with God really means."

He looked to her for understanding and she smiled.

"There is an English composer," she told him, "who wrote music inspired by this journey."

"John Taverner. The Protecting Veil." She was impressed but then he looked on her with great sadness, his face flickering in the light of flames released by Caleb's stick. "You know Ana, revenge runs deep in Arab culture. For peace to come to Syria, everyone must forgive and forget. Syria's diversity must become its strength once more." She didn't want conversation to revert that way again and as he spoke words to her such as a father might to a departing child, a cold shiver ran along her spine.

"Violent extremism, throughout the world," he said, "is generally perpetrated by Sunni Salafi groups. Like Al-Qaeda and its offshoots, including ISIS and Jabhat Al-Nusra; Boko Haram, which means, incidentally, western education is forbidden, and al-Shabaab. You know, for five decades, Saudi Arabia has been the official sponsor of Sunni Salafism throughout the world? Even so, ninety percent of Sunni Muslims are not Salafi, for this is considered too rigid, too literalist, too detached from main-stream Islam.

"In the sense that they revolt against history, they are no different – Salafi Sunnis and the Shi'ite extremists sponsored by the Iranian revolution. To them, modernity is the enemy with its ideas of liberty – for men as well as women, democracy rather than tyranny." The Sheikh paused to consider something in the shadows before them.

"And it is a mistake," he added at last, "to think that these extremists can be swayed by compassion. They are terrorists who dehumanise their enemies, who see individuals as representatives of a degenerate adversary. It is up to the rest of the Muslim world to condemn this representation of Islam rather than be humiliated by its successes. Defiance is what will delegitimise groups such as these which thrive on the image they cultivate of being unchallengeable organisations."

Wheat, even oaks grow out of the dust by the side of the road, along with hardy shrubs and poisonous, sweet-scented Oleander. Strange formations rise out of sandstone striped like tigers. Arches, huge mushrooms and mountains like stacks of giant red coins. They pass Dolmans – tombs dating back to the fourth millennium BC, similar to the granite pyres that rise out of Cornwall's Bodmin Moor except these, Caleb informs her, would have been buried underground.

Though so many promises were made, Ana wonders if she will ever see her new friends again. Something blocks her vision of a future. Something that became distant in their desert oasis but looms larger the further they go. Tuan at least, will always turn up like a bad penny and, chastising herself with a fond smile, for the unfortunate turn of phrase his image conjures up, she worries about him. He should have crossed the border from Lebanon into Syria by now and she prays he makes it safely back with Aadil and his sister.

And Ishtar. She left for Ma'aloula over a week ago, contrary to everyone's advice. "My husband languishes in a Syrian prison. Family and friends struggle to survive under siege by fundamental Islamists and you expect me to wait here until it is all over?" Ana will not allow herself to consider how likely Caleb is to follow.

Fortresses built by Muslims, Crusaders, Mongols, Mamluks and Ottomans, perched high on conical hills and ridges at the intersection of vital trade-routes, stand testament still, to centuries of mankind come and gone. Births, lives and conflicts that have passed, people reduced to the dust from which they came.

"Jerash." Caleb startles her out of her sombre mood and she sees their way through fresh eyes in his company. The roads here are lined with fig, olive and cypress trees and in the distance, welcoming mountains are covered by woods and orchards. Mimosa blossoms here in the spring, he tells her and it is easy to imagine the glory of Roman times. He stops for them to dismount and they wander, hand in hand along empty Roman streets, up staircases and through an amphitheatre that would have seated thousands. She touches crumbling columns that were built millennia ago, sculptures, colonnades, facades and ancient, almost perfectly preserved mosaics.

Colourful depictions of mystical creatures, exotic people, slaves, dancing girls, hunting scenes, elaborate buildings and maps. And all the while they come closer to destruction that still lives. An evil force that would destroy even this.

"Tell me the starfish story." Somehow she hears Caleb clearly above the purr of the engine and wonders if she can make herself heard as he does. They are nearly there now and she knows he is trying to distract her.

Why now? But she does understand. For too long she has wondered. What is the point? Nearly three years have passed since this terrible conflict began with no end to it in sight. Only something worse looming out of the terror. Everything she and so many others worked so hard for, suffered for – seems lost, insignificant now and yet, once she believed in the story and it kept her going. She hesitates but the vision returns and she tells him what she sees.

"A man was driving past one day when he noticed a small boy on the beach. Again and again, the boy bent down, picked something off the sand and hurled it into the Ocean. The next day he was there again and the next. Curious, the man parked his car and headed for the shore. He saw that the beach was littered in every direction, so far as the eye could see, with starfish and that these were what the boy was saving. The man watched for a while, wondering and then he said, "what's the point? There are so many. How can you possibly make a difference?"

"Made a difference to that one," the boy replied, throwing another into the water, "and to that one...and that one."

The sun is beginning to set as they come into view of the sprawling, messy desert camp that is Za'atari and Ana's dread is overcome by excitement at seeing the children again. Here is still Jordan, after all and, though this predominantly tent city has problems of its own, it is not blood-soaked Syria.

For safety's sake, they come unannounced. Only Jan, the United Nations official in charge, has been informed. It has been almost a year. Ana has died a thousand deaths since last she was here and yet, nothing seems to have changed. Ever the optimist, he greets them with enthusiastic warmth and speaks of "the most fascinating project on earth when it comes to the development of camps." Some of its streets are now paved, most of the camp has electricity and everyone has access to clean water. True, it is still squalid, barren and crime-ridden, and most of the shops and businesses here are unauthorised but Za'atari has transformed from a refugee camp to an informal city, complete with its long awaited hospital for women and children. Soon even, to boast a Safeway, "residents will be able to shop for groceries in the same comfort as anywhere in the world!"

From a population of one hundred and twenty thousand, neighbourhoods have emerged, gentrification, a growing economy, and Jan is optimistic that the camp is not far off evolving from a transitional population centre to a city that can benefit its host country. "This is a dynamic place which is giving the refugees a sense of ownership and dignity," he concludes and Ana feels the hope in her revive.

Jan congratulates them on their pregnancy, offers them refreshments and advises that they wait until morning to see the children. He tells them how he understands discretion to be vital and how sorry he is for their suffering. "The children are thriving. And the dog, of course. Has become quite a celebrity in fact. As have you. Best you leave before everyone knows you're back."

"Is Kai still here?"

Jan shakes his head. "His mother is sick, but he plans to come back." A pang of guilt finds its mark and Ana examines the floor. "We emptied your tent when it looked like you weren't coming back. I've kept your possessions safe."

"Thank you."

"Another time you must be my guests, but for the duration of this stay it would be best if you to blended in with the volunteers." Of course. She would far rather be back where she started, out of Jan's limelight and the last thing they need is for any whiff of Caleb's presence to reach the Israelis.

The night is cold and restless, this tent exactly like the one she occupied before but with bedding for two. They snuggle in, drawing warmth from each other and comfort from the random conversations that spring up in the small hours. She must have fallen into a deep sleep however, for she wakes to a watery blue sky, bright sunshine streaming in through the open flap of their tent and Caleb on his knees beaming down at her as he places a mug of something steaming next to her mattress.

"Morning, beautiful." She smiles dreamily, watching the turbulence in his dazzling eyes, emotion refining the features of his aristocratic face. She lifts her hands to allow her fingers free access to his wavy black hair and, as his lips close in on hers, cradles the back of his head, pulling him closer.

Hand in hand they wander through this sprawling city of tents and prefab trailers, the thin wintry sun lending a deceptive brightness to dirty grey. People in Za'atari have been planting small gardens around their makeshift homes, scratching out the dirt, saving up water and planting seeds. Even the occasional seasonal tree puts in an appearance and sparkling decorations, for Christmas is now less than a week away.

A tanker truck carrying water roars by and, dodging the sheet of muddy water it throws up from the road, Ana lifts their fragile map above her head. Lileth has been given a trailer. With serious mental health problems herself and seven young children to care for as well as their dog, she is considered to head an especially vulnerable family. So many trailers and tents, most adorned with some distinguishing feature that speaks of home away from home, no doubt creating a recognisable pathway to those who live here. But though it all looks so familiar, Ana is lost.

Some men are busy moving a trailer, precariously perched on repurposed fenceposts with wheels at either end and she wonders at the ingenuity of people who seem capable of making so much out of nothing. They stop to watch as slowly, carefully, the group manoeuvres their load to form the third side of a rectangle with a courtyard in the middle. A place, no doubt, like others they have passed, that will be lovingly fashioned for extended family and friends to gather.

Something licks Ana's leg and she jumps but, as her heart starts to race, Caleb puts reassuring hands on her shoulders, laughter spilling from his eyes. He nods, glancing behind her. "Look who's found us."

He watches them patiently from the shadows, tongue twitching in a steaming mouth, tail beating a triangle in the mud. Twice the dog she knew, he has padded out and tufts of colourful hair – grey, black, white and tan, sprout from bald patches. One ear still stands stiffly to attention, the other flopping untidily into his eager face and he transfixes them with piercing blue eyes, fidgeting eyebrows begging for attention. When she goes to stroke him, however, Asalan turns away and they are compelled to follow.

An icy wind whips the desert, rippling through canvas, spinning dust and litter into the air. A reminder of how recently it covered everything with snow and, in its churning of the vast puddles that obstruct their route, of how it brought heavy rains to drown the tents.

Leading them to a group of young children playing barefoot in the mud, Asalan heads straight for a shock of blonde curls, thin arms wrestling with the heavy sludge of a hole that threatens to engulf it. The child glances at the dog. "I wondered where you'd got to. You should be helping me!" Asalan barks, shooting the visitors a look of resignation and, dumping himself in the hole, gets to work.

Great dollops of wet mud fly in all directions, sending the children wild with delight and, as they dodge his missiles, chastising loudly, Asalan seems to realise that they are goading him on.

"Ana!" Dua runs towards her and the blonde child looks up. He wipes his dripping nose with the back of one hand, covering his face with a fresh coat of mud and jumps to his feet, uncertain of whether to be excited or afraid. Then, with a joyful smile, he launches himself at Caleb, throwing his arms around his legs.

"Saad. You look so well!"

The little boy beams. "He only speaks with Asalan," Dua explains and Ana balances on her haunches so they can see each other properly. They have changed so much.

"You look great," she tells him and he beams, nearly throwing her off balance as he flings his arms around her.

"You too." He steps back and looks at her benevolently. "I'm glad they didn't kill you and that the doctors made you better again."

Ana nods, momentarily speechless. "And I'm so glad you got here safely. How is your new home, Dua?"

He stares at her, his eyes dark and troubled. "It's not home. My mummy and daddy aren't here. But Rahim and his family are kind. They look after us and we have enough to eat. I have new friends.

"Ibrahim is seven." Dua hesitates, something terrible looming as he searches her face. "The aid workers found him before it was too late." He waits for her to say something.

"Too late for what?"

"He saw them torture his parents and tried to hang himself. He wanted to die that way, rather than let Assad's army kill him slowly." Dua's green eyes widen further in the shadows. "Did Assad's army kill my mummy and daddy too?"

Ana shakes her head. "I don't know what happened to your parents, Dua, but we'll do whatever we can to find them." She watches until she is sure it has sunk in. "Do you have any other family?" He shrugs. "Ibrahim is lucky to have you as a friend." Dua nods, emotion overwhelming his capacity to speak. "And these are your friends too?" She waves a hand at the other children watching them warily and he nods again. He takes her hand and she resists the temptation to scoop him up, stroking it discretely instead as Caleb does hers, when she is in need of reassurance.

She points to Asalan, contentedly chewing a bone by the side of his hole. "Asalan's happy. Saad found treasure for him in the ground."

A smile chases away the pain in the little boy's face, for the dog looks so comical. "It's only a bone he lost but I saw him hide it." He lets go of Ana's hands and runs to his old friend, burying his face with a kiss in the fur of the dog's ungainly head. "Rahim and Foued are at the market," he shouts back. "They'll be glad to see you!"

Music throbs from the barbershop. The freshly shaved young man emerging from it, greets them with an enthusiastic smile as they stop to avoid bumping into him. Smartly dressed, with a briefcase and loaded rucksack, he looks set for a day at the office.

Teenage boys steer handcarts packed with wood and kitchen appliances through a crowded street lined with shops and businesses of all kinds. Bright lights flash from a kiosk selling sweets and candy-floss. Aromas of barbecuing meat, fresh bread and sweet spiced coffee waft with that of unwashed bodies, on the chilly wind.

In a tin shack they spot a young boy with one arm missing from the elbow down. He struggles to empty large canvas World Food Programme sacks, freely distributed, into the back of a pickup truck with Jordanian colours. Clearly this grain is headed elsewhere to be sold illegally. They stop to speak with him but he has no idea of what he is doing beyond this simple task. "What's you name?" Caleb smiles, reassuringly.

310

"Faisal, and yours?" The boy stops what he is doing, rubs his stump and flinches, eyeing them suspiciously and Ana sees that the wound has not healed completely.

"Caleb. And this is Ana."

"Hi. I'm a doctor. Would you like me to take a look at your bad arm?" He hesitates and she crouches beside him. "I'd say some antibiotics would make that better, should I see if I can get some for you?"

Faisal nods. "It happened in the bomb factory," he tells them casually. "We used to go there everyday. To the warehouses where they made the bombs. With all the ribbons we'd collected, nails and other sharp things to put into them."

"What were the ribbons for?" Caleb asks.

"They stuck out and when they all burned, the bomb would go off. One went up in the warehouse." Faisal falls silent and stares at something only he can see.

"Is that where you lost your hand?"

He looks at them vacantly and nods. "My best friend died," he says, his face reddening as tears spring to his eyes. "His head came off. There was blood everywhere. You could see his brains."

Caleb puts a hand on the young boy's arm. "I'm so sorry, Faisal."

"Yeah. I'd seen a lot but that was the worst. The smell was awful. But now I must get back to work."

"Will you be here tomorrow?" Ana asks.

"Most days."

"Then I'll come back with something for your arm, okay?"

Distracted, Faisal shrinks into the corner and Ana follows his gaze to a group of dishevelled children coming up behind her. There is terror in their eyes as if they are running from something. Ana understands them now. Emotionally detached, their ability to reason, assess risk or empathise, severely diminished, they will be operating in survival mode, focusing on their instant needs. Instant gratification. She guesses they have stolen from Faisal

311

already and wonders out hoping to engage their attention but they scatter, disappearing in all directions.

Above, a cascade of wires sprouts from street lights like tangled strands of spaghetti, finding their way somehow, to individual shacks and trailers and the face of a cold moon, its mountains and craters clearly visible, watches over them.

They eat the best baklava they have ever tasted, rolled out on a metal table with a broom handle in a bakery jerry-rigged from a container and a tent. The baker's four year old daughter tells them that she wanted to take the teddy-bear to keep him safe from the snipers "but they wouldn't let me!"

"No, we don't steal from others," her father says, cutting another strip to shape and bake. "We don't take things from other peoples' houses."

"We tried to tidy up," the little girl explains. "So that it won't be so bad when they come home again but everything is mixed up." Full of concern, she turns to her father. "Do you think someone is looking after our house, daddy?" He tells her that he expects so.

They find the boys haggling with a toothless woman far older than her years, over a pile of something green and leafy. A middle-aged man in a dirty white djellabaya and bright red keffiya appears to be arguing their case and, at last, she relents, shrugging in exasperation as she packs a pile of her produce into a plastic bag and hands it over for Rahim's money. "Thank you," he says politely "*Wa alaykum s-salamu wa rahmatu l-lahi wa barakatuh!*" Laughing, as she shoos them away muttering something unintelligible, the children turn towards the next stall. From this one comes the delicious smell of freshly baked bread and as they make their way through the people crowding in on it, a spotty teenager, as thin as a rake comes to view. He throws a flat bread into the air and for a moment, this seems to hover like a white parachute, falling gracefully back onto its sculptor's giant pan. Then, with one swift move, the boy passes it over to the baker in return for another shapeless pile of dough.

The boys are at the head of the queue now. They take two loaves, packing these in with their greens and as they turn, Ana catches Foued's eyes. "Ana?" In an instant, Rahim sees her too and his worn face is transformed by a heart-warming smile. They push their way through the crowd, nearly dropping their hard earned winnings so that Caleb has to rescue the flimsy bag before it catches on someone and tears, and fling their arms around Ana shouting. "*Alhamdulillah!* You came back, you came back!" She hugs them each in turn, taking her time to look at them. They too, have changed so much.

"It's good to see you. You are so grown up," she tells them and they beam with pride.

"We've been busy," Rahim says. "There's lots to do each day with nine mouths to feed and our new home to keep."

Ana swells with pride for them. "And I'm sure you do a great job. How is Lileth?"

"Fine. Stopped taking her tablets when you left but the Australian doctor sorted her out. She still lets me do most of the work 'cause she has the baby to look after."

"Of course. And the girls?"

"Good, thank you. We've a bit more shopping to do then we'll go see them, no?" He looks worried, as if they might disappear again.

"That'd be great."

Rahim frowns and looks intently first to Caleb, then Ana. "We were so afraid," he says, "that you would die. Or worse. We wanted you to live but it is better to die than be tortured in prison. Are you…better now?" He looks at her with understanding, his face reddening, tears forming as he struggles to control his twitching lips, and when she opens her arms, does not hesitate. For well over twenty seconds, they hold each other tight and, despite the bustling crowd, they are aware of nothing else.

A loud tooting makes Ana jump. The others fall back as the crowd makes way for a tatty scooter. A little dog close behind, jumps haplessly for meat hanging tantalisingly just out of reach from its pannier. Ana looks back to Rahim still considering her. "I'm well Rahim and we are very happy. Caleb and I are married and we are expecting babies. Twins!"

"Twins?" He looks dazed. "Really?" She nods and the look of confusion on his face gives way to a broad smile. "That's amazing!"

"Indeed." A cheer goes up and she notices, with horror, that this hasn't been a private reunion after all. These people are here because of, not despite them, and now, very noisily, they celebrate their good news. Feeling very conspicuous, Ana pulls the scarf around her face and blushes but thanks them all the same.

"Where to next, Rahim?" There is an edge to Caleb's voice and, as the two boys lead the way, their well wishers part to let them through.

They pass a pet-shop, a home-made ice-cream parlour, a bridal shop, a wooden bench covered with citrus fruits, apples and dates, and some children selling second-hand clothes from a corrugated tin-shack. Finally, Rahim stops at a stall selling meat, glancing with pride back to his guests. He makes a show of asking what the butcher would recommend and pales without flinching when he gets the final bill.

"Can I pay?" Caleb asks discretely, crouching beside him. "It is a special occasion after all and we would really like to contribute." He pushes the money into Rahim's pocket.

"I'll pay you back."

"When you earn more than me Rahim, you can pay me back."

It would have taken forever to find Lileth's trailer for it floats in a sea of them to the east of the camp where electricity hasn't yet arrived. Not even via the three hundred or so kilometres of illegal wires stealing it from the public lighting system at an unsustainable cost of almost $500,000 a month, Rahim informs them. Also, that there are frequent demonstrations because of this, the Eastenders believing it to be unfair that they shouldn't have the same as everyone else. Rahim and his family are just grateful, however, for a solid roof over their heads, "to keep the heat in, the water, rats, snakes and scorpions out." But unrest is a problem and one of Foued's classmates died because of it recently, overwhelmed by teargas when the guards struggled to put a riot down.

Here everything looks quite new and fresh. Hardly any gardens have sprung up and there are none of the satellite dishes that clutter the skyline in other parts of the camp. The girls are sitting on the steps leading up to their open doorway, playing with dolls made of recycled waste. Creating clothes for them from pieces of tin foil, plastic wrappings, scraps of material and ribbons, and an elaborate tale for them to enact, of a handsome prince coming to rescue them from the evil president's guards.

Completely lost to their make-believe world, it takes Rahim to break their trance and, even then, they place their dolls carefully to one side before jumping up to greet them. The sound of a woman humming, stops and Lileth calls out. "Who is it girls?" Her covered head appears at the open window then little Aamina, bright eyes shining from a chubby face in her mother's arms. They reach the door and hesitating, though the children pull them on, Caleb bids their mother good-day. "Ana? Is that you?"

"Yes and this is Caleb."

"Caleb?" Disbelief transforms into joy. "You saved my children! All this time I've waited to thank you."

"I'm sorry I couldn't come all the way," he replies. "I needed to go back for Ana as soon as it was safe to leave the children. I knew Rahim could handle the final leg."

"Yes, yes, I know. He told me all about it. He is a good boy." Rahim beams.

"But now you are here. Come in, please!"

As the children throw themselves onto mattresses and bedding piled neatly at the far end, the adults stand in a cold bare rectangular cabin. Everything but the ceiling is lined with linoleum designed to look like wood and in the corner opposite the door, someone has tidied plates, bowls, mugs, cutlery, a camping stove, a cooking pot, and a washing-up bowl. There is a plastic bag overflowing with clothes, a bar of soap, paper, pencils, a few toys and a bag of nappies.

"It is not much," Lileth apologises, "but you are welcome to make yourselves at home." They thank her, seating themselves on the floor with the children and Lileth perches on a mountain of bedding. "You look so well. Ana, you are with baby?"

"Two babies, would you believe?" Ana turns to Caleb, anxious to dispel potential misconceptions before they arise. "My husband, Caleb," she says then, turning back to Lileth, "you look great! And to think, now you have six children to look after, as well as their dog, and little Aamina."

"Thank you and congratulations. Yes, it is hard. We had a good home and a comfortable life back in Syria before the war. My husband was a surgeon. We were well respected and, though there were injustices, we had what we needed and more. But here... This is not living. It is existing. Making it from day to day until..." We can go back home is what she wants to say but they all know there is nothing to go back to. "But it could be a lot worse. We have shelter, food, healthcare and the children are beginning to make something of their lives. The older ones go to school, there are playgroups for the little ones and maybe some day soon, I will find work to supplement our rations. Then we will buy furniture, a toilet pot, maybe even a washing-machine like the others."

"You don't need to work mother," Rahim reassures. "Give me a little longer and I'll bring some money home." He turns to Ana settling down beside her husband. "What do you think?" he asks. "I'm planning to start a bicycle repair business. I used to look after our bikes at home, so know what to do. I'm sure it won't be long before the outside world sends us more bicycles. I could start by working from home, get a shed when we have enough money. Foued could help, couldn't you?" His brother nods enthusiastically. "The girls could make drinks to sell our customers while they wait. Perhaps, in time, we could open a coffee shop with a library so people could come and read. Wouldn't that be great?"

"That's a brilliant idea Rahim! I can see it now."

"You will still go to school?" Caleb asks.

"Of course. Education is most important."

"Ana?" Lileth passes the baby to Rahim and Ana rises to her embrace. "Thank you so much for going after them…my sons."

It feels wrong to take the credit when others have sacrificed so much. Ahmed, who paid with his life. Father Hans starving with his flock. Mo'amin struggling to save the wounded in besieged Old Homs. Tuan, risking his life in Syria. Caleb and, of course, little Rahim, who had the courage to take the initiative in the first place, but Lileth has waited a lifetime to thank her and now Ana acknowledges that gratitude for them all.

"I'm sorry for what they did to you and so grateful for your courage and perseverance. Thank you."

"In England we say, every cloud has a silver lining. There are many very special people I would never have met – including the love of my life, a camaraderie I would never have experienced and a thousand lives I would never have lived if I hadn't gone into Syria. For those things and the joy of seeing your family reunited, I will be forever grateful." One of the girls starts to clap, the others quick to join in, laughing and cheering so that the little cabin seems to swell with pride and happiness and Ana knows at last, that it really was all worth-while.

Later, leaving Lileth to feed Amina and the girls to rearrange the cabin, the boys take their guests to one of the kitchens and together they cook the food they bought from the market. A delicious stew to be shared with bread and water by candlelight. In the unaffected joy of the occasion, Ana sees that Rahim's extended family has reached some kind of compromise with its fate. Afterwards, as they head for one of the communal washing areas however, the bowl filled to overflowing with dirty dishes, mugs and cutlery, Caleb's phone rings and the fear with which she started the day, returns with a jolt to the pit of Ana's stomach.

He puts the bowl on the floor, frowning as he retrieves the phone from somewhere deep within his leather jacket and Ana waits with bated breath. "Hi. You okay?" He nods. "Tuan," he says, trying to hide his concern. "You sure?…Can we bribe them d'you think?" He shakes his head, lines of worry working their way into his face, fear darkening his eyes. Unconsciously he puts a hand over his mouth, drawing it down to smooth the stubble on his chin as he considers Ana. "Can I call you back?" he asks at last and nods. "Fifteen minutes." He pockets the phone and looks around at them all watching him. "Boys, could you take the bowl? We'll catch up."

He takes Ana into his arms and peers into her face. "Aadil is in prison," he tells her. The world spins and Ana closes her eyes, gasping for air. "Ana?" She feels him lower her to sit on the ground and, as she puts her head between her knees, the blood rushes back along with the implications of what he tells her. She sees the pain in his eyes and pulls herself together. "I have to go but I'll be back. In days at most."

"When?" She hears herself ask though the answer is obvious.

"Tonight. Now. I'll take the bike and be back before the week is up." She shakes her head, looking to the ground and sees Aadil. She remembers the way he lifted her from the deepest depression with his upbeat humour and beaming smile. The way he never complained even beyond exhaustion, a never-ending human catastrophe unfolding before him. His compassion. His ability to see the good in everyone and how he never lost hope. And, as she considers what he probably suffers, waves of nausea rise with an unbearable pain in her stomach. Caleb puts an arm around her.

"How long?"

"Four days."

"Do we know where he is, how he is?"

"Yes." Caleb does not elaborate and she looks with horror into his face.

"Please come back to me Caleb."

"I promise you, I will. Ana, you need to be strong for our babies, if not for yourself. Will you do that for me?" She nods. Caleb is all that matters now and he must be free of worry for her if he is to focus. Though she longs for reassurance, she would rather live in ignorance until this is over than know the truth. He kisses her, helps her up and for a precious moment they hold each other tight.

"I'll see you off," she says at last and, taking her by the hand he leads her to the wash-house.

Their chatter killed in an instant, the children stand to attention as soon as the adults enter. "Do you remember Aadil?" Caleb asks and Rahim nods. "Well," Caleb hesitates, but Rahim would guess the whole truth whether he told it or not. "I'm afraid he is in prison and they need my help to get him out." Rahim looks shocked. "Would you do something for me while I'm gone?" He nods gravely, a deep frown furrowing his brow. "Would you look after Ana? She and the babies are more precious to me than anything in the world. You know how to find a doctor if she needs one and Jan Schilz?"

"Of course. Don't worry. I'll make sure she gets the care she needs."

"And that she doesn't do anything she shouldn't?"

Rahim looks at her sheepishly. "I'll do my best."

Full of dread, she holds him close. "I love you Caleb. Whatever happens, somewhere I will be waiting for you." There is so much more to be said but nothing that won't betray her greatest fear and, though they both realise it, to give it voice would be to empower it. He kisses her one last time, hypnotising her with his eyes then, steeling himself, mounts his motor-bike and starts the engine. He looks at her and smiles, his face reflecting unbounded love, gratitude, hope and fear and, in the heat of his passion, her hands resting on her twitching belly, she watches him disappear into the star studded night.

She moves entranced through the days that follow for there is nothing she can apply herself to wholeheartedly. It is as if colour has leached out of the world so that she sees it in various shades of black and white. Without Caleb she is lost, like a ship without a compass, wandering aimlessly from one anchorage to another. Tossed about by stormy seas. Aware of a destination but unable quite to fix where that might be and when she is alone at night, the terrors return to haunt her.

By day she does what she can to help Lileth and the children, meeting the casualties of Syria's war as a neighbour rather than a therapist. Realising no longer – politics, freedom fighters, terrorists, dictators or armies, but only the fragility of civilisation and human life. The lives these people had were the lives she, her family and friends have. They owned corner shops, farmed, worked in factories, built houses, taught, healed. They raised their children, cared for their disabled, sick and elderly, kept their homes and celebrated that which brought them joy. None of them expected to be running for their lives, leaving everything they had – comfort and respect for poverty and humiliation.

All she wants to do is cry. Of course, she would be emotional. She is pregnant after all but deep down, though she will not acknowledge it, she knows her depression stems from certainty that she will never see Caleb again. When she wakes herself in the night screaming, dripping with cold sweat, terror coursing through her, she tries to remember. To imagine him wiping the hair out of her face, calming her with his steady voice, entrancing her with those magical eyes, holding her until the trembling subsides and her heart settles back into her chest.

Sometimes, with their babies moving inside, memories of a desert oasis return and she truly feels him, but when she is dragged before that white door, nothing can save her, for it has only to open and she is lost forever. From the depths of her unconscious the stench of hell rises, something bloody trembles still beating before her and, though she feels life inside her grow, her own is ebbing away.

"When I sleep," Rahim tells her, " I dream I'm back at school playing with my friends." It is late and she should be back in her own tent but tonight they insisted she stay. They are worried about her. Rahim has heard that she wakes, screaming in the night and he doesn't want her to be alone. She tried to reassure them, to explain that she does not want to add to the burden they already carry but there was no dissuading them. The children have put the mattresses together to make space for her between the two big boys and now all three of them lie on their backs holding hands, watching the flickering candle-light on the ceiling while Lileth tells the little ones a bedtime story. "It's as if the souls of my friends are living in my heart."

A gust of wind hits the side of the cabin like a fist and the hammering of rain intensifies, momentarily drowning out all else.

"And in a way, Rahim, they are," Ana says as the noise dies away again. "Those we knew and lost, live on in our memories. They affect how we see the world, the choices we make, the way we behave. In a way they continue to live through us."

The wind shrieks around them, shaking the trailer as if testing its weight so that they would have missed the knock had it not been for Asalan. Barking loudly, he jumps from his cosy spot between Dua and Saad and heads for the door, friendly tail rocking his whole body. In an instant Rahim stands beside him. "Who is it?" It is too noisy outside for anyone to hear. He opens the door a fraction and a blast of cold wind showers them with freezing rain. "She's not here." He tries to shut the door but a force far greater than his, pushes him to one side and Ana jumps to her feet. The little ones huddle together, the girls cowering in the farthest corner, Lileth clutching Aamina as she stands defiantly before them. Foued rushes to the rescue but, wide-eyed, Ana raises her hand, shaking her head with a frown to stop him coming closer then turns to the intruders and Rahim.

Four of them, dressed all in black that reveals little but the glint in their eyes. They wear pakistani style tunics, trousers tucked

321

into leather boots, belts bristling with weapons and menacing balaclavas. Without thinking, Ana heads for Rahim, pulling him away so that she stands between them. "What do you want?" Though dread fear threatens, her voice remains remarkably calm.

"You Ana?" She nods. "Come with us."

"Where to?" He lunges towards her but Rahim gets in the way.

"No. Go away. Get out of our home or we will call the police!" The intruder pulls a knife, long and curved. Its evil blade gleaming in the flickering light seems to take on a life of its own but Rahim is quicker and, though he dodges it, he still stands before her. Lileth screams and Ana pushes him away.

"Stop, please! I'll come with you but please leave the others alone." She says it in Arabic though they spoke English and the one who appears to lead, frowns. He waves the blade millimetres from her face and she holds her breath, forcing herself not to flinch. She feels the babies inside her move and the sudden urge to weep, but still she stands her ground, watching, waiting, willing them to do the right thing then, when she has their undivided attention, she drops her head and gaze in demure submission. "Please may I speak with the child before we go." The one with the knife at her chest nods, retreating slightly and Ana turns, dropping to her knees before Rahim.

"Rahim, trust me and do as I ask. Stay here and take care of your mother and the children. Remember the things we talked about. Pray for me and never lose hope. One day we will see each other again but it is not for you or I to decide where or when that will be. Do you understand?"

THEN THEY CAME
FOR ME

It must be many hours since they threw her bound and gagged, with a dark sack over her head, into the back of a pickup truck. Though she has no idea where they are headed, it seems likely to be somewhere in Syria. They stopped once, not long after leaving Za'atari and she guesses that would have been the border. She tried to draw attention to her plight but her muffled cries were lost to the wind, her feeble attempt to kick cold metal, met with one brutal blow. Something hard with sharp edges that rendered her unconscious for goodness knows how long. Now she lies in a pool of freezing water, sharp needles piercing every taut muscle, joints stretched to their limits, helpless to brace herself against the unpredictably violent movements of the truck.

She has no idea who has taken her or why. How did they even know where she was? Dark thoughts enter her head, black simmering eyes haunting her in the darkness. The wind rattles the flimsy cover above her and she draws consolation from the protection this affords against the rain. Desperate to empty her bladder, she considers the life inside her and weeps bitter tears. The magic spell that held so much promise, is well and truly broken.

Lileth begged them for mercy. "She is pregnant. Her husband is away. Please, let her be!" But they knocked Rahim's mother to the ground and would probably have killed her had Asalan not come to her rescue. He got such a thrashing, poor dog. Ana can still hear him whimpering and prays the children will be able to save him. They will be devastated if he dies.

323

She can no longer feel her hands or legs. Waves of agony crescendo to excruciating shocks like electricity with every bump and turn and, as she struggles to breath, her consciousness fluctuating, all hope fades away. Here in the back of this miserable truck, trussed up like some animal heading for slaughter, she will suffocate. Her life, as well as the two who take sustenance from her even now, will come to an end.

She must have passed out, for though her situation is the same, they are no longer moving and the engine has stopped. She hears men shout, the crunch of footsteps, rope being drawn then the cover pulled back and, despite the dark sack-clothe, is overwhelmed by blinding light. Rough hands take hold and excruciating pain shoots through her, every joint and muscle screaming for release. She feels herself being lifted and thrown unceremoniously onto the hard ground, daggers slicing through muscles, ripping her joints apart as she lands, then nothing.

At first, when she regains consciousness, it seems that little has changed. Still she lies on hard cold ground unable to move, her contorted body begging for release. Sweat pours off her though she shivers with cold, her drenched clothes leaching the last of her body-warmth into the wintry day. She closes her eyes wondering how much longer. Why? If they wanted her dead, surely they would have killed her by now? So why treat her this way?...Who?

Someone approaches, the sound of footsteps ringing sharp and echoing. She begs to be released but her voice is reduced to a faint mumble. Someone grabs hold and her bonds tighten. She thinks she will go mad with the pain but then the pressure eases slightly and suddenly, she is free. She tries to move but falls back paralysed, unable to feel or control any of her limbs and then the blood rushes back into them and she screams, for this agony is even more unbearable than what came before.

For an age she lies, shaking violently, helpless to do anything to recover herself. More footsteps. Men's voices. Animated conversation in Arabic but, unable to focus on anything but the searing heat ripping through her body, Ana hears nothing of what they say. Something tugs at the sack over her head then that too, is gone and she looks up to dirty grey ceiling, faint daylight illuminating blooming rosettes of mould on dirty whitewashed walls. Slowly, gingerly, she sits herself up, rubbing her swollen wrists and peers into the gloom.

She sees a soldier or policeman perhaps, dressed in uniform she does not recognise and her head spins. He is angry and appears to be admonishing her abductors in no uncertain terms as they simmer broodily from their sombre attire. He comes towards her, apologising for the way she was treated and unties her gag. "Believe it or not, we are not all savages here," he says. There is something familiar about him though she is sure they have never met. She wastes no time.

"Where am I? Why am I here?" He looks perplexed and she notices that his uniform, dirty, creased and torn, only partially conceals cuts and bruises and that he smells of sweat and urine. "Who are you?"

"Unfortunately, a prisoner like yourself. Baltasar is my name. We are somewhere in Syria, probably not far from, perhaps even in, Ma'aloula, my home town and I would say you must be pretty valuable to someone, judging by the fact that you are definitely not a local girl."

Baltasar? Ma'aloula? "Do you speak English?"

He nods.

"Do they?"

He shrugs.

What if this is a trick? Has he been planted to get information from her? If he's genuine, he won't answer personal questions for fear of putting those close to him at risk. She decides not to put her hypothesis to the test. "Why are you held prisoner?"

"Ma'aloula was taken over by jihadists."

"How long have you been here?"

"Weeks."

"Have they treated you well?" He closes his eyes. "Do you know what they intend to do with you?" He looks to the floor and shakes his head gloomily. "And me?" Nothing. "Do you know who's holding us?"

"ISIS." Her heart lurches and she forces it down. It's like they're on drugs, the twenty-three year old fighter repeats in her head and she tries to silence him. They charge at you in groups of three hundred and, though we shoot them like sheep, the next day there are twice as many.

He spoke of children as young as ten being put under social pressure to volunteer as suicide bombers, serve as prison guards with the job of whipping prisoners, or sleeper cell agents to inform on rival groups or government forces. An eleven year old machine-gun wielding boy they rescued had been recruited by ISIS after his father and brothers were killed by Iraqi security forces. They have a lot of hope for children like him, the fighter said. ISIS believes it will conquer all of Iraq and Persia and liberate Jerusalem. It has rewritten regional history and assigned itself the mission of reversing the Western conspiracy to divide Muslims through the Sykes Picot agreement. It was ninety eight years ago that the Allies of World War One forged a secret agreement to carve up the territory of the Muslim lands, it reads.

There is a commotion at the door. Whilst they were distracted, someone else arrived and though she cannot see him clearly in the gloom, the hairs stand up on the back of her neck. Two of her abductors approach. One of them points a rifle at her, gesturing with it that she should get up. The other takes her wrists and cuffs them behind her back. He jerks his head towards the door, pushing her forward and with one last look, conveying all the questions she could not ask before she is blindfolded, Ana turns once more to meet her fate.

They force her to her knees and she shrinks back, overpowered by the stench of rotting flesh. Flies buzz around her and she closes her eyes with dread as they remove the blindfold. They prod her between the ribs with something sharp and she has no choice but to open her eyes. She has to see to save herself from falling into it.

Propped up against a stone, the man is frozen in the position he was murdered and she stares at his headless neck. Streaked with yellow fat, muscles turn from deep red through grey to green, the chords of bare tendons and vertebrae glaring white in the cold sunshine. Sick with horror, Ana stares at the ground and retches, aware only at some subconscious level of the mobile phones they hold up to film her.

Someone grabs her by the throat, metal flashes before her and she feels something sharp against her skin. They take it away then bring it closer, slowly so she can focus on it, this barbaric blade with its serrated edge and now they press it against her just enough to slice her skin. Her breath catches in her throat, her heart shaking her whole body but then, knowing she is about to die, a strange calm descends on her. She closes her eyes, praying that the knife is sharp, her murderer skilled and thinks of Caleb.

Blood trickles down her neck and she panics. Why are they taking so long? Please God, make it quick! In agony she waits. The knife slices through her. She feels the pressure of it increase and waits in terror, for it to dig deeper then, suddenly, it is gone.

She keeps her eyes screwed tightly shut for she knows they are playing with her, prolonging the torment. On the edge of sanity she waits for what comes next, knowing that it is completely out her control. Her fate, that of Caleb and their twin babies hangs, literally, on a knife's edge, dependent on the whim of some screwed up excuse for a human being and there is nothing she, or anyone else can do about it.

Air rank with fear rushes past and something hits the ground with a thud beside her. Petrified, she peers through her eyelashes, retches and screws her eyes up tight. She sees now that the corpse was also dismembered. She shuffles on her knees, turning away and no-one stops her. Heavy breathing crescendoes beside her. With increasing dread, she opens her eyes.

He stares at her in abject terror though he has clearly survived this before. Baltasar. But now, somehow, they both know his time is up and she cannot help herself. "Do you know Caleb?" she whispers and he nods. His eyes widen and he stares at her, beseeching but he says nothing. "I will tell your family," Ana says, "that you were a great comfort to me in my darkest hour, of the kindness you showed me and the courage with which you died."

"Tell them how much I loved them," Baltasar adds and she nods, determined, despite her tears, not to shut him out. And all the while they film.

The one with the knife comes closer. A black monster with a glinting slit for eyes. It laughs, taking the blade to it's victim's throat and Ana can bear it no longer. Screwing up her eyes, she hangs her head and does her best to shut out the sounds as well. A muffled scream. Gurgling as Baltasar drowns in his blood and his last torturous gasp for breath. Jeering and laughter. The thud as his head hits the ground and hissing as his heart empties its body of blood. She folds, burying her face in her lap. They cannot hurt her now. There is nothing left but the irresistible desire for oblivion.

She doesn't notice them haul her to her feet, march her back inside and free her, or the passage of time as she languishes in pitch black on that cold hard floor. Only the blinding light when they come for her and that there is someone else in this new place. They put bread and water on the concrete floor but, despite the flutter in her belly that begs for sustenance, she cannot eat or drink.

"You again!" She recognises that voice and, though unable yet to place it, unspeakable terror rises from deep within. Wondering if this is hell, she opens her eyes and looks around a bare room apparently hewn from rock. Ancient frescoes peer down from a domed ceiling and fittings on the whitewashed walls suggest that these too, were once decorated. There is no furniture apart from the chair he sits on.

He leers at her hungrily, this monster that has committed unimaginable atrocities and it comes back to her in a flash. Shabiha. He was there. In that Damascus death cell with her. One of them that caused her so much pain. Sentient again, she trembles before him. What makes it worse is that he speaks to her in English. From this she deduces that he is educated like she is, the epitome of her greatest fear. "What wouldn't you, or those close to you, be capable of, in extreme circumstances?" he seems to be saying and she is incapable of considering the positive side of this equation. She forgets those she has seen commit staggering acts of bravery and the redeeming power of love, for here, she is surrounded by those who serve the devil.

With his massive, tattooed muscles, shaved head, bushy black beard and white trainers, he tells her how he likes to pump iron at the gym before heading for the nightclubs of Latakia, Syria's Mediterranean port. He tells her that when his master, the *mualem* calls, he leaves his wife and children at home and forsakes his drink of local arak. "If I get a call from my boss, my whole day has changed," he says. "I don't know when I'll be back."

How clever – to make her consider that his 'normal' life is not that unlike any she might know, to compound the agony he inflicts with the knowledge that he does this despite being capable of some compassion for, surely, he must care for his family and friends? That he considered her deserving of such punishment despite the shred of humanity that remains in his warped mind. That in some remote way they are similar and she could become what he is. She shudders, fighting back waves of panic and nausea, and then that image returns to haunt her. The white door with its peeling paint. Though it remains, thank God, firmly closed, it still has the power to terrify her beyond anything else and she trembles in excruciating pain.

He must have noticed she wasn't paying attention and it would seem that his need of this outweighs his desire to hurt her, unless he is truly blind to her distress, for he brings her out of the trance by putting a pistol to her head. Hard, so that she cries out and will bear the mark of it for weeks to come. She stares at him in abject terror and that seems to satisfy him. "You will listen to me," he tells her and she nods, desperately trying to ignore the movement in her belly that would remind her of who else is at stake here.

"So then I take my weapons," he waves his hand proudly over a pile of Kalashnikovs, pistols and grenades as if showing off a newborn son, "given to me by our god, Assad, and join the others. Our gang has over one hundred in it." Imagine that! Ana shudders. Imagine, as an innocent, traumatised civilian trying to protect your loved ones, your children, being faced with a gang like that, who will shoot, knife and hack them to death, leaving some beheaded, or worse.

"I grew up in poverty," he tells her, "like many of us Alawites and for that we make the Sunnis pay. My story is similar to all shabiha. I was born in a small village and didn't finish school. Instead I went to work with my father on our lemon farm." He was recruited into Syria's security forces during military service, where uniformed officers worked with thugs in regime-sanctioned smuggling. He and his gang lived the gangster high life, smuggling food, cigarettes and commodities from Latakia into Lebanon at massive profit, luxury cars, guns and drugs back in for his Syrian masters. "My job is to defend Assad and his family and keep power for the Alawites," he tells her proudly and Ana wonders why her opinion of him matters. For one thing however, she is grateful. Apart from the pistol to her head, so far he hasn't touched her and she guesses that has something to do with Qassem.

He tells her his name – Abu, and that Sunnis have held power wrongly for one thousand four hundred years. That the balance was only restored when Hafez-al-Assad seized power in 1970 and manned his security forces with Alawites. "I know Sunnis will take revenge for what we've done," he tells her. "I'm fighting to guarantee a good future for my sons and grandsons. So this is the final battle. Win or die." Now Ana sees her chance. It would appear that his discourse is not motivated purely by sadistic lust but that at some level he does actually want to impress her.

"So why am I here Abu? What crime have I committed that deserves the punishment you meted out to me?"

He looks at her and laughs. "What you are guilty of is irrelevant," he tells her. "I have a job to do and I enjoy my work." "But how would you feel if it was your wife, your sister or your daughter who was treated in the way I was?"

"I would hunt the perpetrator of such a crime down and his family, and show them no mercy! I would make the parents watch me torture their children before I dismembered and beheaded them, then I would do the same to them." His eyes glint with avaricious madness and Ana sees no point in reasoning with him after all. Abu is just another tool, carefully crafted over years, poisoned from childhood by a cocktail of religious indoctrination, minority paranoia and mafia crime. Created by a government that uses systematic torture to spread panic and push the country into civil war.

And for Ana now also, there is no escaping the horror of it all, for with the return of the peeling door comes a voice in her head. It could be Abu, or any one of his murderous associates, but she heard these words first from a former officer in Syria's feared military intelligence. "They have no problem torturing a child to death," he said. "All they know is that he is not from their sect. The regime has planted sectarianism inside them since the 1970s to make sure they are loyal to the regime, their highest god. They have only one problem with what they do. The murdered person has only one soul. They wish a second soul could return to the body so they could continue the torture and satisfy their hatred."

QASSEM

He stares at her with lustful disdain, his dark eyes flashing, a strong hand caressing his thick black beard. "You are with child," he tells her as if this should be a great revelation. "My child." She wants to scream, NO! But something holds her back. If he believes the babies to be his, maybe he will see to it that they come to no harm.

They have brought her to his rooms, appropriated from the unfortunate residents of Ma'aloula, whose home this once was. She saw terrible things on the way for, this time, they did not blindfold her. Impaled, decomposing heads and crucified bodies.

Sick with horror and bitter hatred, she struggles to do what she knows she must. Focus, understand his game and stay one step ahead. The odds are stacked against her but she has nothing to lose.

He brings his grime-lined face close to hers, blasting sweet decay and she shrinks back, avoiding mesmerising brown eyes that are disturbingly familiar. He puts a hand on her belly and she pushes it away. "Twins!" he exclaims with a satisfied grin and she shakes her head, wondering how he can possibly know. "I will see to it that they have a good Muslim upbringing. They will be pillars of the Islamic State, followers of the mighty Caliph." At least then, she assures herself, he has no intention of killing me until my babies are viable. But he hasn't finished. "And you are truly mine."

"I will never be yours," she hisses, recoiling from him and he laughs, a glint of anger touching his dark eyes.

"Why do you think you are still alive?"

"Because you are an evil, sadistic monster who takes pleasure in the suffering of others."

"My intention is to discipline you. To tame your wild spirit and see to it that you recognise your true master."

Her fury knows no bounds. "You are not and never will be, my master!"

His eyes darken and he nods. "We shall see about that." He says it with unnerving calm, turning away as he snaps his fingers and, from no-where, come his minders. Four of them. Dark hairy men with avarice in their eyes. They bind her hands and feet with cord and throw her onto the bed. Then, with another click of Qassem's fingers, they are gone.

"So, what did my brother do with you?" Holding himself prostrate above her, Qassem leers, licking his lips hungrily and Ana shakes her head, gasping for breath. He waits, watching in delight as she grapples with what he has just told her.

"No!" She says it to herself, determined not to let him brainwash her, not to give in to him and yet,…those eyes. She closes hers but they are still there. Haunting, mesmerising and chillingly familiar.

Qassem grows impatient. "Sargon, or Caleb, as you call him, is my brother. Soon he will be here to tell you so himself."

"What do you want with Caleb?" Intolerable yearning vies with dread fear.

Qassem ignores her. "You will be mine until the day you die," he informs her coldly and she goes rigid with his touch. "If you please me, I will keep you comfortable and safe. I may even allow you to mother our children. Now show me how you responded to my brother."

"No!" she shrieks. "It's *haram*. I'm married." She uses the word deliberately for it means forbidden not only in the secular sense but also under Islamic law. "The Qu'ran forbids sexual relations outside of marriage."

"Except with those whom your right hand possesses. Have you read the Qu'ran then Ana?" She has. Parts of it anyway. In the early hours when she could not sleep. She found it dense, poetic, dictatorial, often conveying mixed messages. There were many verses about Jihad and enemies but also others about kindness and mercy, compassion being a defining characteristic of the divine. Women were mostly described as wives, captives and slaves as 'those whom your right hand possesses', and the Qu'ran gave their owners licence to use them freely.

"Because that will make your conversion to Islam easier."

Ana shakes her head defiantly. "What are you Qassem?" she demands. "One of Assad's foot-soldiers or a slave to Isis? Have you found another calling to satisfy your greed more completely?"

"Neither."

The twinkle in his eyes serves only to infuriate her further. "And what about Abu? What are shabiha doing in the middle of the fundamental Islamic siege of a Christian town?"

"Abu is useful to me. He thinks I'm a double agent, that this is all some elaborate front. A political coup to curry the sympathy of the world for his master and that, when Assad takes Ma'aloula back, they will rewrite its history to meet his ends.

"Makes no odds to me. When I don't need him anymore, I'll give him to the others to do with as they please."

"So you're a triple agent?" He shrugs, his dark eyes holding her in a spell she dare not break. "But what future do you have with Isis?"

"DAESH cannot fail." He watches her with icy deliberation as she considers whether he uses this acronym deliberately to test her. A pejorative Arabic version of the group's name which is hated by the jihadists, it suggests one who sows discord and treads underfoot. Qassem nods. "It will build a caliphate extending throughout the middle-east starting in Iraq."

"Iraq?"

"You westerners are so naive! You believe that overnight, Iran can transform from your deadliest foe to an ally in your fight against us. You say that Iran is the world's leading state sponsor of terrorism. It is behind Hezbollah, Hamas and Assad, and is busy developing nuclear weapons to further its war against the West, to bring about the destruction of Israel. Yet you do not see how it works to prevent the birth of a unified Iraq that could threaten its regional dominance, how it has been using Shia militias to foment sectarian strife since the fall of Saddam. Through its puppet Maliki, it has succeeded in alienating the sunni minority so badly that this turns to Daesh for protection."

"There are some who say Daesh is a creation of Iranian and Syrian intelligence," Ana challenges, "that most of its members don't know they're being manipulated…"

Qassem's eyes narrow. "So how will they control this monster they have created?"

A cold shiver runs through her but Ana holds her ground. "They don't have to. Eventually the world will rally to do it for them."

He smiles with a nod, bringing his lips close to hers and she snatches her head away from him. "So you blow with the wind?" He shakes his head slowly. So close. She thinks she will burn in the heat of his body, suffocate under the weight of him and that smell… She forces herself to look at him and chooses her words carefully. "Why did you torture me?"

"For my brother."

Her stomach lurches. She scowls at him. "What do you mean?"

"You'll see."

"Why does he deserve to suffer at your hands?" Angry storm clouds gather in his eyes and she has no choice but to look away.

This room could belong to any house in her world. Comfortably furnished in deep warm reds and lush greens, it has a thick pile carpet, a dressing table loaded with cosmetics, perfume, hairbrush and comb, two armchairs and this bed with its cast-iron frame. She looks up to him watching her, desperate to distract him for his eyes are hooded, full of carnal lust.

"So, Daesh will use Iraq as a springboard into Syria?" She blurts. He considers her carefully and raises himself to a more comfortable position. The muscles of his arms bulge, stretching the sleeve of his black tee-shirt, and she marvels at the skill of his tattooists, for only now does she see the scars they sought to conceal.

"Yes, and most of the Arab world will support us, covertly of course. Most significantly, Turkiye which has strategic significance to us. Do you know why that is? Why Erdogan will tell the world he will help it fight us but fail to act on his words?" She nods. Turkiye's prime minister is already altering laws to maximise his power over its people, cracking down on dissent and intimidating his opponents. She knows he considers men to be superior to women and that he would see Daesh victorious sooner than concede power to the Kurds.

"And do you see how clever Assad is?" Qassem persists. "That he will prevail?" She nods. "By eliminating any legitimate threat to him and allowing extremists like us to rise from the ashes of his civil war, Assad is creating a monster to threaten the whole world which, as you say, will have you all rallying behind him to defeat. Only we will not be defeated. For we are not merely a state or even a religion, but an ideology, whose seeds, sown in every country, have germinated and grow even now, to strangle you in your own beds. You will submit to us, to me, Ana."

He bears down hard against her and, panicking, Ana wriggles and squirms until she falls from beneath him onto the floor. But before she can even consider escaping, he is on his knees beside her and the cruel steel of a long curved knife gleams in the soft light above her. She closes her eyes, holding her breath and waits, willing it to be over, but only a gust of air makes her flinch. There is nothing else. Her nostrils fill with his musky heat, her heart catching in her throat and she thinks she will choke on air turned solid around her.

His lips touch her mouth and she snatches it away. "I am pregnant – it is haram!" she blurts but he ignores her. The blade of his deadly weapon skims a sensitive earlobe and, though she holds herself rigid, she trembles, helpless beneath him.

In a physical sense he doesn't kill her after all but, as he leaves her weeping silently into the carpet, time begins to disintegrate with Ana's mind. She doesn't notice when at last someone comes. A woman with something long and dark which she pulls over Ana's head, gently releasing the cords that bind her, helping her up and leading her by the hand but, as they leave the bedroom, the angry voice of a man frightens her gentle carer away and Ana is bound with shackles around her ankles and wrists.

They take her to a bathroom and close the door behind her. It is modern with a toilet, sink and shower of pale green complimented by the lush red of a thick pile rug on a stone floor. There is a window and now Ana's heart skips a beat for, unbelievably, no-one thought to take the key from its lock.

The window opens the second time she tries it and she waits for the onslaught with bated breath. They must have heard her forcing it. No-one comes. She climbs onto the toilet seat and peers out, her eyes straining against the dark, her ears amplifying every little sound. The wind howls through the hills, something blown rattles against the walls and a dog barks in the distance but there is no-one standing guard outside.

Her heart pumping so hard that it makes her whole body shake, she hauls herself onto the window sill and freezes. Still nothing. She lifts her legs and scrambles unceremoniously over the edge, dropping with a thud to the ground. Her jilbab catches on the window-latch, tearing with a sickening sound that must be audible for miles in the sudden brief silence of the night.

She stands motionless, straining to hear through the howling wind and the deafening heartbeat in her throat. Still no-one comes.

With a deep breath, she steels herself and runs. Blindly at first, as if the flames of hell itself where on her tail, the devil and his demons breathing fire down her neck. The chains that bind her, force the shackles deep into her flesh, tripping her mercilessly so that she has no choice but to compromise the size of her steps but she compensates with an increased rate and soon falls into an uneasy rhythm. When she has no breath left, she braces herself, hands on knees, neck extended, forcing her chest to restrain itself for she will suffocate rather than give herself away.

She hears shouting. It is so dark and she has no idea where she is. She peers behind an ancient wall wondering if all the residents of Ma'aloula fled, certain they would help her if they could.

The noise crescendoes. Shouting, swearing, barking, guns firing. She sees a light in a window and runs to the house, hammering on the door. From nowhere something takes flight and rams into her, winding her, throwing her off balance. Sharp teeth tear through flimsy nylon, sinking into tender flesh and she shrieks as much in terror as pain. "Please... help me!" But the light has gone out. No-one comes.

She tries to force the door but dead-weight pulls her back. Noise rises to a deafening pitch. Another set of razor teeth close in on her like a vice, forcing her down. Vicious snarling, panting, hot putrid dog breath and saliva. Gaping jaws, the faint gleam of fangs and sickening crunch as they meet bone. She raises her forearm to protect herself but the weight of them overwhelms her and she sinks, exhausted to the ground. Men shout. A sharp command then a gun firing into the air. Merciful release as the dogs let go and back off, snarling in ferocious disappointment. Footsteps on gravel. Angry voices. Heavy breathing. Terror. Pain. Nausea.

Perhaps it is the first blow that takes her mind again, for it is so hard across her face that she sees stars. They pull her to her feet then knock her to the ground. Her belly contracts and something wet trickles down her legs. The dogs bark so close she feels their spit against her skin and the heat radiating off them. Her nostrils fill with the stench of them, the unwashed, oil and gunpowder.

More blows. Fists, feet, rifle butts. Excruciating pain. A voice. His voice. Bright lights. She braces herself but has no strength left and is powerless to protect herself. She feels herself sinking, floundering in thick mud that closes over her, cloying, suffocating.

Her babies cry out for a chance to live, Caleb calls and then there is nothing.

Something pounds inside her head, determined to split it open. Pain pulses along her spine and through her body, waking dead arms and legs, making her fingers and toes fizz. Bracing herself against it, she forces herself to be still.

Intricate patterns of green, blue and yellow spin before her eyes, the blood vessels in her eyelids highlighted in purples and reds. A deep throbbing in the pit of her stomach rises with her nausea and she retches, her body convulsing against cold metal, gulping in of a cool breeze.

She opens her eyes, squinting against bright sunlight flooding the room from an open window. Squeezing out her tears, she shivers then freezes, the chill of something far worse than the wintry day, catching her with rising awareness.

"Don't ever try to escape from me again!" Seething with anger he can barely control, Qassem tears down the last of her defences.

They keep her bound hand and foot in a windowless carpeted room with no furniture and a bucket to use as a toilet. Five times a day they bring her water to wash, a dirty towel and a prayer mat, watching as she performs Salat, variously mocking or trying to correct her amateur attempts. Only the one who comes in the late afternoon seems to take these obligatory Muslim prayers seriously himself, explaining each time he lays his prayer mat next to hers, how this ritual, which forms the second Pillar of Islam, is over one thousand four hundred years old and connects Muslims everywhere with all who have ever uttered these words and made the same movements throughout Islamic history.

It would seem her captors share their own food with her for some of it is good. Bread, cheese and spicy stews but, especially on the rare occasion when Qassem forces it into her, she vomits most of it straight back up. Her thirst is relentless however, and she drinks hungrily of the gritty water they bring, wondering if her deadly fatigue is in part, due to diabetes of pregnancy and if her kidneys fail with the last vestiges of hope.

Occasionally she sees another woman or women. Ana cannot tell if she is the same for even her hands and feet are covered in black and she hurries by, casting her eyes to the ground as if to avoid Ana's gaze.

From time to time they take Ana to the bathroom and, turning the shower on full, she scrubs herself raw as if she could wash him away but then they take her back to his rooms and all her efforts are wasted. Only in her nightmares does she have the strength to resist, kicking and screaming as they drag her to the white door, the terror that wakes her before they ever reach it, augmented by his attacks when they are together, for it never fails to rouse him.

Sometimes when she is alone, her mind plays tricks on her, rising above her senseless body to roam freely as if nothing could hold it. Windows, doors, walls and ceilings melt away and she wafts like a summer's breeze, invisible to bored guards and eager hounds. Or she goes to where the babies lie safely cocooned deep within. Fully formed miniature humans, mature enough to recognise their mother's voice. Her voice. Contented smiles break out on their tiny faces as the warmth of her love washes over them and, marvelling at their resilience, Ana wonders how they don't tangle themselves up when they do somersaults inside her.

Fierce emotion rouses her, when she considers them like this but, no matter how she struggles, working at the locks with broken fingernails and forcing raw swollen limbs through cold metal, she cannot free herself.

She almost becomes accustomed to Qassem's unpredictable moods, watching him warily when he returns, shuddering to think whose blood he carries and how. Standing naked before her, she sees that the scars extend over much of his body. Burns, puncture wounds and the deformities of badly healed bone and then she contemplates the story his body would tell her if she could read it.

Sometimes, when he wakes in the early hours screaming, trembling in a cold sweat, she wonders at the terrors capable of turning a small boy into a monster and at what happened to make him hate his brother so. Why, when they shared a womb did they go such different ways? What if it had been Caleb instead of him, who suffered whatever fate he did? And then she dreams of the two of them. "How does it feel to know she serves me in my bed?" she hears Qassem ask and his brother's moans when they hurt him, torture her more than anything else.

RESCUE

Lifetimes pass and Ana's sanity fluctuates with her awareness. Physical discomfort, disgust, shame, hatred, terror, reality and imagination blur. Time ceases to exist.

"We have a visitor," Qassem tells her with glee one day, stroking her swollen belly, as he reclines on one elbow beside her, his eyes narrow with expectation. Her heart lurches. The deal is Caleb's life for hers but Qassem will never honour his side of the bargain. "Don't you want to know who it is?" She nods, adrenaline sending her heart into overdrive and he jumps to his feet laughing. "You'll see."

Taking his rifle from where it stands propped against the doorway, he mutters something to those waiting outside and leaves her to fret. Two guards enter, leering, mocking her with lewd comments then laughing loudly at their jokes. She resists the temptation to spit on them. She wonders if she has woken from a deep sleep, why she is so weak and, spurred on by the memory of Caleb, prepares herself for a fight to the end. Death is infinitely preferable to slavery. Their children need never know the misery of human existence.

They unfasten the cuffs on her ankles but not her wrists, put a collar around her neck, attach a chain and lead her like a dog down the stairs. Pale rectangular spaces on the walls speak of pictures that once hung there. Family portraits perhaps, such as she would have had on their walls had their dreams been allowed to come true. She wonders what they would have been like, these children she bears. Whether they would have been brave, strong-willed and compassionate like their father or weak and submissive like herself.

She trips, grabbing the collar with both hands as her minders pull her back. Winded, she gasps for breath and forces herself to focus. Not here, not yet.

They take her through a living area devoid of almost all furniture, colourful dents in faded rugs speaking clearly of where this once stood, to what looks like a throne and Qassem presiding preposterously over all those gathered before him. Ana laughs out loud and they pull her back, choking her so that she coughs and splutters. He narrows his eyes and stares at her, the flame in his eyes igniting and they throw her to the ground beside him. "Perhaps I should have disciplined you more thoroughly," he mutters contemptuously then turns to his audience. Men, mostly dressed in the same pakistani style pyjamas and bristling with weapons. Qassem clicks his fingers and a door opens at the back of the room.

She comes dressed from head to foot in black, the confident beauty she once radiated, bowed in resolute submission, her eyes dark with anguish. She nods at Ana then raises her head to Qassem. "What have you done, son?" she asks, her voice husky with emotion and he leans forward, one hand gripping its arm-rest, the other stroking his beard.

"Son? Now you call me son?" His voice rises with his temper. "Yes," she hesitates. "You were once that to me and I loved you equally. You and Sargon. Please Qassem!" She falls to her knees and prostrates herself before him. "It doesn't have to be this way."

"You should have thought of that long ago." Fury raging in him, Qassem raises his eyes and claps his hands. A group of men disappear from the back of the room.

"He did what you asked, fully aware of the price he would pay." Ishtar hesitates. "Great men do not make bargains they cannot keep," she says loud and clear.

"And what do you mean by that?"

"The video you sent me, Qassem. We watched it together, Sargon and I." She rises and turns to face his men. "We watched Baltasar beheaded and how you threatened Ana with the same. Together we came just as you demanded, to pay for her freedom with Sargon's life."

"He was too afraid to come alone?"

"What was I to do?" She turns back to him in distress. "My children are my world. Baltasar. You, Qassem. Sargon, his wife and the children she carries. He begged me to stay but I came to plead for his life. Please Qassem, if you are a great man, you will show them mercy for your mother's sake."

Qassem snorts his derision and clicks his fingers once more. Bound hand and foot, they drag him in. Caleb or Sargon as his mother calls him. Clearly what they have done to him has taken time. Days at least. Probably weeks. Ana's heart catches in her throat. Tears prick and anger rises with her grief. He was here. In all that time when she was so lonely without him, he was here being treated worse than she, for her sake. She sees Qassem as he stood before her in the bedroom, with fresh eyes, the sadistic satisfaction on his face as confirmation that it was Caleb's blood he carried.

They bring him closer and dump him at his bother's feet. "Well? You wanted to see her. Now take a good look."

Caleb frowns. He forces himself to his knees, bracing every muscle, perspiration dripping from his contorted face. Catching his breath as he trembles with the effort of holding himself this way, he opens his eyes and turns to Ana. "I'm so sorry," he whispers and she turns in fury to their tormentor.

"How could you? Your own brother!"

"Less of a brother than most I have met."

"You're twins! You shared your mother's womb!"

"He sired you both, that monster!" Ishtar adds with vehemence.

Qassem turns to her and grins. "Like father, like son. You have only yourself to blame, Ishtar. Unlike me, you had a choice." He surveys his audience. Testosterone charged brutes with violence in their eyes, fundamental ideology as their excuse, watching the scene unravel with sadistic hunger, and glances at Ana. "Tell her," he commands. "As my wife, she needs to learn obedience and loyalty."

Ishtar hesitates.

"NOW!"

He leans forward to loom over her, his knuckles turning white as he grips the arm rests and she jumps, bowing her head to avoid his terrible eyes.

"We had been married two years," she tells the floor.

"Speak up woman!"

She looks at him in angry defiance, rising to her full height as if she could equal him. "Baltasar was a year old. We were staying with friends. Bedouin in the Jordanian desert when he came, like a tornado blackening the sky, turning everything upside down. Evil, merciless devils – they took three of us from the camp. He enslaved me as you have Ana, and I fell pregnant.

"An old lady helped me to escape. I was late into my pregnancy and huge, for though I did not know it at the time, it was twins I carried. You two," she adds quietly with a frown. She looks to Caleb on his knees before her then into Qassem's eyes. "I'm sorry," she says, "but I had no choice. How do you think it was for me, having to give one of you up?"

"I'm sure it broke your heart."

"It did." Closing her eyes, Ishtar counters his mockery with a whisper.

"Would you like to elaborate?"

"My husband, who had been trying to find me, was waiting with Baltasar back at the camp. He had never given up hope that I might return. We went into hiding but the shock sent me into premature labour. You were born in a tent in the Jordanian desert. By some miracle you survived but before I was well enough to

345

travel, he found us. We fought for you both but the odds were always stacked against us.

"It seemed odd at the time, that he should allow us to keep one of you…"

"So, you see? You!…Are responsible! For what I have become. For the deaths of Baltasar and Sargon!"

"No Qassem, please! You have the power to be merciful. Do what is right."

Qassem looks to the ground with a frown then, the colour rising in his cheeks, stares at her wide-eyed and scowls. "Did you ever consider how I was suffering at his hands and those of his devils as you call them?" Ishtar nods. "How I struggled, lonely and afraid, to survive his violent tempers? His brutality? It was because of you. He blamed you! I. BLAME. YOU!" His finger shakes as he points at her but Ishtar does not flinch and her answer comes with the calm assurance of one who has gone over those events, reliving her options and the agony of her decision, countless times, always to reach the same conclusion.

"I'm sorry for what you suffered, Qassem but I loved you equally. I love you still for, whatever you have become, you are my son. I have died a thousand deaths for you but I am not to blame."

"So, of the two of us, it was me you chose to sacrifice. And now it is my turn." He flicks his head at Caleb and surveys the room. "Look at me and listen carefully. All of you. Today I pass sentence on you, Sargon. For your crimes against Islam: apostasy, blasphemy, murder, and for what you caused me to suffer. You will watch me take Ana, in the sure knowledge that I will own her for ever and that our children will devote themselves to Allah through service to the Islamic State. Then she will watch me crucify and behead you."

"No!" Ana rises to confront him. "Qassem, please don't do this. We are your only true family. This is the woman who carried you. She nurtured you for nine long months and loved you despite her suffering. She would have died to save you. Your fate could as easily have been Sargon's. It was not what she wanted for you. It was your father who made you suffer, not Ishtar. For whatever crimes we are supposed to have committed, we have suffered enough. Please, use your power to show us mercy."

Qassem laughs at her but his eyes spark with anger.

"Qassem," his voice weak and broken, Caleb struggles to make himself heard. "It wasn't my fault. I came back for you but the flames beat me back. I knew you couldn't have survived that and I needed to get the others out before it was too late."

"Well, it would appear the phoenix rose from those flames. Do you have any idea what they put me through, those bastards that run your so called democracy?" He looks at Ana as if she is personally responsible. "I begged them to put me out of my misery. A bullet would have ended it all but they scraped me from the ashes of my deathbed and nursed me back to life without anaesthetic or pain relief. I was strong. I didn't die in the fire like I should have. For three endless years I suffered at their hands and during every second of that time, with every insult, every torture, my determination for revenge grew. I have survived a thousand deaths for this moment and now I will be vindicated. I will see you die Sargon, knowing that Ana will be mine to the end of her days and that her children will learn the true meaning of sacrifice for the sake of Allah."

"And what of your pledge to free Ana in exchange for Caleb's life?" Somehow, Ishtar manages to keep her voice steady. "Are you to be known from now on, as a man who does not keep his word? Someone who cannot be trusted? What sort of a leader does that make you?"

"A strong one whose vision is not blinded by pity."

"And what of justice and compassion? Is there no room for those in your distortion of Islam? Or is religion merely an excuse for your barbaric cruelty? Poor Qassem, was mine the only true love he ever knew? Do you satisfy yourself with conquests when you could have so much more?"

"Enough woman! Hold your tongue or it will be parted from your head. The sentence has been passed. Tomorrow at midday it will be executed. You, Ishtar, along with everyone else here, will pay witness and then we will see who is the true king. After that you will be free to go. Now take them away."

"Wait." Pale and exhausted, Caleb can barely hold himself up. "I am innocent of your charges. If you are of signifiant rank in this movement, as your brother I have the right to a proper trial. Show us the evidence that condemns me and Ana, my wife. For what crimes do you punish her? Show your followers that it is more than revenge you seek, that their work here has been for something other than your sadistic lust."

Qassem rises, his black eyes flashing, the knuckles of his clenched fists white.

"How dare you defy me!" he hisses. "Here, I am the law. Tomorrow you will feel the hand of justice."

"Brother, please! At least spare Ana for she has done you no harm. Look at her. What sort of justice demands a pregnant woman be held in shackles, tortured and raped? Ana has nothing to do with this. Take my head and have your revenge but let her go."

"She is mine and there is nothing you can do about it." Qassem looks casually beyond Caleb with a nod and Ana's anger rages above despair.

"So, do your followers know what crimes you are guilty of Qassem? How do you justify raping a pregnant woman in the name of Allah?" she demands. "That is haram! And who do you really serve? Syria, Isis, Allah or Assad? Do they know you as an officer in air force intelligence, that you held and tortured me at Mezzeh airport along with many other unfortunates opposed, as you purport to be, to the Assad regime? Do they understand why the Shabiha take orders from you, Qassem?"

He scowls at her but his eyes flash and not one of his followers raises an eyebrow either to her accusations or the way he punishes her.

She waits in the half-light for Qassem to return, willing that time to pass though every fibre of her being resists. Slim though it may be, there is still a chance and she will do anything to save Caleb. She has prepared herself to beg and plead. Panic hits and she twists her wrists, forcing them through cold metal, ignoring the searing pain in her shoulders, the burning of skinned flesh. But they have bound her so tight that there is no slack in the chains for her to work with.

She wonders about Caleb, focusing all her attention on him as if she could find him this way. Imagining she can tune into his thoughts, she tells him how much she loves him. That, whatever happens, she will wait until they are together again.

A deafening flash of light startles her out of her trance, people crashing about down below, then footsteps on the stairs. She braces herself as the door flings open but it is neither Qassem nor one of his brutes who confronts her now. She closes her eyes and tries to shake sense into her head but, when she opens them again, the vision has not altered.

"Ana. Thank God you're alive!" Sapphires blaze from his dirt-stained face. In full combat gear, he bears an automatic rifle in one hand and a bunch of keys in the other. Ana cannot believe what she is seeing.

"What has the fucking brute done to you?"

"Father?"

He fumbles awkwardly with the keys as he comes towards her. A shadow looms behind him and she screams. "It's okay," he barks. "They won't be bothering us for a while. M eighty four crash-bang grenades. Blinding, deafening, disorienting. The world will be spinning for them right now. If they try to stand, they'll fall. The others will finish them off before they recover their senses. Now, which one is it?" He interrogates her with his eyes and she stares at him blankly.

She looks at the keys and recognises one of them. "That one. Wrists." The key turns easily in the lock. "What you doing here father?" She must be hallucinating.

"Ishtar," he says, as if that is explanation enough. "Recognise any of the others?"

They work their way rapidly through the keys and within minutes she is free. She rubs her wrists, shaking her hands to get the circulation going and her father tells her that it's rude to stare. "We need to get out of here before all hell breaks loose."

Ana panics. "Qassem?"

"Your brothers' job to deal with him, mine to get you."

"Chris? Daniel?"

Her father nods. "Yep, both here. Family effort this one. I wasn't going to get help from the Israelis, that's for sure. Not exactly in their good books anymore."

"Oh." Ana shakes her head, images flitting through her mind of her kid brothers at the monster's mercy. But they are big boys now. "Caleb?" Her father pulls her to her feet but her legs have neither feeling nor strength and she crumples. He helps her up again.

"Tuan's going for Caleb." Hope rises like a warm glow within her though her head will insist on shaking its disbelief and Ana smiles through her tears. "Come," her father says gently. "We must go."

She follows him down the stairs, peering into the rooms they pass. For so many hours she has listened to the enemy chatting and laughing down here, as if this was any ordinary job and wondered if, at the end of their stint, these savages went back to wives, children, homes – as if they hadn't been brutalising their victims. Now they lie completely disorientated, rolling about on the floor. Her father stops at the front door, holding his hand up to keep her back and peers into the gathering dusk then, gun cocked, he steps out, scanning the field before ushering her on.

Seconds is all it takes. Had she not hesitated, it would have been too late but freedom is another world and she was bewildered. He takes her from behind, forcing his hand into her mouth so that she almost chokes, pressing cold steel into her back. Instantaneously a single shot takes her father to the ground and Ana screams into rigid flesh. The monster tightens its grip on her, its knife slicing through cotton until it whispers against her skin.

The world lights up with a deafening roar and she is propelled into it, helplessly bound by human flesh and steel. Past her father's inanimate body. Silence. Only the rush of the wind through deserted streets, catching her dress so that it flaps against her legs.

"Let's see how precious you really are." Qassem raises his head to shout at the mountains. "If you want her, come and get her." He pushes her forward, along a street she knows so well for it has haunted her since her doomed attempt to escape.

"Don't be an idiot Qassem!" Chris? "We have you covered. The only way you get out of here alive is by co-operating with us." They stop moving. "Let her go, Qassem!"

"She goes down with me!" He pushes the knife into her back, pulling it down to slice tender flesh and releasing her mouth so they can hear her scream.

"Don't you fucking hurt her!"

Qassem laughs.

"Let her go and we will talk."

"My life for hers? Do you think I was born yesterday?"

"We will spare your life if you let her go."

Wild laughter rocks Qassem's huge body and Ana quakes in his arms, a terrible wailing emanating from somewhere as the knife zigzags across her back. She closes her eyes and catches her breath, willing herself calm.

"You are surrounded. Your men are dead or incapacitated and Assad's army is assembling on the plains to retake Ma'loulah. This is your last chance. Release Ana and we will not harm you. Surrender or die."

Qassem shakes his head, the rumble of mirth rising in his

belly as the tension in his muscles grows. "No! You listen to me. If you touch me, she dies. Do exactly as I say." He waits but only the howling wind rises in response. "Bring me the Shabiha in the range-rover."

"Yes. We'll do that now. Don't hurt her."

She sees Caleb, his hands high above his head, walking unsteadily towards them, feels the knife move against her skin and freezes. Then she realises. If he had a gun, Qassem would have shot him by now. She twists herself free of the hand at her throat but he doesn't seem to notice. "Idiot!" he hisses. "He'll have it as soon as I've finished with you." He hauls her before him effortlessly without altering the pressure of the knife against her skin. A sudden burst of gunfire makes her jump but Qassem remains as steady as rock. "Abu and the range-rover. NOW!" He screams.

"Calm down. He's coming." Chris's voice again.

The sound of an engine starting, a car closing in on them. She sees it out of the corner of her eye for now Qassem holds her so tight that she cannot move her head.

"We're going for a ride baby but don't go thinking lover boy is getting away with this. I will personally see to it that he serves his sentence."

Qassem carries her before him like a shield, his grip on her throat falling in with his footsteps. Mustering all her strength, Ana waits. The pressure on her throat relaxes and she bites, as hard as she can, into hard calloused fingers. As she expected, the effect is almost negligible, but for a moment, he is distracted and that is all they need.

"You'll pay for that."

The world explodes around them and he takes her with him to the ground. She does not hesitate. Arching her back away from the knife, she jackknifes and he loses his grip on her. She sees stars and darkness threatens but she ignores it. She staggers to her feet and starts to run but her skirts trip her and he is quicker than she. His hand comes around her throat but before it can choke the breath out of her, she turns to face him. She sees her father in the distance, rise from the dead, blood dripping from a gash in his head, one eye buried in a mass of swollen flesh. Wriggling herself free, she ducks and, at that moment, he fires. Flames leap in slow motion from the barrel of his gun, the shock-waves tearing at her eardrums, searing heat rushing past her face and history repeats itself. Her father takes a direct hit and falls lifeless to the ground.

She feels herself being dragged, hears a vehicle draw up behind them and focuses all her effort into pulling away. For a moment the knife loses her skin but Qassem is so much stronger than she is. He pushes it into her arm, twisting mercilessly and all her strength melts away. He reverses towards the range rover and Abu opens the door to the back seat. Still holding Ana like a shield before him, Qassem throws himself in and slams the door.

"To the plains," he shouts and Ana squirms, suffocating beneath the weight of his arm, wriggling to escape his cruel blade. Something catches her face like a breath of fresh air on a hot summer's day and she freezes. It moves away and she follows, oblivious to any restraint, and then it happens. Without warning. An explosion. Excruciating pain in her arm. Screaming. Blood everywhere. Something pulling at her legs. Someone gathering her in their arms. Her head falls back and she sees him. Qassem. Lying unconscious in the back of the range rover, a dark cloud blooming in his chest.

"Sorry love, had to shoot through you to get him." American. "Only a flesh-wound. You'll be alright." An engine roars to life as wheels spin in wet mud. "Don't mind him. Won't last long where he's going anyway. We're off home if that's alright with you."

"Ana?" Caleb's eyes brim.

"Later mate. Let's get out'a here 'for it's too late."

Waves of pain and faintness threaten. She is hardly aware of the crescendoing pulse, only its blissful gusts. But then the force of it hits her hard and she has no choice but to look. A helicopter with twin propellers at either end of the wing it hangs from, rotating with increasing speed. They lift her up to receiving arms and lay her next to the inanimate body of her father.

"Father?" She strokes his face, suddenly overwhelmed by emotion for he is clearly dead. "Father!" She closes her eyes and the tears flow. Uncontrollably. For now that he is no longer here, she understands. He couldn't help himself, just as she wouldn't have, had Qassem had his way. But her father loved her and, though she never believed it until now, he did know her after all.

Her consciousness begins to fluctuate. They have closed the doors to the helicopter and she feels it rising. Faces loom and fade away. Her brothers. So different to how she knew them but recognition lies in their eyes. Chris and Daniel. Tuan. The roar rises to deafening pitch and, as Caleb takes her hand and lays himself down beside her, darkness falls.

JANUARY 2015

She watches them work out how to fit the cups inside each other and claps as they tip them out to shrieks of excited joy. "Clever! Can I have the red one please?" Ilyas picks it up passing it from one hand to the other then hands it over with a chuckle and his sister finds another.

At eight months, they're doing well despite the insults they weathered in the beginning and Ana is so thankful. She has everything so many lost. Family, good health, love, security and, above all, something she will never again take for granted. Freedom.

They let the twins have this Birthday present early. Though he intends to be back by then, Ana hadn't wanted Caleb to miss out. Unbearable emptiness catches in the pit of her stomach and she wonders where he is, praying that soon he will be back.

Not the twenty-first of May, his Birthday, after all. There was no way they were going to hold out that long and her obstetrician wouldn't have allowed it, anyway. Far too risky to allow the babies to go to term. They came in their own time. Sooner than the planned Caesarean, though that was how they were delivered in the end, despite her best efforts at getting them out naturally. They took everyone by surprise and, in any case, she had wanted at least to try. She suffered greatly, labouring to bring them into the world naturally but, despite her failure, thankfully they arrived undamaged.

Ilyas hides a ball under a cup, laughing and clapping as his sister finds it but then she rubs her eyes, raising her arms for a cuddle. They're tired. Its time for some milk and a nap. Dani topples onto her knees and crawls towards her. She climbs onto her lap, laying herself down so that she can watch her mother's face then, lifting her top as Ana makes herself comfortable with the sofa behind her, takes a breast in both hands and begins to feed. "It's alright Ilyas, your turn next," Ana reassures and, putting an arm around him, wonders how ever she would have managed without them.

She cared so diligently, Aadil's sister, not only for her brother when he was so sick, but also Ana and the babies for, though he was the quickest to recover, there were times when even Caleb's great strength failed. Without her help, Ana would never have succeeded in nursing, for her milk was slow to come and the babies ravenously hungry. Yes, Naida will make a good nurse. A fresh smile warms Ana's heart. Now that Aadil is so much better and Caleb away, they delight together in that self-appointed role of helping his family. Small recompense they are quick to counter any gratitude, for the sanctuary provided them here in London and help wading through the bureaucratic trap that will eventually, they hope, grant them permission to stay.

Ishtar was a great help too, of course. Ana had been too unwell to attend her father's funeral. Ishtar went in her place and returned to Ma'aloula soon after Assad's troops took it back from the Jihadists. Then she joined them in London, taking Ana's place in caring for Caleb. It hadn't been just physical, Ana's disability. Still she struggles to come to terms with what happened. Even now, sometimes she doubts him, Sargon, as she sees him then. Could he have become what Qassem did? Could he have prevented his brother from becoming the monster he is? But then Caleb smiles, dispelling all doubt and, when he leaves, he takes part of her with him.

Absentmindedly, Ana strokes the fair hair that tickles her nose. Thick and curly like hers. From their father, the children have inherited mesmerising brown eyes and olive skin.

She wonders about Rahim. How he and his family are getting on in Germany with their Persian taxi-driver uncle. A kind man who specialises in helping the disabled and elderly rather than Botany, the degree in which he excelled prior to his urgent need to emigrate. He has a daughter at medical school. Germany has already granted Rahim and his family citizenship. They have the probability of a good future there.

Dua and Saad were not so fortunate. Somehow, while she and Caleb were unable to prevent it, these little ones came to Lebanon and the last she heard, they were living in a refugee camp with a childless couple. Adults rendered penniless, dependent. Stuck in a poor country without enough work for its own, let alone the visitors who swell its population by a third. Now that their UNHCR food allowance has been slashed, they will have barely enough for a meal a day and it will be the children who get sent out to beg and labour long hours.

It has been a vicious winter in Lebanon. Violent storms and subzero temperatures aggravate the misery of those already struggling to survive. Ana is haunted by images of toddlers walking barefoot in thick snow. A little boy sobbing as he searches for his parents and others battling with their carers to repair flimsy shelters. Since the conflict in Syria began, over ten million have fled the fighting, half of them under the age of sixteen.

Ilyas pulls away, Dani wriggles on her lap and, realising with a start, how tightly she holds onto them, Ana forces herself to relax.

Prayer. That's what Dua means, Caleb told her as they lay together worrying about the children one night. And, daily, she does pray for him. For them both. That Caleb will find them before it is too late and that he and she will be allowed to give them the future every child deserves.

There is a knock on the door, followed by Aadil's cheerful face. "Alright if I play the piano?"

"Of course." He plays beautifully. It calms the twins and gives Ana such joy to see how he fascinates them, how the notes weave their magic within their growing brains. He has come so far and will do well, Aadil. No doubt he will earn his place at the Royal College. She will never forget that first time in hospital when she found him sorting buttons.

His fingers caress the keys and, cruising along the furniture to reach him, Ilyas holds onto his stool, putting a hand up to feel the vibrations of the piano. The Moonlight Sonata, one of their favourites.

All shapes, colours and sizes. He sat there staring at them. "Won't talk," the nurse told her, "except to ask for buttons." Ana closed her eyes to him then, too distressed to approach him at first, images of hell confronting her with the realisation that he had gone through it alone. Perhaps this is why now he does the music such justice for he knows, as Beethoven did, what it means to suffer.

He told her later. After she watched him sort the buttons by colour into piles, comforting him when he broke down. Of how his grandmother used to do this, "make me sort the buttons when I was upset. She had a whole jar of them. Once I'd sorted them into piles, she'd make me thread them, all of one colour together, tied so tightly they couldn't escape. Then she'd cut the threads, mix them up and make me start again. I always felt better afterwards. All my troubles melted away. It was magic.

"I miss my grandmother. She died you know. At the beginning of the war. I went to see her one day, like I always did and found her. It was a bomb."

Ana watches them now. A young man of fourteen years, who has lived through more than many far older and her own children still blissfully unaware and, as the tears prick, takes a satisfied baby to her cot. When she returns Ilyas sits, still spellbound, at Aadil's feet and she busies herself with a bit of tidying up. The headline of a newspaper catches her eye. February 2013, almost two years ago. Another article that should have been tidied away with their growing collection about Syria.

Three thousand civilians are still trapped in Homs, she reads. Rebel held areas have been under siege for eighteen months and Assad continues to pursue a policy known as 'surrender or starve.' A second round of peace talks are planned to take place in Geneva. Both Assad's forces and the opposition have agreed to attend but the jihadists are not part of the dialogue and they are doing most of the fighting now.

It's over – the siege in Homs. And Father Hans is dead. Assassinated. Not by Assad's regime after all, or so it has been made to seem, but by jihadists. And now they have their Caliphate with the self-appointed Caliph Ibrahim. A murderous tyrant who, far from being consensually elected by his people and the most morally excellent of his time, uses religion as cheap armour to acquire political power and impose a medieval form of Islam on his victims. Who forces the rest of the world to acknowledge his state through acts of brutality and terrorism. So Qassem's predictions come true. Ana shudders to think how close she and her children were to becoming a part of that and, in the light of the savage treatment inflicted on minority groups, with the recent publication of a guide to raping child slaves, what exactly that would have meant.

Then there is Kai. Never far from her thoughts, her heart lurches whenever she considers him and she is filled with dreadful guilt. He didn't go back to his sick mother but after her. Into Syria. And there he disappeared. Nobody knew where he was until now. They have been sent a proof of life video. From ISIS. Every day Ana's stomach ties itself into knots on his account as she prays for an end to his suffering. That his ransom will be paid. She could not bear his fate if it was not.

The phone rings and Ana jumps, rushing to pick it up as the room falls silent. "Please let it be Caleb! Tell me he's safe and well and that he's found the children." But it is Olivia, her teacher friend, recently back from a project in Lebanon run by Save the Children. "An accelerated learning programme that helps children out of school two years or more, to catch up," she enthuses. "You should see it Ana! For the first two weeks it's almost impossible to deal with them. Getting them to stand in a straight line is a major feat and they fight all the time, but slowly they settle and you see the difference in them. They start washing their hands and brushing their hair. They say 'Good morning' and try not to get their feet dirty. It's as if they step back into reality."

A warmth spreads from deep inside, bringing a smile to Ana's face and a fragile peace settles in her heart for, in the words she knows so well, Love never gives up. Its faith, hope and patience never fail.

STARK NUMBERS –
NOVEMBER 2014

Since the start of the conflict in Syria, over 215,000 have been killed and the country has regressed by more than four decades from second to third world.

75% live in poverty.

More than 50% live in extreme poverty.

54% unemployment.

More than 50% of children are not in school.

45% of the population – over ten million are displaced. The world's largest source of refugees.

An estimated 10.8m people are in need inside Syria.

3.2m refugees in neighbouring countries.

MARCH 2016

Estimated number of people in need of humanitarian assistance inside Syria: 13.5 million

In hard to reach/besieged areas: 4.5 million

Estimated number of internally displaced: 6.5 million

Number of refugees – registered & awaiting registration: 4,598,594

Lebanon: 1 069 111. In Lebanon, where there are no official camps, many refugees live in sub-standard shelter such as garages and tents.

Turkey: 2 503 549

Jordan: 636 482

Iraq: 245 022

Egypt & North Africa: 117 658

The Syria conflict has triggered the world's largest humanitarian crisis since World War II.

An entire generation of children is being exposed to war and violence, deprived of basic services, education and protection.

Civilians continue to be the primary victims of the conflict. Torture, rape and sexual violence, enforced disappearances, forcible displacement, recruitment of child soldiers, summary executions and deliberate shelling of civilian targets have become commonplace.